An Armada Three ✔ KU-714-874

Three Great
Hardy Boys Stories

ROSS FULTON
CAMERON YOUTH CLUB
HOUSE, PLANEFIELD RD
INVERNESS IV3 5DN

ARMADA

Hardy Boys® Mystery Stories in Armada

* For contractual reasons, Armada has been obliged to publish from No. 57 onwards before publishing Nos. 47–56. These missing numbers will be published as soon as possible.

The Hardy Boys® in

66 The Submarine Caper
67 The Four-Headed Dragon
68 The Infinity Clue

Franklin W. Dixon
Illustrated by Leslie Morrill

ARMADA

This Armada *Hardy Boys*® *Three-in-One* was
first published in the U.K. in Armada in 1988
by William Collins Sons & Co. Ltd

Armada is an imprint of
the Children's Division, part of
the Collins Publishing Group,
8 Grafton Street, London W1X 3LA

Published pursuant to agreement with
Simon & Schuster Inc., New York, USA

Printed and bound in Great Britain by
William Collins Sons & Co. Ltd, Glasgow

The Hardy Boys® in

The Submarine Caper

The Submarine Caper was
first published in the U.K. in a single volume
in hardback in 1982 by Angus & Robertson (U.K.) Ltd,
and in Armada in 1983

Contents

1 Surprise Collision

"Remember my friend Alfred Wagner?" Gerhard Stolz asked Frank and Joe Hardy, who were staying at his Munich apartment. "You met him when I took you to his auto repair shop a few weeks ago. He's got a serious problem."

"What happened?" Joe asked. "Is *Ludwig II* giving him headaches?" He was referring to the mini-submarine Wagner had invented and was building in his spare time. It was named after the inventor's favorite king, which resulted in plenty of teasing from his friends.

"No. *Ludwig II* is fine—in fact, it'll have its maiden run next week," Gerhard replied. He was a slender man of medium height, who now creased his forehead into a thoughtful frown.

Frank looked at him questioningly. "What is it then?"

"Wagner is afraid that someone has copied the blueprint for his sub."

Frank whistled. "That would be very serious, indeed. What makes him think his plans were duplicated?"

"He found an empty film container under his desk and put two and two together, even though he can't prove it. I went to see him last night because my battery needed to be recharged. That's when he told me someone was after his sub. He had noticed a while ago that his papers had been disturbed. After that, he locked them into a drawer, but he says it happened again."

"Are you sure he's not imagining things?" Joe inquired.

"I doubt it. He's a very trusting person and it takes a lot to rouse his suspicion." Gerhard Stolz poured himself a second cup of breakfast coffee.

"I promised Alfred I'd look into the matter," he added.

Stolz was a well-known investigative reporter who had met Frank and Joe's father, a famous New York detective, many years ago. The two had become good friends, and when he heard that the

10

boys wanted to spend a summer in Germany to sightsee and brush up on their language skills, he invited them to stay with him and his wife Rita. Eighteen-year-old Frank and his brother, who was a year younger, were accomplished amateur detectives themselves, and found Stolz's work fascinating.

Frank was about to ask Gerhard whether Wagner suspected anyone in particular, when the phone rang. He picked it up and after listening for a moment, handed it to Gerhard. "It's your paper, the *Herold*."

"Oh, thanks. I'll take it in my study."

Frank waited until Stolz picked up the extension, and then quietly hung up. He flopped into a chair and grinned at his brother. "Your turn to do the dishes today!"

Joe grimaced. "I was hoping you'd forget." He cleaned the table and was just about finished with his chore when Gerhard rushed back into the kitchen.

"Boys, would you do me a favor?" he asked. "I have to catch a ten o'clock flight to Frankfurt. Would you drop me off at the airport?"

"Sure," Frank said. "What's up?"

"Tell you on the way. Go ahead and start the car. I'll be right down."

While Stolz hurried into the bedroom to pack a

few things, the two boys left the apartment. They did not wait for the elevator, but ran down the stairs into the garage. Gerhard owned a blue Mercedes, the car he usually drove, and a silver-gray Porsche, which he loaned the boys during their visit.

Frank slipped behind the wheel of the Mercedes, while his blond brother climbed into the back. Then they drove around to the front door and waited until Gerhard arrived with his suitcase and joined them.

"Why is the paper sending you to Frankfurt?" Joe asked eagerly. "Do you have to investigate an interesting case?"

Gerhard smiled. "No. I'm only going there because my final destination, the little town of Glocken on the Rhine River, has no airport."

He told the boys that in Glocken a number of priceless paintings had been hidden during World War II and could not be found afterwards. Now the hiding place had been discovered by accident, and the townspeople were planning a festive ceremony, in which the paintings were to be removed from the hiding place and escorted to the museum.

"That's all I know," Stolz said. "I was asked to cover the story, and accepted because it won't take much time. Besides, I'm getting a nice weekend trip to the Rhine."

"Look at him!" Frank grinned at their friend, while he pushed a strand of dark hair off his forehead. "Goes off on a fun weekend and leaves his company home!"

Gerhard laughed. "Well, it's not quite like that. I have to do some work, and you'll hardly die of boredom in Munich. You two always find something to keep you busy."

"We were counting on you to take us to the movies!" Joe protested.

"Tell you what," Gerhard said, suddenly serious. "Why don't you drop by Alfred Wagner's and see if anything new has developed?"

"We'll be glad to," Frank offered.

"Great. And mention to him why I couldn't make it myself. I'm sure he'll understand."

"Business first," Joe said with a chuckle.

Gerhard made a face. "I do have to earn a living."

"How about Rita?" Joe asked. "Does she know about your trip?"

The journalist slapped his hand against his forehead. "Oh, I forgot to leave her a note! Please tell her what happened, will you? I'll be back Sunday night."

"You'd better bring her some flowers," Frank advised his friend. "Maybe then she'll forgive you for rushing off like this."

"Good idea!"

After Gerhard Stolz boarded his flight, Frank and

Joe drove directly to Alfred Wagner's. The inventor's garage was located on the outskirts of town next to a small lake, which he used for the experimental runs of his sub. Adjoining his repair shop was a charming old frame house where he lived with his mother and sister.

Frank parked the Mercedes behind a red Alfa Romeo.

"Oh, look at that beautiful car!" Joe exclaimed. "I'd love to have a set of wheels like that."

"So would I," Frank agreed, as the boys got out. They admiringly surveyed the elegant sports car before entering the large, noisy shop. They walked in between cars with open hoods, and past half a dozen mechanics who were working on them.

"*Guten Tag*," several of the men smiled in greeting as the visitors made their way to the end of the shop, where a small wooden cubicle served as Wagner's office.

The boys had almost reached it when the door flew open and a young girl stormed out. She collided head-on with Joe, who was standing right in her path!

2 Danger on the Autobahn

The girl glared at Joe, who mumbled an apology. Still looking angry, she hurried away, her long blond hair bouncing as she moved

"How do you like that?" Joe asked, looking after her. "I wonder what's bugging her?"

Just then, an impatient voice sounded from behind. "What are you doing here?"

The Hardys whirled around and faced a short, wiry man with a head of unruly dark hair and metal-rimmed glasses. He was Alfred Wagner.

When he recognized them, his tense expression dissolved into a smile. "Oh, it's you, boys," he said. "Sorry I shouted, but I'm beginning to get suspicious of everyone. Did you hear the story about my drawings?"

"Yes," Joe confirmed. "That's why we're here. But what was wrong with that pretty girl? She almost ran me over."

Wagner shrugged. "Who knows? Anyway, she was too nosy for me. Said she was a reporter, but I didn't believe her and told her to leave."

"Good for you," Frank said.

"Why don't you come into my office?" Wagner suggested. "It's tiny, but nicer than out here in the shop."

The brothers followed him into the small room. Papers and drawings were strewn all over and folders lay on the floor. Here Wagner worked on his many inventions, which he enjoyed far more than running the car repair business he had inherited from his father.

Frank told him about Gerhard Stolz's trip and asked Wagner if he had an idea of who might have copied his plans for the mini-sub.

"I don't like to suspect anyone," Wagner replied. "For years, I've been leaving my papers in here and no one has touched them. Now I have to lock them up, and even that doesn't seem to help."

"Perhaps you should invent a safe that can't be cracked!" Joe grinned.

"You're right. But first I'll have to complete my sub. Come on, I'll show it to you."

Wagner led the boys to a shack next to the garage. At the far wall, a rising door opened up to the lakefront. On a rack near the door was the yellow mini-sub. It was about twenty-one feet long, six feet high, and was shaped somewhat like a turtle. It could be lowered by means of a winch into a narrow canal of water and driven right out of the shack into the lake.

A young man in overalls was climbing out of the hatch with a wrench in his hand. Wagner introduced him as his assistant, Rolf Meier.

"We'll just have to modify a few things," the inventor told his visitors proudly. "But *Ludwig II* should be ready for its first test run in a week or two. If you want, you can come along."

"Great!" the boys cried in unison, and Frank added, "Just think, Joe, of all the things that little sub can do! We can go a lot deeper with it than with our diving suits."

"Yes, to about fifteen hundred feet," Wagner said. "But not in this puddle. All we have here is a depth of sixty or seventy feet, with mud, algae, and garbage at the bottom."

He locked the shack and invited the boys to his house for coffee and cake. They met his mother and

sister, then everyone sat down on the patio, where Frau Wagner served freshly baked *Apfelkuchen*.

As Frank helped himself to a second piece of the delicious apple cake, he asked, "Herr Wagner, I understand there are various mini-subs on the market. Do you have any idea why someone wants *yours* so badly that he'll resort to a criminal act?"

"I've asked myself the same question," Wagner replied. "My invention contains only a few improvements over the others. The reason must be that *Ludwig II* is very inexpensive compared to other boats of its size and capacity."

"How come?" Joe asked.

"It's made of fiberglass. The special shape of the body makes it possible to avoid using steel, which is heavier and costlier."

"Are you planning to build more of these boats if the test run is successful?" Frank asked.

"No, I'm not interested in that. I want to sell the license to a large manufacturer. The manager is a friend of mine, and we already wrote up a contract."

"Then it must be the competition who's trying to steal your plans," Frank declared. "Once your friend begins to market these subs for a low price, other manufacturers will be in trouble."

Everyone agreed that this made sense. Then Joe inquired as to how the culprit had been able to get to Wagner's drawings.

"Unfortunately, that was no problem," the inventor admitted. "I have simple locks on my office door and my desk drawers. And I'm really not sure who has the keys to what locks. That's why I think the spy might be one of my employees." Wagner looked unhappy at the thought.

"Would anyone have a chance to sneak into your office, perhaps at lunchtime?" Joe asked.

"No, too many people are around then. But often one of the men will stay late, and at that hour, Meier and I usually work in the shack. The person could easily walk into my office unobserved, or even come during the night, for that matter. I do know several mechanics have their own keys to the shop. I'm just not sure what other keys they might have."

After thanking the Wagners for their hospitality, Frank and Joe drove back to Gerhard's apartment. Rita Stolz heard them coming and opened the door. She was a slender, pretty woman with short, reddish hair.

"I'm glad you're here," she greeted them. "Gerhard just called a minute ago. He wants you to join him in Glocken."

"In Glocken?" Joe exclaimed, puzzled. "I wonder why?"

"I have no idea," Rita replied. "He didn't give me

any details. Just said he needed you by tomorrow noon, and it would be best if you could leave now and get there before morning."

"Looks as if his nice, pleasant weekend was just a dream," Joe said with a grin, as the Hardys began to pack a few things. "I'm sure he has a problem or he wouldn't have called for us."

Soon the boys were on their way with Joe driving. Traffic was heavy until they reached the Autobahn to Nuremberg. From then on, they whizzed along at top speed. They changed places at a rest area, and Frank took the wheel. But they hit heavy traffic once more, and by the time they could move freely again, it was already dark.

Another car was behind them and stuck like glue. Its headlights irritated Frank, causing him to say angrily, "One more inch and that guy'll hit our trunk!" The boy moved into the right lane to let the car pass. The driver pulled up, but when he was about parallel with the Hardys; he pushed toward the right lane, getting perilously close to the young detectives.

"That crazy idiot!" Frank cried. "He's cutting us off!"

They were forced further and further to the right. Finally, Frank braked hard in order to avoid driving onto the shoulder. The Porsche started to fishtail and turned around almost 360 degrees! Finally, it stopped with screeching tires.

Their knees shaking, the boys climbed out and pushed the car to the side. The other driver was nowhere in sight by now.

"Wow!" Frank wiped the perspiration off his forehead. "Did you ever see anything like this?"

"That lady was out of her mind," Joe agreed, as he walked around the Porsche to check if there was any damage. Luckily, everything seemed to be in order.

"Lady?" Frank asked. "I only noticed the red sports car. I didn't see the driver."

"I couldn't swear to it, but I think it was a woman with long blond hair," Joe said. "Well, at least nothing happened." He took the wheel again, and passed Frankfurt. Finally, he turned off the Auto-bahn to drive along the Rhine River. They arrived at their destination late at night. The Hotel Glocken-hof was in the picturesque town square. Joe parked across the street since the parking lot was full.

"We'd better leave our things in the car till we're sure they have a room for us," Frank said, and the two boys walked into the lobby. They asked for Gerhard Stolz and were directed into the dining room, where the reporter was talking to Herr Dietrich, the owner of the hotel.

Stolz greeted them with a friendly smile, introduced them to Herr Dietrich, then ordered something for them to eat. Much to their relief, the kitchen was still open.

"How was your trip?" Gerhard inquired.

"Don't ask. We almost got run off the road," Joe replied, and described the incident on the Autobahn. However, when a huge platter with salads and cold cuts arrived, the boys did not let the recollection spoil their appetite. They dug in with gusto.

Then Joe asked why Gerhard had called for them.

"It's a long story, and we'd better go to bed now," Gerhard replied. "Tomorrow morning we'll have plenty of time. The festivities don't start till early afternoon. We can do some sightseeing and I'll tell you what's happening, okay?"

"Seems we have no choice," Frank replied with a grin. "But I have to admit, I could use some sleep."

"I reserved a room for you," Gerhard said. "It's right next to mine."

The boys went outside to get their luggage. They had only gone a few steps when Frank called out, "Joe! Look over there!"

His brother stopped short and saw a shadowy figure tiptoe away from the Porsche and disappear around the corner. Quickly, Joe chased after Frank, who had already started to pursue the stranger.

Suddenly, Joe heard a yell. Flying around the corner, he ran straight into someone who was just getting up from the ground. The two crashed to the sidewalk!

3 A Mysterious Clue

"Hey!" Frank sputtered and clutched his right side in pain. "Can't you watch where you're going?"

Joe scrambled to his feet. "How was I supposed to know you were sitting around the bend letting that man escape?"

"Listen to this! First I get knocked on the head by some creep, then you come along and run me over, and to top it all off, you yell at me!"

"When you're finished complaining," Joe said with a grin, "why don't you tell me what happened?"

Just then the boys heard footsteps, and the next moment, Gerhard Stolz walked around the corner. "Here you are!" he called out. "I saw you running off and couldn't figure out what was going on."

"We noticed someone tampering with the car," Frank replied. "I think he had a tiny flashlight. Anyway, when he saw us coming, he ran off. I caught up to him and grabbed him by his jacket, but he punched me in the head and took off."

"What did the man look like?" Gerhard asked.

"Couldn't see much," Frank admitted. "Not enough light. But he was young, and dark-haired. I think he wore a mustache. But I doubt that I'd recognize him in daylight."

"Let's check the car and see if he did any damage," Gerhard suggested, and the three returned to the Porsche. A short inspection revealed that nothing was missing.

"We'll drive into the lot now," Frank suggested. "It has emptied out a bit."

He and Gerhard climbed into the Porsche. Just before Joe got in, he noticed a handkerchief a few feet away. Thinking it might have something to do with the stranger, he picked it up and put it in his pocket, making a mental note to study it in the morning. Then, anxious for some rest, Joe squeezed into the car, every muscle in his body aching. Frank drove into the hotel lot, and the boys took their suitcases to their room.

Completely exhausted, they fell into bed. Next

day after breakfast, Gerhard asked the hotel chef to pack a lunch for them. The three walked through the quaint old town into the vineyards that rose up directly behind Glocken.

As they climbed up the vine-covered mountain in the early morning sunshine, Frank said, "Gerhard, I can't wait any longer. Won't you tell us why you wanted us to join you?"

"I will. But first let me bring you up-to-date on what I learned from Mayor Reimann about those paintings. You see, there's a little museum in Glocken containing old documents, woodcuts, tools, and furniture, the usual local antiques. Before World War II, however, the museum owned a veritable treasure—five very valuable paintings by the Sexton."

"The Sexton?" Frank asked. "Who's that?"

"A medieval painter. His name is unknown, but apparently he was the sexton in this town. He never signed his pictures but marked them with a little bell. He is said to have painted eight masterworks and five of them were here in the museum."

"I bet those paintings are worth a fortune!" Joe exclaimed.

"Oh, yes, a few million dollars," Gerhard replied.

"What happened to them?" Frank asked.

"They were put away during the war," Gerhard

answered. "But unfortunately they were hidden so well that afterward no one could find them. All people knew was that Mayor Altenberg and three other men took the paintings to a secret place one night."

"And those men didn't remember where they put them?" Joe asked.

"All four died. For years, the town and the surrounding area were searched systematically, but the treasure was never found."

"Apparently, it has been found now," Joe said. "How come? Did the old mayor visit the new mayor in his dreams and tell him about the hiding place?"

Stolz grinned. "No, nothing that far out. The daughter of Mayor Altenberg cleaned up her father's library and found a piece of paper in an old volume. The note was in her father's handwriting and revealed the hiding place."

"Where is it?" Frank asked eagerly.

"In the wine cellar of his home. From there, a secret door leads to a room in which stands a huge wooden chest. The paintings were placed inside after being packed in a waterproof metal container."

"Mysterious notes and secret doors," Joe said. "Sounds like a great mystery!"

Gerhard nodded. "And the paintings aren't the only things that were hidden," he went on.

"What else?" Joe asked eagerly.

"A collection of gold coins called *Joachimstaler*. It belonged to the former mayor of Glocken."

The three stopped and rested for a moment, turning around to look at the town. Talk of the missing paintings and coins ceased abruptly.

"Oh, what a view!" Joe cried out. "Wait till I take a picture!" He pulled out his camera, adjusted the setting, and looked through the viewfinder. "It's dusty," he said, pulling a handkerchief out of his pocket. "What's this—" He stared at the handkerchief, then let out a low whistle.

Frank and Gerhard looked at him in surprise.

"I almost forgot!" Joe cried out. "This handkerchief may belong to the guy who sneaked around our car last night. I picked it up from the street, but I was so tired that I just put it in my pocket and forgot about it."

Gerhard examined the silk handkerchief. "What an unusual pattern," he said, "light blue stripes with something like suns in between them. They have long rays and faces. Strange."

"Somehow this pattern rings a bell," Frank said. "Maybe I'll remember later what it reminds me of."

The group continued on and Joe said, "Now we know all about the paintings and the coins, but you still haven't told us why we were supposed to come to Glocken, Gerhard."

"I received an anonymous phone call yesterday,"

Stolz explained. "A man said, 'You'll be in for a surprise when the hiding place is opened tomorrow!'"

"A surprise!" Frank repeated. "Do you know what he means by that?"

"I haven't the vaguest idea. In a few hours we'll know more. I have a hunch there'll be trouble, that's why I called you. Things like that are right up your alley, aren't they?"

"You bet!" Frank grinned. "But suppose it was just a practical joker who phoned you?"

"I think there's more to it than that. Why would he call me, of all people? Anyway, I have to go back to Munich tomorrow afternoon. If there's a mystery to be solved, will you take over?"

"We'll be glad to," Frank replied with a grin. "Besides, it's so nice here we wouldn't mind spending a few days, would we, Joe?"

Joe agreed, then suggested they stop for lunch.

"By the way," Gerhard said, after taking a big bite out of his sandwich, "did you get a chance to talk to Alfred Wagner yesterday?"

"We sure did," Frank said and repeated in detail what happened. With a grin, he mentioned the young lady whom Wagner had asked to leave his shop. Suddenly, Joe held up his hand.

"Frank! The Alfa Romeo!" he sputtered. "Remember it wasn't there when we left Alfred's place?"

Frank realized what his brother was getting at. "You're right! I had a hunch that the incident on the Autobahn was no coincidence! She must have pushed us over on purpose!"

"What are you talking about?" Gerhard wanted to know.

"Remember, we almost got killed yesterday by a blond girl in a red sports car," Joe replied. "And now I recall that in front of Wagner's garage there was this red sports car—an Alfa Romeo!"

"Our attacker and the girl might have been one and the same person!" Frank added.

"But why would she do a thing like that?"

"Maybe to scare us. She's no reporter. She probably belongs to the group who copied Wagner's drawings! She could be working with one of his employees."

"You've got a point there," Gerhard had to admit.

On the way back to town, the three discussed Wagner's problems and his suspicion that the culprit might be one of his mechanics.

"We'll have to check all of them out," Frank decided. "Starting with Alfred's assistant, Rolf Meier."

The trio returned from the vineyards and soon

found themselves in front of the mansionlike home of the former Mayor, Helmut Altenberg, which was located in a small valley outside of town. Between the house and the wine cellar, which was built into a hill, was a wide yard. It was now full of gaily chattering people. Flags flew in the wind, a brass band and a school choir were ready to perform. The festivities had just begun.

Gerhard and the Hardys made their way through the crowd and joined a group of reporters who were led down into the wine cellar by a guide.

In the dark, cool room, Mayor Reimann greeted the people from the press and introduced the honorary guests—government representatives, the city council, members of the state assembly, and, of course, Doris Altenberg, a trim, dark-haired woman with a friendly face, who held her father's letter in her hand.

"Here at the end of the cellar," Reimann declared, "you see the bottom of a keg built into the wall. It's five feet high and seems to be merely a decoration. However, from the note, we learned that it is really a door to another room. Fräulein Altenberg will now open it according to the directions her father left behind."

As the woman stepped toward the wall and counted the boards, everyone stood in silent anticipation. Then Doris Altenberg pressed a certain spot and the heavy oak door sprang open!

Large spotlights had been set up and were now directed into the secret room. It was empty, except for a wooden chest in the middle. Tension was high as the woman walked over to it, opened the lid, and looked inside.

Suddenly, Doris Altenberg turned pale and let the lid fall in its place. "It's empty!" she whispered. "There's nothing in this chest!"

4 Taler, Taler

There was a stunned silence at first, then a storm seemed to break loose. Shouting and gesticulating angrily, the guests pushed toward the wooden chest to look inside.

A government representative turned to the mayor. "If this is supposed to be a joke, I don't get it!" he snarled.

"Did *you* fake the note, or did Fräulein Altenberg?" another man cried out.

"Why don't you admit that you arranged this whole thing just to get some free publicity for your tourist trade?" a reporter commented snidely.

The beleaguered mayor denied the accusations vehemently. "You had better watch what you're saying!" he cried out. "We have expert testimony that this note is, indeed, written by Mayor Altenberg!"

Doris Altenberg, who had been standing frozen in utter shock, began to defend her father and protested loudly against any allegations of forgery.

The news spread quickly to the crowd outside, and people began pushing into the cellar, blocking the entrance. Finally, Reimann managed to be heard above the unruly mob.

"Please leave immediately," he called out. "The ceremony is herewith canceled. I'll make sure that the matter will be investigated properly."

With the help of the local police, he managed to evacuate the cellar and persuade people to go home. Gerhard, Frank, and Joe realized immediately that this was the surprise the anonymous caller had been hinting at. They surveyed the room carefully. It was smaller than the wine cellar, and the back wall had crumbled. Now a mountain of debris formed the end of the room.

"Once this must have been a section of the wine cellar," Gerhard said. "Then part of it caved in, and they just built a new wall and put in a secret door."

When everyone had left, Mayor Reimann asked Gerhard Stolz if he could help him clear up the mystery. "Of course, the police will be working on the case, too," the mayor assured him. "But with your experience as an investigative reporter, you might be able to uncover a clue."

"I'm sorry," Gerhard replied, "I have to return to Munich tomorrow. But my two young friends will be glad to assist you." He introduced Frank and Joe and told the mayor about the many mysteries they had solved in their own country.

Reimann accepted the offer and assured Frank and Joe of his full cooperation.

At dinner that night, Gerhard and the boys discussed the mystery. "I wonder if Altenberg himself was the thief," Joe spoke up. "Of course then he wouldn't have written that note."

"I think his daughter is innocent, too," Frank added. "Otherwise, she would've destroyed the letter."

"Before we come to any conclusions," Gerhard said, "we'll have to find the answer to a number of questions. Let's assume the pictures and the coins were in the same container. When was it stolen? Who had the opportunity to take it? How could it have been removed from the cellar without anyone noticing?"

"Also, someone knew ahead of time that the pictures and the coins weren't there," Frank said. "The anonymous caller. Who's he and how did he know?"

"And what was he after?" Joe added. "Is he involved with the paintings, coins, or both? We should find out more about the gold *Joachimstaler*, too."

"Wait a minute," Gerhard said and stood up. "I'll be right back."

When he returned, he smiled. "I just phoned a well-known coin dealer in Frankfurt who's a friend of mine. He'll see us tomorrow at noon, even though it's Sunday."

The following day, the three detectives parked the Porsche in front of the coin dealer's home. Joe, who had squeezed into the narrow back seat, stretched and complained about being stiff before ringing the doorbell. Lothar Rehm, a tall man with white hair and thick eyeglasses, greeted the visitors and led them into his study on the second floor.

"Well, Gerhard, what mystery are you working on this time?" he asked with a smile.

Gerhard explained their mission, and the dealer looked thoughtful. "That's strange, indeed," he said. "You see, *Joachimstaler* or *Schlicktaler* are really silver coins that were minted in the Joachimstal in Bohemia in the sixteenth century."

"Is that why they're called *Taler*?" Frank asked.

"Right. The coins became so popular that they spread throughout the country and Europe. Via Spain, the *Taler* was brought to America—"

37

"And that's where it was called 'dollar!'" Joe put in.

"That's correct. But let's get back to the *Joachimstaler*. Count Stephan von Schlick, who ran the mint, had a couple of hundred gold coins made around 1520. Those were not intended as currency. Instead, he used them as gifts for royalty such as Emperor Karl V and King Ludwig I of Bohemia."

"That makes them very valuable, I suppose," Gerhard Stolz put in.

"It depends on their condition. A collector may pay between a thousand and four thousand dollars for one. There are four editions of the gold *Joachimstaler*, with slight variations only an expert can detect. If you have all four, they increase in value."

"Do you have any?" Frank asked.

"No. But I can show you a picture." The dealer took a large volume from a bookshelf. "Here's one. On one side there is the holy Joachim with the Schlick family's coat of arms at his feet, and on the other side stands the Bohemian lion with its oddly stylized double tail."

The three visitors studied the picture and memorized each detail of the coin. Finally, Gerhard spoke up. "Lothar, has anyone ever come in here to sell you gold *Joachimstaler*?"

The dealer wrinkled his forehead. "Not that I

remember. But strangely enough, someone visited me just the other day and asked if I had *bought* any of the coins recently, and from whom. Of course, I didn't tell him anything."

"Do you know his name?" Frank asked.

Herr Rehm shook his head. "I don't think he ever told me."

"Do you remember what he looked like?"

"Yes. He was around fifty, short and heavyset, with a round face and bald head. Wore a light tan suit. And I noticed another thing. Part of his left ring-finger was missing."

"That's a great description, Herr Rehm," Joe said. "I'm sure this man is connected with our case."

"Lothar," Gerhard said thoughtfully, "would you give *us* the information you refused him?"

"Sure," the dealer replied. "I don't mind telling you. Let me run downstairs and check."

When Herr Rehm returned, he was shaking his head. "I only bought three gold *Joachimstaler* in the last ten years," he reported, "and all of them from other dealers. I acquired them for customers whom I have personally known for a long time."

"If you think of anything else that might help us," Frank said, "please call us at the Glockenhof in Glocken."

The dealer promised to do so; the visitors thanked him for his help and then left. Frank and Joe drove Gerhard to the Frankfurt airport and, while they waited for the boarding announcement, discussed the case.

"If somebody found the metal container and sold the coins," Frank said, "he could have gone to a different dealer. Matter of fact, he could have sold them anywhere in the world!"

Gerhard nodded. "I'll try to check with other dealers in the country, at least."

"And the guy who wanted to know if Herr Rehm sold any coins," Joe said. "How does he fit into our case?"

"He may suspect that the container was found and the coins were sold, and he wanted to find out by whom," Frank replied.

Gerhard agreed. "In any case, your next step should be to find out as much about the paintings as you can, and to search the secret cellar closely. Maybe you'll get an idea how the paintings and the coins could have been removed."

A few minutes later, Stolz boarded his flight for Munich, and the boys drove back to the quaint town on the Rhine River.

When Frank put the key into the lock of their hotel room, it would not turn. "That's funny," he

said. "I could have sworn I locked up." He opened
the door, stepped inside, and gasped.

The room was a mess! Drawers had been pulled
out, the closet door stood open, and their things
were strewn all over the place!

5 The Ransacked Room

Joe, who was looking over his brother's shoulder, whistled. "We had a visitor!"

"Seems he did a thorough job of ripping everything apart!" Frank fumed. "Come on, let's see if he left a clue."

Carefully, he examined the doorknob, the handles on the drawers, and pieces of furniture for fingerprints. "Nothing." He sighed. "Our visitor was a pro. I wonder how he got in."

Joe walked to the hall door, checked the lock from the outside, and discovered a few scratches.

"Forced entry," he declared dryly. "Well, I guess we have no choice but to clean up. At least that'll tell us if anything's missing."

Grumbling, the boys began to straighten up.

They found that Joe's old camera had disappeared.

"Luckily, I didn't leave the new one in our room," the boy declared. "The old camera wasn't worth much. I don't even know why I brought it with me."

"Perhaps the thief only swiped it because he couldn't find what he was really after," Frank spoke up.

"What do you mean?"

"Do you still have that handkerchief you found near our car?"

Joe opened a bureau drawer. "Oh, no!" he cried out. "I put it in here, but it's gone! Now I get the message. The intruder came to retrieve the handkerchief and took the camera to make it look like a burglary!"

"Exactly," Frank agreed. "The handkerchief must be very incriminating for him to have gone to all this trouble. If only I could remember where I've seen the pattern!"

Joe nodded. "It looked familiar to me, too. But I don't know the answer."

The boys reported the incident to Herr Dietrich, who was flabbergasted. He wanted to call the police, but Frank persuaded him that since the loss was so small, it was hardly worth it.

"Do you know if any other rooms were broken into?" he asked.

"Oh, no. Of course not. One is enough! This is the first time something like this has happened in my hotel!"

"It won't happen again," Frank assured him. "We're convinced that this was not an ordinary thief. He came for a special reason." Quickly, he told Herr Dietrich what had happened the night before. The boys left and were about to cross the lobby when the clerk at the reception desk waved to them.

"You had a phone call this afternoon," he said. "Unfortunately, the man didn't leave his name."

"No wonder," Joe grumbled. "He only called to make sure we weren't in our room. Did he ask for our room number?"

"Well—no. He asked to talk to Mr. Frank Hardy in room 17. I told him you had room 25, and wouldn't be back before late afternoon. Why? Did I say the the wrong thing?"

"No, no," Joe assured him. "Everything's okay."

The boys discussed the strange phone call over dinner that night. "How'd the thief get my name?" Frank wondered.

"Maybe he saw it on our luggage in the car," Joe reasoned. "You think he's in cahoots with the blond girl who drives the Alfa Romeo?"

"Possibly. Or he may have something to do with the mysterious disappearance of the paintings."

Suddenly, Frank changed the subject and started to talk about the delicious food and the picturesque town of Glocken. Joe, assuming his brother did this on purpose, looked around casually. He noticed an elderly gentleman at the table next to theirs—he had been there the night before.

After the boys left the dining room, Frank said, "Did you see the guy at the next table? He listened to every word we were saying. When I mentioned the paintings, he literally pricked up his ears!"

"Well, everyone's talking about the paintings," Joe said. "But if he was really listening, he might have picked up something last night when we had dinner with Gerhard. Our names, for instance."

"Right," Frank said unhappily.

Next morning after breakfast, the boys walked to the city hall to see the mayor. "Do you have a clue yet?" Reimann asked them anxiously.

"Not so far," Joe admitted.

"Don't feel bad," Reimann assured him. "The police haven't gotten anywhere, either."

"Could you tell us about the history of the paintings?" Frank asked.

"I'll try," Reimann said. "Unfortunately, I came here just a few years ago and can only repeat what I was told."

He reported that Mayor Altenberg had decided to put the paintings in a safe place after the first air raid by the Allies. "Altenberg confided in three colleagues, and one night they brought the treasure to a secret place. It was not to be recovered until after the war, when there would be no more danger of its being destroyed. Altenberg asked his co-workers not to reveal the hiding place to anyone."

"Who were those people?" Frank inquired.

"One was the deputy mayor, Palm. The second was Councilman Schmidt, and the third one was a man named Blendinger. He was in charge of the museum."

"And all four perished in the war?" Joe asked.

"I'm only sure about Altenberg," Reimann replied. "He was executed by the Gestapo because he wanted to turn the city over to the Americans in 1945."

"How terrible," Joe murmured.

"Schmidt is said to have been killed in combat, and Palm supposedly died of natural causes. That leaves Blendinger, who is rumored to have drowned in the Rhine River. But his corpse was never found, only his clothes."

Reimann paused for a moment, then went on, "Herr Lechner might be able to tell you more. He was here during Altenberg's tenure. He's out today, but tomorrow he should be back to work."

The Hardys thanked the mayor and left the city hall. Immediately, Joe began to talk about Blendinger. "Do you think he stole the paintings and left his clothes at the riverbank so people would think he was dead?"

Frank shrugged. "Let's go see Doris Altenberg. Maybe she can tell us something, and also let us search the wine cellar."

The boys left their car where they had parked it and walked through the narrow streets toward the huge east gate set into the wall around the city. A slightly rising path led from there to the Altenberg house.

A German shepherd barked furiously when they arrived. "Kaiser, shut up!" Doris Altenberg called out as she appeared in the doorway.

"Are you by any chance the Hardy boys?" she asked with a friendly smile. "Herr Reimann told me you had offered to help find the treasure and would probably come to see me. Please come in." She led the boys into a large, airy living room furnished in heavy oak. On the walls hung a collection of spectacular photographs of the surrounding area.

"Did you take these?" Frank inquired.

"Yes," Doris replied. "It's a hobby of mine. I have my own darkroom in the house."

"Have you always lived here?" Joe asked as they all sat down.

"No. I was only five when my father was shot, and my mother died a few days later. I was brought up

47

by my aunt in Lüdenscheidt, but always spent my school vacations here."

"Who took care of this house?" Frank inquired.

"Karl and Lina, our housekeepers. They've managed the place all these years and are like parents to me."

"Would they have noticed it if someone had gone into the cellar?" Frank asked.

"We've asked them that before," Doris replied. "They insisted that they would have."

"Could we talk to them ourselves?" Frank asked.

"Certainly. I'll go find them. Be back in a minute." A few moments later, Doris returned with Karl and Lina.

They were in their seventies, with white hair and friendly faces. After they had been introduced to the boys, Frank asked, "Could someone have sneaked into the cellar without you noticing it?"

"No way," the old man replied. "We never left the house alone in all those years. For a long time, our married daughter lived here with her family, but now they've moved to Düsseldorf."

"How about at night?"

"The dog would have barked."

The boys were disappointed. Apparently, the intruder could not have gotten into the place!

6 Futile Chase

After Karl and Lina had left the room, the boys continued their conversation with Fräulein Altenberg. "I have a nephew in Frankfurt who's studying art," she said. "He wanted to write a paper on the paintings and could hardly wait to see them. He's very disappointed."

"Do you think we could search the cellar?" Frank inquired.

"Of course. But let me settle another matter first. Where are you staying?"

"At the Glockenhof."

"Why don't you come and move in here? I'd love to have the company of young people, and it might facilitate your investigation."

"Oh, that's very nice of you," Frank said, "but we don't want to impose—"

"Nonsense. Go and get your things, then you can do all the sleuthing you want."

Grateful, the boys hurried back to their hotel. They were in the middle of packing their clothes when they heard approaching footsteps that suddenly stopped in front of their door. But no one knocked and the footsteps faded again toward the stairs.

"You think someone was on the wrong floor?" Frank finally asked. He was in the middle of changing his clothes and at this point stood in his underwear. He went to the door and opened it just a crack. No one was in the hallway. Frank was just about to shut the door again, when he saw a note tacked to the outside.

YOU SNOOPING AMERICANS, GO HOME
OR YOU'LL BE DEAD!

With a quick call to Joe, Frank rushed out of the room and ran down the hallway. "I'll get this creep!" he vowed under his breath. Suddenly, he saw a figure clad in underwear running toward him, followed by a tall, slender youth with blond hair. He stopped short and suddenly realized he himself was the fellow in the underwear, running toward a huge mirror next to the stairway. The youth behind him was his brother!

Joe rushed past Frank, yelling, "Dummy!" in his brother's direction and then turned down the stairs. There he met an old man with a bent back who was on his way down, balancing himself with a walking stick. When he heard the boy behind him, he turned and said in a hoarse voice, "Careful, young man! I almost got run over by another guy a couple of seconds ago!"

Joe stopped and caught his breath. "What'd he look like?"

"Red hair and shabby clothes. A bum!" The old man squinted through his eyeglasses. He had a gray beard and a hat pulled low over his forehead. "The fellow raced out of here as if the devil himself were after him," he added.

Joe thanked him, then hurried across the lobby and through the door into the town square. He looked in all directions, ran to the next block, and looked around again. No red-haired man was in sight!

Disappointed, the boy shrugged and returned to the hotel just as the old man came out.

"Didn't find him, eh?" he rasped. "What's going on, anyway? Oh, well, young people today—" He shook his head and shuffled down the street.

Joe went into the lobby and asked the desk clerk

if a red-haired man had left the hotel a short time before.

The clerk shook his head. "No. The only person besides you that I saw in the last five minutes was that old man."

"Is he a guest?"

"No. Never met him before. I had gone to the office for a moment. He must have come in when I wasn't at the desk."

Suddenly, the truth dawned on Joe. The culprit had been the old man! He had put the warning on their door, then made up the story about the red-haired bum to divert attention from himself.

Joe ran out into the square for the second time and tried to spot the man. There was no sign of him anywhere. Grumbling, Joe returned to the hotel and went up to their room. On the way, he met his brother, now fully clothed, looking a bit embarrassed.

Despite his disappointment, Joe had to laugh. "Too bad the mirror was there," he said, "otherwise the good citizens of Glocken would have had the pleasure of watching you chase a crook in your underwear!"

"Go ahead and laugh," Frank said. "Where's the crook?"

Joe shrugged. "I lost him." Quickly, he told his brother what had happened.

"I guess we both blew it," Frank said as they went back to their room.

"That old man wasn't old," Joe added. "Otherwise he couldn't have disappeared so quickly. That getup he wore was a disguise!"

"Well, he did it all for nothing!" Frank declared. "We're not leaving!" He took the note from the door and looked at it closely. The message had been printed on a piece of white cardboard with a red crayon.

Quickly, the boys finished packing and went into the lobby. On the way, they met the elderly man who had listened to their conversation in the dining room the previous two nights. He looked curiously at their luggage.

"You're leaving Glocken already?" he asked.

"No, we're just changing our lodging," Joe replied.

"You're the Hardy boys, aren't you?" the man went on. "My name's Julius Braun."

"How do you know who we are?" Frank asked suspiciously.

"Oh, word gets around. I know you're investigating the case of the missing pictures."

Frank answered evasively, wondering what the man had overheard when he sat at the next table in the dining room.

"You're probably curious why I'm interested in this," Braun went on. "You see, I'm an art dealer and would just love to see the famous paintings while I'm here on vacation."

He asked a few more questions, but the boys did not volunteer anything, and finally the nosy art dealer walked away.

Before Frank and Joe left the hotel, Frank called Gerhard to tell him of their change in lodging. Their friend was worried about the latest developments and advised the boys to be very careful.

"I have some news too," he added. "I checked with various newspapers this morning to see if they had sent a reporter to Alfred Wagner last Friday. One of them, the *Isarpost*, did."

"You mean the blonde really *was* a journalist?" Frank asked.

"Right. I went to talk to her. She's still mad at poor Alfred."

"Then she wasn't that crazy driver on the Autobahn?"

"No. She couldn't have been. The Alfa Romeo doesn't belong to her. She drives a Volkswagen."

"Wait a minute. You're saying that the sports car belongs to another blonde?"

"Yes. She could be acting as a contact between one of Wagner's employees and whoever wants the sub plans. Suppose she happened to be there when you arrived, overheard you talk to Wagner, then followed you all the way to the Autobahn?"

"She must have hidden well in that case," Frank replied. "We didn't see another blonde at the garage. Matter of fact, the reporter was the only girl there!"

"H'm. I'm going to Wagner's right now," Gerhard went on, "and try to find out who owns that red Alfa Romeo. Talk to you later!"

On the way to the Altenberg house, the boys discussed what they had just learned. When they went through the town gate, a red sports car suddenly came out of a side street and moved in front of them.

"Joe, look, an Alfa!" Frank cried out.

"Only the driver isn't a girl," Joe replied. "But he has a Munich number. Let's follow him!"

Just then, they were caught in a minor traffic jam on the other side of the gate, and the boys had no choice but to pull up close to the red sports car. They were worried about being noticed by the driver, who was adjusting his rear mirror, his head slightly turned.

He was a young man, dressed in a white shirt under a green pullover. On his head he wore a jaunty green cap. His face was dark-complexioned, and his small mustache made him look like a Spaniard.

"Frank!" Joe whispered excitedly. "I think that's the guy who sneaked up to our car the other night!"

Just then, traffic loosened up and the car in front began to move. Frank followed. Instead of turning into the lane that lead to the Altenberg house, they drove down a street paralleling the Rhine River.

The young man drove slowly, forcing Frank and Joe to keep a safe distance.

"How long is he going to creep along like this?" Joe muttered impatiently when the red car leisurely headed into a curve. Two more curves followed right afterward, and by the time the boys came out of the last one, the street ahead of them was empty!

7　A Horrible Discovery

"Step on the gas, Joe!" Frank cried out. "He's not going to get away that easily!"

The Porsche shot forward. But less than three miles ahead, they found themselves in a small town, and wound up behind a large truck that trundled along at a snail's pace. It took a while before Joe could pass it and resume his chase.

"If this keeps up, we'll never catch the crook!" he muttered angrily as he stepped on the gas again. But after a few miles, they both had to admit that their chase was futile, and that the red sports car had vanished without a trace.

"I'm sure that guy drove slowly on purpose," Frank declared. "He knew the road and figured that in that series of curves he could get rid of us!"

"I bet it's the same car we encountered on the Autobahn. Only this time it had another driver."

"For all we know, the driver was the person who put the warning sign on our door, disguised as the old man," Frank said. "Apparently he wants to get rid of us. One way or another!"

"One thing I can't figure out," Joe said, "is why they followed us to Glocken. As long as we're not in Munich, they have nothing to worry about!"

Frank nodded. "Well, at least we know now who's after us. A Spanish-looking man and a blond woman, who drive the same car."

When the boys arrived at the Altenberg home, Kaiser barked loudly, but less ferociously than before. Apparently, he was getting used to them. Doris Altenberg showed them their room on the second floor. They were impressed with their comfortable accommodations filled with antique furniture. They unpacked their clothes quickly, then Joe plopped down on one of the high brass beds. He almost drowned in the fluffy feather comforter.

"Boy, I love these," he declared. "It's like sleeping on a cloud. Don't wake me up early tomorrow, okay?"

"We've got work to do, Joe," Frank said. "And if you don't rise voluntarily, I'll use that jug of water over there!"

"Sadist!"

"Come on now, it isn't nighttime yet. Let's search the cellar," Frank urged.

The police had found no clues in the secret room, but had deduced that the theft must have taken place a long time ago because of the dust and cobwebs on the old chest.

Frank and Joe got powerful flashlights from their car and climbed down the dimly lit staircase. The secret door was unlocked, and they entered the hiding place.

"Spooky, isn't it?" Joe said. "Like a tomb!"

The beams of their flashlights moved over the heavy chest to the caved-in back wall.

"Let's start over there," Frank suggested.

Carefully, they poked around the debris and searched among the rocks and crumbling stones.

"Apparently, the cellar once reached pretty far into the hill," Joe said. "You can't even determine where it ended anymore."

Finding nothing in the pile of rocks, they examined the walls and floor, hoping one of the cinderblocks might be loose and hide a secret. But they had no success. Suddenly, they heard a scratching sound near the door. They turned their lights in that direction and stared into a pair of glowing eyes!

Joe was so surprised he dropped his flashlight. "W-what—" he muttered.

Frank, who had recognized the eyes, chuckled. "Here comes the ghost of the Sexton!" he intoned in a deep voice. But then he clicked his tongue. "Kaiser, what are you doing here? Come over here!"

The German shepherd hesitated, wagged his tail, then finally moved close enough for Frank to pet him.

"That critter scared me to death!" Joe complained and picked up his flashlight.

Kaiser walked around the cellar and sniffed here and there. When he reached a pile of debris, he suddenly whined and began to dig.

The boys watched him with curiosity. "What's there, Kaiser?" Frank asked. "Are you looking for a bone?"

The dog paid no attention. Instead, he continued digging furiously with his front paws.

"Maybe he's on to something," Frank said. "I'll get a shovel!" He ran off, while Joe tried to calm the excited animal. Soon Frank returned with a spade and dug into the pile of stone. After a while, he stopped, wiping perspiration from his forehead.

"Nothing there," he declared. "That dog's crazy."

But Kaiser continued to whine and kept scratching in the debris. Frank resumed digging with his spade while Joe held the flashlight. Suddenly, something white came into sight.

"What on earth is that?" Joe asked. "It really looks like a bone!"

Frank put aside the spade, and the boys dug with their hands. "That's not only one bone," he declared, "that's a whole lot of them—pelvis, thigh—" His voice trailed off as the Hardys stared at each other in horror.

"It's—it's a human skeleton!" Joe whispered finally. "I told you, it felt like a tomb in here!"

Taking Kaiser along, the young detectives hurried out of the cellar and into the house, where they told Doris Altenberg about their find.

She instantly called the mayor and reported what happened.

"Too bad we don't know when the cellar caved in," Reimann said. "It could have been hundreds of years ago! Well, I'll phone the police right away, and we'll be out there as soon as possible."

Fifteen minutes later, the mayor arrived with two uniformed officers. They excavated the skeleton and took photographs.

"We'll have to send all this to Frankfurt for further evaluation," the mayor declared.

A clue had been uncovered in the shape of a wedding ring on one of the skeleton's fingers. It bore the name "Bertha" and the date 19·5·40.

"Let's check the records and see who got married that day," Frank suggested.

Reimann promised to take care of it. "The medical examination of the skeleton might also help to identify the victim," he said.

"Do you think he was murdered?" Frank asked.

"Either that, or he was killed when the wall crumbled. His skull is crushed."

After Reimann and the two officers left, Frank and Joe tried to find an answer to the riddle. But after a while they gave up. They were just crossing the yard to the house when Joe spotted a round figure walking along the street.

"Look who's coming," he said. "Our nosy friend, the art collector."

"Lovely place!" Braun called out when he noticed the boys, and described in detail the walk he had just taken. When he stretched out his left hand to indicate the way, the brothers suddenly made a startling discovery. Part of his left ring-finger was missing! Julius Braun was the man who had asked the Frankfurt coin dealer about gold *Joachimstaler*!

8 Two Hunches

"Oh, excuse me, Herr Braun," Joe said with a wink at his brother. "I forgot something."

He ran into the house and up the stairs to their room. Quickly, he got his camera from a drawer, put the telephoto lens in, and went to the window. He was hoping that Frank would still be talking to the art dealer.

As he looked out, he saw the two engrossed in conversation, but Braun's back was turned to the window! Cautiously, Joe tried to get Frank's attention by moving the drapes. When Frank finally glanced up, he put a finger to his lips and held up the camera.

Frank got the message. Slowly, he began to shift

his position. Without being aware of it, the art dealer followed suit. Finally, Joe was able to take a half dozen pictures from the window. When he was finished, he whistled contentedly and went downstairs again.

As Joe approached, Braun was just saying goodbye to Frank. Once he was gone, both boys laughed gleefully.

"That was a great idea!" Frank complimented his brother. "Although it wasn't easy for me to push that guy around into the right position!"

"I bet Braun's the man who visited Herr Rehm," Joe said. "And I don't believe he's here on vacation. Probably has something to do with the missing treasure."

"But why would he go to Frankfurt to inquire about gold *Joachimstaler*? Do you believe he got the same anonymous tip as Gerhard?"

"*He* could be the anonymous caller!" Joe pointed out. "But that doesn't make much sense. Why would he tip us off about the theft?"

"I have no idea."

"Well, I have all the things I need to develop the film," Joe said. "Then let's take the prints to Frankfurt to verify that Braun's the man who talked to Herr Rehm."

Doris Altenberg let Joe use a large, walk-in closet she used as a darkroom, while Frank went to the post office. He wanted to talk privately to his friend in Munich.

"Things are happening in Glocken, eh?" Gerhard said, impressed with the boys' new findings. "But what the connections are, I can't see just yet."

"I can't either," Frank admitted. "Did you find out about the red Alfa Romeo?"

"One of Alfred's mechanics, a man named Tarek, remembered working on it," Stolz replied. "A young man, who sounds like your friend with the little mustache, came in for a minor repair. No one had ever seen him before, and he didn't give his name."

Frank was disappointed. "Well, at least we have his license number. Of course, it may be a fake, or the car may be stolen."

"Let me have it anyway," Gerhard said. "I'll try to check it out with the Motor Vehicles Bureau. Now I have a request. Could you drive down to Düsseldorf tomorrow and do a little sleuthing for me? You're a lot closer than I am."

"Sure. What is it?"

"I'd like you to visit a company called Lemberg Werke. Alfred told me they approached him a couple of months ago and wanted to buy his plans for the sub. He declined."

"Oh, I see," Frank said. "And because they didn't

get anywhere, he thinks they may be trying to acquire the plans illegally now."

"It's possible," Gerhard said thoughtfully. "See what you can find out. Meanwhile, I'll look for the spy in Alfred's organization."

Joe was busy all evening developing his pictures, which turned out very sharp and clear. His brother, meanwhile, read a brochure Fräulein Altenberg had given them. It was dated before the war and contained pictures and detailed descriptions of the missing paintings. Among them was a wooden triptych Frank liked especially.

Before the boys went to bed, they wrote a letter to Herr Rehm, planning to mail the photographs since they had no time to drive to Frankfurt and deliver them. They posted the letter early next morning, then went to City Hall to see Herr Lechner. They were directed to a stuffy little office, where a thin, elderly man with white hair greeted them and offered them two straight-backed chairs.

"The mayor told me you'd be coming to see me," he began.

"Yes. We'd like some information on Mayor Altenberg," Joe replied. "Also on Herr Blendinger."

"Helmut Altenberg was a fine man," Herr Lechner said. "Everyone liked him a lot. Had a summer home in the Bavarian Alps, in Bad Waldsee. When he wasn't there, he'd let his staff use it. Almost all municipal employees were up there at one time or another."

The boys listened politely to the old man's memories. However, they were most interested in Blendinger, who had disappeared into the river one day. As soon as he had a chance, Joe brought up the subject.

"Well, they never cleared up what happened," Herr Lechner replied. "There was no trace of Blendinger except his clothes. He probably drowned while swimming. Water was pretty cold already, because it was in September. Yes, in September 1944."

"Wasn't it unusual for him to go swimming so late in the year?" Frank asked.

"Not for Blendinger. He was an oddball anyway, especially since his wife died. Lived all by himself, and nobody knew him very well."

"We have a theory," Frank said. "Perhaps he left his clothes on the riverbank to pretend he drowned, but really took off with the paintings."

Lechner pulled on his right earlobe. "H'm. An oddball Blendinger was, but a thief? I doubt it. Yet, as I said, no one really knew him well. But if you're looking for a suspect, I know one. Unfortunately, it's been proven that he's dead."

"Who's that?" Joe asked.

"Wilhelm Schmidt, the councilman. After he was called into the army, Herr Altenberg found out that Schmidt had embezzled quite a bit of money. When the police were about to arrest him, in the summer of '44, the report came that he had been killed in combat. Probably better this way for his wife and his son Heinz, who was only a little boy then."

"Where's Frau Schmidt now?" Frank wanted to know. "I'd like to ask her some questions."

"Can't. She took off for South America after the war with her son. Had relatives there. I have no idea what became of her."

Herr Lechner also told the boys that Palm, the deputy mayor, had died of a heart attack a few months after the paintings were hidden. The boys thanked the elderly man for the information and were about to leave, when Joe suddenly had an idea.

"Excuse me, sir," he said. "I just remembered something else I wanted to ask you. Do you know Frau Blendinger's first name?"

"Of course," the old man said, raising his eyebrows. "Her name was Bertha."

Bertha! The name on the ring of the skeleton they found in the secret wine cellar! Was it possible the dead man was Blendinger?

Quickly, Joe told Herr Lechner why he had asked.

"Well, well," the old man said, shaking his head. "I can't believe all this happened in our quiet little town. Tell you what. I'll check the records right now and see if I can find Blendinger's wedding date."

While Lechner looked in the files, Frank and Joe talked to each other in low tones. If the dead man was really Blendinger, why were his clothes found on the riverbank? There was only one explanation for this—*murder*! After the murderer had killed Blendinger, he put the man's clothes on the grass, buried the corpse in the pile of debris in the cellar, and disappeared. But how could he have gotten into the cellar without anyone noticing him?

"The dead man could also be someone else," Joe spoke up. "Maybe Blendinger was the murderer and thief, and left his own ring on the victim's finger!"

Frank looked at his brother admiringly. "Not a bad deduction!"

Finally, Lechner returned. "Congratulations," he said. "The date is correct. You were right, it must be Blendinger's wedding ring."

Frank asked Herr Lechner to tell Mayor Reimann about their discovery, then the boys thanked the old man and left. When they returned to the Altenberg house, Kaiser greeted them with a loud bark.

"Thanks, pal," Frank said and patted the dog. "You helped us a great deal!"

Suddenly, the boy had an idea. He ran into the garden, where he had seen Karl weeding the vegetables. Joe followed.

"Karl, did you always have a dog in the house, even before you got Kaiser?" the young detective asked.

"Oh, yes," the old man replied. "You need a dog in a place like this. I've been here for a long, long time, and we've always had one."

"Are you sure you had one in September 1944?"

Karl frowned. "Let's see—which one did we have in those days? Prinz, that's it. How—how'd you guess, young man? That must have been the time when Prinz was so restless at night and barked all the time. One morning we found him dead— poisoned!"

Joe realized what his brother was getting at and asked tensely, "Did you ever find out who killed the dog?"

"No. Probably someone who was bothered by the noise. The poor animal! Anyway, we didn't get another dog until a few weeks later."

The boys thanked the man and hurried into the kitchen, where they quickly ate a sandwich prepared by Lina. Then they started their trip to Düsseldorf.

"That was quite a brainstorm you had," Joe said admiringly to his brother.

"Well, I realized that the theft could have taken place right after the war. And Kaiser wasn't alive then!"

"Of course not. And the fact that the previous dog was poisoned proves that someone could have gotten into the cellar without Karl and Lina being aware of it. And it all happened at the same time Blendinger drowned!"

"Maybe the thief forced him to reveal the hiding place of the treasure and killed him afterward," Frank said.

With moderate traffic on the Autobahn and a short break for a snack, it was three in the afternoon before they reached the Lemberg Werke. It was a small company, and looked clean and neat.

The Hardys had decided to introduce themselves as reporters for a youth magazine. The receptionist asked them to wait a few moments. Someone would be with them soon to give the information they wanted.

The boys sat down in the lobby. People came and went. A young man in a white lab coat looked at them curiously as he waited for a folder at the receptionist's desk. Finally, a well-dressed man in his forties walked up to them. "What can I do for you?" he asked with a friendly smile.

Joe said they were writing a series of articles for their magazine about mini-submarines. "We'd like to mention the boat your company is developing," he added.

"I'm sorry I can't help you with that," the man said. "We did have a mini-sub division, but we discontinued the development about two months ago."

The boys looked at him in surprise. If the company was out of the mini-sub business, there was no reason for them to steal Wagner's plans. They wondered if the man was telling them the truth.

"What made you give up your project?" Frank asked.

"Internal reasons," the man replied curtly. "I really can't talk to you about it."

The boys tried for a few more minutes but had no luck. Disappointed, they thanked the man and left.

"We're really no wiser than before," Frank muttered as they walked outside and looked around. Just then the man in the white lab coat, whom they had seen in the lobby before, came out the door and walked past them. Without turning his head, he said, "Wait for me at Maria's at five o'clock!"

9 News at Maria's

The Hardys were speechless for a moment as they stared after the man. Then Joe made a move to follow him. Frank held his brother back by the arm and pulled him into the street.

"Don't!" he whispered. "Maybe we'll learn something!"

The boys climbed into their car, and Joe shook his head. "I don't get it. How does this guy know who we are? And why didn't he just tell us what was on his mind?"

"He might have overheard us at Lemberg Werke," Frank replied. "Perhaps he knows something about the mini-subs but doesn't want to be seen with us so as not to risk his job."

"Then maybe our trip wasn't in vain after all," Joe agreed. "Let's go to Maria's! I suppose it's a café or a restaurant. Actually, I hope it is. Can you believe I'm hungry again?"

Frank chuckled. "So am I!"

He started the car and drove to the next intersection. Maria's Coffee Shop was on the other side on the left. After parking the car, the boys went inside.

It was a small place with tables on each side of the room. Frank and Joe sat down and ordered hot dogs with potato salad.

Soon the little restaurant filled up with people who had just left work. The Hardys waited with growing impatience for the mysterious young man. He walked in a few minutes past five, said hello to some friends, then sat down at the boys' table.

He introduced himself as Peter Hauser, ordered a cup of coffee, then grinned broadly at the young detectives. "How much is it worth to you to talk to me?"

Frank and Joe stared at each other. They had not expected to pay for the information.

Frank cleared his throat. "I think we'd better tell you what this is all about," he began. "My name's Frank Hardy, and this is my brother Joe. We're working for Gerhard Stolz, the investigative reporter. You might have heard of him."

"I sure have," Hauser said. "Does that mean

you're not really with a youth magazine at all?"

"That's right. We just pretended to be reporters to get some information from Lemberg Werke without arousing suspicion." Frank told the young man the reason for their visit, and Peter Hauser shook his head in surprise.

"And here I thought I could make a few bucks off two rookie reporters. But this is even better. So you're working on a case of industrial espionage? I wouldn't be surprised if this guy Steiner was behind it."

"What do you mean?" Frank asked. "Who's he?"

Peter Hauser explained what had happened to the development of the Lemberg mini-sub. The company had been urged for several years by their South American representative in Buenos Aires to design a small sub that would be able to submerge to a depth of fifteen hundred feet.

"The Argentinian representative, Willy Steiner, felt it was a great idea. Two years ago, we hired half a dozen people to work on the project, among them a friend of Steiner's—a younger man named Heinz Kroll—and myself. We developed different designs, and just as we were ready to build a prototype, the whole thing was called off!"

"So it's true that Lemberg discontinued the sub," Joe said.

"Yes. In spite of all the money that we put into

it," Hauser replied. "Later, I learned the reason from Heinz Kroll."

"I think I know what it was," Frank spoke up. "Management heard about Alfred Wagner's mini-sub, which was superior to their own. So they tried to buy Wagner's."

"And when he refused to sell, they just dropped the whole project," Joe added.

Hauser nodded. "Exactly. Willy Steiner was furious. He made a special trip over here, and argued with Herr Lemberg endlessly. Finally, Lemberg kicked him out."

"I don't see why the man we spoke to wouldn't tell us that," Joe declared.

"Maybe he would have if you hadn't claimed to be reporters," Hauser said. "I don't think he wanted the affair written up in the press. In fact, there's something else going on now that even he doesn't know about!"

"What's that?" Frank asked eagerly.

"Willy Steiner decided to continue developing the mini-sub on his own, together with his friend Heinz Kroll and a man named Oskar Jansky. Both were with Lemberg but left. They're building their ship in Munich—I don't know their address, though. Later, they're going to test it in a little Bavarian lake."

"How do you know all this?" Frank asked.

"From Heinz Kroll," Hauser replied. "He wanted me to go with them. Initially, I pretended to be interested, just to find out what they were up to. He promised me the world, too. He was really ticked off when I said no."

Hauser ordered another cup of coffee and took a long sip. "I had no intention of working with these people. For one thing, I can't stand Heinz Kroll. He's a slippery character, that one. And Jansky I don't trust, either. Besides, the whole thing looked rather fishy to me. Heinz claims that our company didn't handle Wagner right, but that Steiner didn't have any trouble."

"Sure he didn't," Frank said. "He didn't ask Wagner to sell his plans—he just took them! We'll have to stop those crooks before they get too far. I hope we won't have any trouble finding them in Munich."

Joe asked the young man what the three suspects looked like. Hauser said he had never met Willy Steiner, but Jansky was about six feet tall, skinny, and had gray hair. When he described Heinz Kroll, the Hardys gaped in surprise. There was no doubt that he was the man whom they had seen in the red sports car!

Frank and Joe thanked Peter Hauser, who promised to let them know if he heard anything further from Kroll. Then he shook hands with the Hardys and grinned. "I never thought I'd be helping Gerhard Stolz with one of his investigations!"

The young detectives decided to drive back toward Glocken and call Gerhard from a rest area later because it was too early to catch him home. They stopped near Limburg and went to a telephone booth.

Rita Stolz answered. "Gerhard isn't here," she said. "I have no idea where he is. Said he'd eat out. Shall I leave him a message?"

"Please," Frank said. "Tell him we have some important news for him. We'll try to get in touch with him later."

"Okay. Oh, wait a minute. I just noticed that Gerhard left a note for you on this telephone pad. It says, 'Alfa license number phony.'"

"Thanks, Rita. Good thing it doesn't matter now in view of the new development."

It was late at night when the boys arrived in Glocken. Joe had tried to reach Gerhard once more, but he hadn't returned.

Next morning after breakfast, the boys drove to the post office. Doris Altenberg had offered them her telephone, but they did not want to take advantage of her hospitality. Joe went into a booth and dialed Gerhard's number, but there was no answer.

When Joe walked out, his forehead was creased in

thought. Then he heard a low whistle. He realized that it came from Frank, who stood in the town square waving to him.

"What's up?" Joe asked after he hurried to his brother.

"I just saw Herr Braun come out of the Glockenhof," Frank replied. "See, there he is. Let's follow him for a while. Maybe something interesting will turn up."

Joe agreed. If the art dealer should notice them, they could just walk up to him and start a conversation.

Braun did not seem to be going anywhere in particular. When he came to an intersection, he suddenly stopped and looked intently down into the side street. Frank and Joe glanced into a shop window, watching the little man out of the corners of their eyes. Just then, Braun rushed around the corner in a flash!

10 A Bird Flies Away

"After him!" Joe urged.

But Frank held his impulsive brother back. "Wait a minute. If we run around the corner, he'll realize we're after him. Let's cross the intersection and just look down the side street in a casual manner."

The boys pretended to be deep in conversation as they crossed the street. Frank glanced past Joe and whispered, "He's halfway down the block talking to a guy in a blue car. They're too far away for me to really see much. Now Braun's getting into the car. Drat, they're taking off! Too bad."

Joe turned and saw the car round the next corner, but neither he nor Frank could read the license number. There was no way to follow the art dealer, because their Porsche was parked in the town square.

"Do you think that character in the blue car has something to do with the gold *Joachimstaler* and the paintings?" Joe asked.

"Who knows?" Frank replied. "Maybe he was just a casual acquaintance of Braun's."

"Perhaps we should call Herr Rehm in Frankfurt," Joe suggested. "He must have the photos by now. Perhaps he'll be able to identify Braun."

"Good idea," Frank agreed, and headed for the next phone booth. A few minutes later, he emerged with a smile. Lothar Rehm had confirmed their suspicion: the man with the missing part of his finger was the art dealer! Now the boys were convinced that Braun had some connection with the theft of the paintings, but they still were not sure why he wanted to know who had sold gold *Joachimstaler*.

"Maybe he'll be back at the Glockenhof this afternoon," Joe suggested. "We can pay him a visit and try to find out what he's up to then. Now I suggest we go back to the Altenberg house. Maybe Gerhard called and left a message."

But Gerhard Stolz had not called. Instead, a telegram was waiting for them. Frank opened it and frowned. "Listen to this," he said to his brother and read the message. " 'Clues lead to Vienna stop will go there for a few days stop Gerhard Stolz.' "

"Vienna?" Joe asked. "That's strange. Do you think Steiner and his gang took off for Austria?"

Frank shrugged. "Too bad we can't contact him. We have so much to tell him!"

"I can't figure out why he sent a telegram instead of calling us," Joe declared.

"Maybe he didn't want to disturb Miss Altenberg so early in the morning," Frank replied. "The telegram was phoned in at six-thirty."

The boys spent the rest of the morning helping Karl with his work in the yard. After lunch, they drove back into town and went to the Glockenhof, asking to see the art dealer.

"Herr Braun?" the clerk said. "Sorry, but he's gone."

"Gone?" Frank and Joe echoed.

"He checked out about an hour ago. He had planned to stay longer, but apparently something important came up. He left in a hurry."

"Do you know where he went?" Frank inquired.

"No. I don't even know where to send his mail."

"Maybe he'll call you. Then we'd be able to get in touch with him," Joe said. He told the surprised clerk that they needed to talk to the art dealer because he could help clear up a theft. The young man promised to phone them if he heard from Braun.

"So our bird flew away," Frank muttered as they left the hotel. "I bet that stranger in the blue car had something to do with it."

Joe nodded. "Too bad. Well, let's go see Herr Lechner while we're here. Perhaps he and the mayor have some more news on Blendinger."

At City Hall, the elderly official gave them two yellowed photographs of Blendinger and a group shot that included Helmut Altenberg and Wilhelm Schmidt. If Blendinger was still alive, the boys were told, they might be able to recognize him from the pictures of him as a younger man.

The boys thanked him and left his office. They decided to call Gerhard in Munich to find out more about his trip to Vienna.

"While you call," Joe said to his brother, "I'm going to have some ice cream. I'm hungry."

He went to a small café on the square while Frank disappeared into the telephone booth in front of the post office. As Joe was ordering an ice-cream cone at the counter, a customer stood up and passed him on the way to the door. He was elegantly dressed, with dark glasses, a mustache, and shiny black hair.

Just then, the clerk handed Joe his ice cream. He took it absentmindedly, then suddenly jumped off his stool and rushed after the mustached man. "Hey, wait a minute!" Joe called out.

Several passersby turned their heads as the young detective ran out of the café. The stranger, meanwhile, kept walking straight ahead. Finally, Joe caught up with him and blocked his way. He pointed to the man's breast pocket that showed part of a blue-and-white-striped silk handkerchief with a sun pattern, exactly like the one he had found near their car the first night in Glocken!

"Excuse me, sir, but where did you get this?" Joe asked.

The man retreated from Joe's pointing finger and stared at him indignantly. Then he tried to pass the boy.

But Joe blocked his way again. Ice cream was dripping down the young detective's fingers, and pedestrians began to crowd around the two, staring curiously. Suddenly, the Italian owner of the café rushed toward them and yelled, *"Al ladro! Al ladro!"* Joe paid no attention to him. He was too busy trying to find out about the strange handkerchief, while desperately licking his melting ice cream.

The café owner, feeling ignored, became very agitated. He let out a stream of words in Italian that Joe could not understand.

Just then, Frank came out of the telephone booth

and pushed his way through the crowd. When he reached his brother, he stared in surprise. The Italian was gesticulating wildly and pulling on Joe's arm, while the younger Hardy was trying not to get ice cream all over himself and the café owner.

Frank could not help but burst out laughing. Suddenly, a police officer appeared on the scene. The Italian quickly turned to him for assistance, while Joe looked at his brother with a despairing shrug.

"Instead of helping me, you're laughing!" he accused Frank. "Don't you see I'm in trouble?"

"Sorry, but all this is kind of funny," Frank replied. "What happened?"

Quickly, Joe explained the reason for his predicament. Meanwhile, the policeman could not make heads or tails out of the Italian's complaint. He was pleased when Frank turned to the mustached stranger, who apparently spoke no German either, and tried to tell him in English what was going on.

Soon everyone calmed down. The stranger realized that Joe had not meant to attack him, and the café owner was paid for the ice cream. The Hardys found out that the man Joe had followed was from Argentina and that he had bought his handkerchief, the cause of the trouble, in a shop in Buenos Aires.

When the Hardys were finally back in their car, Joe said, "I had a hunch I'd seen that pattern before.

It reminded me of the Argentinian flag, even though that has only one white and one blue stripe with a sun in the middle."

"Right," Frank added. "And now we know why Kroll wanted to retrieve the handkerchief. It pointed to his connection with Argentina."

"Hey, where are you going?" Joe asked suddenly, when he realized that his brother did not turn toward the Altenberg house but continued straight ahead.

"I just had an idea," Frank replied. "Remember, this is the road where Heinz Kroll gave us the slip with his Alfa. We assumed he just stepped on the gas and took off, right?"

"Right. What are you getting at?"

"Well, perhaps he hid somewhere along the way and let us pass. There could be a little alley we missed because we were looking at the street straight ahead!"

"It's possible," Joe agreed. "I'll check the right, you take the left."

Shortly after the curves where the red sports car had disappeared from sight, the boys noticed a turnoff. It was hardly more than a footpath leading into a small valley. Meadows bordered it on both sides, and there was a little vineyard that no one seemed to have tended for years. The boys immediately spotted tire tracks in the dusty road. A car had driven there recently, and both Frank and Joe were sure it was the red Alfa Romeo.

The path turned left, and they saw a wooded hill ahead. Then an old mine came into view. DO NOT ENTER. DANGER! was written on a sign along the road.

Frank parked the car in the shadow of an oak tree, and the boys got out to look around.

"Strange place," Frank muttered.

"You're right," Joe agreed. "There's the entrance, and up there is the foundation of an old building."

"I wonder if Kroll hid here?"

"Let's investigate," Joe suggested and got a couple of flashlights from their car. As they approached the mine entrance, they noticed several more tire tracks on the ground leading inside. The boys went over to the marks and studied them carefully.

"I think these were made by the same car coming and going several times," Frank declared.

"I agree," Joe said. "And I bet it was the red Alfa Romeo!"

Cautiously, the young detectives moved toward the entrance and looked into a large antechamber. They gaped in surprise. Inside, in the semi-darkness, stood the red sports car!

They held their breath and listened, but heard nothing. "I don't think Kroll's in here," Frank whispered finally. "Come on."

They turned on their flashlights and began to examine the elegant little Alfa. Joe opened the trunk with the key he found in the ignition. A collection of license plates was lying inside! Frank, meanwhile, was checking the interior of the car. He discovered an old gray suit and a hat. When he opened the glove compartment, he said excitedly in an undertone, "Joe, look! Here's your camera. And what in the world is that?"

As Joe hastily walked over, Frank pulled out a strange object. Dangling in his hand was a wig with long, blond hair!

11 A Trap!

"A wig!" Frank exclaimed triumphantly. "That explains the blond woman on the Autobahn!"

Joe nodded. "This guy really fooled us, didn't he!" Then he spotted the clothing inside the car. Quickly, he checked the suit pockets and pulled out a pair of glasses and a phony gray beard. On the floor of the car, he saw a walking stick.

"Now I get it!" he exploded. "Heinz not only impersonated the blond woman, he was also the old man who put the warning on our door! Apparently, it had nothing to do with the art theft, after all!"

"There's one thing I don't understand, though," Frank spoke up.

"What's that?"

"What is Heinz Kroll doing in Glocken? And why does he want to get us out of town? He should be happy we're here and not in Munich!"

"True," Joe agreed. "I don't have the answer to that, either."

Suddenly, it dawned on the boys that they had been talking freely with each other. What if someone was eavesdropping? They quickly turned off their flashlights and stood still to listen. After a minute of dead silence, Joe said, "I don't think anyone's around. What are we going to do next?"

"I'd like to check out this mine," Frank replied. "Perhaps we'll find some more clues."

"Or Kroll himself. But we'd better be careful."

Their eyes had become used to the semidarkness, and the boys saw a narrow tunnel at the end of the antechamber.

Cautiously, they went into the passage. It was just wide enough for them to walk side by side. After a few steps, they had to use their flashlights. The tunnel went straight ahead for about twenty yards, rising slightly, until it curved to the left. At the corner, the boys switched off their lights and listened tensely. There was no sound anywhere. They put their flashlights on again and continued.

Now the passage became narrower, and large boulders dotted the floor here and there.

"I hope we don't get hit on the head by one of these," Frank whispered.

They came to a cross tunnel and listened again. There was no sound. The air had become noticeably cooler and more humid, and a moldy smell pervaded the area. Suddenly, they heard a loud rustling! The noise stopped as abruptly as it had begun, and the Hardys were petrified. Was something or someone lurking ahead of them?

They stood stock-still for a while, but finally Joe turned on his flashlight again and walked closer to the cross tunnel. Just then, a shadow shot out of the dark, rushed past them, and disappeared through the entrance.

"Wow!" Frank muttered and wiped cold perspiration from his forehead. "A huge rat! I almost had heart failure because of that thing!"

When the boys had recovered from their scare, they beamed their lights into the short cross tunnel. Joe touched one of the huge, wooden supports.

"They must be ages old," he said. "I wonder how strong they are at this point." He pushed the beam with his hand, and little stones rained down on them from the ceiling. Instantly, the two jumped out into the main passage.

"Are you tired of living?" Frank hissed. "Let's not tempt fate, eh?"

Joe grinned sheepishly, and the two continued their investigation. The ground beneath them rose and fell, and after a few more bends they came to a cross tunnel that had no visible ends.

They stood a while, listening in the darkness, then Frank suggested, "We'd better go back. Otherwise we'll get lost!"

Joe nodded and was just about to put his light on again when suddenly he stopped short. "Wait a minute," he whispered. "What was that?"

Tensely, the Hardys strained their ears and heard a mumbling up ahead.

"Voices!" Frank said excitedly. "Let's go a little closer!"

The boys held on to each other and tiptoed ahead. Approaching a dim shimmer of light, the Hardys heard the voices of two men. The tunnel turned sharply and the young detectives realized that the men had to be just beyond the bend.

Suddenly, Frank stopped and pulled Joe by the hand. He thought he had heard steps behind them. They listened again, but all was quiet, so they advanced a few more steps.

"—have to go! These young snoopers are beginning to become a real problem!" a man said.

"I warned them, and that's it. If they don't get out of town now, we'll have to take drastic measures."

"I bet that's Heinz Kroll," Frank whispered. "But who's he talking to? Willy Steiner or Oskar Jansky?"

"Let's get them and find out!" Joe whispered back. "They'll be so surprised that we'll have a good chance of overpowering them."

Frank nodded, and with a loud war whoop, the Hardys charged ahead, ready to attack their enemies. Aggressively, they barreled around the bend, but suddenly stopped dead in their tracks. There was no one at the other side of the tunnel!

A flickering storm lantern stood on the floor, lighting up a tape recorder that was slowly unwinding.

"Get back!" Joe cried out. "It's a trap!"

But it was too late. Suddenly, a tremendous explosion filled the area. Stones and boulders flew through the air as the tunnel behind them collapsed. Both boys were thrown to the ground and passed out momentarily.

Then there was nothing but black stillness. After a while, Joe moved and coughed. "Frank, are you okay?" he called out fearfully. "Are you hurt, Frank?"

"I think I'm still in one piece," Frank croaked. "But my ears are ringing like a million bells!"

Joe got up and switched on his flashlight. He was lucky it hadn't been damaged. Through a slowly settling cloud of dust he saw his brother, who sat on the ground shaking his head. Then he got back on his feet, knees trembling from the frightening experience.

Joe beamed his light in the direction from where they had come. There was nothing but a mass of rocks, boulders, dirt, and crushed supports. The tunnel was completely cut off!

"We're trapped!" Frank exclaimed, his face white as a sheet. "We'll never get out of here again!"

"We could try digging," Joe suggested lamely.

The boys put their lights on the ground and started to move the debris with their hands. Soon they were perspiring and gasping from the effort. A huge boulder was lying in their way, and was impossible to move.

"This won't work," Joe said. "The cave-in might be ten or twenty yards long!"

Frank leaned on the wall, exhausted. "That means we'll have to find another exit."

"If there is one," Joe muttered. He picked up the storm lantern, which had fallen over, and lighted it with a match. "This way we can preserve our flashlights," he declared.

Tensely, the boys walked forward. They passed

another cross tunnel, but soon reached the end of the main passageway. There was a wall of debris where the tunnel had apparently caved in long ago.

"I feel like a trapped animal!" Frank sighed. "We can't give up, though. Let's examine the cross tunnel."

The boys hurried back, fighting a feeling of panic. The first cross tunnel ended soon, but the second one was a narrow, low passageway that led down into a cavelike room. From there, three more tunnels branched off in different directions. With newfound hope, the boys investigated them, but all three came to an end after a few yards.

Discouraged, the young detectives returned to the cave and sat down on a large boulder.

"We should've known there wouldn't be another exit," Joe wailed. "Kroll set the trap at the right spot!"

"And we were stupid enough to walk right into it," Frank added. "This creep must know the old mine like the back of his hand. I wonder how come?"

"We'll never know the answer," Joe's voice trailed off. He was overcome with the feeling that their situation was hopeless, and that they were buried alive.

Frank, too, was overwhelmed with his own helplessness. "We won't be discovered missing until tomorrow. And then, who would think of looking for us in this abandoned mine? Even if someone had the idea, it could take days for a rescue team to get to this spot! By that time, we will have died from dehydration or lack of air!"

12 A Surprising Development

Joe pointed to the lantern that stood on the ground. "We'd better put it out. We'll need the oxygen."

Frank nodded. Suddenly, he stared at the light and rubbed his eyes. "Hey, Joe! Maybe I'm dreaming, but I think the flame's flickering a little. You know what that means? A draft! There must be an opening somewhere!"

Joe slapped his brother on the back and jumped up. "You're brilliant, Frank! How come I didn't see that? Now I can even feel the draft!"

With renewed hope, the two prisoners searched for the opening. Soon they discovered a crack in the ceiling of the cave, but it was high up and so narrow that no one could possibly squeeze through it.

Joe sighed in despair and slumped back onto the stone, while Frank's mind worked rapidly.

"Cheer up, little brother!" he cried suddenly. "There has to be another opening somewhere. Otherwise there wouldn't be a draft!"

This brought Joe to his feet again, and the two carried the flickering lamp through the narrow passageway into the main tunnel.

"Up there, under the ceiling somewhere, must be the other hole," Frank declared and directed the beam over the pile of debris. "I can't see where else it would be."

"So let's dig," Joe said.

Quickly, they started their task, which was extremely difficult without tools. The boys worked in shifts, since there was not enough room for both of them. After one had been digging for ten minutes or so, he stopped for a rest and the other took over.

Slowly, they progressed until Frank loosened an especially heavy boulder and moved it aside. There was nothing behind it. His hand reached out into empty space!

"We've broken through!" he cried out. Then he added cautiously, "But we're not outside yet. I think this is another passageway."

Their flashlight batteries were weak and the light beams rather thin at this point, so they could not really tell where they were after they had slipped through the hole and worked their way down the pile of debris on the other side. Frank lighted the lantern again and held it up. Suddenly, both boys cried out in surprise. They were standing in a low-ceilinged room with a huge wooden chest in the middle!

"I don't believe it!" Joe exclaimed. "We're in Fräulein Altenberg's secret wine cellar!"

"At least we're safe," Frank said, and sighed in relief.

They went into the other cellar, flew up the stairs, and were about to rush out into the yard when they found the door locked.

"That's all we need," Frank grumbled, and banged his fists against the wood. Instantly, Kaiser began to bark. It seemed like an eternity until footsteps were heard and a man's voice said, "Who's there?"

"Frank and Joe! Please let us out!" Frank yelled.

The door was unlocked and the boys saw Doris Altenberg and Karl standing in the yard. Lina came running up, and the dog jumped around the boys in excitement.

"You look like you've been rolling in dirt!" Lina cried out. "What on earth were you doing down in the cellar? Did someone lock you in?"

"We were worried about you," Doris added. "It's rather late—"

But Frank and Joe suddenly felt too exhausted to explain. They pleaded for a shower and a night's sleep, and promised a detailed report of their adventure in the morning.

The following day their hosts were amazed to hear where the boys had been.

"The mine?" Karl asked, his eyes growing wide. "I never knew you could get into the cellar that way. And who would have ever thought of looking for you there?"

"What kind of mine is it?" Frank asked. "No one mentioned it to us before."

"It's been abandoned since World War I," Karl replied. "At that time, iron ore was mined there, but after a terrible accident it was closed down. Since then, no one ever goes near it."

"It seems irresponsible to have just a little warning sign by the road," Frank said. "We'll have to tell Mayor Reimann about it."

"Yes, you do that," the old man agreed. "I know the entrance used to be boarded up, but apparently the panels have rotted away."

"Or the crooks removed them so they could trap us more easily," Frank said.

"Those terrible, terrible men!" Lina cried, her voice trembling. "You'll have to report them to the police at once!"

102

"We will," Frank promised. "But first we want to see if our car's still at the mine."

"No!" Lina turned to Doris Altenberg. "Doris, don't allow those boys to go near that place again! It's suicidal!"

But Frank and Joe were convinced that their enemies had left the mine by now, thinking the boys were locked in the tunnel forever. Doris agreed with them, and offered to let them use her car.

Right after breakfast, Frank and Joe left.

"Now we know how the thief got into the cellar to steal the paintings," Joe said on the way.

"Of course," Frank agreed. "The tunnel was probably dug just for that purpose, then the cave-in was engineered in 1944."

"Good thinking, Frank. This would fit into our theory about Blendinger's disappearance."

"What I'd like to know is how come we didn't notice the draft while we were checking out the cellar?"

"There wasn't any. The crack in the ceiling of the cave could have been caused by the explosion!"

Both boys were deep in thought while Joe turned onto the narrow path leading into the valley. "Something I can't get out of my head," Frank finally said. "Heinz Kroll and his partner, whose voice we heard on the tape, must know the mine extremely well in order to trap us like this. Don't you think that's odd?"

"Why? They may have discovered the place accidentally, or heard the local people talk about it."

"But what if it wasn't accidental? What if they've known the mine for a long time, or someone drew them a map?"

"It's possible. What difference does it make?"

"A big one," Frank said excitedly. "If they know the mine so well, they might also know about the tunnel to the secret cellar. In other words, the Kroll gang might have had something to do with the theft of the paintings!"

Joe whistled. "Not a bad deduction. It would explain why Kroll wanted us out of Glocken! But on the other hand—he's involved in the industrial espionage case at Wagner's!"

"Right. Don't ask me how come he features in both mysteries!"

The boys reached their destination and, though they were convinced that their enemies had left, proceeded quietly and carefully. They parked the car some distance from the mine behind a clump of bushes, then slowly crept toward the entrance. Their suspicion proved correct. The Alfa was gone.

Only the silver Porsche still stood under the oak tree.

"Let's see if anything is missing," Frank suggested.

"Missing?" Joe said with a grin. "Quite the contrary!" He pointed to his old camera in the passenger seat. Otherwise, everything seemed to be untouched.

"Very clever," Frank declared. "Now it looks just like an accident. 'Curious kids entered abandoned mine and were trapped by landslide. Rescue discontinued because of excessive danger.'"

Joe chuckled. "Wait till Kroll sees us. Will he ever be surprised!"

"First we'll have to find them," Frank reminded his brother. "I suggest we go to Munich and start searching."

"Good idea," Joe agreed. "There's nothing else for us to do here now anyway."

It was decided that Joe would bring back Fräulein Altenberg's car and start packing, while Frank would call Rita Stolz from the post office.

When Frank spoke to his friend's wife, he was surprised to hear that Gerhard had not been in touch with her. Rita was worried, and so was the Hardy boy.

When he arrived at the Altenberg house, Joe had

packed almost everything. The smell of veal roast permeated the house, and Doris Altenberg invited them to stay for lunch. Gratefully, the boys accepted.

They were all standing in the kitchen when Karl came in.

"Doris, guess who I just saw in town," he said. "Heinz Schmidt!"

Frank stared at him. "Are you talking about the son of the former councilman who was killed in the war?"

"That's right," Karl confirmed. "First I didn't know who he was, because I hadn't seen him since he was a little boy. But afterwards I realized that it had to be Heinz. He looks just like his father. He's driving a sports car. Must be doing well in South America."

Joe almost exploded with excitement. "What kind of car was it?" he urged. "What did it look like?"

"I'm not familiar with the various makes of automobiles, young man," Karl said with a grin. "All I know is it was a little red sports car!"

13 The Man in the Lobby

Frank stared at his brother. "Joe! Did you hear that! Heinz Kroll is probably Heinz Schmidt!"

"I heard. Karl, can you describe Heinz to us?"

After the old man had given them a good idea of what the man looked like, there was no doubt in the boys' minds. Schmidt was indeed Kroll!

"Karl, you've been a great help!" Frank said. "You've given us our best clue yet!"

"Boys," Doris Altenberg interrupted, "would you mind telling me who this mysterious Kroll is? Or would you rather not reveal your findings since I'm still a suspect?"

The young detectives assured her that they never

for a moment believed that she was involved in the thefts.

"We just didn't mention Kroll by name because we didn't realize he had something to do with the paintings," Joe said. "Only as of this morning do we suspect that the two cases we're working on might be connected."

"Two cases?" Doris asked, amazed.

"That's right." Quickly, Joe told her about Alfred Wagner's mini-sub and the reason for their trip to Düsseldorf. He also mentioned the Argentinian handkerchief and the warning they had received at the hotel.

"It all didn't make much sense until now," Frank added. "But since Heinz Kroll is really Heinz Schmidt, the puzzle falls into place. One thing I can't figure out, though. How did he have access to the paintings?"

"Perhaps his father told him where they had been hidden," Fräulein Altenberg surmised.

"That's possible. But Heinz was only a little boy when Wilhelm Schmidt died."

"Maybe Herr Lechner can shed some light on this matter," Joe suggested.

"And let's not forget Blendinger, either," Joe said. "His role in all of this is still a mystery." He sighed. "I can see that we have a lot of work ahead of us."

"You'll figure the whole thing out," Doris said. "You've already discovered a great deal, and I'm sure you'll eventually find the pictures."

"The gang probably sold them a long time ago," Joe said. "I doubt they stole them just to look at them."

"Of course not. But I have a feeling they had trouble finding a buyer," Doris insisted. "There's a good chance that the paintings are still in their possession."

"What makes you think so?" Frank asked.

"Easy. If they had accomplished their goal, they wouldn't try so desperately to get you out of the way. They wouldn't have to, because by now they'd be long gone!"

"Excellent reasoning!" Frank said admiringly. "You're quite a detective, Fräulein Altenberg."

After lunch, the boys thanked their hosts and said good-bye. On the way out of town, they stopped at City Hall to talk to Herr Lechner. He told them that the skeleton they had found in Altenberg's cellar had indeed been identified as Blendinger, and that Frau Schmidt's maiden name was Kroll.

"With his father's reputation, Heinz apparently didn't want to use his name, so he adopted his mother's maiden name," Frank surmised.

Next, the boys called at the mayor's office. Mayor Reimann told them that the town of Glocken, with the help of state authorities, posted a reward of ten thousand marks for the person who found the paintings.

"Wow!" Frank said after they were on their way to Munich. "That's a lot of money. Just think what we could do with that!"

Joe grinned. "We could stay in Germany for another year! Wouldn't that be great?"

After a couple of hours, Frank took the wheel. Joe was glad, since he was getting tenser and tenser the closer they got to Munich. "I just don't understand why Gerhard didn't call," he said. "That's not like him. And this telegram—" He reached into the pocket of his jacket, which he had rolled up and put on the narrow seat behind him. The telegram was not there! Joe turned around and looked in all his pockets, then searched the floor of the car.

"The telegram's gone!" he finally called out. "Did you take it, Frank?"

"Of course not."

"I put it in my pocket yesterday and left the jacket in the car when we went into the mine."

"But we checked everything this morning. Didn't you notice it then?"

"I didn't think of looking for it," Joe admitted. "No doubt Heinz Schmidt took it!"

"Why would he do that?"

"Because it was phony and he didn't want it to be

found!" Joe replied. "I had a funny feeling all along that there was something fishy about that telegram. I'm sure Gerhard didn't send it. One of the Schmidt gang did!"

"That means Gerhard isn't in Vienna after all!" Frank said.

"Right. Who knows? Maybe he walked into a trap and they kidnapped him!"

Frank put his foot on the gas and shot along the Autobahn as fast as he could, since there was no legal limit to restrict his speed. When they came close to Munich, he said, "Why don't we stop at Alfred Wagner's? Maybe he knows what happened."

Joe agreed, and the boys parked in front of their friend's garage. They found Wagner alone in his office, poring over his drawings. The mechanics had gone home some time ago.

"Mr. Wagner, do you know where Gerhard is?" Joe blurted out.

"I thought *you* could tell me," the inventor retorted with a frown on his face. "I was wondering how come I didn't hear from him. I've been trying to get in touch with him since yesterday, but no one answered the phone."

Quickly, the boys told him about the telegram and their suspicion that Gerhard Stolz might have walked into a trap.

"When did you see him last?" Joe inquired.

"Monday," came the reply. Wagner took off his glasses and polished the lenses. "He was here and checked my personnel files. Tuesday morning he called and said he suspected a certain person."

"Who was that?" Frank asked eagerly.

"He didn't tell me, because he wasn't sure. He was planning to trap the guy and find out who his boss was at the same time."

"How was he going to do that?" Joe inquired.

"He made me lock some old drawings in my desk. Then I was to tell everybody in the shop that I'd designed an improved piece of equipment for the sub."

"Oh, I get it," Frank exclaimed. "He wanted to watch the spy when he came in to photograph your papers, and then follow him."

"If only we knew whom he suspected," Joe said with a sigh. "Did anyone work overtime Tuesday night?"

"Possibly," Wagner replied. "I went home at six, because Gerhard had wanted me to. I sent Meier home, too."

Which doesn't mean that he didn't return later, Joe thought. He was still suspicious of Wagner's assistant.

"And yesterday everyone came to work?" Frank inquired. "No one acted suspiciously?"

"Not that I noticed," Wagner said. Unable to give

the boys any further information, he shook his head in frustration. The boys patted him on the back encouragingly, saying they'd keep at it, and quickly left his garage.

It was after seven when they came to a halt in front of the reporter's building. Frank rang the doorbell of their friends' apartment, but no one answered.

"Rita must be out," he declared, "and we don't have a key for the downstairs door!"

"Let's wait until someone either comes out or goes in," Joe suggested.

Soon a woman opened the door for them on her way out. Joe held it while Frank unloaded their luggage and put it into the elevator.

When they were finished with their bags, a tall, muscular man came down the stairs in a hurry. He wore a straw hat and thick glasses, and carried a leather briefcase. When he saw the boys at the elevator, he gave them an angry look, mumbled something unintelligible, and ran out the door.

"I wonder what's bothering him," Joe said as they took the elevator up.

Frank shrugged. "He was probably annoyed that we tied up the elevator and he had to walk down."

When they arrived in front of the Stolz apartment, Frank unlocked the door and both boys went inside. Joe sniffed. "Too bad," he said.

"What?"

"Rita isn't here, and yet I can smell her perfume. She must have just left. I really wanted to talk with her."

Just then, they heard a moan from the living room. They ran inside and gaped. In an armchair was a bound and gagged figure.

Rita Stolz!

14 A Telltale Initial

The boys ran up to Rita and freed her as fast as they could.

"Thanks," she murmured. Frank got a glass of water from the kitchen and gave it to the distraught woman, while Joe massaged her wrists.

"Big man," Rita stammered between gulps of water. "Wore glasses. Left only a few moments ago."

Frank and Joe stared at each other. Both immediately thought of the tall stranger who had run out of the building when they were loading their luggage into the elevator.

"Did he wear a hat and carry a briefcase?" Frank asked.

Rita nodded.

"He couldn't have gone far yet!" Joe declared, and rushed to the telephone. He called the police, where Gerhard Stolz was well known. The sergeant on duty promised to send a squad car at once to look for the fugitive.

"Would you like to lie down?" Frank asked Rita.

"Oh, yes," the woman said, and the boys helped her to the couch, putting a pillow under her head. "I'll feel better in a minute," she added with a little smile. She touched her aching jaw and rubbed her swollen wrists.

"With Gerhard you're never safe," Rita said. "I wish he didn't always have to get involved with criminals."

"How do you know it wasn't just a regular burglar who had no idea that the apartment he broke into belonged to a famous investigative reporter?" Joe asked.

"I know. Why else would he have searched the desk, taken nothing, and then ripped out the top sheets of Gerhard's note pad?"

"In that case, he doesn't sound like an ordinary thief to me, either," Frank admitted. "How'd it all happen?"

"I had just walked in when the stranger jumped me from behind the door. I struggled to get out of his grip, but he shoved a gag in my mouth, then

117

bound my hands and feet with a piece of rope."

"So he was already in the apartment when you came home," Joe said. "Then he must have broken the lock."

"No, he didn't," Rita stated. "He had a key. When he left, he locked up from outside."

Suddenly the truth dawned on Frank. The "burglar" belonged to Schmidt's gang! No doubt they took the key from Gerhard Stolz after they lured him into a trap!

"Now I get it," Joe said at the same time. "He got the key from—"

Frank shoved his elbow into his brother's ribs. He did not want to worry Rita with the news that her husband had fallen into the hands of a gang of ruthless criminals.

Just then the doorbell rang. Two policemen arrived, dragging a struggling man along with them. He was the stranger the boys had seen in the lobby!

"And I'm telling you, you made a mistake!" the man protested loudly. "I'm going to file a complaint against you!"

Rita stared at the trio and held her ears. "What's this all about?" she asked. "I'm still upset after this brutal attack, and I wish you'd come sooner so you could have caught the intruder, and—"

"But Rita!" Frank interrupted. "Isn't *that* the burglar?"

"Of course not. I never saw this man before!"

"See, what'd I tell you?" the stranger cried triumphantly.

Joe apologized to the man for the mixup, but explained that the description of the "burglar" had fit him perfectly, and that he had run out of the building in such a hurry that the boys had suspected him.

"That's because I wanted to catch the train home!" the man shouted. He was still angry and told the group that he had been waiting for fifteen minutes in front of Herr Huber's apartment on the same floor. "I guess Huber forgot we had an appointment," he grumbled. "So I finally decided to leave. Figured I could catch the early train, but the elevator was occupied."

The policemen explained that they had had no trouble finding the man, because he was running along the street.

"I'm really sorry you missed your train," Frank said. "But perhaps you could be of great help to us. Did anyone come out of this apartment while you were waiting?"

"No," the man said, surprised. "But wait—when I got off the elevator, a man was waiting for it. He took it down."

"What's he look like?"

"He was tall and strong, even though he was no

youngster anymore. I think he had a sort of pinched mouth and flat nose. He was wearing glasses, and had on a gray or very light blue suit."

"That's the one!" Rita spoke up.

The police wrote down the description, then thanked the man for his help. He left, somewhat mollified, because the officers assured him that he had been an important witness.

Rita now told the police about the break-in. "The intruder went into my husband's study, searched through the desk, and finally ripped some sheets from the note pad. I could see him through the open door from the living room."

The officers were puzzled. They searched the apartment, found nothing disturbed, and Rita confirmed that there was nothing missing.

"Don't bother looking for fingerprints," she added. "The man wore gloves."

After the officers left, she disappeared into the kitchen to prepare dinner. Frank and Joe, meanwhile, went downstairs to bring their car into the garage.

"Don't you think the intruder was part of the Schmidt gang?" Joe asked his brother.

Frank nodded. "Schmidt probably wanted to know if we passed on any clues to Gerhard, so he sent someone to check the place for evidence."

"The description fits neither Heinz Schmidt nor what we know of Oskar Jansky," Joe reasoned. "So it must have been Willy Steiner."

"Probably. However, the gang might have other members that we don't know about."

"Look," Joe said as they drove into their parking slot in the garage, "Gerhard's Mercedes is gone. I guess that's not surprising."

"I remember he once told us about a good friend of his who's the top detective in the Munich Police Department," Frank said. "His name is Sepp Schirmer. I think we should call him. I bet he can help find Gerhard."

"Good idea. But let's do it from a booth. We'd better not upset Rita."

The boys returned to the lobby where they found a telephone booth. Frank got Schirmer's number out of the telephone book and dialed.

The detective was home and listened carefully to Frank's report. Then he sighed. "I don't like this," he said. "I'm going back to the office after dinner, and I'll send someone to the airport right away to check all the passenger lists. Also, I'll alert my department to be on the lookout for the suspects. What's the license number of Gerhard's car?"

Frank gave it to him, and Schirmer went on. "Perhaps I'll find something in the reports from the last two days. If you hear anything, let me know right away, will you?"

Frank promised to do so and hung up. Then the two boys returned to the apartment. Rita had set the table and dinner was ready. Despite all the excitement, the three pitched heartily into the delicious meal. Later, the boys offered to clean up while Rita rested on the living room couch.

They were drying the dishes in the kitchen when Rita suddenly burst in excitedly. "Look what I found!" she cried out, holding a piece of paper in her hand.

Frank took it and stared at it in surprise.

" 'W. WORRIED ABOUT THE DISAPPEARANCE OF S.,' " he read. " 'CALLED REPEATEDLY. T.' "

"Wow!" Joe exploded. "I bet that's a message from Schmidt's spy!"

"Sure. W. for Wagner, S. for Stolz, and T. is the spy! Maybe Wagner can give us a clue as to what T. stands for."

Frank hugged Rita and kissed her on both cheeks. "You're terrific," he said. "This is a fabulous clue! Where'd you find it?"

"It was lying near the living room couch. Apparently it slipped out of the man's pocket while I was struggling to get away from him." She looked at the boys expectantly. "Are you going to call Wagner?"

"No," Frank said. "I think we should go see him in person."

Frank and Joe rushed out and soon arrived at Wagner's garage. As they had hoped, the inventor was still in his office despite the late hour.

"Do you have an employee whose name starts with T?" Frank asked after a quick greeting.

"T?" Wagner wrinkled his brow. "Yes, I do. One of my mechanics is named Tarek. Why do you ask?"

"Because we think he's the spy for the Schmidt gang!" Frank showed the inventor the slip of paper Rita had found in the Stolz apartment.

"But how can you be sure it's Tarek?" Wagner asked.

"We'll have to set a trap," Frank said. "But first I'd like to find out if the message was written in this office."

Wagner had two typewriters. One of them, an older model, was often used by his staff.

Quickly, the boys compared the typeface. There was no doubt—the message had been written on the older machine!

"Suppose we confront Tarek with the facts," Joe suggested. "He might give himself away."

"No, I have a better idea," Wagner spoke up. "One of you should call the guy and pretend to be Schmidt. Maybe that'll work."

"Great!" Frank agreed. "But why don't we set a trap, so he not only gives himself away, but we can catch him in the process?"

They tried to figure out how to trick the criminal. Finally, it was decided that Frank should call Tarek and tell him to come to the office.

The boy tried to imitate the first voice he had heard on the tape in the mine and said, "S. left a report in W.'s office. We'll have to get rid of it before morning. Please take care of it right away." He hung up before the man had a chance to reply.

Joe laughed. "Now all we have to do is to plan a nice reception for the crook. I can't wait until he gets here."

"Neither can I," Wagner said. He told Joe to hide in a closet in his office, near the light switch, and leave the door slightly ajar. Then he and Frank crouched behind a car in the garage.

Fifteen minutes later, they heard a noise outside. A key turned in the door, and Frank tapped gently on the office window to warn his brother.

Joe clenched his teeth. I can't let him escape! he thought. This man knows where Gerhard is!

Through the window in the office door, he saw the muted beam of a flashlight moving along the floor. The intruder approached the office, opened it, and walked straight to Wagner's desk. He directed his flashlight to the drawers. Joe reached through the closet door and switched on the light. At the same time, he yelled, "Stop! Don't move!"

The intruder whirled around. His flashlight clattered to the floor as his eyes were blinded by the bright glare of the fluorescent ceiling lamps.

15 A Late-Night Row

Alfred Wagner and Frank rushed from their hiding places at the same moment.

"Tarek!" Wagner shouted, grabbing the man by the shoulders and shaking him angrily. "*You* are the crook! *You* photographed my drawings and sold them to Kroll. You might as well admit it, lying won't help you one bit!"

Tarek, a short, stocky man around thirty, was deathly pale. He had not recovered from his initial shock yet.

Frank walked up to him and carefully checked him for weapons. Tarek did not carry any. The boys tied the intruder's hands behind his back and pushed him into the closest chair.

"Where's Gerhard Stolz?" Frank demanded.

"I—I don't know exactly," Tarek stammered. "Somewhere on the other side of the lake in a house."

"You'd better tell us all you know," Joe added, staring at the man coldly.

Tarek said that a few months ago, when he was in a local restaurant, a young man had offered him five hundred marks for "fixing" a stolen car. "Burning off the motor number and painting it a different color, you know," Tarek explained.

"It was an Alfa Romeo and you painted it red, didn't you?" Frank asked.

"Yes," Tarek admitted. "I needed the money, so Heinz Kroll—that was the name of the young man—brought me the car and I worked on it after hours."

"You should be ashamed of yourself to do a thing like that!" Wagner scolded.

"Next day an older man contacted me and put me under pressure," Tarek continued. "Threatened he'd tell the police about it if I didn't get him the drawings for your mini-sub."

"And that was Heinz's partner, Willy Steiner," Frank guessed.

"I don't know. He never told me his name. Anyway, I had no choice but to go along with it. I took a camera the man gave me and had an extra key made to the office. With that, I could come in any time and take the photographs."

127

"How did you hand over the film?" Joe asked.

"Further down on the lake is a little park. I left my car there when I came here at night to take pictures. On the way home, I left the exposed film in a hollow oak tree."

"And how did your boss know when to look?" Wagner inquired.

"I told him ahead of time," Tarek replied. "I'd go to the park at lunch hour and sit down on a certain bench. If I had a message for him, I stuck it under the bench with chewing gum. He gave me his orders the same way."

"But you made a mistake!" Frank said. "You signed your notes with T., and that's what gave you away."

Tarek started to curse, but Frank did not give him any time to ponder his error. Instead, he wanted to know what happened to Gerhard.

"When Herr Wagner mentioned his new invention on Tuesday," Tarek said, "I decided to photograph it the same night. Everything went fine until I put the film into the hollow oak. Suddenly I heard a rustling in the bushes behind me! I almost had a heart attack, I was so frightened."

"What happened?" Wagner prodded.

"My boss came out of the bushes with another man. Then I saw Herr Stolz lying on the ground, unconscious."

"The other man was probably Oskar Jansky," Joe said to his brother. Then he turned to Tarek.

"Why did the two men follow you?"

"When they got my message at noon, they thought it might be a trap. That's how they were able to catch Herr Stolz. They caught him while he was waiting to catch them!"

"What did they do with him?" Frank pressed.

"They carried him to a boat and took off across the lake," Tarek replied. "That's why I think they're holding him somewhere on the other side. It was too dark for me to see which house."

"We'll see if the police buy that story," Frank said.

Alfred Wagner took the cue. "That's right. We'll call the authorities right away. All houses across the lake will have to be searched."

Frank went to the telephone. He contacted headquarters and asked if Detective Schirmer was still there. He was told the officer was on his way home, so he asked the sergeant on duty to have the prisoner picked up and to leave a message for Schirmer to call Wagner.

Now they had no choice but to wait. However, Joe was impatient and worried about his friend, who had been in the hands of the criminals for two days by now. Suddenly, he had an idea.

"I want you to come with me and show me exactly

where the two men went," he said to Tarek.

"And don't think of running away," Frank added. "Don't forget, there are three of us against you."

Tarek glared at him angrily, but offered no resistance as the boys led him through the barn and out to the lakeshore.

The other side of the lake was hardly visible in the darkness. Tarek pointed diagonally across toward a clump of trees. "They stopped near there," he said. "I think there's a house behind those trees. And there's another one to the right, directly on the shore."

Frank turned to Wagner after a whispered conversation with his brother. "May we borrow your rowboat? This way we can find out which house Gerhard is in before the police arrive."

Wagner nodded with some hesitation. "Okay, but be careful, will you?"

The boys promised.

"Wait just a moment," Wagner said. "I want to get my gun from the house so I can keep this bird here under control!" He ran off and returned in a couple of minutes. Pointing the gun at Tarek, he said, "Now move. Back into my office!"

Frank and Joe hurried to the little dock, loosened the boat, then rowed out into the lake.

"Let's not head straight for the house," Frank

advised. "We'd better cross the lake and then advance along the shore."

Once they had reached the other side, they let the boat drift and listened for any telltale sounds. After a while, Frank said. "Come on, we don't have any time to lose."

Silently, they rowed along the shore to the group of trees. The house that stood to the right of them on the shore looked uninhabited.

"Let's try the other one first," Frank suggested.

The boys noticed a small boathouse behind the low-hanging branches of a weeping willow. Cautiously, they approached it. Joe shone his flashlight through the open door and saw a rowboat tied up inside.

The boys fastened their own craft to the dock and climbed out. Joe noticed a long piece of rope trailing on the other boat. Maybe we can use that, he thought to himself, and cut it off.

A narrow, rising path led from the boathouse through the trees. Frank and Joe saw a faint streak of light after a while and realized it came from the house.

"Sh!" Frank warned. "Let's sneak up without any noise!"

As the boys got closer, they heard a murmur of voices. They followed the sound to the window, which was covered by heavy drapes allowing only the small beam of light to escape.

The young detectives pressed closely to the wall underneath the window and listened. A man said something unintelligible, then another replied in a harsh tone, "Five hundred thousand isn't enough!" The boys gaped at each other. It was one of the voices they had heard on the tape!

The first man again said something they could not understand, but he sounded as if he were pleading. Finally came the reply.

"I'm telling you, it isn't enough. I have better offers. And don't forget, a hundred thousand advance at signing of the contract!"

"I bet that's Willy Steiner!" Joe whispered to his brother. "He's probably arguing about the price of the paintings!"

"Or the drawings for the mini-sub," Frank guessed. "Maybe—"

"Sh—" Joe interrupted his brother. The soft-spoken man argued desperately, but the boys could not make out his words. Joe pressed his ear closer to the window, but Frank pulled him back.

"Be careful! Your head was showing above the glass!"

Frustrated, the young detectives waited, not daring to move or breathe. Then the hard voice was heard again. "Okay, you have till tomorrow night to

132

talk to your client. Then I want an answer. Good night. Heinz, will you see our guest out, please?"

"Heinz Schmidt is there, too," Frank murmured.

"Let's go to the front door and check out the visitor!" Joe suggested, and was about to move, when suddenly the yard was bathed in light!

Someone had opened the drapes above them and was staring out into the night!

16 A Violent Fight

Frank and Joe held their breath and did not move a muscle for fear of being discovered.

But then the drapes were drawn again, and the man retreated into the room. Joe let out a lungful of air. "Wow!" he whispered. "That was a close call!"

Quickly, they crept around to the front, where a large yard separated the house from the street. A path bordered by bushes led from the door to the gate at the end of the yard.

The boys were just in time to hide behind a shrub when two men appeared in the doorway. Frank and Joe recognized Heinz Schmidt, but the face of the visitor, who was short and heavyset, was in the shadows. The men shook hands and talked for a moment in low voices.

"I don't think Heinz will accompany the visitor out to the street," Frank whispered. "Why don't we try to catch the little guy?"

"Good idea!"

The boys crept toward the street and stopped behind some dense shrubbery near the gate. They did not have long to wait. Schmidt closed the door behind him after disappearing into the house, and the visitor walked toward them. When he was passing the boys' hiding place, Frank suddenly jumped up and grabbed him in a headlock, which stifled the man's scream.

With a gurgle, he collapsed on the ground as Joe kicked his legs out from under him. He struggled furiously for a while, then lay still. Joe tied his hands and feet, then Frank loosened his grip around the stranger's throat and gagged him with a handkerchief.

"Good work, partner!" He grinned at his brother.

The boys dragged their victim behind the bush and shone a flashlight into his face.

"Hey, Frank!" Joe whispered excitedly. "It's Herr Braun, the art dealer!"

"Some art dealer," Frank grumbled. "Wants to buy stolen property! Maybe it was Steiner he was talking to in the street in Glocken before the two of them took off in the blue car."

"Possibly, but what do we do next?"

The brothers moved out earshot of Braun and debated. "In order to get into the house, we'll have to lure Heinz Schmidt and Steiner outside," Frank declared. It was decided that Frank would wait near the house, while Joe would ring the bell at the gate. When the men came out to see who it was, he would distract them with a cry for help.

While Frank hid, his brother went to the gate and pushed the bell. The door opened and he cried, "Help! Please help me!"

Heinz Schmidt stuck his head out the door and looked into the yard. He heard Joe's cry and stepped out, but stood still after a few yards and listened. Obviously, he did not know what to make of the sudden interruption.

Too bad he's alone, Frank thought; Willy Steiner is still inside. He watched with bated breath as Schmidt advanced a few more steps and stopped only three yards away from him. The young detective made a quick decision. He jumped from his hiding place, grabbed the man by the neck, and pulled him to the ground. Schmidt kicked furiously but Frank, who had the advantage of the surprise attack, kept the upper hand.

"Joe, quick!" he called out.

Joe was already on his way to the house when he heard his brother's cry. He ran up and tied Schmidt in the same manner as Braun.

"I'm glad you brought that rope," Frank said when the job was done, and Joe had shoved his handkerchief into Schmidt's mouth.

Joe nodded. "I had a hunch we might be able to use it. Now we have to get number three!"

The boys carefully approached the house. They walked inside and found themselves in a long, narrow hallway. The floor was covered with an old carpet, and the walls were decorated with rifles and sabers.

Frank was about to close the front door, when the wind blew it shut with a loud bang. The boys froze.

"What's the matter, Heinz?" came the harsh voice from one of the rooms in the back.

Desperately, the boys tried to figure out what to do. Finally, Frank mumbled something unintelligible, while both Hardys went up to the room from which the voice had come. They pressed themselves flat against the door frame.

"What did you say?" the voice came again. Apparently, the man realized that something was wrong. A chair scraped and then heavy footsteps neared the door. The next instant, a tall, strong man appeared in the doorway.

Frank jumped him, twisting Steiner's right arm

backward and shoved his knee into the man's back.

Steiner moaned, then kicked Frank in the shin. Frank loosened his grip in pain and was thrown against the wall by his enemy. Joe smashed into Steiner headfirst and pushed him against the door frame. But the impact was so great that Joe fell down himself.

Quickly, Steiner ripped a gun from the wall and pointed it at the boys.

"Oh, no, you don't!" Joe cried before the man could pull the trigger. He rammed his fist into Steiner's stomach. The rifle clattered to the floor, and the man collapsed with a groan. Both boys pounced on him, carried him into the room, and tied him to a chair.

"That's the guy who attacked Rita," Joe pointed out. "He's the right size and he has the flat nose and pinched mouth the other man described." A pair of horn-rimmed glasses lay on the desk.

Steiner, who had wagged his head in a daze, suddenly stared at the boys with hatred. "It's you? I can't believe you snoopers—"

"You're surprised, aren't you?" Frank asked. "You thought we'd be dead by now."

"Next time I'll make sure you are!" the man hissed.

"There won't be a next time. And now you'd

better answer a few questions, Herr Steiner. Where is Oskar Jansky?"

"Jansky? I wish he were here." Steiner's lips twisted into a sardonic smile. "But today he isn't. Heinz—"

"He's outside, tied up neatly," Frank said. "What did you do with Gerhard Stolz?"

After a small amount of prodding, Steiner admitted that Gerhard was held captive in the basement. A steel door led to it from the hallway.

Frank sighed in relief. "Take his keys, Joe." he said. "We'll search the house later."

"Let's call the police, though," Joe advised, as he fished a key ring from Steiner's jacket pocket.

Frank went to the telephone. He called Wagner's garage first to find out what had happened, and was told by a policeman that everything was under control. Wagner would explain everything later.

Frank quickly reported where he and Joe were and that they had captured the chief crooks.

"Detective Schirmer is on the way here," the policeman said. "As soon as he arrives, we'll get over there."

"Just a few more minutes and the police will be here," Frank announced after he had hung up. Then he and Joe hurried into the hallway.

They found the cellar door, unlocked it, and

turned on the light. Then they rushed down the steps and checked each room in the basement. In the last and tiniest one stood a metal cot. Gerhard Stolz lay on it, his hands and feet bound to the frame!

"Gerhard!" Frank cried hoarsely.

The prisoner turned his head and smiled weakly. The boys cut the ropes that bound the reporter and gently helped him sit up.

"What did these creeps do to you?" Joe exclaimed. "Have you been down here long?"

Gerhard nodded while Frank massaged his wrists. Suddenly, there was a hollow *bang* upstairs. The boys jumped up and looked at each other in alarm. Frank rushed out and raced up the stairs. The metal door to the hallway was closed and locked from the outside!

Angrily, the boy rattled on the doorknob and banged his fists against the panel but in vain. Disgusted, he returned to the others.

"How stupid!" he muttered. "I left the key in the lock. But I still can't figure out who did this. We had these guys tied up safely!"

"Maybe Jansky was in the house after all," Joe surmised.

"You're right. Now we can only hope that the police come soon."

Just then, the boys heard footsteps in the yard,

and a car engine roared to... Quickly, Joe stepped on the cot and looked out the small cellar window. He saw Heinz Schmidt slam the car door and take off in a cloud of dust.

"There they go!" Joe cried out. "All three of them!"

"Don't worry, boys," Gerhard said softly. "I'm just glad that you two are unhurt."

"Oh, we're okay," Frank said.

"Those men told me you were trapped in a caved-in mine!"

"Well, actually we were," Joe admitted, and started to retell their adventure. After a while, they heard a car drive up and stop in front of the house. A loud thumping told them the door was being forced open. Frank ran upstairs and banged his fists against the metal cellar door while Joe helped Gerhard slowly up the steps. Moments after the captives heard the front door burst open, someone began working on the cellar door.

It finally swung open, and a tall, broad-shouldered man in a baggy suit stood outside, looking dumb-founded.

When he noticed Gerhard Stolz, his face brightened. "Gerhard, I'm glad to see you! And these boys must be Frank and Joe Hardy."

"They are," Gerhard said and introduced the young investigators to Detective Sepp Schirmer.

"Where'd you hid~~~ ~~~ crooks?" Schirmer wanted to know.

"The~~~ ~~~ away," Frank replied, crestfallen. He ~~~ ~~~bout the criminals' escape. Unfortunately, he could not give a good description of the men's car.

Schirmer sighed. "Let's hope we can catch them," he said, and ordered one of his officers to report to headquarters. The other men began to search the house.

"I have no idea what the gang will do next," Gerhard said. "They never mentioned a word about their plans."

He gave a quick recounting of his capture, but his friend saw how exhausted he was and how difficult it was for him to speak.

"Tell the details later," Schirmer advised, "when you feel better. Right now I want you to go home and rest!"

Joe supported the motion wholeheartedly. "Rita's worried to death," he said. "I know she can't wait to see you."

At first Stolz did not want to leave, but finally he admitted that he had been knocked unconscious for a while and needed to relax and sleep.

"I'll get someone to drive you," Schirmer said. "He can—"

Just then a policeman came up to the group and stammered, "Boss—I—eh—outside—"

"What's the matter, h…

The man looked embarrasse…

man in the yard. He was tied up and g… inquired.

"Braun!" Frank cried out and slapped h… and this head with his palm. "We forgot all about him!"

"Who's he?" Schirmer asked, perplexed.

"He calls himself an art dealer, but we know he's not honest. He was trying to make a deal with Steiner, probably on the stolen paintings."

"He might be able to help us find the gang!" Joe added.

Hans cleared his throat. "No, he can't. He—he disappeared!"

17 Underwater Danger

Four pairs of eyes stared at the hapless man. Then Schirmer thundered, "Would you mind telling me how a man who's gagged and bound can disappear?"

"When he took off, he wasn't bound anymore—I mean, I had untied him," Hans stammered. He explained that he had heard muffled sounds in the bushes and discovered Braun. The art dealer, after being relieved of his gag, had insisted he was a victim of Schmidt's gang.

"Braun's not stupid," Frank said.

"I untied him," Hans went on. "Then he told me there was another prisoner in the backyard. He would show me where. We went there, and while I

144

searched for the man, Braun raced off into the bushes."

"Next time, don't be so trusting," Schirmer grumbled and dismissed the officer. Then he turned to the boys with a sigh. "Now we lost all of them!"

"Maybe not," Joe said suddenly. "Unless Braun has friends in town, he must be staying in a hotel. Suppose we check all the hotels in Munich to see if he's taken a room?"

"Good idea," Detective Schirmer said. "I'll call my assistant at headquarters. We have a list, and he can put a few people on the job. It'll take quite some time to call every hotel in town."

A half hour later, Schirmer's assistant phoned to report that they had located a man who matched Braun's description and who had checked into the Hotel Continental under the name of Herr B. Julius.

"That's our man!" Frank cried out. "Let's go over to the hotel right away and have a little talk with him."

While Joe accompanied Gerhard Stolz home in one of the squad cars, Frank, Schirmer, and two officers rushed to the Hotel Continental near the main railroad station. After the detective identified himself, the night clerk revealed the art dealer's room number. "Herr Julius just got in a few minutes

ago," he volunteered. "He seemed to be in a hurry!"

When Schirmer and his group knocked on Braun's door and were admitted, they saw that the art dealer had been packing his suitcases!

"It seems you're planning to move out in the middle of the night," Schirmer declared. "Well, we'll be happy to put you up at the local prison for a while!"

Braun protested vehemently and turned to Frank. "You know me!" he cried. "Please clear up this misunderstanding!"

"Misunderstanding?" Frank asked. "You might as well admit that you were trying to buy the stolen paintings that belong to the Glocken Museum! We heard you!"

Braun turned ashen.

"And how about Herr Rehm, the coin dealer in Frankfurt?" Frank pressed on. "Why did you ask him about gold *Joachimstaler*?"

Braun mumbled something about police brutality, but did not resist any further. He was taken to headquarters while one of the officers drove Frank to Stolz's apartment.

Gerhard was already sleeping when the boy arrived. Rita had called their family doctor, who had examined the exhausted reporter and insisted that he have plenty of rest.

In the morning, Gerhard felt much better. He had just finished eating a hearty breakfast when the telephone rang. Joe answered. It was Detective Schirmer. Unfortunately, the police had not found a trace of the gang, and Braun was not talking. "But we've discovered Gerhard's car," he reported. "It was parked near the airport."

"Apparently, they wanted to create the impression that Gerhard left it there," Joe commented.

"Right. I'm going to have somebody get the car. Why don't we all meet at Schmidt's place at noon? By that time, we may have picked up another clue."

"Fine. We'll have to get our Porsche at Wagner's house anyway."

Joe wanted to tell Gerhard about his conversation, but Rita stood in front of his bedroom door like a sentry. "Psst!" she warned. "He's sleeping again. Don't disturb him."

"Okay," Joe said. "When he wakes up, tell him we're at Wagner's."

The boys took the subway and a bus to the inventor's house and found Wagner in his office. Frank and Joe immediately told him everything that had been happening. Then, eagerly, they retrieved the Porsche and drove around the lake to Schmidt's place. In the daylight, it looked rather unkempt. Schirmer was already there and told them that the house had been empty for quite a long time before Schmidt and Steiner had rented it.

"It's a great hiding place," the detective said. "The neighbors had no idea what was going on here."

The group went to investigate a wing of the house they had not searched the night before. A connecting door led into it from the hallway. When they saw that the entire area consisted of one large workshop, they gaped. In the middle sat the half-finished body of a mini-sub!

"That's what the gang built from Wagner's drawings!" Frank cried out. "They copied his boat!"

Schirmer nodded. "And all the plans are still here on the drawing board. Apparently, the crooks didn't have enough time to take them along."

The three inspected the boat from all sides. As far as the boys could determine, it was an exact replica of *Ludwig II*. None of them, however, could figure out what the crooks intended to do with it.

"Jansky was probably working here last night when you two arrived on the scene," the detective guessed. He pointed to a bell next to the door. "It's connected with a button underneath Steiner's desk. He must have maneuvered himself toward it along with the chair he was tied to while you were in the cellar."

Frank grimaced. "I suspected something like that. We should have known it was fishy when

Steiner revealed Gerhard's hiding place without much hesitation."

"Do you have any clue regarding the paintings yet?" Joe asked the detective.

Schirmer shook his head. "I found nothing in the house. But I'm having the whole property searched. Also, we're keeping the place under surveillance in case the crooks return."

The boys drove home for lunch. Gerhard was sitting up in bed reading the newspaper. "I'm really feeling great," he said, "but Rita won't let me get up yet."

After eating ham sandwiches, the boys went downstairs and washed Gerhard's Mercedes, which had been delivered by a police officer. Sepp Schirmer came by later in the afternoon, and Gerhard told again in detail how he had been taken prisoner by the gang. His report matched that of Tarek's.

"I was attacked in the park from behind," he said. "When I regained consciousness, I found myself on the cot in the cellar."

"How did you know Tarek was the spy?" Frank asked.

"He was the mechanic who worked on the red Alfa Romeo, but claimed he didn't know the name of the owner. I remembered that when I checked out Alfred's employees. At that point, I also learned that Tarek had recently spent more money than he made."

"The old story," Schirmer said.

Gerhard nodded. "I made some notes about him on my desk pad."

"Too bad Steiner got here before us," Joe put in. "Otherwise we would have found the information."

Next morning, Alfred Wagner called. He had tested *Ludwig II* for the first time, and the little boat had passed its maiden run with flying colors!

Elated, the inventor invited the boys and Gerhard to come along on his next trip. They accepted enthusiastically, even though Rita was anxious.

"Gerhard, you must promise me not to go down in the sub!" she said. "In your condition, that is not a good idea. Suppose something happens—"

"In that little lake?" her husband laughed. "But I promise you anyway."

The three drove to Wagner's, full of excitement. They found him in the barn, with the door to the lake open.

"Hi, everybody," the little man said happily and shook Gerhard's hand. "I'm so glad to see you well again!"

"I'm fine," Stolz told him.

"Rolf Meier is out on the lake," Wagner went on. "See, here he comes." He pointed to a spot on the water where the surface was suddenly broken by the rising sub. Then the bright yellow craft moved toward the dock and stopped in its little slip. Rolf climbed out of the hatch, fastened *Ludwig II* with a rope that Wagner tossed him, then jumped out.

"Everything's just working fine," he reported. "We're ready for our first passengers."

"Okay, boys, all aboard!" Wagner grinned.

Frank and Joe climbed down the hatch and Wagner followed. Then Rolf untied the boat. While he and Gerhard waved, Wagner closed the hatch behind him before taking his place beside the controls. Frank and Joe sat behind him. They could see through the large, rounded pane in front of them.

"Here we go!" the inventor called out. He started the diesel engine and slowly drove out into the lake. When they were about in the middle, he cut the engine and opened several valves to let water into the buoyancy tank.

"We'll have to take on ballast in order to descend," he explained while the boys watched excitedly. Slowly, the water rose above the boat and surrounded them.

Wagner kept his eyes on a small indicator showing the amount of ballast in the tank. Finally, he pushed a button and closed the valves. Then he switched on the electric motor and pushed the steering rod all the way forward. The boat began to descend like an elevator! First they could see through the water around them, but after a few yards it turned dark green in color.

"Now watch!" Wagner said and drove around in circles. He made a figure eight and went up and down. Finally, he switched on the bright headlight, took on additional ballast, and descended to the bottom of the lake.

"Rather dreary down here," Joe said as they skimmed over algae and other vegetation.

Wagner nodded. He pushed a button to activate the pump that would empty the ballast tank so they could rise again. But suddenly the electric motor stopped and the headlight went out. There was nothing but silent darkness around them!

The boys froze for a moment. They did not dare move, afraid to upset the boat's balance. It was a terrible feeling to be caught at the bottom of the lake without power!

Wagner, however, did not panic. He switched on a flashlight. "We'll fix it," he said confidently. "Probably a short circuit somewhere." He played the beam on the main switch, which also served as a circuit breaker. Indeed, the breaker had tripped! Wagner bent down under the dashboard and direct-ed his light on the maze of wires.

"Ah, there's the culprit!" he called out when he

found a loose connection. "Joe, there's a toolbox beneath your seat. Want to hand me a screwdriver and a pair of pliers?"

"Sure." Joe opened the box and gave Wagner the implements. As the inventor started to fix the wire, they suddenly felt a slight impact. They had run aground!

The Hardys stared at each other uneasily, afraid to think of what would happen if Wagner was unable to repair the damage.

But the little man had no such doubts. Calmly, he kept on working, then stood up to switch on the main breaker. The headlight flooded the lake and they could hear the pump humming. The boys sighed with relief.

"We'd better get some fresh air now," Wagner said with a smile and handed Joe the tools. Then he grabbed the steering rod and brought the boat up. It was not long before he had eased *Ludwig II* into its slip and they climbed out.

Gerhard Stolz was worried when he heard about the mishap, but his friend calmed him down.

"No reason to be upset," he said. "We do have a spare battery for a real emergency."

After a short break, Wagner and the boys went on a second trip.

"This time I'll show you the claw," the inventor said when they were hovering just above the lake bottom. "It's a very useful tool, which scientists can use to collect stones or samples of underwater life."

The claw was a mechanical arm with a hook on the end. It was built into the hull of the ship behind a small sliding door and could be operated from the dashboard with a pistol-grip control.

Eagerly, the boys watched through the window as the claw extended, curled up, swayed from side to side, and opened and closed.

"Unfortunately, there isn't much in this puddle that's worth bringing up," Wagner said. "The best you can hope to find is an old shoe or a bunch of rocks." With a grin, he pulled in the claw.

When they were on land again, Gerhard asked Wagner if he would like to accompany them to the Schmidt house. He wanted to show him the half-finished boat.

"Sure, I'm dying to see it," Wagner said. "Come on, we'll take the rowboat over."

Frank and Joe looked disappointed, and the inventor laughed. "Don't you have enough of the sub yet? If you want, you can go down with Rolf again. Maybe he'll teach you how to steer it."

The young mechanic said he would be glad to, and the boys eagerly climbed into the sub again. Meanwhile, Stolz and Wagner rowed toward the house on the other side of the lake. They inspected the workroom, and Wagner was utterly indignant when he saw the copy of his boat. "It's exactly like *Ludwig II*, down to the last detail!" he grumbled.

Later, Detective Schirmer joined them, and they discussed the tangled mystery for a long time. When Gerhard and Alfred finally returned to Wagner's place, it was already dark. There was no light in the garage and no sign of Frank, Joe, or Rolf.

"Do you think they're still in the lake?" Gerhard asked uneasily.

"Let's see if the boat's here," Alfred replied. But the sub was not in its slip! Wagner went into the barn and turned on the light. He noticed a slightly sweet odor. "H'm, I wonder what that is," he said.

Gerhard hurried over to him. "Chloroform!" he cried out, his face tense. He rushed through the barn and into the garage to Wagner's office. Three motionless figures were lying on the floor—Frank, Joe, and Rolf Meier!

18 Hunt for a Truck

Gerhard Stolz kneeled down and felt for Frank's pulse. "Thank goodness he's alive!" he exclaimed.

Just then, the boy began to move, and seconds later the others regained consciousness also, sitting up and blinking their eyes.

"Wh-what happened?" Frank stammered and looked around.

"That's what I'd like to hear from you," Gerhard replied. "But you'd better take it easy until you completely recover from that dose of chloroform you got."

Frank grimaced. "Oh, I remember now. We were attacked after we came back from our trip. First Joe got it when he entered the barn to turn on the light, then myself when I went looking for him. Apparently after that, it was Rolf's turn."

"Did anyone see the attacker?" Gerhard asked.

"I did," Joe replied. "It was Heinz Schmidt!"

"Why can't these criminals leave us alone!" Wagner wailed desperately. "Now they even sank my sub!"

"No, they didn't," Gerhard replied. "I'll bet they stole it!"

He called the police while Frank and Joe looked around for clues. Wagner found that the winch had been used to pull the boat out of its slip. "They probably trucked it away," he concluded.

Frank and Joe discovered tire tracks in the lawn. "Must have been a huge truck," Frank declared. "The driver had to run over the grass to turn the corner."

Shortly, Detective Schirmer and his officers arrived. He ordered the men to photograph the tracks. "But it won't help much," he grumbled. "What we really need is a description of the truck." He radioed headquarters and asked that every patrol car be alerted to look for a large truck with a boat on it.

"What I'd like to know," Frank said, "is why did the crooks want Alfred's sub in the first place? They must have a special reason."

No one had the answer, and finally the boys and

Gerhard said good night to Wagner and the officers and drove home.

On the way, Frank said, "You know, I just had an idea. Maybe the Glocken paintings are hidden in some lake, and the gang wants *Ludwig II* to retrieve them!"

"I thought of that," Gerhard said. "But it probably would be just as easy for a few men to go down in divers' outfits. They wouldn't need a sub for that."

"That's true," Frank admitted. "I just mentioned it because Schmidt and Braun were negotiating about the paintings."

"We don't know whether they were really talking about the pictures," Joe put in. "Braun claims to be an art dealer, but perhaps he really isn't, and they were discussing the boat plans instead."

When they arrived at the apartment, Rita stood in the open door. "I don't believe it!" she scolded. "Gerhard, yesterday you were ill in bed, and today you're already out again until all hours of the night chasing crooks!"

Gerhard hugged her and grinned. "Don't worry," he said. "I feel just fine. A little hungry, perhaps—"

"Well, come on in. I have dinner waiting." Rita led the three to the dining room table. While they were eating a delicious roast she had prepared, they told her about their adventures at the lake.

Suddenly, the phone rang. It was Detective Schirmer. "A company by the name of Bally Transport just reported one of their trucks missing," he said. "It's dark blue with white lettering and has a trailer."

"The crooks may have dumped the trailer somewhere," Gerhard guessed.

"That's what I think," Schirmer agreed. "I'll call you in the morning if I hear any more."

Next day after breakfast, he had further news. "We found the trailer in a rest area along the Autobahn," he said. "But what's more, the driver showed up, near Rosenheim. I couldn't quite figure out his story, so he's on his way here. Want to come over with the boys around twelve? Maybe we'll get something out of the man."

Gerhard and the Hardys arrived at Schirmer's office at noon, eager to talk to the driver. He was a tall, gray-haired man with a pale face and a day's growth of beard.

Detective Schirmer smiled at the three. "Herr Bauer here was on his way to Ulm yesterday to pick up a load," he filled them in. "When he stopped at a rest area, he was approached by two men, apparently Jansky and Schmidt, according to his description. They started to talk to him, and suddenly, one of them shoved a chloroform-soaked rag in his face."

The driver took up the story. "When I came to, I was lying behind the cab, gagged and bound. It seemed as if a heavy piece of machinery was being loaded. Then one of the men started the truck."

"Did they say anything about where they were going?" Frank asked.

"No. And they pulled a sack over my head so I couldn't see. They drove for a long time, then went along a bumpy path before halting again. At this point they dragged me out of the truck and carried me into the woods, where they left me."

"How did you manage to get away?" Joe inquired.

"I finally loosened my ties," Bauer said and showed them his bruised wrists. "Then I wandered for hours until I found a small village near Rosenheim."

"Could you show us on a map where your attackers left you?" Schirmer asked.

Bauer nodded and indicated the general area.

"I'll send some men down there right away to question people," Schirmer decided. "Perhaps the truck stopped at a local gas station, or the men ate in a restaurant."

Gerhard and the boys returned home. After lunch, they pored over a map in Gerhard's study. "I wonder why the gang dropped the driver where they did," Gerhard said.

"Well, they couldn't get rid of him before they

picked up the boat because that wouldn't have given them enough of a lead," Frank guessed. "If he was found too soon, the police would have been too close behind."

"Right. On the other hand, they wouldn't want to leave him too near their destination, either," Joe added. "It seems to me they'd drop him off somewhere along the way."

"You mean, their goal is north or northeast of Rosenheim?" Gerhard asked.

Frank held up a hand. "I doubt it. It was probably a trick to lure us into the wrong direction!"

"I bet you're right!" Joe cried out.

Gerhard bent over the map again. "They can't cross the border, so they must have driven into the Bavarian Alps," he finally said.

Frank snapped his fingers. "The young man in Düsseldorf, Peter Hauser, said Schmidt wanted to test the boat in a little Alpine lake!"

Joe nodded. "But which one?" His fingers began to trace the various lakes. Suddenly, he stopped. "The Waldsee, that's it! The Altenbergs have a summer house in Bad Waldsee!"

He told Gerhard that this house had often been visited by the municipal employees of the town. "Probably the Schmidts were there, too! Heinz may have known the lake ever since he was a child!"

"Why don't you call Doris Altenberg and ask her?" Gerhard suggested.

The boy did, and she confirmed the fact that the Schmidt family had often stayed in Bad Waldsee.

"Would you like to use our house when you go there?" she asked. "If so, I'll call the neighbors. They have the key."

"That would be great," Joe said. "Thanks a million!"

It was decided that Frank and Joe should leave right away and start looking for clues in Bad Waldsee. Gerhard, who had some urgent business to take care of, would follow in a day or two.

Half an hour later, the Hardys were on their way. It was dusk by the time they reached Bad Waldsee. The Altenberg house was at the edge of the resort, directly on the lakefront. They got the key from the neighbors and made themselves at home in the simple but attractively furnished chalet.

Next morning, Frank suggested taking the rowboat out that was docked at the boathouse to investigate the lake. "I brought Gerhard's binoculars," he said.

Joe nodded. "And to look authentic, we'll take a fishing rod from the boathouse and throw a line once in a while."

The young detectives rowed around the lake for

four hours without finding the slightest clue to the gang. Finally, Joe became hungry. "I could eat all the trout we *didn't* pull in this morning," he declared.

The boys returned to the house, tied up the boat, then went to an old restaurant where they had *Bratwurst* and potato salad. After lunch, they visited the police to inquire about the truck and the criminals. However, there was no news.

"Maybe the crooks needed gas or went food shopping," Frank said when they were out in the town square again. "Let's check out all service stations and groceries."

"Okay. Why don't you take the northern part of the town while I take the southern," Joe agreed. "We'll meet again in an hour."

In the end, even this effort proved fruitless. No one remembered seeing the men or a dark blue truck with white lettering.

"Now what?" Joe asked.

"Let's go around the lake and question people in other places," Frank advised. "Maybe the gang avoided Bad Waldsee on purpose."

For the next few hours, the young detectives continued their search in gas stations, restaurants, and food markets. They learned nothing.

They worked their way about three quarters around the lake, and drove through a stretch of woods. They could not see the water until the street wound down again to a romantic little inlet. A small restaurant with a few wooden tables on a veranda was right next to the shore.

"Let's take a break!" Joe exclaimed. "This looks so inviting."

"You're right," Frank agreed and parked the car.

When they sat down, an elderly man, in leather shorts called *Lederhosen*, approached them. Apparently, he was the innkeeper himself. *"Guten Tag,"* he said with a friendly nod of his head. *"Was darfs denn sein?"*

The boys ordered apple cider, and the man brought them two large glasses. Lingering by their table, he asked what brought them to the town, explaining his family had lived there for generations.

Joe told him they were chasing three thieves and described the men and the truck. The innkeeper shook his head. He had not seen them.

Frank sighed. "If they're here, they probably came in at night, so nobody would notice them," he concluded.

The innkeeper raised his eyebrows. "When did you say these people arrived?"

"Saturday or Sunday," Joe replied.

"Well, I didn't see the truck, but maybe I heard it!" their host declared. "I woke up from the noise at three o'clock in the morning on Sunday! The truck went right up to Bear Lake!"

The man pointed to a small street that wound behind his restaurant and up a steep hill covered with fir trees. "Come to think of it," he added, "it never came back, either. I wonder what it's doing up there?" He creased his forehead.

The boys almost jumped with excitement. They finally had a possible clue to the whereabouts of the gang!

19 The Secret of Bear Lake

"What a crazy notion, to drive a truck up that steep, little path," the innkeeper sputtered. "And at night yet! I didn't even realize till now that it hasn't come back yet. Maybe the driver broke his neck!"

"Perhaps he returned another way," Joe suggested.

"There isn't any. At least none a truck could use. You fellows don't know Bear Lake!"

Their host explained that it was a long, still lake farther up in the mountains, about half an hour away. At the end, there was a huge cliff rising out of the water. The rest of the lake was bordered by dense, dark-needled trees. "The lake's incredibly deep and the surrounding woods so dark that no one likes to go there. Especially after the landslide."

"Landslide?" Frank asked. "Was that recently?"

"No, no. It was soon after World War II. A piece of the cliff crashed into the lake."

Frank asked the innkeeper to give them directions to Bear Lake, and the friendly Bavarian went to get a piece of paper and a pencil. Then he drew them a detailed map.

The little street behind his restaurant rose straight up the mountain, where it reached a plateau in the woods and continued until it forked about three hundred yards before the lake.

"The left branch goes to a small clearing on the shore, the right one to a hunting lodge and a boathouse," the man explained.

"Who owns the lodge?" Joe asked.

"The Count of Kranichstein. His grandfather used to hunt bears up there every season. But now Count Leopold only spends a few days a year at the place. Otherwise, hardly anyone goes there."

Joe grabbed his brother's arm. "You see how it all fits? I bet the gang is up there with *Ludwig II*."

"With whom?" the innkeeper looked puzzled.

The boys quickly explained about the stolen mini-sub, then shook the man's hand. "You've been a great help!" Frank said. Then he looked at his brother. "Maybe we should have some dinner before we leave."

"Good idea," Joe agreed. "I'm starved."

The innkeeper laughed. "Good idea. We can't send you up to Bear Lake on an empty stomach." He hurried into the house to prepare a meal. Joe, meanwhile, went to call Gerhard from a pay phone. When he returned, a platter of smoked ham sat on the table. Then the innkeeper brought a loaf of bread and three fried eggs for each boy.

"Gerhard wasn't home," Joe reported. "Rita will give him the message. I told her where we were going, and that I'd come back here after we locate the crooks. I assured her that we'd call again in a couple of hours or so."

When the boys had finished their meal, they paid their host and climbed into the Porsche. Joe took the wheel. The closer they came to Bear Lake, the more cautiously he drove, trying to listen for any sound around them. At the fork, he turned left and finally switched off the engine. They pushed the car into dense underbrush, then continued on foot to the clearing.

The sun had disappeared behind the mountains, and it was starting to get dark. They could barely make out the hunting lodge between the trees on the other side of the lake.

"You know, it's really kind of spooky up here," Joe said. "Very desolate and somehow depressing. No wonder that—"

Suddenly, Frank held up his hand. Someone had turned on a light in the lodge!

"There they are!" he whispered. "Come on!"

The boys did not want to walk along the street in case the gang had rigged up some kind of alarm system. So they crept through the woods around the lake for almost an hour, using their flashlights sparingly.

Finally, they saw a dim glow of light and realized they had reached their destination. Noiselessly, they moved up to the window from which the light came. The shutters were closed. Joe peered through a crack and saw the back of a man who was sitting at a table. Then he recognized Steiner's harsh voice!

"I don't know, Heinz, but it seems that everything's going wrong," the man complained. "We finally find the thing, and the claw doesn't work!"

"Well, we fixed it," Heinz said soothingly. "Now we shouldn't have any more trouble."

"I hope not. In two hours we should be up again, then we'll sink the sub and take off."

"And Stolz and his two foreign snoopers are out of luck!" Heinz sneered.

Steiner laughed. "As for Jansky—" His voice fell to a whisper, and the boys could not hear the rest of the sentence. Suddenly, Steiner spoke in his regular tone again. "Oh, good, Oskar, there's the chow. Heinz, why don't you turn on the radio?"

The Hardys heard a chair scraping, then the voice of a newscaster. They retreated until they were out of earshot.

"Did you hear that?" Frank whispered. "I bet Steiner is about to do Jansky in once he doesn't need him anymore!"

"We won't let him!" Joe vowed. "We'll have to prevent him from getting 'the thing' from the lake, whatever it is. And we'll have to save *Ludwig II*. But how?"

"We can't call the police," Frank said. "By the time they'd get here, the crooks'll be long gone. So we only have one choice—to hide the boat and call for help later."

"Okay, let's go!"

The boys hurried to the lakeshore. Next to the boathouse, they noticed the stolen truck and a car parked between the trees. Quickly, Joe noted the license numbers.

The moon was shining, and in its light they discovered *Ludwig II* next to a small motorboat on the dock. Set into the hull of the boat was a square instrument with a complicated dial system.

"Could be some kind of echo sounder," Frank suggested. He climbed onto the sub and opened the hatch. Suddenly, he realized that their plan had a weak point.

"Wait a minute," he whispered to Joe, who was about to loosen the ropes. "First we have to put the motorboat out of order!"

"You're right," Joe said, scratching his head. "And the two vehicles, too, so the crooks can't leave before the police come."

"Let's take the rotor out of the distributor of the car to start with," Frank said. He was just about to jump onto the dock when they heard a loud shout. Frantically, Joe called, "Frank, they're coming!"

When Frank looked up, he saw that the door to the lodge was open and someone was approaching them with a flashlight. The boy did not lose a second. He jumped through the hatch, squirmed into the pilot's seat, and switched on the light and the engine.

He heard Joe follow him into the sub and accelerated. The craft moved away just as a man ran screaming and gesticulating onto the dock. Oskar Jansky was only a few feet from the sub!

"Wow, that was a close call," Joe said. He watched as the sub gained speed and moved out into the lake.

Just then, spotlights came on at the dock. "They're going to follow us in the motorboat!" Frank cried out.

"Let's go down," Joe suggested.

Frank cut the engine and let water into the tank while Joe locked the hatch. They had watched Rolf Meier and knew exactly what to do. Before the motorboat reached them, they were out of sight.

"Trouble is," Frank said, "we can't stay down here forever."

"Not forever," Joe admitted. "But perhaps long enough so Gerhard will find us. He'll worry when he doesn't get my call." The boy noticed a map on a hook in the wall and unfolded it. It was a home-made but exact chart of the lake with a dozen crosses on it. Most had black circles around them. Only one was circled in red. Next to each cross was a number.

"That probably indicates the depth," Joe said. "Really incredible, because all are around six or seven hundred feet!"

Both boys now pored over the map and tried to figure out the significance of the crosses. Suddenly, Joe snapped his fingers. "I've got it!" he said. "The 'thing' Steiner mentioned must be made out of metal, because I think the instrument in the motorboat is a magnetometer! A cross was made for every location where a metallic object was found on the bottom of the lake."

Frank nodded. "Then the gang took the mini-sub and checked those locations. A black circle around

173

the cross means the 'thing' they were looking for wasn't there—"

"And the red circle means they hit pay dirt! I bet it's those paintings in their metal container! But how did they ever end up here?"

"Who knows? Say, Joe, why don't we bring up the box ourselves? I'm sure we're not too far away from the spot!"

"Good idea!"

With the help of the boat's compass, they figured out the direction, then took on more ballast and switched on the headlight. They descended while Joe watched the instruments.

"One hundred meters, one fifty, one eighty—" The boy became tense. "One eighty-five—hold it right here."

Frank stopped the boat as they reached the bottom. They used a large boulder as a point of reference, then began a systematic search. The uneven ground was covered with a layer of black muck. Slowly, they proceeded, now and then seeing a rotted tree trunk or a clump of algae. A few times, they thought they saw the metal container, only to find that it was a large rock when they came closer.

After an hour, Joe changed places with his brother and began to pilot the boat. Minutes later, Frank discovered the box.

"Over there, to the right!" he directed. Both

boys were jubilant. There, half-sunken into the black mud, was a square, metal container with two handles. Were the missing paintings inside?

"I hope the claw works," Joe whispered tensely as Frank manipulated the grip. Slowly, he directed the mechanical arm toward the container, grabbed the box, and carefully retracted the claw. The container came easily out of the mud. Frank locked the claw into position, and the brothers broke into whoops of joy, slapping each other's back and jumping up and down. However, their exalted mood soon diminished when they remembered the quandary they were in.

Joe checked the instruments and became worried. "We only have enough oxygen for another hour," he announced. "Maybe we should go up and look around."

Frank agreed. "If the crooks are still waiting for us, we can always submerge again."

Joe nodded and brought the boat up to a point just below the surface. They had cut all lights, and now strained their eyes to see through the window.

The lake seemed deserted, and there was no light in the lodge.

"The gang skipped!" Frank cried out.

Joe was not so sure. "It could be a trap," he said cautiously. "Let's stay away from the boathouse."

The boys decided to continue underwater to the

clearing, then hide the box and go for help in their car. Using the chart and the compass for directions, they reached the designated area with no problems. The water was deep enough for them to pull right up to the small strip of land. Carefully, they maneuvered the box onto the ground, then jumped out of the sub.

"Don't move or I'll shoot!" a loud voice suddenly commanded. The boys whirled and stared into the blinding beams of two flashlights.

A clicking sound proved the threat had not been an empty one. There was no chance for them to attempt an escape.

Someone stepped up behind them and tied their hands and feet. When they had gotten used to the glare of the lights, they recognized Heinz Schmidt and Oskar Jansky.

"You went straight into our trap," Schmidt sneered. "When we found your car, we knew right away where to expect you!"

The boys heard the motorboat start up at the boathouse and Schmidt went on, "Thanks for bringing up the paintings, by the way. My father will be thrilled to get them back."

"Your father?" Frank was puzzled. "He was killed in the war!"

Schmidt smirked. "He arranged it so everyone believed that. Pretty clever, eh?"

"So Steiner is really Wilhelm Schmidt?" Joe asked.

"That's right," Heinz replied.

"But we saw photographs where he looks completely different!"

"A little plastic surgery can do wonders. Now, no more revelations, even though you two won't have a chance to tell anybody. You're through with snooping once and for all."

He grabbed Joe and, together with Jansky, carried him into the sub. The boy struggled fiercely, but Schmidt's fist landed in his face as he was shoved through the hatch down into the passenger seat. Frank immediately followed.

They could hear the motorboat pull up. Jansky came into the sub, started the diesel engine, and drove out into the lake. He would not answer any of their questions. After a while, he cut the engine and left the ship without a word. In his place, a large, elderly man appeared through the hatch. He was strong looking, had a flat nose, a pinched mouth, and wore glasses. *He was Willy Steiner, alias Wilhelm Schmidt!*

"I warned you, you pesky kids!" he thundered. "But you didn't listen. Now you're finished!"

"Why don't you give up, Schmidt!" Joe cried out bravely. "You'll never get out of this valley, the police are already on their way!"

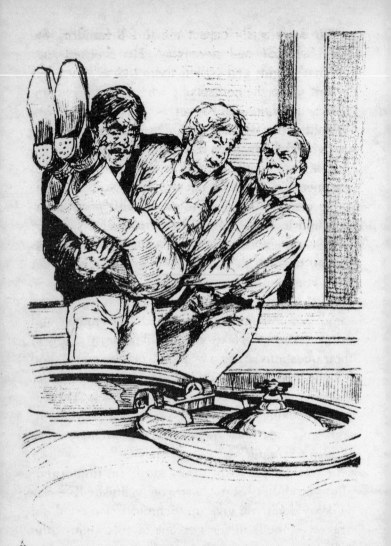

"You don't really expect me to fall for that, do you?" Schmidt said derisively. He checked the prisoners' bonds and pulled them tighter, then he stepped up to the controls.

"You've got enough oxygen for half an hour," he declared with a devilish grin. "No one will ever see you or Alfred Wagner's mini-sub again!"

With that, he turned the knob that opened the ballast valves. Then he cut the lights and scurried up through the hatch. The cover fell shut behind him and was sealed from the outside.

Frank and Joe were caught in the slowly sinking submarine!

20 Amphibian Arrest

The boys were almost paralyzed with terror. They began tearing frantically at their bonds, but the ropes only cut deeper into their flesh. They had no time to lose. If the sub crashed to the bottom of the lake, it had little chance of sustaining the shock.

Finally, Frank controlled himself enough to think clearly. "Joe, the toolbox!" he cried out. "Maybe I can reach it!" He wriggled into the right position and, after many unsuccessful attempts, managed to pull out the drawer underneath the seat. Quickly, he felt for a knife, then started to work on Joe's bonds in the dark. The task was made almost impossible by Frank's own tight bonds. But finally he cut the cord, and soon both Hardys were free!

Within seconds, they had closed the ballast valves, started the electric motor, and activated the pump to empty the water tank. They were just in time—the boat was only ten yards above the bottom of the lake!

"Wow!" Frank exclaimed and wiped the perspiration from his forehead. "I'm glad we made it. Do you think the boat would have stayed in one piece after hitting the bottom?"

"I bet it would have been smashed to bits and us along with it," Joe replied. He shuddered at the thought, then took a deep breath. "We'd better get some fresh air before the oxygen runs out."

Cautiously, they ascended. When they reached the surface of the lake, they saw the headlights of a car coming through the woods from the lodge.

Frank unlocked the hatch cover and looked out.

There they go, he thought.

The next moment, the whole forest seemed to come alive! Two shots cracked through the night, shouts were heard, and the headlights went out. Then a maze of flashlights flared up and moved all over.

Frank stared at the scene in amazement. "Joe, the police are here! Let's get going!" he cried out.

Soon they reached the shore and climbed on land. The noise had stopped, and after a few steps, Frank held his brother back by the arm.

"Someone's coming!" he whispered.

A twig rustled, then broke. Tense and alert, the Hardys pressed themselves against an evergreen. They noticed a shadowy figure sneak down to the water's edge about fifteen feet away from them. After a silent signal to each other, they let out a war whoop, jumped the stranger, and pulled him to the ground.

Gerhard Stolz and Detective Schirmer heard their cry and rushed to the scene. "Don't let him get away!" Schirmer exclaimed.

The Hardys took a closer look at their captive. It turned out that the shadowy figure was Wilhelm Schmidt!

"Good work, boys!" Schirmer praised, as he handcuffed the man. "He almost escaped!"

Gerhard put his arms around the young detectives. "Am I glad to see you!" he said. "I was worried when I didn't hear from you, so Sepp and I came up here as fast as we could."

"I'm glad you did," Frank said with a grin.

"How did you catch this guy?" Gerhard went on.

"With the help of *Ludwig II*," Frank responded and pointed to the mini-sub. "We made an amphibian arrest, so to speak."

Everyone laughed, then Joe asked, "What about the other two crooks?"

"They're in custody already," Stolz replied.

"And the paintings?"

"We have them. They even unpacked them for us. As we suspected, the coin collection belonging to Mayor Altenberg was in with them, too!"

"I'm sure Doris will be delighted to get it back," Frank said.

"Why don't we go to the hunting lodge and talk there?" Schirmer suggested and dragged the handcuffed prisoner with him.

When they arrived, they found a pot of coffee steaming on the stove, and the two other prisoners under the watchful eye of a police officer.

The Hardys told Gerhard and Detective Schirmer what had happened to them, and the reporter shuddered when he heard how the criminals had intended to get rid of the boys. "That's attempted murder!" he exclaimed. Then he turned angrily to Wilhelm Schmidt. "Steiner, you're going to spend the rest of your life in prison for that!"

"Steiner?" Joe repeated. "That's really Wilhelm Schmidt, the former councilman of Glocken!"

The crook let out a string of curses when Frank explained what they had heard from Heinz.

But no one paid any attention, and Schirmer turned to Jansky. "You may be able to get an easier sentence if you tell us what you know. First of all, how did you ever get into business with Schmidt?"

The man sighed.

"Don't think you owe the Schmidts anything," Frank spoke up. "They were going to get rid of you the minute they didn't need you any longer."

"That's right," Joe added. "We overheard them say so when we eavesdropped here at the window earlier this evening."

"I had a hunch they'd do that!" Jansky stormed. "I was a fool to trust them!"

He had been hired for a huge salary, he now revealed, but had seen little of it. It was not until later that he found out what the Schmidts were up to. By that time, he was so involved that he could not back out.

"Schmidt was obsessed with the treasure in the lake," Jansky went on. "In order to retrieve it, he needed a sub because it was down so deep. And he had to transport the craft to Bear Lake without attracting attention. So he tried to have Lemberg develop one. That would have been the easiest way."

"Oh, now I see why he was so upset when the firm dropped the project," Joe spoke up.

Schirmer looked at Schmidt. "Then you had Tarek steal Wagner's drawings, and you built a copy of *Ludwig II*."

The criminal did not reply.

"As soon as he had retrieved the paintings, he was

going to sabotage Wagner's sub and sell the plans abroad," Jansky revealed.

"Very clever," Gerhard Stolz admitted. "This way he would have killed two birds with one stone."

Jansky nodded. "When he heard from Tarek that Wagner had become suspicious and had asked you for help, he sent Heinz to the garage to give Tarek instructions. Both stood near Wagner's office when the Hardys arrived. Heinz overheard that Stolz was in Glocken, and why. When he told his father about it, Wilhelm sent him after the boys to keep an eye on them."

"He decided to do more than that," Joe said. "He tried to kill us on the Autobahn."

Jansky shrugged. "He happened to catch up with you and took advantage of the opportunity. The interlude with the blond girl reporter had given him the idea of buying the wig, by the way."

"That did confuse us for a while," Frank admitted.

"But when he broke into our hotel room, he made a mistake," Joe added. "That's when we realized the meaning of the Argentinian handkerchief."

"The red Alfa helped, too," Frank said. "It's such a conspicuous car."

Wilhelm Schmidt turned to his son. "You see, what'd I tell you!" he hissed.

185

"So *you* didn't make any mistakes?" Heinz scoffed. "You left Tarek's note in Stolz's apartment!"

"Shut up!"

Schirmer rubbed his hands together. "Thanks. That explains the attack on Rita Stolz!"

Jansky continued with his story and admitted that Schmidt and he had overpowered Gerhard Stolz and dragged him into the cellar of the house on the lake. Then he had taken Gerhard's Mercedes to the airport and sent the Hardys the telegram. Schmidt had gone to Glocken the same night, where he asked Heinz to scare the young detectives by putting a threatening note on their door. When it did not work, the two set up a trap in the old mine, where Heinz was to lure the boys.

"But that wasn't necessary," the young man said with an evil grin. "They came on their own! I had been there setting the trap when they showed up. I'd call that perfect timing," he added sarcastically.

His father ordered him to be quiet, but Heinz shrugged. "For what? It's all over anyway."

Now he and Jansky both admitted that they had engineered the theft of the truck and the attack in Wagner's workshop. The motorboat with the magnetometer was also stolen but taken to Bear Lake earlier.

"What I don't understand," Gerhard said, "is why the container with the paintings was hidden almost two hundred meters below the surface of the lake!"

"No one planned it that way," Heinz said. "My father had stashed it at the foot of the cliff where there was a small promontory only ten meters deep. But when he wanted to retrieve the treasure, he realized that the landslide had pushed the box way out into the lake."

Schmidt now admitted that during the war he had heard about the investigation Altenberg had started against him, and, being guilty, wanted to avoid punishment. He had managed to exchange identification papers with a dead soldier and sneaked back to Glocken at night without anyone seeing him. He had been familiar with the old mine ever since he was a child and suspected that one of the tunnels led near the Altenbergs' wine cellar. He had dug for weeks to break into the cellar, while his wife supplied him with food.

"And then Fritz Blendinger found out about your scheme, didn't he?" Frank asked.

"H-how did you know?" the criminal stammered. Then, realizing he had nothing to lose, Schmidt admitted that he had killed his former colleague because he was on to him and also took credit for poisoning Altenberg's dog.

After Schmidt had concealed the paintings in Bear Lake, he fled to Argentina, where his wife and son followed. His wife died soon after her arrival. Many years later, Schmidt found a buyer for the paintings and came to Germany.

"That buyer was Braun?" Joe inquired.

"No. I had offered him the pictures, too, but he refused. Now I could have extracted any price from him."

"Why is that?"

"Because he was recently commissioned by a South American collector to buy them," Schmidt replied.

Two days after the capture of the criminals, the Hardys were having coffee and cake with Gerhard and Rita in their Munich apartment, when Sepp Schirmer dropped in.

"I wanted to tell you that Braun confessed," the detective said after pouring himself a steaming cup. "The tip about the surprise at the Glocken ceremony came from him!"

"We wondered about that," Frank said. "But what was his purpose? To confuse us?"

"No. He was hoping the tip would get you on Schmidt's trail and lead you to the paintings. Schmidt had once offered Braun a gold *Joachimstaler*, but had not revealed his name. And he had hinted that he had possession of the paintings. When Braun heard about the public opening of the secret wine cellar in Glocken, he instantly connected Schmidt's story with those pictures. That's why he came to the ceremony."

"So by tipping off Gerhard, he thought Gerhard would be interested in the case, and find the pictures for him, because now he had a customer for them?" Joe asked.

"Right. Then he met Schmidt in the street in Glocken and made a deal with him directly."

Gerhard Stolz grinned. "Well, that winds it up, boys. Now I can write my report for the *Herold*."

"Only it'll be more exciting than you thought, won't it?" Frank said.

Gerhard nodded. "And you and Joe will become international heroes besides getting a ten-thousand-mark reward! By the way, what are you going to do with all that money?"

"I'd like to do some more traveling," Joe suggested. However, he would soon find out that there was no time for travel once he and Frank got involved in a case called *The Four-Headed Dragon*.

The Hardy Boys® in

The Four-Headed Dragon

The Four-Headed Dragon was
first published in the U.K. in a single volume
in hardback in 1983 by Angus & Robertson (U.K.) Ltd,
and in Armada in 1983

Contents

1 Surprise Attack

Frank and Joe Hardy were working on a chemical experiment in the laboratory above the Hardy garage when the phone rang. The boys paid no attention. It would be picked up by their mother.

But then Mrs. Hardy's voice came over the intercom. "Frank or Joe, get the phone. It's Chet. He says it's very important!"

Frank reached for the receiver. "He's probably stuck somewhere and wants a lift."

But Chet had no problem this time with his troublesome old jalopy. "Frank, my father found Sam Radley wandering around our farm," he said, his voice tense. "Sam doesn't seem to know where he is. He mumbles, but we can't understand a word."

Frank glanced at Joe, who had heard Chet's excited voice. "Tell you what to do, Chet. Call the First Aid Squad, and—"

"Oh, I already did that," Chet interrupted in a hurried tone. "The ambulance is on the way. I also called Sam's apartment three times, but there was no answer. Guess Ethel is out shopping."

"What's Sam doing now?"

"My father and Iola managed to get him into a chair and my mother made him a cup of coffee. But he won't drink it. He just stares into space with his hands on his knees. I tell you, it's scary. Frank, I have to go. Here comes the ambulance. They sure are quick."

"We're going to drive to the hospital right now!" Frank said before Chet hung up.

Then he turned to his brother. Joe was already putting away the equipment they had been using for their experiment. Frank buzzed the main house on the intercom.

"Yes?" Aunt Gertrude replied.

"Joe and I are rushing to the hospital," Frank told her. "Sam Radley's been hurt. Tell Mom, will you?"

"I will," Aunt Gertrude said and cut off the conversation immediately. She never asked questions during an emergency.

In a minute, the boys were in their yellow sports sedan and moving down Elm Street.

"I wish Dad were here," Joe said.

"We'll notify him as soon as we can," Frank told his brother.

Sam Radley and his wife, Ethel, were good friends of the Hardy family. Sam and Mr. Hardy, who had once been an ace detective on the New York police force before he went into private practice, had been working together for years.

Frank thought of that as he turned into Main Street. A siren shrieked behind them. He looked back. "Here comes the ambulance!"

Quickly, he pulled the car over to the curb and stopped. The ambulance tore by on the way to the hospital.

As Frank was moving out into the mainstream of traffic again, someone honked the horn frantically behind them. He slammed on the brakes as a large black sedan swerved to miss them and almost hit an automobile coming from the opposite direction. The black car did not slow down, but continued after the ambulance.

Joe let out his breath. "That was close!"

"That driver never even looked back!" Frank complained. "Too bad there's no patrol car around. A cop could have nabbed him for speeding and

197

going over a double line. Did you get a look at the driver?"

Joe shook his head. "Not a peek. I tried to catch the license plate number, but the car was going too fast."

Frank moved ahead cautiously. "My theory is that guys like that get caught eventually. I just hope it happens before he kills someone because of his recklessness!"

They arrived at the hospital a few minutes later, and met Dr. Kelly in the lobby. "How's Sam Radley?" Frank asked.

"Oh, is that who's down in emergency?" the physician asked.

The boys nodded.

"I'm on my way there now. You two sit in the lobby. I'll get back to you as soon as I've examined the patient."

Twenty minutes later, the doctor reappeared and sat down. "It's an odd case," he said. "Sam seems to be in shock, and yet it's not quite that, either. He doesn't have any wounds and, as far as I can discover, no broken bones. I'm going to have X-rays taken, though, to be sure."

"Can you make an educated guess as to what it might be, Doctor?" Frank asked.

Dr. Kelly knitted his brow. "This is no diagnosis, you understand, but his condition is somewhat like concussion. I served three years overseas with the army, and I've treated soldiers who were too near a shell when it exploded. They were not hit, but they received the shock of the blast. Sam reacts like those soldiers—mumbling, incoherent, nearly motionless—the thousand-yard stare."

"Thousand-yard stare?" Joe asked.

"He doesn't seem to see what's directly in front of him, but is looking at something far away," the doctor explained. "Very common for soldiers who have been in combat for many days. Just why Sam should be affected that way is a mystery to me. Has anyone contacted Sam's wife?"

"Chet Morton tried to phone her, but she's not in," Frank replied.

"Well, I suggest that you contact Mrs. Radley as soon as you can. Her husband is in no great danger, but she should be here. Perhaps, if he sees her, he'll snap out of his condition."

Dr. Kelly left, and Frank and Joe went to a phone booth to call Ethel Radley. After the phone had rung ten times, Frank hung up.

"Why don't we go over to the apartment?" he suggested. "Maybe a neighbor has an idea where she went."

"Good thinking," Joe agreed.

On the way, Frank snapped his fingers. "I should have thought of it before! Do you remember the automatic answering machine the Radleys bought last month?"

"Sure," Joe said. "Sam made us call them three times to make certain it was working."

"Then why didn't it answer?"

"Maybe Ethel forgot to turn it on when she went out."

"That's not like her," Frank said. "She's so careful about everything."

"Could be the machine is on the blink," Joe suggested.

"It's possible, but I have a feeling something's wrong." Frank smoothly pulled up in front of the Radley's apartment building and the boys rushed into the lobby.

"Did you see Mrs. Radley go out this afternoon?" Frank asked the doorman, who was sweeping the floor.

"No, I didn't," the man replied. "I only came on at four o'clock, though. She hasn't gone out since then."

"Thanks." Joe jabbed the elevator button. It seemed forever until the doors opened on the lobby floor. Frank punched the button marked "17" and up they went.

The Radley apartment, 17E, was at the end of the hall. The boys walked rapidly toward it.

"Look, the door's slightly open," Joe cried. He marched in, followed by Frank.

It was dark in the living room. "Where's the light switch?" Frank asked tensely.

"A little to your right, I think," his brother said.

However, Frank did not have time to turn on the lights. There was the sound of heavy footsteps from the other side of the room, then three bodies slammed into the Hardys.

Frank and Joe had been trained to react quickly when ambushed. Joe seized the right arm of the nearest attacker and pulled the man to the floor on top of him. Then he twisted in a way that would have made his high school wrestling coach proud of him. Now he was on top.

Frank was pinned to the wall by two other assailants. He kicked sharply and felt his shoe make contact with an ankle. One man screamed and released his grip. Frank turned his attention to the other fellow, swinging a skillful right cross to the stranger's head.

But the battle came to an abrupt end. Joe couldn't hold down the stocky man beneath him. The thug heaved the boy off to one side. Then the intruder, whose ankle had been kicked, growled, "Let's get out of here!"

The three rushed for the door. They retreated so

quickly that neither Frank nor Joe were able to stop them.

Frank managed to reach the door just as the trio was disappearing into the elevator. He saw only their backs, but he noted with satisfaction that one was limping badly.

"I'm going after them!" he called out to Joe and took up the pursuit. If he were lucky, the elevator would stop several times on the way to the lobby. He raced to the fire exit stairs and flew down as fast as he could.

Maybe someone with a lot of luggage will hold up the elevator, Frank thought. Perhaps someone will move a piece of furniture—

But his wish did not come true. When he arrived in the lobby, panting and out of breath, the elevator doors stood open, and there was no sign of the three men. The doorman was nowhere in sight, either.

Frank rushed out to the street, but the men had disappeared without a trace. Disappointed, the boy went up to the Radley apartment again. Everything was quiet as he entered, and the light was still off. A chill went down Frank's spine. Had something happened to his brother?

2 *Night Scare*

Frank switched on the light. "Joe, where are you?" he cried in alarm.

"Over here," came a muffled voice from behind the couch. Joe slowly emerged, looking disgusted.

"Are you hurt?" Frank asked.

"No." Joe rubbed his neck. "But that guy flipped me as if I were a pillow, even though I'm taller than he is and outweigh him by a few pounds. Anyway, I landed on my head and blacked out for a minute." He surveyed the room. "What a mess!"

Pictures had been ripped off the walls, chairs and the couch had been overturned, drawers had been pulled out and their contents heaped on the floor.

Even the carpet had been taken up and tossed in a corner.

The kitchen, bathroom, and bedroom were in the same condition. The most serious damage was in the spare room Sam used as an office. The cards that the detective had carefully compiled for many years on hundreds of criminals had been taken out of the file box and now littered the room from wall to wall. The automatic answering machine had been smashed.

"Well, whatever those thugs were looking for they didn't find," Frank observed. "Otherwise, they'd have been gone by the time we arrived."

Just then they heard a thumping from the office closet. Frank leaped to the door and flung it open. Ethel Radley was lying on the floor, her hands and ankles tied and her mouth taped. She had been kicking her heels against the door.

They freed her from her bonds and carried her to the living room couch. Joe brought her a glass of water. She sat quietly for a few moments, her eyes closed.

At last, she looked at the two anxious youths and said, "I never thought I would get out of that closet."

"Can you tell us what happened," Joe asked, "or would you like to rest some more?"

"No, no." She shook her head to clear it. "I'm all

right. I want those people caught before they hurt someone else. I went out to shop and returned a little after one o'clock. Two of them were already here, going through everything. They tied me and put me in the closet. All afternoon I listened to them moving around, smashing things. I tried to hear what they were talking about, but caught very little of their conversation. They were discussing a dragon, that much I could hear."

Joe and Frank stared at her in amazement. "A dragon?" Joe asked.

"Yes."

"Do you remember anything else? What they looked like? If they referred to each other by names?"

Ethel Radley thought carefully. "It all happened so quickly that I had only a slight impression of their appearance. One was tall with dark hair and another was fairly short. It was this last one who tied me up. He was very strong."

"Sounds like my sparring partner," Joe said wryly, remembering how he had been tossed. "But there were three of them. You didn't see the third man?"

"No, he came in later." She knitted her brow. "Wait a minute. The phone range. They answered it and probably talked to the third man."

"How did they do that?" Frank asked, perplexed.

"We called twice and they didn't pick it up."

"It must have been a code," Ethel suggested. "It rang three times and then stopped. Then it rang again after a minute and one of the men said, 'That must be Carl.'"

"Carl," Joe repeated thoughtfully.

"Anyway, one of them picked up the receiver and listened. Then he said. 'Well, follow the ambulance and find out where they're taking him.' Then he hung up."

Frank and Joe looked at each other. "That must have been the black car that almost hit us," Joe said.

"You know something about this?" Ethel asked.

Frank explained what had happened, then said gently, "Do you feel better now?"

"Oh, yes."

"I'm afraid I have some more bad news for you. Sam was found wandering around the Morton farm. He didn't seem to know where he was. The ambulance took him to Bayport Hospital."

"What!" Ethel's hands flew to her face. "Poor Sam! How is he now?"

"Physically he appears to be all right," Frank replied. "But he's disoriented. He still doesn't know where he is. That's why we've been trying to get in touch with you and why we came here."

"I have to go to him!" Ethel cried.

The boys helped her to her feet. "We'll drive

you," Frank said and took her arm. Although she was still shaky, she managed to walk out to the car.

Sam's condition had not changed. Ethel sat by his bed, anxiously watching her husband's face. "You two can run along now," she said with a wan smile. "I'll stay with him."

"You ought to eat something after what you've been through," Frank said. "We'll have a meal sent in to you."

"Thank you," she said.

"If Sam says something that you can understand, would you please write it down?" Joe handed her a pencil and a page from his notebook. "Don't worry if it makes little sense. You never can tell when a clue will pop up."

A twinkle returned to Ethel's soft gray eyes. "You sound just like Sam."

"And our father," Frank remarked. "Which reminds me that we have to get in touch with him. Come on, Joe."

The youths stopped at the hospital coffee shop to order a hamburger and a soft drink for Ethel. Then they started home.

As they drove down Main Street, Frank said, "I wonder what Sam was working on. If we knew that, we'd know how to proceed."

"Maybe Dad has an idea."

Fenton Hardy, an internationally known detective, was often asked by the federal government to help on difficult cases. At the moment, he was in Alaska working with the FBI.

When the boys arrived home, Aunt Gertrude called to them from the kitchen, "Dinner will be ready in ten minutes!"

"We have to phone Dad first," Frank told her as he and Joe headed for the study.

"Your mother is talking to him right now," Aunt Gertrude informed them.

"Here they are," Mrs. Hardy said into the phone as her sons entered. "Don't hang up. They'll tell you what's been going on." She looked at the youths curiously. "As a matter of fact, I would like to know, too. I've been waiting all afternoon for a phone call from you."

"Sorry, Mom," Frank apologized as he took the receiver. "Everything happened so quickly, we didn't have a chance."

He related the events of the past few hours to his father.

"That's just terrible," Mr. Hardy said in a troubled voice. "I don't know what Sam was working on. It must have come up very recently. I spoke to him three days ago and he mentioned only a few routine things. Of course, he might have been trying to contact me since, but I've been away from the office. I had to go underground and even the

FBI didn't know where I was." Mr. Hardy spoke calmly about what must have been a dangerous assignment.

"I'm flying home immediately," he continued, concern in his voice. "Fortunately, my work in Alaska has been completed. The case is not solved, though. We'll have to pick up clues somewhere else. Good-bye, Frank, I'll see you tomorrow."

"Good-bye, Dad. Have a good flight."

Frank had just put down the receiver when Aunt Gertrude stuck her head into the study. "If you don't come right now, the food will be cold," she announced.

The two women asked questions all during the meal and Frank and Joe answered between bites of delicious lamb stew.

"I'm glad your father is returning," said Mrs. Hardy. "It seems as if he's been away a month."

"Not to change the subject," Aunt Gertrude remarked, which meant she was going to do exactly that, "but did you hear about the hurricane that is approaching North Carolina? I hope it won't veer and hit Bayport."

Mrs. Hardy smiled. "There are lots of hurricanes at this time of year, and most of them amount to nothing. Anyway, North Carolina is a long way from here, Gertrude."

"That's what everyone said several years ago,"

Miss Hardy said tartly. "And look at the hurricane we had then."

Frank chuckled. "I don't think you should worry about something that might never happen."

"Oh, you're right," Aunt Gertrude replied. "But I believe in the Boy Scouts' motto: 'Be prepared.' I'm going to lay in a supply of canned food and condensed milk early tomorrow morning just in case we lose electricity again."

After dinner, the boys phoned Sam's hospital room. Ethel Radley said that, although the detective was resting more easily, there was little overall change in his condition. She had not been able to make out any words from her husband's incoherent ramblings. Dr. Kelly had been kind enough to have a cot set up for her and meals sent in. She would let them know immediately if Sam awakened.

"But do me a favor," she added. "I haven't called the police about the break-in yet. Will you do it for me?"

"Sure," Frank promised. He reported the incident to the sergeant on duty, then he and Joe went out to the garage laboratory and completed their chemistry experiment. It was their way of relaxing.

Later, they sat in the kitchen, drinking cocoa and going over the mysterious events of the afternoon. They came up with several theories, but rejected each one after careful consideration. At last, unable to find a suitable answer to Sam's delirium or the invasion of the Radley apartment, they went to bed.

They were awakened three hours later when Aunt Gertrude shook them. Joe snapped on the table lamp between the two beds, but their aunt put her finger to her lips to command silence and switched off the light.

"I've been listening in bed to my radio earphones in case there was any new information about the hurricane," she whispered. "When I took the earphones off, I heard noises downstairs."

The boys stared at her. "I don't hear anything," Joe stated. He and Frank knew how vivid their favorite aunt's imagination could be, especially coupled with the possibility of a hurricane. The sounds, they suspected, might be a figment of her imagination.

"How could anyone get in?" Frank asked. "We have a burglar alarm system. No one could—"

"I know what I heard!" Aunt Gertrude insisted in her usual tart manner. "Now, do you want me to go look or will you?"

The boys groaned inwardly, but slid out of their beds and went to the landing. There they became wide awake in an instant. From below came very faint but unmistakable sounds in the study. They retreated to their bedroom.

"Please phone the police, Aunt Gertrude," Frank

whispered as he and Joe pulled on pants and shirts in the dark. "Then go to Mom's room, tell her what's happening, and lock the door. We're going downstairs."

Aunt Gertrude gripped their shoulders. "On second thought, maybe you'd better wait for the police!"

"The burglars may get away if we do," Joe pointed out.

"Then be very careful. Don't take any unnecessary chances!" Aunt Gertrude slipped out of the room noiselessly.

Frank and Joe slowly crept down the carpeted stairs. Frank stopped at the right side of the room their father was temporarily using as a study, since his study upstairs was in the process of being redecorated. Joe took his post at the left.

"Well, there's nothing about the four-headed dragon here," came a low, rough voice from within. "Let's try the other rooms."

The boys instantly remembered the reference to dragons by the burglars of the Radley apartment, but their thoughts were interrupted by another voice.

"I don't like this, not with those kids upstairs."

"Oh, you're always scared, Carl," a third man sneered. "That's all they are, kids."

"Strong kids," Carl reminded them.

There was a soft snort. "I handled one of them this afternoon all right."

Joe clenched his fist, aware that he was listening to the man who had tossed him in the Radley apartment. We'll see who wins the second round, he said to himself.

"We can't stay here all night yakking," said the first man, who was obviously the leader. "Come on, let's get moving."

The Hardys tensed as the door opened. Then, as the masked intruders emerged, Frank snapped on the hallway light and he and Joe jumped the strangers.

For the second time in a few hours, they were battling the same crooks, but now they had the advantage of surprise. They were fighting evenly, too, because one of the men broke loose from the melee and ran out the front door.

Joe once again found himself struggling with the smallest of the gang. He pinned the thug against the wall. The man's mask fell off to reveal a face crossed with scars.

Then Joe heard a thud. Out of the corner of his eye, he saw Frank on the floor, his assailant standing over him with a blackjack. The man raised the weapon for another devastating blow. With a shout, Joe released the small man and hurled himself at Frank's opponent.

His fist caught the crook's chin and the man staggered backwards. The thug recovered quickly, though. He held the blackjack high, menacing Joe, who was standing over Frank's inert form!

3 *Warning in the Woods*

But the blackjack never fell. "Let's get out of here, Slicer," the man called to his unmasked companion.

The other needed no further persuasion. Together, the two backed toward the now open front door as Joe glared at them, his fists ready.

"We'll meet again, sonny," the small man growled just before the burglars disappeared into the night.

As soon as they had left, Joe turned his attention to his brother. To his surprise, Frank was still conscious, although he was very groggy.

"Go . . . after . . . them, Joe. Don't . . . worry about . . . me."

"Mom, Aunt Gertrude!" Joe shouted. The two

women appeared at the head of the stairs. "Frank's been hurt! Take care of him, will you? I'm going after the burglars!"

"No!" his mother cried, but Joe was already out the door. He saw the thugs getting into a black car across the street. Joe sprinted for the garage, opened the door, and jumped on his motorcycle. One pump of his foot and the bike roared.

Down the driveway the youth drove and into Elm Street in pursuit. The black sedan went a few blocks and turned into Main Street.

Maybe I'll see a patrol car, Joe said to himself. The small city was quiet. They passed stores, houses, and gas stations where not a light showed— but there was no sign of the police.

Joe stayed two blocks behind the sedan, trusting that the criminals would not spot him. Apparently, the three men felt safe and did not look back. After passing through the business district, they turned onto a country road, going well below the speed limit.

The driver probably doesn't want to draw any attention to himself by going fast, Joe thought.

They drove on for a couple more miles. Just after they passed the entrance to the Morton farm, Joe's motorcycle began to sputter and lose speed. Finally, the engine quit and he drifted to a stop.

Joe knew very well the reason for the engine's

failure and scolded himself. He had been low on gasoline and had delayed filling the tank!

He pushed the cycle into the bushes. When he was sure it could not be seen from the road, he started jogging home. As he passed the Morton farm again, he thought of turning in to borrow Chet's car. But it would not be fair to wake the family.

Fifty minutes later, he turned into the Hardy property. Lights were on downstairs and a patrol car was parked in the driveway.

Aunt Gertrude, Mrs. Hardy, Frank, and Police Chief Collig, who had been a friend of the family for many years, were in the study. They looked up as he entered.

"Well, what happened?" Frank asked.

Joe shrugged his shoulders and told them the story of the empty gas tank. "So I wasn't able to accomplish anything," he concluded. Then he turned to his brother. "How are you?" he inquired.

"He should be in bed," Mrs. Hardy put in, "but he insisted on waiting for you."

"The police took me to the hospital," said Frank, "and I was checked out, X-rays and all. No concussion or anything like that. I must admit, though," he went on with a wry smile, "that I have a whopper of a headache."

"Sergeant Moore informed me about the break-in of the Radley's apartment and Sam's condition," Chief Collig spoke up. "I'm sure these crooks are professionals and won't be easy to track down. You have the most sophisticated burglar alarm system I've ever seen, yet they managed to dismantle it without your knowledge. It takes an electronics genius to do that."

"You're right," Frank said. "And both times the intruders mentioned something about dragons. Do you have any idea what this could refer to?"

The chief shook his head. "None. I've never heard of anything like this."

"Did you see Sam, Frank?" Joe asked anxiously.

Frank shook his head. "Ethel was sleeping on the cot and I didn't want to disturb her. A nurse told me, though, that his condition has not changed."

Chief Collig rose. "Nothing more to be done here for the present," he said. "Just one question, Joe. Did you manage to get the license plate number of the black car?"

"I wasn't able to pull up close enough," Joe replied. "I was afraid they might see me if I narrowed the gap."

Chief Collig nodded. "That was wise. But we have very little to go on, except that one of the thugs, Slicer, is small and has a scarred face.

Another is called Carl. And something about dragons. I don't mind saying I'm glad your father's returning today. It's not that I don't admire your talents, boys, but I suspect that this particular gang is very dangerous!"

Frank and Joe had always been early risers, but this morning, exhausted by the events of the previous night, they slept until nine. They would have remained in bed even later if they were not awakened by a bustle from downstairs.

Coming into the hall, they were met by Aunt Gertrude. "You'll have to get your own breakfast," she informed them, "and please don't get underfoot today. Mr. Rogers is on his way over to start laying new carpeting, and your mother and I are getting the house ready for the work."

"We won't be in the way," Joe promised. "We'll be going to get my motorcycle."

When the boys had finished eating and were on the way out, Aunt Gertrude burst into the kitchen followed by the carpet dealer, Mr. Rogers, and a stranger.

"We also want carpeting in here," she declared. She cast a sharp eye on her nephews. "Leaving?" she asked.

"Yes," Frank said. "Hello, Mr. Rogers."

"Hello there, Frank, Joe. I'd like you to meet my new assistant, Ben Ebler."

The large, broad-shouldered man with the genial, smiling face held out his hand. "It's a pleasure meeting you," he said. "I read about your exploits in the California newspapers. You certainly have acquired quite a reputation for yourselves."

"You're from California?" Joe asked.

"I've lived out there for ten years, but originally I'm from Boston. I like California, but my relatives are here in the East, so I thought I would return to my roots for a while."

"Is Curt away on vacation, Mr. Rogers?" Frank inquired. Curt Gutman had been Rogers's assistant and carpet layer for many years.

"Just came back," Mr. Rogers replied grumpily. "He would be on this job, but when I arrived at my store this morning, I found a note from him. Said he had to go to Philadelphia immediately to visit a dying aunt. Humpf, I didn't even know he had an aunt. Never mentioned her. Anyhow, it was lucky that Ben came in with letters of recommendation from some of the best rug dealers on the West Coast. I hired him on the spot."

"I'll be around here for a few days," Ben explained, "but I'll do my best not to get in the way of anything you're doing."

"Well," Aunt Gertrude exclaimed, "nothing will be done if we stand here gabbing all morning! You boys said you were on your way out."

Frank winked at Joe. "We're already gone, Aunt Gertrude."

They rode off in their yellow sports car. When they were approaching the Morton farm, Joe suddenly yelled, "Stop, Frank! Quick!"

"What's the matter?" Frank pulled over to the side of the road and jammed on the brakes.

Joe didn't hear him. He had his head turned and was staring after a gray car that had just passed them going to Bayport. "I think that was him!"

"Who?"

Joe turned back, scowling. "Remember the guy that knocked me out at Sam's—Slicer? I'm pretty sure he was driving that car!"

"Then let's go after him!" Frank suggested excitedly.

"There's no chance to catch him," Joe said gloomily. "He was going fast, well over the speed limit. Anyway, maybe it wasn't him. I only had a quick glance at the driver."

"Well, if it was Slicer, they have more than one car!"

Joe nodded, and the boys got out. They easily found the spot where Joe had left his motorcycle. He was struggling to pull it out of the bushes when a cold voice remarked, "You are trespassing on private property!"

A young man, not much older than the Hardys, appeared from the woods. Joe smiled at him. "I thought this was part of the Morton farm."

"It is not! It is the Sayers' estate!"

Joe started to explain that he had run out of gas in the early morning and was forced to hide the bike in the bushes, but the other interrupted him rudely. "Please, no excuses. Do not set foot on the Sayers' property again or it will mean trouble for you."

With that dire warning, the young man crept back into the foliage. Joe looked at Frank, puzzled. "Now what do you think that was all about?"

"Your guess is as good as mine. He's a foreigner, that much is for sure. I couldn't make out the accent, though. Could you?"

Joe shook his head. "Eastern European would be my guess."

"Another thing puzzles me," Frank said. "The Sayers' property has been deserted for years, except for Emile Grabb, the caretaker!"

4 A Dangerous Scheme

Joe filled the gas tank and started the motorcycle. He noted with satisfaction its steady roar. Apparently, the bike had not been affected by its night out.

"Let's stop in at the Mortons," suggested Frank. "I had only a few words with Chet yesterday. Maybe I missed something about Sam in the rush or Chet forgot to mention an important clue."

"Good idea," said Joe.

Frank drove up the dirt road leading to the farmhouse, followed by Joe on his motorcycle. Chet's pretty, dark-haired sister, Iola, came out of the kitchen door, wiping her hands on an apron. "Hi, Frank, Joe. Chet's out on the tractor, but he ought to be here in a few minutes. Come on in. I've just made a cake and you can sample it."

"Glad to," Joe said, getting off his bike. "Only don't you think Chet would be a better critic? He's had a lot more practice at cake testing than I have."

The pixie-faced girl's eyes twinkled as she laughed. "Oh, his appraisal isn't worth too much. He'll eat *anything*."

She turned serious. "How is Sam?"

Joe was about to tell her when Chet came in. "Wow, chocolate cake!" he exclaimed. "But you've already given these guys most of it."

"Most of it!" his sister protested. "Why, they only had two small pieces."

Chet winked at his two best friends. "Looks like most of it to me," he said, cutting himself a large slice. "Say, how's Sam?"

The boys gave Chet and Iola their meager information concerning Sam's condition and then filled them in on the events since yesterday.

Chet whistled when they were finished. "This is terrible! My father figured that maybe a large branch had fallen from a tree and hit Sam on the head, giving him a concussion. But Dr. Kelly doesn't think so, huh?"

"No head injury at all," said Joe.

"Hello there, Hardys," boomed a voice, as Mr. Morton entered the room, followed by Mrs. Morton. "Glad to see you. How's Sam?"

Once again, the boys repeated their tale. The farmer shook his head. "Well, I hope he pulls out of whatever ails him."

"Say, Dad, did you hear anything about new people moving in next door at the Sayers' estate?" Iola asked.

"Not a word. Is it true? I've been waiting for years to have new neighbors. Always good to have friends nearby to visit and chat."

"I don't think they'll be too friendly, judging by the person we met," Joe said, and went on to describe the threatening young stranger in the woods.

Mr. Morton rubbed his chin. "He doesn't sound very hospitable. But then, they have a right to keep people off the property, I guess."

"By the way, Dad, I saw tracks of the wild dogs near the sheep pen," Chet stated, helping himself to another piece of Iola's cake.

"That high wire fence kept them out, I guess," Mr. Morton surmised, "but they're getting more daring than ever."

"I thought you liked dogs, Mr. Morton," Joe said.

"I do, but I can't say I'm particularly fond of the wild pack that formed about four years ago. Two or three dogs started to live in the woods. I figured they escaped from cruel owners. They weren't too much trouble at first, but now the pack has grown to about fifteen. They've been after our sheep and chickens. Poor mutts, they're really in misery. Most of them are diseased. I've been asking the town government to round them up, but they keep dragging their heels. I'm afraid sooner or later those dogs are going to attack human beings!"

"That's an awful thought!" Frank glanced at his watch. "Mrs. Morton, would you mind if I called home?"

"Not at all. You know where the phone is. Help yourself."

Frank and Joe went into the hall where the telephone was. Frank dialed and their mother answered.

"Come back right away and pick me up," she said. "Jack Wayne just called over the radio. Your father's plane is half an hour away from landing at Bayport."

"We're on our way, Mom," Frank replied.

After saying good-bye to the Mortons, the boys left. They pulled into the Hardy driveway fifteen minutes later.

They ran into the house where their mother was ready and waiting for them.

"Wait a minute," Frank said before they went out the front door. "I want to get my tape recorder. Perhaps we can tape Sam's mumblings." He took the stairs two at a time, almost tripping over Ben

Ebler, who was laying carpet in the upstairs hall. "Sorry," he said.

"Think nothing of it," the man replied.

A few moments later, Frank drove the car out into Elm Street.

"That was a good idea to bring the recorder," Joe complimented his brother. "I hope it works."

When they were walking through the parking lot at the air terminal, Mrs. Hardy pointed upward and said, "That's what I call good timing."

The boys followed her gaze and saw *Skyhappy Sal*, Jack Wayne's silver-winged plane, gliding down. Jack piloted Mr. Hardy whenever necessary. By the time Mrs. Hardy and the boys had walked through the terminal, he was taxiing to the building.

Fenton Hardy was the first off. After kissing his wife, he turned to the boys. "Has there been any change in Sam's condition?"

"Not as far as we know," Joe replied, "but we haven't checked today."

"Then we'd better get to the hospital as fast as possible." The detective turned to his pilot, who had just emerged from the plane. "Jack, we'll run you home so you can get a well-deserved rest."

"Thanks, Fenton, but you go on ahead. I have to leave instructions about servicing the plane first," Jack Wayne said.

"Are you tired?" Mrs. Hardy asked her husband as the automobile moved out of the parking lot.

He leaned back and smiled. "I caught some sleep on the way. Jack certainly knows how to fly a plane smoothly."

"It's like riding on air, right, Dad?" Joe commented.

Everyone laughed, then Mrs. Hardy asked her husband if he would be able to stay home for a while.

He sighed. "I'm not sure when I will be called in again. The Alaska phase is completed and the FBI has to pick up the leads I uncovered elsewhere."

"Can you talk about the case, Dad?" Frank asked.

"Yes, but I have to warn you that you're not to breathe a word about it. The plot is so diabolical that it's almost unbelievable. If the story appears in the newspapers, people might panic."

"That serious?" Mrs. Hardy inquired.

"I would say that the possible destruction of the Alaskan pipeline is indeed serious," her husband replied soberly.

"The Alaskan pipeline!" gasped the boys together.

"None other. A few weeks ago, U.S. Intelligence services picked up strange rumors that Burl Bantler, an American criminal, has been contacting unfriendly foreign governments, claiming that he can destroy the Alaskan pipeline with a secret weapon.

"Apparently, one country—we don't know which—bought the deal, for recently Bantler has been seen in Alaska. That much I uncovered."

"Do you think he's still there?" Mrs. Hardy questioned anxiously.

"No. It seems I just missed him in Nome by a few hours. Now he has left the state, but the word is that he'll return with the weapon."

"He must be stopped!" Mrs. Hardy exclaimed.

Her husband nodded. "He bragged that he doesn't mean wiping out just a section of the pipeline, but the entire thing. I don't have to tell you what effect that would have on our country."

"A good deal of our oil supply would disappear," Frank commented, "until the pipeline is rebuilt, which would take years."

"Right," Fenton Hardy said grimly.

"How do you know that Bantler isn't faking, Dad?" Joe asked. "Maybe this weapon doesn't even exist."

"That's a possibility," the detective admitted, "especially considering that Bantler, besides his other criminal activities, has been a con man. But I doubt that he would try such a scam on a foreign government.

"Second," Mr. Hardy went on, "Bantler has

never before been involved in espionage. I don't believe that he'd get into it if he didn't have a real weapon. Third, why would he go to Alaska after contacting these foreign governments? If the entire thing was a confidence game, he would have gone underground after collecting his money. Or, what's more likely, he wouldn't even have collected if he hadn't had some convincing proof of what he's able to deliver."

The famous sleuth's face was set in rocklike determination. "This man has to be stopped. If not, our country may be in very bad trouble!"

5 Sabotage at the Airport

"It's unfortunate that Sam is injured at this particular time," Fenton Hardy said as he, Mrs. Hardy, and the boys entered Bayport Hospital. "Not only is he a close friend, but he once arrested Bantler and would be able to recognize him. I've never seen the man and don't have much of an idea what he looks like."

"Don't you have a description?" Frank asked, puzzled.

"All I really know is that he's a large man," Mr. Hardy replied. "You see, Bantler is a master of disguises. And Sam, as you know, is a master of seeing through disguises. Probably the best in the country."

Ethel Radley looked worried and tired as the boys and their parents entered the hospital room. Dark rings lined her eyes. "He just doesn't change," she said, when asked about Sam's condition. "He's calmer, but he's still delirious."

Fenton sat by the bed and talked to Sam for a few minutes, but there was no response from the ill man, except a continual, nonsensical mumbling. Finally, the detective rose, sighing. "Let's go and confer with Dr. Kelly."

"Joe and I'd like to stay here, Dad," Frank said, "and tape what Sam is saying."

Mr. Hardy nodded and left the room with his wife and Ethel Radley.

Frank checked the recorder to see if it was in working order before placing the machine on Sam's pillow. Then he and Joe sat back in their chairs. However, Sam was now quiet.

After fifteen minutes had passed, the silence was broken by the shrill sound of the telephone. The boys jumped, startled by the ring.

Joe picked up the receiver.

"Hardys?" asked a rough voice on the other end.

"Who is this?" Joe questioned sharply.

"You're Joe, right? Just wanted to warn you to lay off this case. Don't meddle any more. What you're doing is dangerous!"

Joe recognized the voice. "We don't pay any attention to threats, Slicer."

There was a half-gasp and then a buzz as the line went dead. Joe hung up slowly, shaking his head. "I made a mistake. I should never have mentioned his name. But I did hear his buddy call him Slicer last night."

"He may not have realized that his name had been spoken during the fight," said Frank, "or he may have thought that you hadn't heard it."

Joe nodded glumly. "Now he knows we know his name."

A few moments later, Fenton Hardy came back into the hospital room. "Dr. Kelly is convinced Sam will snap out of it sooner or later," he said, and looked with pity at the man in the bed. "I only hope it's sooner. Did you record anything?"

"The tape just came to an end," Frank said. "I don't know if anything's on it because the phone rang. We'll study it at home."

He told his father about Slicer's call when the telephone rang again. The three of them stared at it.

"Do you think Slicer's calling back?" Joe asked.

"Only one way to find out," the detective declared and picked up the receiver. "Fenton Hardy here. Oh, it's you, John. How did you track me down here? Gertrude told you? Good. What's up? What? Great! That may be the break we've been waiting for! Chicago? Sure, I'll meet you there. Good-bye."

The boys looked at their father expectantly when he hung up, but he held up his hand to prevent questions and dialed again. "Hello, Jack. Sorry to bother you so soon, but the FBI just phoned. Yes, I'm afraid we're off again. Perhaps I should get another pilot for this trip? No? Okay, I appreciate that. I'd rather fly with you than anyone else. I'm off to the airport right now and I'll meet you there. No, no change in Sam. I'll see you."

Once again, he put down the phone. "You two bring the car over to the front entrance. I'll meet you there in five minutes after I talk to your mother."

The boys were full of questions, but they had been trained to act quickly and obey orders during an emergency. They turned on their heels without saying a word and left the room.

Frank had just pulled up in front of the hospital when Fenton Hardy came running out. He jumped into the back seat and they drove to Main Street.

"Go to our house and wait while I pick up some clean shirts," the detective said. "Then we'll continue on to the airport. I'm off to Chicago. That was FBI Agent John Mortini on the phone. An associate of Burl Bantler's has been picked up. He saw Bantler only a month ago, but he isn't talking yet."

"Do we return to the hospital to get Mom after you take off?" Joe asked.

"No, she wants to stay with Ethel this afternoon. Doctor Kelly will drive her home when he finishes his shift at five o'clock."

As they pulled up to the Hardy residence on Elm Street, a car parked at the curb moved away. Aunt Gertrude was pruning roses in the front yard. Fenton Hardy dashed over to her. "I have no time to talk, Gertrude. The boys will fill you in on what's going on." With that, he continued on into the house.

Frank quickly told his aunt about the search for Burl Bantler and his father's trip to Chicago.

She sighed. "He's always on the go. I know what he's doing is very important, but he simply must get a little relaxation sometime. He hasn't had a vacation in years!"

"Who was that in the car pulling away?" Joe asked. "The driver certainly seemed in a hurry."

"Ben Ebler," she said. "He received a phone call just before you arrived. He turned white as a sheet and ran off after shouting to me he had to leave because of an emergency, but would be back tomorrow."

"Poor man," Joe said. "I hope there's no trouble."

Fenton Hardy ran out of the house, shirts tucked under his arm. He gave Aunt Gertrude a peck of a kiss on her forehead and jumped into the car.

She cast an appraising eye on him as Frank started the engine. "You look pale and tired. All this gallivanting around is not doing your health a speck of good. I imagine you haven't had any lunch yet."

"Don't worry, I promise to have a big steak when I arrive in Chicago," he said.

"With plenty of green vegetables," she called as the car backed out onto Elm Street.

"She treats you just like she treats us, Dad," said Joe with an innocent air.

"I'll worry when she doesn't," the detective said, waving good-bye to his older sister. "Now there are some things I want you to do for me," he explained, placing the clean shirts in his suitcase. "Before I left Alaska, I requested the FBI to ask all the police chiefs in the country to send me any data they might have on Burl Bantler—anything, no matter how insignificant. This information will come to our home since I'm never sure where I'll be from one minute to the next. It'll be your job to receive the data and summarize it so that you can give it to me in a nutshell when I phone."

"When will that be, Dad?" Frank asked.

"I can't tell you exactly. I'll try to make it daily and perhaps more often, but I don't know at what time."

They drove directly to the hangar instead of the

air terminal's parking lot. As they got out, they saw a red-faced Jack Wayne gesturing excitedly at Sy Kramer, the head mechanic. The boys had never seen the pilot so angry.

"You know, Sy, that you and I and your own mechanics are the only people allowed to touch this plane, and no one else!" Jack thundered.

"What seems to be the problem?" Mr. Hardy inquired.

"Some guy waltzed in here wearing a white coverall and claimed I sent him to service the *Skyhappy Sal*. He showed a phony note reportedly from me, confirming the order," Jack shouted. He turned back to Kramer. "Sy, didn't it occur to you to phone me and see if it was okay to let this guy work on the plane?"

"Well, he seemed all right," the chief mechanic replied with an embarrassed shrug.

"Seemed all right!" the pilot exploded. "Seemed all—"

"I'm sure Sy believed he was doing the correct thing," Mr. Hardy said in a conciliatory tone, even though tension showed in his face. "Anyway, it's too late now. What should be done next, Jack?"

"I'm sorry to delay the flight, but you'll have to admit this is highly suspicious. I want to go over the plane from nose to tail."

"You're right," Mr. Hardy agreed.

As the pilot walked into the hangar, the detective turned to Kramer. "Sy, what do you remember about this fake mechanic?"

"Well, he had a rough voice. He was small, about five foot five, I would say, but strong, bulging with muscles. His face has a number of crisscrossed scars."

The boys looked at each other. "Slicer!" Frank exclaimed. "You remember, Dad, the thug we told you about?"

"I remember," Mr. Hardy said, his expression grim. "First he searches our house for something, then he tries to sabotage my plane. I wonder why?"

While Jack and Sy worked on the aircraft, Mr. Hardy and his sons went into the terminal to report the incident to the police. When they returned to the hangar a half hour later, Jack walked toward them, his overalls greasy. "Lucky Sy mentioned this guy," he said. "I found a small leak in the fuel line. It was so tiny that I was fortunate to discover it."

"What would have happened if you hadn't?" Mr. Hardy asked.

"We would have run out of fuel in about an hour or a little after. That would have been in the Great Lakes area. If there'd been an airfield nearby, I might have been able to glide in, but in all probability we would have crashed into the water!"

6 Vicious Dogs

Mr. Hardy's face was grim but calm. "Did you find anything else wrong, Jack?"

"The plane's okay now," the pilot replied. "I'll stake my life on it." He grinned. "Come to think of it, that's what I'm doing, right?"

The detective smiled. "If you say the *Skyhappy Sal* is in good shape, then it must be. Let's go!"

The boys watched the plane taxi down to one end of the runway and then roar along the concrete until it lifted off into the cloudless sky, heading west.

"Dad sure asked the million dollar question," commented Frank as they walked back to the car.

"What's that?" Joe asked.

"Why Slicer sabotaged his plane. Does what's

happening have something to do with the Bantler case?"

"It's possible," Joe admitted.

On the way home, they saw a familiar figure on Main Street, kicking the tires of an old, battered jalopy. They pulled up to the curb and Joe called, "Chet, what are you doing?"

Chet gave the tire a final, powerful kick and looked up at them. "This dumb old thing is giving me trouble again."

The brothers laughed. "The car isn't human, Chet," Frank said. "It doesn't know what it's doing."

"Or not doing," Joe added, smiling.

"Well, it sure acts like it does," Chet grumbled. "I tell you, this jalopy's got a grudge against me. Lucky for me I met a stranger who has more sympathy than you two." He waved toward the upturned hood, which came down with a sudden slam.

"I'm afraid, son, that you have carburetor trouble," Ben Ebler said. "Oh—hi, there, Frank and Joe. You know this unfortunate young man?"

"We have watched him eat anything in sight since he was in kindergarten," Joe explained. "With luck, we'll be watching him doing that for the rest of our lives."

"I'm still growing," Chet defended himself.

"In all directions," Frank observed, glancing significantly at his friend's stomach. "Coach won't like that when you go out for football."

"Oh, I'll be in shape by the first game," Chet replied airily. "Say, how about taking me to Gordon's Garage?"

"At your service," said Joe. He opened the trunk and took out a towline, then Frank pulled their sports sedan in front of Chet's old jalopy.

"Can we drop you anywhere?" Frank asked Ben as Chet and Joe attached the line.

"No, thanks," Ben replied. "Haven't got far to go."

"Aunt Gertrude was concerned that you had to leave so suddenly this afternoon," Frank went on. "Nothing serious, I hope."

"Family problems out of town," the man explained. "But everything is cleared up now. Tell your aunt I'll be at your house bright and early tomorrow morning." He waved good-bye and sauntered down the street.

"Nice guy," Joe said as he hopped back into the car, while Chet got behind the wheel of his disabled jalopy. "Helping a total stranger is what I call real kindness."

At the garage, Mr. Gordon looked grim after he had examined the engine. "That Ebler fellow diagnosed it just right, Chet. Needs a new carburetor. I don't have any in stock. It'll take at least a week to get one."

After Mr. Gordon had told him the price, Chet looked unhappy. "I've just lost my appetite," he said to Frank. "Could you drive me home?"

"Your wish is our command," Frank replied. "But Joe will be your chauffeur. I'm going home to find out if anything's on the tape we have on Sam."

The boys climbed into the sports sedan, and Joe tried to comfort his friend. "Maybe you can make some extra money cutting lawns," he suggested.

Chet sighed. "You realize how many lawns I have to cut to pay for a new carburetor? It'll take me all summer!"

Frank laughed. "That'll keep you out of mischief!"

Chet gave him a withering glance as Joe pulled up in front of the Hardy home to let Frank out. Then the two drove on to the Morton farm. Just as Joe was about to turn into the lane leading to the farmhouse, they heard cries for help ahead.

"Someone's in trouble!" Joe exclaimed, passing the Morton entrance. They went over a small bridge and reached the spot where they thought the cries had come from, but could see no one.

"Maybe somebody's playing a joke," Chet guessed.

"We'd better check," Joe said, his head hanging

out of the car. He switched off the engine, then Chet, too, heard the calls.

"It's coming from the woods," Joe declared. "Let's go!"

He dashed in among the trees, followed closely by Chet, who was fast despite his size. They had gone a hundred yards when they came into a small clearing. A young woman had her back to a tree and was staring horrified at a pack of wild dogs. The animals, saliva dripping from their mouths, were growling as they slowly advanced on her.

"Don't shout any more!" Joe called to her. He walked a few steps toward the dogs and then began to jump and yell.

The animals turned. They were malnourished and covered with sores. Some were so thin that their ribs were pushing against their skins. Joe knew they were to be pitied, but all he felt was fear. He had hoped that they would flee when he and Chet burst upon the scene, but they apparently saw them as other and better victims. One dirty white-and-brown mastiff, obviously the leader, pushed through the pack and advanced on the Hardy youth while Chet backed off in fear.

Joe thought quickly. "I'll draw them off!" he yelled at Chet. "Get her in the car and go for help!" Then he ran deeper into the woods, pursued by the

pack that now started to howl, excited by the hunt.

Chet reacted quickly. He rushed to the terrified young woman and seized her wrist. "Come on!" he shouted in her ear to shock her out of the horror that made her motionless. Together they fled toward the road.

When they reached the car, Chet ran around to the driver's side. However, his feet became tangled in a vine and he fell to the ground. He struggled to rise, but by the time he had settled himself behind the wheel, he discovered that the girl had disappeared. He looked wildly around, but there was no sign of her. Quickly he backed the car up to the entrance of his home, then shifted into drive and shot up the lane.

He jumped out of the car and burst into the living room where Iola and his father sat reading the newspaper. "Joe's being chased by the wild dogs out in the woods!" Chet called out.

Mr. Morton sprang up without a word and began to unlock the gun cabinet to get his shotgun. Iola ran for her jacket, while Chet dialed the phone. Fortunately, Frank answered right away at the Hardy house. Chet tersely told him of Joe's plight and Frank promised to come immediately. Chet hung up just as Iola returned and Mr. Morton finished loading the gun.

The trio ran out to the Hardy's car. Chet drove

back to the spot where the boys had run into the woods. He was surprised to see the young woman and a man her age running toward them.

"My friend, Tonio," she said breathlessly, waving at her companion. "He knows the way of the woods."

"That's why you left?" Chet asked as he, his sister, and father emerged from the car.

She nodded. "He will be of great help."

"I can track," Tonio confirmed. "I was brought up in forest land." Chet noted that he, too, spoke with a foreign accent.

"We need all the help we can get," said Mr. Morton. "Is this where you went into the woods, Chet?"

"That's right. You can see where we trampled through the bushes."

"Then lead the way."

Chet plunged into the underbrush, the others on his heels. Soon they came to the clearing where he and Joe had found the mysterious young woman facing the vicious animals. But now there was no trace of either the younger Hardy or the dogs!

"What do we do?" asked Chet helplessly. "I can't remember in what direction Joe ran."

"Wait!" Tonio ordered, holding up his hand.

They all held their breath for a full minute. "I don't hear anything but birds," Iola said at last.

"Nor do I," said Tonio. "I thought we might hear the baying of the pack. I shall have to find the trail."

He walked around the clearing for a few minutes, his eyes intently on the ground. Twice he moved out of the glen in a specific direction, but each time he returned, shaking his head. "I thought that was it, but I was wrong."

The stillness was broken by a faint whir from the road that became louder and louder until they recognized it as the sound of a motorcycle. Then the vehicle's engine stopped and they heard Frank call, "Chet!"

"In here, Frank," returned his friend. In a few moments, Frank burst into the clearing. Chet quickly told him that the young woman and Tonio had come to help find Joe. Frank recognized Tonio as the unfriendly stranger that had accosted him and Joe that very morning, but he said nothing.

"I have it!" Tonio exclaimed. "Come!" They followed him into the foliage.

A thick mist had settled in the forest and it was growing dark quickly.

"I hope he can see the trail," Chet whispered to Frank, his eyes on Tonio, who was now bending low while steadily moving ahead.

After he had left the glen, Joe had managed to keep ahead of the pack by running as fast as he could. He was getting tired, though, and knew he could not maintain the pace. The dogs were gaining on him. Already the leader of the pack was snapping at his heels.

About a mile from the clearing, Joe came to a rapidly running stream that divided the Morton property from the Sayers' estate. He was faced with the decision of whether to jump in and try to swim to safety or not. Too much of his strength had ebbed away, so he grabbed the low-hanging branch of a tree and swung himself up. The leader of the pack made a desperate leap, but his teeth snapped on empty air an inch from Joe's leg.

Joe paused a moment to recover his breath, then slowly climbed two branches higher. Beneath, the animals howled for a few minutes. Then they sat and quieted, waiting for their prey to return to the ground.

"Not today, fellows," Joe said to them, "if I can help it."

The trees were closely bunched along the bank of the stream. Perhaps, he told himself, I can get away by moving from tree to tree. Gingerly, he reached out to the next one and grabbed a branch. Over he swung.

His pursuers silently moved until they were beneath him again. He went to the next tree and then the next, but they always followed.

He traveled safely through ten trees, but the eleventh was a mistake, which he realized immediately. It had been dead for a long time and needed only a violent storm to bring it down.

The branch he landed on cracked beneath his weight. He almost followed it down, but at the last second he was able to seize another. It, too, creaked dangerously. Afraid that it might not hold him much longer, Joe removed his shoes, tied the laces together, and hung them around his neck.

The beasts below growled in anticipation. Was the stream deep enough? He didn't have time to wonder. As the branch crumbled, he jumped, landing feet first in the water.

Luckily, it was at least eight feet deep. When Joe's toes struck bottom, he pushed himself up. He emerged just in time to hear a crash behind him. He looked back and saw to his horror that the dead tree had fallen into the stream. The swift current was rushing it toward him. He flung up a hand to escape it, but managed only to partly divert it. The torn end of the rotten trunk struck him a glancing blow and he slipped into unconsciousness!

7 Narrow Escape

Fortunately, Joe was unconscious only for a moment. The cold water revived him and he floated down the stream as the wild dogs ran along the bank. Their mouths were open and their sharp teeth gleamed.

Joe tried to swim to the other bank, but gave up after a few strokes. He was too exhausted from running and from the blow on his head.

I'd better just float for a while until something turns up, he said to himself. Unfortunately, what turned up was a slowing of the current. The water had been too swift for the dogs to swim in, but now the leader saw its chance. It dove in and paddled after the Hardy boy. Joe saw to his horror that the beast was thirty yards away and gaining rapidly.

Then came a stroke of luck Joe had been hoping for. Before him loomed a small island. It was fortunate that the tide was out; otherwise, it would have rushed up the small river from Barmet Bay, completely submerging the little mound of mud and twigs.

Wearily, Joe pulled himself onto the land and turned around. It was only a matter of seconds before the dog reached the island. It came out of the water, its scraggly fur dripping, and advanced on Joe as the pack on shore howled with anticipation.

Joe frantically looked around for a weapon—a rock, a branch, anything, but there was nothing but slippery mud!

Meanwhile, Tonio led the way through the darkening woods, the rest of the party following closely. Suddenly, they heard the howling of the dogs ahead of them. "They're not far away!" Tonio called out.

"I just hope we're in time," Chet muttered, panting. He shivered, not from the cold air, but from thinking about the diseased and hungry wild animals. Frank, by his side, said nothing. His mouth was set in a grim line as they quickened their pace.

Joe took his shoes from around his neck as the pack leader came nearer and nearer. He put his right hand around the knot that tied them together, then swung the shoes above his head.

The stalking beast stopped, startled for a moment. A low and steady growl arose from its throat. Its hind legs went down and its entire body tensed for action.

Then the dog sprang through the air in a mighty leap. Joe was prepared for the charge and timed his blow just right. The heavy shoes caught the animal on the jaw and it fell to one side, landing on its back, yelping.

Joe turned to face the beast, his shoes again swinging for the next blow. But he never had to deliver it. The dog scrambled to its feet and quickly jumped back into the water.

Just then, the rescue party came into view. Mr. Morton sized up the situation in a split second, lifted his shotgun, and let off a blast above the heads of the dogs. Away they ran, followed by the mastiff, whose tail was between its legs.

"Am I glad to see you!" Joe yelled.

"Can you get over here," Frank asked, "or do you need help?"

Joe looked at the span of water. "Are you kidding? Sure, I can." He put his shoes around his neck again and plunged into the wide stream. Frank eyed his brother anxiously. It was evident by his slow strokes that the younger Hardy's energy had been depleted by the efforts of the past hour. Happily, though, Joe did not have to swim all the way. His feet touched bottom and he was able to walk the last twenty feet.

When he arrived, his friends and Frank pounded him on his back and pumped his hand.

"Better get up to the house," Mr. Morton said, "and put on some dry clothes before you come down with pneumonia." He looked around the clearing in which they were standing. "You know, something's funny here, though. Something I can't put my finger on." He frowned thoughtfully, then cried out, "I have it! There was an old shed here. My father built it a long time ago to store wood he cut, and for axes and saws. I've never used it, but I saw it last winter. Now it's gone!"

"I think we should leave," Tonio suggested. "The dogs might return."

"I doubt it. They're scared to death. They may be capable of attacking a single person or helpless animals, but not a whole group." As he spoke, Mr. Morton walked around the clearing, his eyes glued to the ground. "What's this pile of dust?"

He leaned down and picked up a handful. "This is where the shed was. Did you ever see anything like this?"

Everyone except Tonio, who held back, gathered

around the farmer and stared at the dust. "It's as if a billion termites had a banquet," he said, and shook his head.

"I think your friend is shivering," Tonio said, and pointed at Joe.

"You're right." Mr. Morton glanced at the Hardy boy, who was, indeed, shaking. "We can talk about this mystery later," the farmer said, and took off his heavy jacket. He put it over Joe's shoulders. "Come along."

Soon the party arrived at the farm. Mrs. Morton was standing in the door. "I was getting worried. I came back from shopping and no one was here. You didn't even leave a note," she said.

"Didn't have any time." Mr. Morton told her what had happened.

"Those dogs!" she exclaimed. "I just hope the township government will listen to you this time and round them up. Chet, you better take Joe up to your room."

While Joe and Chet were gone, Iola and Mrs. Morton busied themselves in the kitchen. Mr. Morton, Frank, and the two strangers sat in the living room. Conversation was attempted by both Frank and Mr. Morton, but Tonio's attitude cast a pall over the scene. He sat buried in a chair, hands in pockets, and staring at the ceiling. The young woman threw him imploring looks to improve his manners, but he ignored her.

When Joe came downstairs, however, the atmosphere was lightened by the sight of the younger Hardy wearing his friend's clothes.

Frank laughed. "You look like a circus clown."

Joe looked at himself in the mirror and, seeing the baggy trousers and oversized wool shirt, grinned sheepishly. "I guess I do."

"Those clothes look all right," Chet protested.

"On you they do," his smiling father replied.

"They're warm and dry, anyhow," Chet said defensively.

Just then Mrs. Morton and Iola bustled in, carrying trays of sandwiches. Everyone took something, even Tonio, who mumbled his thanks.

"I would like to thank you for rescuing me from those horrible dogs," said the mysterious young woman to Joe and Chet. "You risked your lives to save mine."

"All in a day's work," Chet said airily. Then, glancing at Joe, he added shamefacedly, "Of course, Joe did the most."

"Are you from around here, dear?" Mrs. Morton asked the young woman.

The stranger's smile lit up her dark eyes. "No, both Tonio and I are from thousands of miles away. Permit me to explain. My name is Maquala Krazak and my friend is Tonio Mossesky. At the moment we, my father, and my uncle are your next-door neighbors."

"You are staying at the old Abby Sayer mansion?" Mrs. Morton asked, her eyes widening.

"For the time being," Maquala said with a touch of sadness in her voice. "It seems we are always on the move, but I shall be sorry to leave Bayport, for it is a very nice place. We lead what might seem exciting lives to many people; however, it is far from pleasant to be always running from agents who are following us, even in this country, escaping from prison, and—"

"Maquala, they don't care to hear about all that," Tonio broke in. "Anyway, it is getting late and your father—"

"To the contrary, we are very interested," said Mrs. Morton. "Please go on, my dear."

Tonio receded into his sulk as the Mortons and the Hardys leaned forward to hear the story.

8 Telephone Trap

"We are Huculs," began Maquala.

"You are what?" asked Iola.

Maquala laughed. "I know you're puzzled. Not many people outside of Eastern Europe have heard of us. The Huculs are the people who live in the Carpathian Mountains. Some of us live in Poland, some in Czechoslovakia, and others in Romania, but we are one people with our own culture.

"My father, Dubek Krazak, is a great scientist. That's not only my opinion, but scientists all over the world say so. It that not true, Tonio?"

Her friend gave a short nod, but continued staring at the ceiling.

"All the countries behind the Iron Curtain want

him to work for them. Believe me, they have tried many times. They have begged him, they have offered him a soft life, and they have threatened him. But he has always refused to serve them. He hates oppressors and loves the democracy he has never enjoyed until he came to this country."

"How long ago was that?" Iola asked.

"Only a few months back," Maquala replied. "When Father was young, he fought against the Nazis. After the war, he fought other oppressors. He has been a leader of the Resistance and, oh, what a price he has paid! What a price we all have paid!

"Neither I nor Tonio have ever known a permanent home. Often we have been awakened in the middle of the night to flee minutes before the secret police arrived.

"Sometimes, we were not quick enough and my father and my uncle, Alessandro, were arrested and taken off to prison. My mother and Tonio's mother and father died in prison. But my father and my uncle always escaped."

The girl sighed, then continued. "A few months ago, it became obvious that there was no place in Eastern Europe we could stay. My father had become too well known. Also, he is crippled as a result of the tortures he has endured, and his health is poor. Thus, it was decided that we should come to the United States. We rented the Sayer house, but we might have to move on soon. My father has been told that secret agents are searching for us even here. Meanwhile, he is working on an invention that he hopes—"

Tonio stood up abruptly. "Maquala, I must insist that we leave. Your father will be very worried."

He held her coat and she rose reluctantly. "I suppose you're right," she said. "Again, I wish to thank you, Joe, for what you did. You saved my life. You were very, very brave."

Tonio's hostile eyes flashed at her praise of the younger Hardy. Joe noticed the Hucul's annoyance and said, "If it hadn't been for Tonio, I would have been the one who might have been killed."

"Yes," joined in Frank, "I don't see how you could track through those dark woods, Tonio. You're a great woodsman."

The young man was not pacified by the compliments. He mumbled something no one could hear and began to hustle Maquala towards the door.

"Please come again," Mrs. Morton invited. "After all, we're next-door neighbors."

"I don't think that's possible," replied Tonio stiffly. "We are very busy."

But Maquala smiled. "Thank you. I will try. It becomes very lonely sometimes."

"Well, I guess we ought to be going, too," said

Frank. "We're expecting a phone call from Dad."

"What will I wear home?" said Joe in dismay. "I mean, my clothes are still wet and—"

"Oh, you can wear mine and return them to me later," said Chet generously. He examined Joe carefully, from the baggy trousers to the tentlike shirt. "No matter what anyone says, you really look great."

"Oh, go soak your head," Joe returned good-naturedly. He playfully tapped his friend on the arm. "Say, I never saw you run so fast in my life as you did in the woods. You ought to go out for the sprints next spring."

"I have talents I haven't even discovered yet," Chet agreed, puffing himself up a little.

When Frank and Joe walked in the front door of the Hardy house, they found Aunt Gertrude carrying a large basket of papers. "These are telegrams," she said grumpily, "from police all over the country. They've been arriving every five minutes all afternoon. Something about a man called Bantler." Then she stared at Joe in amazement. "Where did you get those clothes? It's too early for Halloween and, anyhow, I thought you had outgrown trick-or-treating."

"Tell you later," Joe said hastily, heading toward the stairs.

Frank took the telegrams into the study where

Mrs. Hardy looked up from the phone. "Ethel Radley just called. Sam is better," she said happily. "He's resting more easily and seems to be coming around."

"Has he awakened at all?" said Frank, depositing the telegrams on his father's desk.

"No, he's still semiconscious, but Dr. Kelly is very much encouraged and believes he'll wake soon."

Aunt Gertrude came in the room with an announcement. "That hurricane I told you about is not going to hit North Carolina after all," she said. "The radio says it has bypassed that state and now is headed north. I just hope it doesn't hit us." She looked around triumphantly. "All of you thought I was foolish to worry about that storm, didn't you? Well, it appears my intuition was right!"

She was so proud that the boys were almost sure their aunt would be disappointed if the hurricane didn't come. But they kept these thoughts to themselves.

"What's your afternoon been like?" Mrs. Hardy asked her sons. "Did your father get off all right?"

"The takeoff was beautiful," said Frank with a meaningful glance at Joe, "and the weather between here and Chicago was reported to be just fine. I'm sure he arrived on time."

"Oh, he did," said Aunt Gertrude. "He phoned

from Chicago while your mother was at the hospital. He had a good trip."

Frank avoided mentioning the fake plane mechanic and the puncture in the gas line. No use worrying his aunt and his mother, he decided. Joe nodded in silent agreement.

"But seeing Fenton off wasn't all you did this afternoon," Aunt Gertrude commented, looking at Joe. "You came home in those funny clothes and your hair was wet, as though you had been swimming."

"Not by choice," Joe said, and launched into an account of the day's events.

The two women listened intently. Mrs. Hardy shook her head when he finished. "I wouldn't want to live in the Sayer mansion. It can't be very comfortable. It hasn't been occupied for years. Emile Grabb has been doing his best to keep it in good condition, I'm sure, but he lives in a small cottage on the grounds. Anyway, what can one person do to maintain such a huge house?"

"All I know about the place is that it is old and spooky and on a high bluff," Joe said. "Who was Abby Sayer, anyway?"

Aunt Gertrude's eyes became misty. "Hers is a sad story, a tragedy, in a way. She was the only child of a wealthy clothes manufacturer. When she was very young, she witnessed a terrible thing—her father's factory being burned to the ground. It was only a short way from her house and she saw all the corpses being carried out."

"Oh, no!" Joe exclaimed.

"She never forgot it," Aunt Gertrude went on. "What was worse was that the people of the city blamed her father, although it was proved it was not his fault. Hardly anyone would speak to the family and she had a lonely and unhappy childhood. It did something to her mind. She somehow had the idea that she was being haunted by the ghosts of the workers who had died in the fire."

"That's terrible," Frank said sympathetically.

Aunt Gertrude nodded. "Anyway, after her parents died, she moved to Bayport and built the mansion. I've never been in it, but I hear that it was the strangest house that was ever constructed."

"It *is* a strange house," said Mrs. Hardy. "My friend Joan MacLeod, whose father was a butler for Abby Sayer, told me a great deal about life there."

"What was it like?" Joe asked curiously.

"Abby Sayer never stopped adding on to the mansion. She had carpenters working all the time. You see, she believed that the ghosts of the dead workers had tracked her down and that she had to make them comfortable or else they would do something horrible to her. By the time she died, the mansion had over three hundred rooms."

"Three hundred rooms!" Joe whistled. "That's a hotel!"

His mother nodded. "Miss Sayer designed the place herself and she certainly dreamed up some very strange architecture, such as passages that led to blank walls, trapdoors, and stairways so small that you have to crawl up them."

"Crazy," Frank commented.

"Wait till you hear what happened each night! Abby had a steeple constructed with a huge clock on top. It only tolled once in 24 hours and that was at midnight. Then the servants would bring the most delicious food to the banquet hall on golden plates. She would greet her twelve ghostly guests as she sat down at the head of the table. Then the servants would leave, shutting the door behind them."

"Twelve invisible guests and herself made thirteen," observed Frank.

Aunt Gertrude chuckled. "The right number for such a ghoulish affair. I'll say this for Abby Sayer, though: she may have been a bit touched in her head, but she had a heart of gold. She provided the money to construct the Bayport Youth Clubhouse. And just look at the way she befriended Emile Grabb. He was an orphan, friendless and alone, as she had been, but she took him under her wing and made him her chauffeur and general aide. He worshipped the ground she walked on. Still worships her, I suppose, for he stayed on after she died to take care of the gloomy place."

"How long ago did she die?" Joe asked.

"I can't remember exactly," Aunt Gertrude said, "but it seems like it was ten years ago or thereabouts. No one has lived in the house since. The story is that her lawyers never could figure what to do with the old place. Now, at last, they've rented it."

Just then the telephone rang. "I'll get it," Frank replied and went to pick up the receiver.

"I'd like to speak to either Frank or Joe Hardy," said a pleasant male voice.

"This is Frank."

"Oh, good. I'm Ted O'Neil and I'm a nurse at the hospital. Dr. Kelly asked me to phone you. Sam Radley is wide awake and very anxious to talk with you and your brother. Could you come over at once?"

"We'll be right there," Frank replied.

"Good," said O'Neil. "Oh, by the way, he was told how you recorded him. He'd like to hear that. Can you bring the tape?"

"Sure will. Say, can I talk to Sam now?"

"Dr. Kelly does not want Mr. Radley to overexert himself," the male nurse said a bit nervously. "As a matter of fact, you'll be able to see him for only a few minutes."

"I understand. Good-bye."

266

Excitedly, Frank related the good news to the others.

"That's great!" exclaimed Joe, rising. "I'll get my coat."

"No!" Mrs. Hardy said sternly. "You're in no condition to go out. You go straight to bed and get a good night's sleep. Otherwise, you may end up in the hospital with Sam."

Joe knew better than to argue with his mother when her mind was made up. Also, he recognized the wisdom of her words.

"All right," he replied, "but, Frank, you wake me when you get home and let me know what Sam said."

Frank drove down Elm Street. The worry of the last two days was partly lifted from his mind. Sam was getting better and might be able to tell him exactly what had happened on the Morton farm. Mr. Hardy was getting a lot of helpful information on the elusive Bantler that might stop the criminal before he could damage the Alaska pipeline, and the mystery of the strange young man who had ordered them off the Sayer property had been cleared up.

Frank paid little attention to a car coming up behind him. When it started to pass, he thought angrily that the driver was being reckless by speeding and crossing a double line.

Then the car cut Frank off and forced him to the curb. Two masked men leaped out and opened the door of his car before he could close the windows and lock himself in.

They pounced on the boy and, even though he tried to fight them off as best he could, they pinned him behind the wheel and pommeled him mercilessly.

"The tape!" one of them hissed. "Give us the tape!"

9 A Sad Story

One man reached into Frank's coat pocket and pulled out the cassette. "Got it!" he cried triumphantly. "Let's go!"

"First, let's give him a lesson he'll never forget," his companion growled. "We'll teach him not to meddle in something that's none of his business."

They continued to hit Frank who was pinned on the front seat of the car. Suddenly, the blows ceased.

"Let him alone!" came a familiar voice.

The Hardy youth looked up and saw Ben Ebler pushing the assailants away from his yellow sports car.

Suddenly, the smaller of the two crooks pulled

out a gun. "Get back!" he ordered Ben Ebler.

The carpet layer slowly put up his hands. "You rats!" he snarled.

"I ought to shoot you," the gunman said.

"Come on," the other urged. "The cops may come by. We've got what we came for."

The gunman hesitated and then backed to his car. "I don't know who you are," he said to Ebler, "but we'll meet again!"

"You'd better hope not," Frank's rescuer advised.

The thugs' automobile roared down the street as Ben Ebler bent over Frank. "You all right?"

Frank shook his head to clear it. "I think so. No broken bones or anything. They didn't hit that hard."

Ebler helped him out of the car. Steadying himself with difficulty, Frank said, "Did you get the license plate of that car?"

Ebler snapped his fingers. "I should have thought of it. Sorry, Frank."

"Don't worry about it," Frank said. "No reason you should think of it. I'm just thankful that you arrived."

"It was lucky at that," Ebler agreed. "I had eaten a heavy dinner and thought I would take a walk to work it off. I saw them cut you off, but I was a block away and couldn't get here any faster. Why do you think they jumped you?"

"I don't know," Frank said casually. "Probably a couple of muggers." Fenton Hardy had taught his sons never to divulge a secret to anyone, no matter how friendly or helpful he or she was.

"Can you go on by yourself?" Ebler asked anxiously. "I wouldn't want you driving with a concussion or anything."

"No, I wasn't hurt that badly. Anyway, I'm turning around and going home. I'm certainly grateful to you, Ben. I hope I can do the same for you sometime."

Ben laughed. "I hope not. I don't look forward to having a couple of gangsters jump me. Well, good night, Frank."

Frank entered the house as quietly as he could. His mother and Aunt Gertrude were watching TV in the study and he could hear them laughing. He slipped into his father's study and used the phone there to call the hospital.

"Do you have a nurse named Ted O'Neil?" he asked the woman at the desk.

"No. We have a Mary O'Neil, though."

"Thank you," said Frank and hung up. Next, he went to the laboratory above the garage. He took a cassette out of a file drawer. The Hardys always made a copy of any original tape as a precaution against theft or misplacement. Stealing the tape from Frank's pocket had done the thugs little good if their purpose was to prevent the Hardys from listening to it.

Maybe there's something I missed when I checked it out this afternoon, Frank said to himself. He put the cassette into a player and turned the volume high. Sam's mumbles became a roar, but Frank was not worried about disturbing anyone because the room was soundproof.

In his delirium Sam had said something that sounded like *sheen* over and over again. Now, with a loud volume, Frank could make out a syllable uttered before that word. "Ma-sheen, ma-sheen," droned Sam.

"Machine!" Frank repeated, snapping his fingers. "But—what kind of machine does he mean?"

He took out the tape and, picking up a portable recorder, went into their bedroom. Joe was sleeping heavily and it took several shakes to rouse him. He looked at his older brother through bleary eyes. "What is it?"

Frank told him about the attack, but added, "That's not important now. Listen, do you hear Sam say 'machine'?" He played a minute of the tape.

"It sounds like it," Joe said. "But it doesn't make any sense!"

"Nothing in this case makes any sense so far," Frank agreed.

They stared at each other in bewilderment until

Joe said, "I'm too tired to think. I'm going back to sleep."

There was no time to think about the tape in the morning, either. Messages concerning Bantler were piling up. The youths sifted through the heaps of telegrams and teletypes arriving from the police of various cities in the United States who had had contact with Bantler at one time or another.

By lunch, Frank and Joe decided they had learned very little about the criminal. Not even the several descriptions given by agencies who had arrested him furnished any clues. Somehow, Bantler had managed to look different each time.

"Probably the only people who can identify him are his friends and Sam Radley," Frank said.

Joe glanced at his notes. "Well, we do know he's a genius when it comes to doing anything that's mechanical. He's a whiz at handling electricity, electronics, plumbing, anything like that."

Just then the phone rang. "What have you learned?" Fenton Hardy asked from Chicago.

Frank told him of their meager results.

"Well, it's better than nothing," his father said, sighing. "We've had a little progress on this end. We've been grilling this former associate of Bantler's for hours. He said that he had met with Bantler a few weeks ago. Bantler was very excited about what he termed 'a big operation, the biggest of my life.'"

"Did the associate say what it was?" Frank asked eagerly.

"No. But supposedly Bantler claimed that if things came out the way he wanted, he wouldn't have to do con jobs ever again. This associate wanted to be included, but Bantler told him he had enough henchmen. The only other thing the man was able to learn was that the operation had something to do with four-headed dragons."

"Four-headed dragons?" exclaimed Frank. "That's what the crooks mentioned when they broke into our house."

"Yes. Odd, isn't it?" said Fenton. "Well, I have to go back to the interrogation. Personally, I think we've squeezed out of this fellow all the information he has, but there's no harm in one more try. How's Sam?"

Frank told him of the operative's improvement.

"That certainly is encouraging," said his father. "I'll be in touch soon."

"You didn't tell him how those guys jumped you last night," Joe said after Frank has put down the receiver.

"He seemed to be in a hurry," Frank explained. "I'll tell him next time he calls. I've been thinking about that tape. How did those creeps know that we had taped Sam? We didn't tell anyone and we talked about it only at home."

"There's no way they could have learned about it," Joe said as they left the lab and joined Aunt Gertrude and their mother in the living room. "Yet they did. Maybe they're psychic!"

Frank laughed. "You mean they are able to know what we are thinking? That's the wildest theory you've ever come up with."

"You have a better idea?" Joe said in an offended tone.

"No," Frank conceded, "but there's got to be a more rational explanation than that."

Aunt Gertrude had a map of the eastern coast of the United States stretched out before her on the table, and pointed at it. "The hurricane is about here." She indicated a spot on the Atlantic Ocean. "And it's coming fast. The radio says it will hit this afternoon unless it veers away."

This time the other Hardys took her seriously. "We'd better prepare for it," said Mrs. Hardy. "It's good you bought those canned goods, Gertrude. Boys, you check the yard, will you, please? See that nothing is left out that might be blown away."

"Will do," said Joe. "There's the telephone again. I'll get it."

"Seems as if the whole world has been calling during the last two days," said Aunt Gertrude.

When Joe picked up the phone, he heard Dr. Kelly thunder from the other end of the line, "How come you contacted a New York City neurologist to come to examine Sam without even having the courtesy of informing me?"

"But we didn't," protested Joe. "We don't know anything about it."

The physician was not to be placated. "Maybe your father requested it."

"No, that couldn't be. He called us just a little while ago from Chicago and I'm sure he would have mentioned it. What did this doctor say, anyhow?"

"How do I know? He came when I was off duty."

"I don't understand," said Joe. "Did he hurt Sam?"

Doctor Kelly's voice lowered. "You really don't know anything about this, do you? There's something very wrong here, Joe. This so-called doctor took Sam away!"

10 The Hurricane

"Whatever happened to Sam in those woods—whatever he knows—must be very important to someone," Joe said as he and Frank drove on Main Street toward the hospital. "It sure took a lot of nerve to pose as a doctor and kidnap Sam in broad daylight."

"Was it Slicer and his friends?" wondered Frank aloud.

"I bet it was," Joe agreed and hit his palm with a fist. "I sure hope we'll catch up with Slicer again. Taking a sick man out of his bed like this is the limit!"

Dr. Kelly was waiting for them in the hospital lobby. "Our suspicions were correct," he said. "I phoned the New York City hospital Morrison was supposed to have come from. They never heard of him, but one of their ambulances was stolen yesterday. Sam was taken away in that hospital's ambulance, according to one of our orderlies whom the fake doctor asked to help with the stretcher! The nerve of it, the very nerve!" The face of the usually genial doctor was a storm cloud.

"What happened to Ethel?" asked Joe. "I thought she was staying here all the time."

"Oh, she was," said Dr. Kelly bitterly, "but she received a phone call in the room just before this Morrison arrived. It was supposed to be from me, asking her to meet me at the cafeteria for lunch so we could talk over Sam's condition. She says it sounded just like me, too."

"Where is she now?" asked Frank.

"She's suffering from shock, poor woman. You can understand why. First her husband is found in a delirious state. Then he starts to recover and is snatched away. I gave her a sedative and put her to bed."

"Was Morrison alone?"

"No. The orderly said there was a driver in a white coat, a small man with scars all over his face."

"Slicer!" the Hardys said together.

"You know him?" Dr. Kelly asked, surprised.

"We've met," Frank replied. "Did you notify the police?"

"Not yet," the physician said. "What with everything happening and taking care of Mrs. Radley, I haven't had a chance."

"Never mind," Frank said. "We'll do it."

The youths used the phone at the lobby desk to call Chief Collig. "I wish Dr. Kelly had contacted me immediately," said the police officer. "We might have prevented the ambulance from leaving the city. It was found five minutes ago out of town on Route 13. No one in it, of course. They must have transferred Sam to a car. We'll send out an all-points alarm."

"What do we do now?" Joe asked as they walked out of the hospital.

Frank shrugged. "What can we do? We have no clues at the moment to follow up. We'll just have to wait to see what the police find. Remember what Dad said: waiting is tough, but sometimes it is the only thing to do."

"I hate to tell him about Sam being kidnapped with all the problems he's now facing," Joe said. "And here comes another problem—Aunt Gertrude's hurricane."

Dark clouds were rolling in from the south. A sharp wind blew over the parking lot and large drops of rain began to fall.

"I know what we should do right now," said Joe when they got into the car. "We should check the *Sleuth*."

"Good idea," said Frank, starting the engine. The *Sleuth* was their motorboat, which was moored at the Bayport Marina. As they headed toward the docks, Joe turned on the radio and they listened to a weather report. The hurricane's center was going right over Bayport, the announcer told them. Winds were going to be very high, accompanied by heavy rain. The only happy note was that the great storm would not last long since it was traveling quickly. It was expected to be out of the area sometime in the night. The name the U.S. Weather Bureau had given to the hurricane, the radio announcer added, was Gertrude.

The Hardys laughed. "Aunt Gertrude's own hurricane," said Joe.

"She'll never get over it," said Frank as they arrived at the dock. The *Sleuth* was in its berth, bouncing up and down in the rough water. One of the lines that attached it to the dock was loose and the boys secured it tightly. Then they made sure the canvas cover was fastened properly.

"Look!" Joe exclaimed suddenly, pointing out to the bay. "Someone's out there!"

Visibility was poor, but Frank narrowed his eyes and peered through the slanting rain. He was barely able to make out a person waving from a drifting boat.

"You run down to the Coast Guard," he shouted above the howling wind, "and I'll go out!"

Joe needed no second bidding. He turned on his heels and dashed for their car. Frank quickly untied the lines securing the *Sleuth* to the dock and tore off the canvas cover. In a minute, the engine was purring smoothly and the boat was heading out of the marina. "I hope I can get there in time," the boy muttered.

The Coast Guard station was half a mile from the marina. Ordinarily, it would have taken only a few minutes to get there, but a tree had fallen across the road. After climbing over it, Joe sprinted the last four hundred yards.

He burst into the building. A chief petty officer glanced up from his desk. "Boat . . . drifting. . . . Frank went after it . . ." Joe gasped.

"Catch your breath first, son," the officer said gently. "If you have an emergency, we'll be able to handle it better when we get a coherent statement."

Joe leaned on the desk for a few moments while his breath slowed. At last he was able to speak. "There's a disabled craft in the bay with someone in it. My brother Frank went out in our boat to rescue the person."

"Commander Morelli!" the officer shouted. "Boat adrift!"

From an inner office came a tall, square-faced man. Joe repeated his story. "Sound the alarm, Pete," the commander ordered the officer. "We're going out in one of the cutters."

Pete bellowed into a microphone, "All hands, hear this! Assemble on cutter three! On the double!"

There was the sound of hurried footsteps from a back room, then a group of sailors pounded through the lobby out onto the dock. In the meantime, the commander was hurriedly putting on foul-weather gear. "Come on," he said to Joe. "You can help us."

Joe ran after the commander and jumped into the cutter. Its engines were already roaring. "Cast off!" came the order and the boat moved through the rough water.

"Hope we can find your brother and the other person," said Commander Morelli grimly. This is a very powerful storm."

Frank gripped the wheel with all his might, but it was still difficult to keep the *Sleuth* on course. The boat was pushed in many directions. Once, it was even twisted back toward shore. While the young detective desperately fought to keep the *Sleuth* pointed out toward the ocean, he often lost sight of the disabled craft. Just when he thought the situation was hopeless, he caught a glimpse of the frightened person through the driving rain.

At last he was only a few yards from the drifting boat. He started to shout, but the words died on his lips as he saw a huge wave smash down on the disabled craft.

Riding up the wave and down the trough on the other side, he stared around wildly. Then he saw to his horror that the boat had overturned! A head was bobbing in the water. Frank gunned the *Sleuth* ahead and drew up beside the swimmer.

He let the wheel go and held out his arms. The stranger grabbed at his hands. Twice the slippery grip loosened and the swimmer fell back. The third time, Frank seized the other's wrists and pulled as hard as he could.

The swimmer fell head first to the bottom of the *Sleuth*, sputtering and gasping, then turned a grateful face toward her rescuer. The boy's eyes widened.

"Maquala!"

"Frank Hardy?" she stammered. "Now—now it is twice I owe my life to your family."

"I haven't saved you yet," Frank replied. "First we have to get to shore."

He turned the *Sleuth* around. Heading back to land went faster than pushing out in the direction of

the wind, but it was no less dangerous. Now waves crashed from behind.

The *Sleuth*'s engine suddenly coughed and died. "What's wrong?" shouted Maquala.

Frank quickly examined the motor. "I don't know, and I don't have time to fix it now."

He went back to the wheel. The boat drifted toward the faintly visible shoreline. He tried to steer in the direction of the marina, but, despite his efforts, they headed toward a rockpile east of the docks. If they hit those boulders in the heavy storm, their chances of survival would be practically non-existent!

The cutter rode slowly through the bay, horn blaring but barely heard above the screaming wind. On all sides of the Coast Guard vessel, sailors kept a keen-eyed watch.

"It doesn't look too good, son," Commander Morelli said to Joe. "We're doing our best, but you'd better be prepared for the worst."

Frank drowned? Joe could not believe it. He and his older brother had been through so much together.

"Boat drifting dead ahead!" a sailor suddenly yelled from the bow.

"Anyone aboard?" the commander shouted back.

"Two people!"

"Then prepare to come alongside her!"

Within a minute they had drawn up to the helpless *Sleuth*. A sailor threw a line down to Frank, who grabbed it and tied it to the boat. Then he helped Maquala start up a rope ladder. Joe reached out and brought her up on deck. He recovered quickly from his surprise at seeing her and grinned. "We seem to be bumping into each other everywhere."

When Frank was certain that the young woman was safe, he started up the ladder. Halfway, his foot slipped and he fell back into the churning water. He was swept away and lost from sight!

11 Amazing Rescue

Maquala, Joe, and the crew looked with horror at the roiling water, but there was no sign of Frank. Commander Morelli shook his head. "Keep your eyes peeled," he ordered his men, but it was obvious by the tone of his voice that he held little hope for the boy's rescue.

The screaming wind rocked the cutter, trying to change its direction toward the shore. "Keep it steady," Morelli told the seaman at the wheel.

Suddenly, an enormous wave reared up from seaward. Maquala and Joe gasped and seized the rail. It seemed to them that the Coast Guard craft would be crushed under the tons of water thundering down on them.

Then it hit. The youths lowered their heads to weather the shock. The water tore at them, trying to loosen their grip and would have succeeded in tossing them into the sea if it had lasted one split second longer. As it passed, there was a thud on the deck.

There was a muffled cry! The crew, Maquala, and Joe looked around and saw Frank lying on the deck, clinging to the anchor line. He was shaking and coughing violently. But soon he realized that he had been miraculously saved, and, once he calmed down, a smile of relief flooded his pale face. "Thought—I'd be done for," he sputtered.

Morelli stared at him in amazement. "I've been to sea for more than twenty years," he yelled above the storm, "and I've seen many odd things, but nothing like this! You're a very lucky person."

He and Joe helped Frank to his feet and walked him into the captain's cabin, followed by Maquala. Here the young people were wrapped in warm blankets, and the commander ordered the cutter to return to the Coast Guard station. It took half an hour for the boat to battle its way through the storm back to the dock.

Once inside the station house, one of the petty officers made some tea for Frank and Maquala. Then Morelli, who had been supervising the securing of the cutter, came in. "I hope we don't have to go out again till this hurricane is over," he said.

He turned to Maquala. "What in the world possessed you to sail out in a storm like this? You're lucky to be alive. If it hadn't been for these boys, you'd never have come back. As it was, you put the lives of my crew and Frank Hardy in great danger!"

The foreign girl lowered her head. "I am sorry," she apologized. "I did not know this storm was going to happen."

The Coast Guard officer looked at her incredulously. "Warnings were being announced over the radio all the time," he said. "You mean you never heard about it once?"

"We do not have a radio," she replied simply.

Morelli was even more astounded. "I thought all kids had radios glued to their ears continually. At least, mine do."

"I do not," Maquala said, "but if I had, I doubt I would have done any differently. I would not have known what a hurricane would be like. We do not have them where I come from."

The commander could see his scolding was not going to be effective. "Well, now you know what they're like. As none of you seem to have sustained any injuries that would land you in the hospital, you can go now. Frank and Joe, we'll keep your boat safe here until after the storm."

"Thanks, Commander," Frank said. "And double thanks for saving my life."

The seaman grinned. "All in a day's work."

"I must go home now," Maquala said as the three of them piled into the Hardys' car.

"You'll catch pneumonia before you get there," said Joe. "First come home with us so Mom and Aunt Gertrude can get you dry."

The young woman shivered. "I suppose I should. I am cold."

She continued to tremble all the way to the Hardy residence. It was a hazardous trip. Ordinarily, it took fifteen minutes to go from the docks to Elm Street. This time, three quarters of an hour passed before the boys saw the friendly lights of their house. They had had to detour several blocks because of fallen trees and telephone poles. The force of the wind was increasing and often they felt it push against them. Joe had a hard time keeping the car on the road.

Halfway up the drive, he stopped. "You two get out and run in. I'll put the car in the garage."

Maquala and Frank needed no second bidding. They jumped out and dashed through the teeming rain.

Joe moved ahead to the garage. As he approached, he pressed the button of the remote control unit and the door swung open. He drove in and had one leg out of the car when he heard the sound of running feet. Before he could react, strong hands grasped the car's door and pushed it back, pinning Joe's ankle.

Joe gasped in pain, but the pressure increased. A flashlight was snapped on and shone in his face. "Stay there real still, kid," came a rough voice. Then Joe saw the barrel of a gun.

"Slicer," he said to the man in the darkness.

"You got it right, Hardy. I've been standing out in the rain for a long time for you and your brother. It ain't no fun standing out in a hurricane. That's another one I owe you."

Despite his agony, Joe saw the humor in the situation. "I suppose that's my fault. I would have come home earlier if I knew you were here."

"You're lucky," snarled the thug. "The boss told me not to hurt you."

Joe winced in pain and looked down at his leg. "Do you think this tickles?"

Slicer snorted, but eased the door slightly. "Now listen carefully. The boss wants me to let you know that this is the last warning. Lay off!"

"Lay off from what?" Joe asked. "We don't even know what you're doing. Anyhow, you have our tape and you have Sam."

Slicer's laugh contained no humor. "Sure we have Sam, but don't give me that stuff about the tape. We know you have a copy. And don't do any more snooping if you want your friend to remain healthy. That goes for your father, too. Got that?"

Joe nodded. "I've got it."

"Last warning, remember. Now I'm going. Don't try to follow me or I may have to use this gun."

The flashlight went out and the man ran off into the rain. Joe hobbled out of the car and limped across the lawn toward the house. "Follow him?" he grumbled. "I couldn't run twenty yards!"

It was fortunate no one was in the kitchen, so he didn't have to explain the limp. He went upstairs and into the boys' bedroom. Frank was changing his clothes.

"You twist your ankle?" he asked.

"Not quite. We've had a visitor." Joe went on to relate the incident in the garage.

Frank frowned. "There's a couple of strange things about this."

"Like what?" Joe said, sitting on the bed and taking off his shoe.

"Why did he say that Dad should lay off? Slicer knows he's out of town since he tried to sabotage his plane. Apparently, he also knows that the attempt was a failure. Also, how does he know we had copied the original tape?"

Joe stopped rubbing his throbbing ankle and looked thoughtful. "I can understand how he found out Dad's plane didn't crash. If it had, he would have read about it in the newspapers or heard about it on television. But how he knew we had another tape is beyond me. It's almost as if he could hear everything that is said in this house."

"Maybe he can," said Frank grimly. "Let's look around."

They searched the room, starting with the closet. They went over every inch of the two bureaus and then the lamps. After fifteen minutes, they found what they suspected under the rug beneath Joe's bed.

Frank held up the small electronic device. "A bug!" exclaimed Joe.

"Yes," said Frank. He dropped it on the floor and crushed the tiny gadget under his heel. "There! Now those gangsters won't eavesdrop on us any more. But that's only the tip of the iceberg. I bet every room in the house has a bug."

"But how?" cried Joe. "Who could have done it?"

"Soup's on!" called Aunt Gertrude from the bottom of the stairs.

"We'd better go," Frank said. "Not a word of this to Mom or Aunt Gertrude, though."

They went downstairs where there was a hot meal waiting. "I thought stew would be just the thing for a wet day," said Aunt Gertrude.

Mrs. Hardy and Maquala entered the dining

room. "It is fortunate that Maquala and I have the same size," said the boys' mother. The girl was wearing jeans and a thick, gray sweater. "She fits into my clothes as if they had been made for her."

Outside the wind howled louder than ever, but Aunt Gertrude scoffed at the noise. "It will be all over by midnight," she announced.

"Did you hear what the hurricane is called?" Joe asked mischievously.

She sniffed. "Gertrude! Oh, yes, I heard about that, young man. I wish they would abolish this habit of naming these terrible storms after people."

"They have to be called something," Frank said.

"The first one of the year should be named 'Awful,' the second one 'Bad,' the third one 'Catastrophe,' and so on," she suggested.

The boys laughed. "Might be a good idea at that," Joe agreed.

The brothers ate ravenously, but Maquala merely picked at her food. Between infrequent bites, she raved about the boys' courage and how they had twice rescued her. Frank and Joe felt somewhat embarrassed about her praise and wished their new friend would change the subject. Aunt Gertrude and Mrs. Hardy, though, listened intently, especially to what had happened in Barmet Bay.

After a dessert of apple pie topped with vanilla ice cream, Mrs. Hardy said, "I think, Maquala, you should spend the night here. It's dangerous to drive in this weather."

The girl turned pale. "I cannot, Mrs. Hardy. My father is not a well man and he worries about me a great deal."

"You could phone him," Aunt Gertrude pointed out.

"There is no phone in the main house," Maquala said. "There is one in the cottage where the caretaker lives, but he does not like us and I fear he would not go out in this weather to carry a message to my father. I thank you for your kindness, but I really must go." She rose. "If you could show me the telephone, I will call a taxi."

"There won't be any taxis running in this storm," said Frank. "Joe and I will take you." He glanced at his mother. "Don't worry, Mom, we'll be careful."

Mrs. Hardy nodded, but her sons didn't see her whitened knuckles, hidden in her lap.

12 A Strange Visit

As before, the boys had a difficult time getting out of their neighborhood. Once on Main Street, however, the driving was easier. It was clear of obstructions and there was little traffic. Moving through the outskirts of the city, they saw that block upon block was pitch dark. "Some of these houses may be without electricity for days," Frank observed.

Joe nodded, then pointed ahead. "Look!" he cried out. They had come to a police road block. Frank lowered his window as an officer approached.

"We're trying to get people to go back to Bayport unless it is absolutely necessary for them to leave," he said. Although he was actually shouting, he could barely be heard above the screaming wind and the rain.

Frank explained their mission. "You're the Hardy brothers, aren't you?" asked the officer. "I guess Chief Collig would let you through if he were here. Okay, go ahead, but be careful. It's a mess."

Frank thanked him for the advice and went on in the heavy rain. The wipers were of little use and he could see only a few yards ahead. He drove slowly, leaning forward to keep his sight on the small strip of visible asphalt.

"You know, we're pretty lucky," Joe remarked.

Frank glanced at him quizzically. "How do you figure that?"

"Suppose this had been snow!"

"Very funny." But Frank had to grin in spite of himself. Trust his lighthearted brother to try to make the best of any situation.

Off to one side there came a sharp crack. A shadow was falling ahead of them. Frank had the impression it was a giant fist until he realized a tree had been torn from the earth. He slammed on the brakes and the car skidded a few feet before stopping a foot from the trunk.

The boys got out of the car to survey the damage. "One second more and it would have crushed us," Joe observed.

Frank shone his flashlight along the length of the trunk. "It didn't go all the way across the road. We'll be able to get around it. I just hope that other fallen trees haven't blocked the way completely."

They crawled ahead for what seemed hours, but Frank's hope was fulfilled. Although there were many trees that had crashed, they were able to skirt them. Once they passed an electrical pole pushed down by the powerful wind. The lines lay on the road, smoking and crackling with sparks of acrid-smelling electricity.

After passing the entrance to the Morton farm, they came to the small bridge. "I sure hope it stands up until we're over it," said Joe.

The twenty-foot high iron gate to the Sayer estate was closed. "If it's locked, we're going to have a hard time getting in," said Joe. He climbed out of the car and walked with difficulty against the wind to the gate. It was not locked, but he had to use all his strength to push it open. Frank drove through and Joe closed it behind them.

"Here at last!" exclaimed Joe as he jumped back into the automobile.

They inched ahead. Before them they could dimly see the enormous mansion, starkly outlined in the rain.

"Who are you?" Without warning, a figure resembling a large, flopping bird came out of the bushes, holding a club. "Stop right there, I say!"

Frank almost drove off the road as he attempted to evade the stranger. The figure came up to the window and Frank saw with relief that it was a man; his oversized rain gear had only made him look birdlike.

"Get out of here!" the man screeched. "This is private property!"

"Mr. Grabb, it's me, Maquala," called the Krazak girl. "These young men have brought me home."

The face was wizened and lined. Darting eyes focused on Maquala. "Oh, it's you," came the querulous voice whose tone betrayed a dislike for the girl. Emile Grabb lowered his club. "I've been on the lookout for thieves. They've tried so often to rob Miss Sayer, but I've stopped them every time."

"You think they'd come in a hurricane?" asked Joe incredulously.

The caretaker looked at him with contempt. "What better time? They would hope to catch me off guard. Miss Sayer's orders are to be especially watchful in this kind of weather." He straightened and gestured toward the mansion. "Go on!"

"He talks as if Miss Sayer were still alive," said Frank, putting the car into low gear and moving foward.

"To him, she still is, I think," Maquala said. "Poor

man. He doesn't like any of us, but I feel sorry for him."

"I guess when you've been taking care of a hotel for ghosts for so many years," said Joe, "it's easy to believe she's still around, watching his every move."

Frank stopped the car and the three got out. As they approached, the front door was flung open and Tonio squinted out into the rainswept darkness. "Who are you? What are you doing here?" he shouted.

"Tonio! It's me, Maquala!"

The young foreigner threw an arm around the girl's shoulders and drew her inside. "Maquala, how worried we have been! We didn't know what happened to you. We called the police from the caretaker's cottage, but they knew nothing. Where have you been?"

"Oh, Tonio, I have so much to tell you." She then began speaking rapidly in a foreign language that neither Hardy recognized. It was obvious, however, that she was relating her experience in the boat, for she pointed to Frank and Joe from time to time. Tonio's frown deepened as he glanced at the brothers.

At last, Maquala stopped talking. Tonio turned toward Frank and Joe. "Thank you for what you have done," he said in a surly tone. "Thank you for saving her life."

"You did the same for me," returned Joe.

Tonio looked as if he regretted that he had trailed the wild dogs. "You go now."

"That's no way to act," Maquala cried. "They took me to their house when I was wet and shivering and their mother and aunt took good care of me. Frank and Joe certainly deserve as much from us."

Tonio was about to retort, but was cut short by a voice from the stairs. "Maquala!" A short plump man bounded down the steps and enfolded the girl in his arms. Once again, the two conversed in the foreign language. Finally, the man came toward the Hardys, a wide smile on his face. He held out his hand.

"You are a million times welcome! I am Alessandro Krazak, Maquala's uncle. I fear she has put you to some trouble and, according to her, you were exposed to a considerable amount of danger." The uncle shook both boys' hands vigorously and then beamed at them, his enormous mustache lifted by his grin. "Come, come into the living room. Tonio, fetch glasses of tea and be sure they are boiling hot."

Alessandro herded the young people through a door while Tonio disappeared in the opposite direction. The "living room" was as large as a tennis court. Faded tapestries lined the walls. The floor was covered with worn Oriental carpets. A huge log was burning and snapping in a fieldstone fireplace.

Alessandro led the Hardys and his niece to two large leather couches before the flames. He amiably spoke to them and from time to time gently scolded Maquala for going out in the boat.

Ten minutes later, Tonio entered, carrying steaming glasses of tea on a silver tray. He solemnly presented the tray to the Hardys. The glasses almost burned the brothers' hands at first and they had difficulty holding them, but a few sips made them warm and comfortable.

Tonio sat on the other couch next to Maquala and the conversation continued. Frank and Joe eventually noticed that Alessandro was plying them with questions while diverting their queries about the Krazak family and life in Eastern Europe. They realized that they were undergoing a gentle but clever interrogation.

At last the Hucul took a large swallow of tea and put the glass down. "I am sure that my brother, Maquala's father, would personally like to thank you for what you have done. However, his health is fragile. He is resting at the moment and I should not like to disturb him."

It was a form of polite dismissal and the Hardys

rose. They were about to say good-bye when a far door opened.

"Maquala, where have you been? And who are these people? You remember my rule about never allowing strangers in this house!"

Joe and Frank turned to see a small, thin man in a wheelchair glaring at them!

13 *The Mysterious Wing*

For the third time, the Hardys heard their exploits told in the mysterious foreign language. The crippled man's grim face never changed expression, but there was a softening in his eyes. He pulled Maquala to him and kissed her. Then he pressed a button on the wheelchair and came forward to the Hardys.

"Please excuse me if my greeting was not proper or polite," he said, "but understand that we have been under a great deal of pressure. Also, I am not the diplomat my brother is. I am Dubek Krazak and I thank you for twice saving the life of my only child. I thank you from the bottom of my heart."

"We were glad to do it, sir," said Frank.

"Good-bye, then. Tonio, come with me. I need

you." With a curt nod toward the Hardys, Dubek Krazak turned and wheeled out of the room, followed by a silent Tonio.

"I think we ought to be going now," said Joe.

"Not yet," said Maquala. "Why, you haven't even seen the house."

"They know best, my dear," said Alessandro nervously. "They have to drive back through the hurricane—"

"Oh, it will only take a few minutes," she interrupted. She looked at Frank and Joe. "Don't tell me you are not burning with curiosity," she teased. "I've heard everybody in Bayport would love to be shown through Abby Sayer's haunted house."

"I'd go through a thousand hurricanes to explore it," Joe said impetuously.

"I don't know if I would go that far!" Frank laughed. "But it's true I would like to see it."

"Then come along," she said.

Her uncle sighed. "I'll come, too."

"There once were over three hundred rooms," Maquala said as they walked through the large circular foyer and up the winding stairs, "but just before Abby Sayer died, one wing burned to the ground. There are still about two hundred rooms." She opened a door in the hall on the second floor. "Look."

The young men peered within. It contained one

white iron bed, a mahogany bureau on which stood an old-fashioned washbowl, and a cedar chest. Facing the single window were two rocking chairs.

"This is a ghost's room," Maquala explained. "Every other ghost's bedroom is the same—exactly the same, the furniture, the bed, the chest, the one window. And each room measures exactly twenty-four feet by twenty-four feet."

"There's no closet," said Joe.

She giggled. "There's none in any ghost's room. I suppose she thought they never took off their ghostly suits and dresses."

Frank didn't believe in ghosts, but he had an eerie feeling as he looked in the stark room. If I stayed here long enough, he thought, I might begin seeing things.

Next, Maquala took them up and down several staircases. "Don't you notice anything similar about the stairs?" she asked at last. They stared at her in bewilderment and shook their heads.

"They all have thirteen steps!"

"This one doesn't go anywhere," Joe said after he mounted one staircase and found himself facing a blank wall.

"Oh, there are a lot of them like that."

"Why?"

The young woman shrugged her shoulders.

"Only Abby Sayer knew. Let's go up to the clock tower. It will be exciting in this storm."

"I don't think we should," Alessandro warned. "It might be dangerous. Anyway, you certainly have had enough excitement in one day, I think."

But Maquala disregarded his objections with a laugh, and climbed a ladder to the trapdoor. The others followed her. "Do you still have your flashlight, Frank?" she asked.

"Right here."

"Good. We're in the attic and there are no lights."

Frank snapped on the flashlight and examined the attic, which seemed as large as a football field. In the center were wooden stairs leading upward.

"We have to go up there," Maquala said and ran to the steps. Alessandro again protested, but there was no stopping the headstrong girl. They climbed within a tall, dark column.

"What's that?" asked Joe as they passed a round mechanism with many large gears.

"The clock," Maquala replied, "but it does not work any more. It is said that it stopped the second the old lady died."

They emerged from the stairs onto a platform. All around them were windows and Maquala was right; the scene was exciting. Dark shadows of trees below them waved bony arms at the sky. Menacing clouds whipped by overhead and the wind rattled furiously at the old windows.

"Look!" whispered Maquala, pointing toward the back of the strange building. They could vaguely see the ocean, its waves mounting high and smashing against the rocks below. "The mansion is built on the edge of a cliff," she said. "Someday it will slip into the sea, ghosts and all!"

Alessandro shuddered. "I think it might happen any minute," he said. "I can feel this tower shaking."

"I can't," his niece declared.

"I can," Frank said. "That's a powerful wind. Let's go down."

"All right," she said. "I have a number of other things to show you, anyhow."

"This sure is the best way to see a ghost hotel," Joe said as they descended. "At night, during a hurricane. It had three hundred rooms once, you say?"

"Yes, until there was a fire. You know, Abby Sayer really wasn't very friendly with her ghosts. She was afraid of them. She used to sleep in a different room every night and not even the servants knew which one she picked. They thought she was in the wing that burned during the fire, but she wasn't. It took a long time to search the remaining bedrooms. When they found her, she was sitting up in bed, petrified."

"How do you know all this?" asked Joe.

"Emile Grabb can't resist telling the story of the mansion when he is asked. I've learned a lot from him."

"You shouldn't put any stock into what that crazy old man says," Alessandro remarked.

"I don't," she replied, "but they are good stories. They help to pass the time."

The group went down to the main floor again and Maquala guided them along a long, dark hall. She pushed open a large door at the end and snapped on the light.

Before them was an immense room with a large table in the middle. There were six chairs on either side and one chair at the head.

"This is where Abby Sayer dined with twelve ghosts each midnight," Maquala said.

Joe and Frank could imagine the scene: the old woman sitting alone at the end of the table, talking to empty chairs.

Maquala switched off the light and closed the door gently. Then she took them back through the corridor. When she approached the foyer, she turned to a small door on her right. "Now you can see the wing that was left standing after the fire."

"No, no, Maquala," Alessandro said, bounding ahead to stop her. "Not that door!"

But he was too late. She was already turning the knob. Suddenly, someone opened the door from the inside and Tonio came out. He closed the door quickly behind him, but not before the Hardys had seen some men on the other side seated around a table.

Joe had recognized one of them—Slicer! A chill ran down the boy's spine, and he looked at Frank to see if his brother had made the same discovery. But Frank's face was calm and impassive.

"You must not go in, Maquala," Tonio said coldly. "Your father is working in there."

She pouted. "I'm never allowed in. You and Father and Uncle go in and spend the day, leaving me all alone to wander around the rest of the house. I don't see why I am barred."

"It's because your father loves you so very deeply," said Alessandro. "He couldn't bear to see you hurt. The work he is doing is very dangerous."

"He never tells me anything," she grumbled. "I don't even know what this invention is that he is working on. I think—"

Her complaint was cut off by a sudden pounding on the front door. "More visitors!" Tonio shouted. He stamped across the foyer toward the door with everyone right behind him.

310

There in the rain stood Emile Grabb, his floppy clothes making him look more like a great bird than ever. He was holding his club threateningly over a bedraggled figure at his side.

"I found this trespasser snooping around, trying to find Miss Abby's treasures, no doubt," he said in his squeaky voice. "He claims to know you, but I think he is lying."

The Hardys almost burst out laughing. The pitiful "trespasser" was none other than Chet Morton!

14 A Coded Message

"Don't hit him, Mr. Grabb!" cried Maquala in alarm. "Why, he's our next-door neighbor."

"That's the worst kind," retorted the caretaker. "Okay, sonny, you can go in, but don't try any funny business. Don't want to catch you taking any of Miss Sayer's stuff."

"Why would I want to do that?" said Chet faintly.

"Come in, come in, both of you. Now what is this about?"

No one had heard Dubek Krazak entering the foyer in his rubber-tired wheelchair.

"I'm here to deliver a message from Frank and Joe's mother," explained Chet. "I almost didn't

312

make it because the bridge collapsed after I went over it and—"

"All right, all right," Maquala's father snapped. "What is the message?"

"Mrs. Hardy wants Frank and Joe to know that their father phoned from Chicago. He said that the informer admitted that he saw Bantler—"

Frank and Joe had been giving their friend frantic signals to stop, but Chet had been too distracted by Emile Grabb to notice. Now Joe interrupted the chubby boy firmly.

"Chet, Dad's messages are always confidential!"

Chet turned red. "Oh, I'm sorry, but—"

"You understand," Frank explained to the others, "that we're not allowed to discuss our father's cases with anyone." He stepped up and pulled Chet aside. Joe joined them.

"Now, what's this all about?" Frank asked in a low tone.

"The informer said that Bantler was going to some hideout on the East Coast for a short time, then would be heading for Alaska to destroy large sections of the oil pipeline. Your father's coming back from Chicago immediately. You've got to pick him up at the airport."

Frank and Joe stared at Chet in amazement.

"Your dad knows about the hurricane," Chet

went on. "It's supposed to be over in a few hours. He'll land as soon as he gets word from Bayport Airport."

"We'd better leave right away," Joe said.

"You can't. As I said before, the bridge collapsed and the only way to get back to town is to detour north about forty miles. And it would be very dangerous since a lot of trees have fallen. I can't even go home because of the bridge, and I live right next door!" Chet's voice had become loud and excited again.

The Hardys did not see the sharp glances Dubek exchanged with Tonio and Alessandro, and the hand signal he gave them. Suddenly, before Joe had a chance to tell Frank and Chet about Slicer, the scientist wheeled himself up to them.

"Since your friend reported that the bridge is down, you boys must stay here for the night, or at least until the storm passes," he said in a friendly tone. "I would never forgive myself if you left and were injured after saving my daughter's life."

"Why, thank you very much, Mr. Krazak," Frank said. "We're happy to accept your invitation."

Joe was glad his brother had gone along with Krazak. Perhaps this way they could explore the mansion!

"But we must let our mother know where we

314

are," Frank went on. "Otherwise she'll be worried."

Dubek Krazak held up his hands in a gesture of helplessness. "I wish we could accommodate you, but unfortunately there is no telephone in this house."

"Mr. Grabb has one, I believe," Frank said with a cool smile.

There was a glint of anger in the scientist's eyes. "I suppose it's all right, if Mr. Grabb will allow it."

The caretaker scowled and scratched his head. "Well, I don't know—" He turned to the Hardy brothers. "Fenton Hardy is your father?"

"That's right."

"I do recall that Miss Sayer thought highly of him."

"Did she know him?" Joe asked.

"Oh, not personally, but she used to read about him in the newspapers. She admired the way he solved crimes. Ought to be more people like him, she said. I guess it's okay to use my phone. Come along!"

Dubek looked at Tonio and made a small nod. The young man said, "I will go with you." He looked sourly at Joe and Frank. "Just in case you fall down and hurt yourselves."

Led by Emile Grabb, the Hardys, Chet, and Tonio trudged out into the wind and rain. It was difficult keeping a sure footing on the dirt drive, which had turned to mud. Joe pretended to slip. "I can't stay up. I shouldn't have worn these jogging shoes. Frank, Chet, let me hold on to you."

He put his arm around Frank's and Chet's shoulders and then said just loud enough to be heard above the storm, but out of Tonio's earshot, "One of the men sitting in that room with Dubek was Slicer!"

"Are you sure?" asked Frank.

"Positive!"

"All the more reason for us to stick around."

At last, they reached the caretaker's cottage by the gate. Emile Grabb opened the door and pointed to the telephone on a small table. "There it is. While you're all here, could one of you help me with a crate in the cellar? I've been waiting for someone to come around and give me a hand."

Chet, who had sunk into an easy chair, made no attempt to get up.

"All right, I'll do it," Joe volunteered. He left with Grabb while Frank went to the phone. "I hope the lines are still up," the young detective said anxiously as he dialed. "Yes, they are. It's ringing."

"Thank goodness," Chet murmured.

"Hello, Aunt Gertrude?" Frank said. "How is it going over there? Yes, I know we didn't bring the garden chairs in. We didn't have time. They're blown over into the next street? We'll pick them up tomorrow.

"Look, we have Dad's message. Chet got through. But the bridge is washed out. We can't get away until the storm is over, and even then we'll have to take a long detour home. Maybe Chief Collig could pick Dad up at the airport. Yes, I said Chief Collig. Tell Mom, will you, that we'll be home as soon as possible."

During the conversation, Chet had stared at his friend curiously. Frank seemed very nervous. Had the remark about Slicer disturbed him that much? He was so keyed up that he kept tapping the phone with a pencil all the time he was talking.

"Are you finished?" Tonio asked when Frank had said good-bye to Aunt Gertrude and put down the receiver. "No one else you have to call?"

"No one else," Frank replied as Joe walked into the room. "Let's get back now."

Chet heaved himself up reluctantly.

"Good-bye, Mr. Grabb," Frank called. "Thanks for the use of the phone."

The only answer was a distant grunt.

They battled their way back to the mansion. The foyer was empty when they returned, but the bright light was enough welcome. However, they had only taken a few steps into the house when they were plunged into darkness.

"The electrical lines must have come down," said Joe, disheartened. "This is getting worse and worse!"

15 Caught!

"Don't be afraid of the dark," said Tonio in his usual nasty tone. "We are prepared for it."

They heard him moving around the foyer. Then a match was struck and a candlewick burst into flame. Tonio held the candle near his chest, giving his face an eerie glow. If this was meant to make the atmosphere more frightening, it failed. Joe and Frank were merely amused.

"Follow me," said Tonio. He led the way up the stairs and down a hall, then opened the door to a bedroom. "Good night," he said.

Frank stood in the doorway with his arms folded. Tonio lingered, apparently waiting for Frank to enter the bedroom, but the Hardy youth remained still. "Good night," he said.

Tonio scowled, turned on his heel, and disappeared into the darkness. Frank watched until he was sure the other had left. Then he took one step into the bedroom.

"I think Tonio meant to lock us in," he whispered. He held the knob in case the young man were to sneak up and slam the door. "Now, let's examine the situation, as Dad would say. Something very strange is taking place in this house. When Tonio came out of that wing we weren't allowed to see, I noticed a ring on the third finger of his right hand—a ring with the design of a four-headed dragon!"

Chet was confused. "So what?" he asked.

"Remember the break-ins at Sam's place and our house? The burglars were apparently looking for something having to do with dragons. We overheard them say so."

"At the time," Joe broke in excitedly, "it didn't make much sense, but now it seems to tie in with what's happening here. Slicer was one of the burglars. He sabotaged Dad's plane, and he's here tonight. If only we knew what he and his gang are up to!"

"Whatever it is," Frank said, "I don't think Maquala's mixed up in it."

"No," Joe agreed. "Otherwise, she would have tried to hustle us out of the house, as her uncle wished. Also, she's being kept out of the wing where her father's working."

Frank nodded. "Well, let's get going. We have to explore the house and get to the bottom of this."

Joe reached into his back pocket for his detective kit that he always carried. The small oilskin packet, no bigger than his hand, contained strong, collapsible tools. He took out a tiny flashlight with a long, piercing beam. "I'm ready," he said.

They crept along the hall, stopping at each room. While Chet stood guard outside, Joe would shine his light around until he and Frank were satisfied that the room was empty except for a bed and a bureau.

At the entrance to the fourth room, Frank seized his brother's arm. "There, over the bed!" he gasped. "Look at that mark!"

The Hardys moved across the room. Joe's light formed a circle around the small and simple drawing of an eye. In a corner were the letters SR.

The eye was the sign Mr. Hardy's operatives used to make a trail for their friends to follow. And the SR had to be the initials of the man who had drawn the symbol.

"Sam Radley!" Joe exclaimed. "He must have

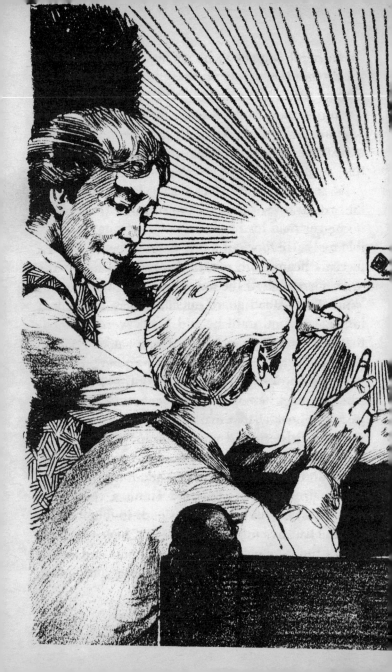

been here! Somehow, he got hold of a pencil and made the sign."

"But where is he now?" Frank wondered aloud.

Before they could discuss that question, there was a crash at the door and Chet tumbled into the room. Joe swung his pencil-sized flashlight around just in time to see Tonio slamming the door shut behind their friend. He took two giant leaps, but as he grabbed the knob, a key turned. They were locked in!

Chet slowly rose from the floor. "I never heard a thing," he groaned. "And I was listening all the time for the slightest sound. All I could hear was you. That guy's like a cat. I'm sorry to let you down."

"Don't take it too hard," Frank said. "Tonio is extremely stealthy. Remember how quietly he went through the woods when we were trailing Joe and the wild dogs? He never even broke a twig. Do you think we can break the door down, Joe?"

"With a battering ram we could," his brother replied. He had been examining the thick oak door. "But I'll try the hinges." He worked on them with his small screwdriver for a few minutes, then stood back, shaking his head. "They're rusted in."

"But we have to get out of here," Chet wailed. He walked to the single window of the room and looked out. "We'll never do it this way, though. It's a long drop and right into the sea. What are we going to do?"

"For the moment, nothing," Frank said. "We'll have to be patient. I think we should relax until help comes."

"Help?" repeated Chet. "How is anyone going to know we're in danger?"

"I told Aunt Gertrude to send the police."

"I listened to you," said Chet, "and I didn't hear you say anything like that."

Frank laughed. "Remember, Aunt Gertrude has been living with three detectives for a long time. She knows Morse code as well as any of us!"

Chet snapped his fingers. "The pencil!" he cried out.

"What are you two talking about?" Joe inquired.

"When Frank was speaking to your aunt, he was tapping the phone with a pencil—in Morse code!" Chet chuckled.

"Oh, good!" Joe said. "What did you tell her, Frank?"

"That we were in danger and she should tell the police."

"Good thinking!" Chet said happily. Soon, however, his expression became worried again. "But suppose they don't get here in time? Just in case you

324

forgot, there's a hurricane out there and the bridge is washed out."

"Let's hope for the best," Frank advised. "Meanwhile, how about some sleep? We'll need to be alert later." He looked at his watch. "It's nine o'clock," he said. "I'll stand watch till eleven, then one of you can take over."

"I'll do the second watch," Chet volunteered. "If I take the last one, I'll be so hungry that I'll probably eat the furniture."

"I'd flip you to see who gets the bed," Joe said to his friend. "But it's so dark I can't see what side of the coin is up."

"Don't you think the ghost might object?" Frank teased.

"Ghost?" Chet quavered. "What's this about ghosts?"

Joe explained how Abby Sayer had run a "ghost" hotel. "So you see, this room really belongs to a ghost."

"You can have the bed," said Chet. "I'll sleep on the floor."

"Come on, Chet," said Frank. "We were only kidding. You don't believe all that nonsense, do you?"

"Oh, no," Chet said, "but I think I'll be more comfortable on the floor. Anyway, if there really *are* ghosts, it won't make much difference whether I believe in them or not."

No amount of argument would dissuade him from lying on the hard floor. It didn't seem to disturb him, though, since in a few minutes, both he and Joe were breathing heavily in a deep sleep.

Frank spent his watch thinking about the possibilities of escape if the police did not arrive in time. Suppose the three of them charged whoever opened the door, and then ran in different directions? One or two might be caught, but the other boy would be able to get help. The young detective didn't put a great deal of hope in the plan, but it was the best he could think of.

When he woke Chet at eleven, his friend leaped up in shock. "What's up? Who are you?"

"It's Frank."

"Oh." Chet put his hand to his head. "It's all true, then? We're in the Sayer house?"

"We are."

"And we're locked in a room and there's a hurricane going on?"

"Right again."

"I thought it was a dream," Chet said mournfully. "Is it my turn for a watch?"

"You're batting a thousand," said Frank.

"I'm so tired." Chet yawned loudly. "I didn't sleep a wink."

"If you didn't sleep, how could you have had a dream?" asked Frank.

Chet thought it over. "Sometimes I dream when I'm awake."

"You do that most of the time," teased Frank, lying down. "Anyhow, I'm going to sleep. You don't have to worry about the ghost, Chet. It walked through the wall, looked at you and Joe, and said, 'Excuse me, I didn't know this room was occupied.' Then it tipped its hat and flew up through the ceiling."

"Very funny," said Chet sourly. "I don't think this is the time for humor. There are weird people in this house, we're locked up, and the biggest storm in the world is going on, and you start making jokes. If you ask me, I—"

He broke off as he realized he was talking to himself. Frank was already sleeping heavily.

The next hour was a torture for Chet. He imagined he heard all kinds of noises. He had never minded facing a flesh-and-blood opponent he could see, but sitting in the dark, open to attack by ghosts, was almost too much to bear. Even though he told himself that he didn't really believe in spirits, he was still a little frightened.

When he heard the old clock in the mansion's tower begin to toll, he actually jumped off the floor. Joe and Frank awoke immediately.

"That clock hasn't worked for years, according to Maquala!" Frank exclaimed.

"Ten . . . eleven . . . twelve!" Chet counted in a trembling tone.

"And thirteen!" Joe cried as the bell struck an extra time.

"Thirteen o'clock," said Chet after a moment of silence. "A ghost midnight. They'll be going to dinner now."

The quiet was broken by the sound of a key turning in the lock. The door was flung open and the three young men confronted Dubek Krazak in his wheelchair. His cold, poker-faced expression had changed to one of concern and fear.

"You must leave here immediately!" hissed the scientist. "You are in great danger! I cannot explain now because you have not a minute to spare. Tonio—" he pointed to the young man beside his chair who was holding a candle, "will guide you. Go anywhere, but get away from this house if you value your lives!"

Dr. Krazak then backed up, turned, and disappeared into the darkness of the corridor. Tonio beckoned, and the Hardys and Chet followed him. For a fleeting moment, Frank wondered if they were being led into a trap.

Tonio took them to the top of the stairs leading down to the foyer. "I can't go any farther," he whispered. "I have to protect the old man. Get out of here and bring the police as fast as you can. Good luck!" With that, he ran down the hall.

"Come on," said Frank. "Keep your light off, Joe. We don't want to get spotted." The three youths went down the stairs as silently as possible.

"I think the door is straight ahead," Joe said. They moved in that direction. "I've got it!" he whispered as his hand made contact with the doorknob.

There was a chilling chuckle behind them and three flashlights turned on simultaneously. The youths spun around. They could not make out who was holding the lights, but they could see gun barrels pointing at them. "Look who we have here," a familiar voice sneered. "Frank and Joe Hardy!"

16 The Dungeon

"Slicer, light some candles," commanded the voice. There were the sounds of movement and a match being struck. Six candles were lit and placed on tables around the circular foyer.

"Say, there's the guy who helped me with my car!" Chet said, staring at the leader.

"Ben Ebler!" gasped Joe.

Frank bit his lip. "I should have known when we found that electronic bug. Who else had the chance to place it in the house?"

"Very clever deduction," the ringleader scoffed.

"Not clever enough," Frank said ruefully. "It's only now that I realize what your real name is. You're the man who can manage to look different each time he's photographed, the man who is a genius at electronics. You're Burl Bantler!"

The other gave a small bow. "One and the same. But, as you say, it's a bit too late to discover that fact. Yes, it went off just as I had planned. We hit a few snags here and there, such as our failure with your father's plane. But, on the whole, it was a fine scenario."

"You look on what you do as a play or a movie?" asked Frank.

"That's exactly what it is," exclaimed Bantler excitedly. "A good crime is one that is designed and carried out flawlessly. Quite like a stage play, but with the addition of danger. I am both the director and lead actor."

Joe looked at Slicer and the other crook, a tall, dignified-appearing man. "Some cast!" he said.

"Let me introduce them," said Bantler. "I believe you and Slicer Bork have met on several occasions. The other is—or was—a real actor, although not too successful until he joined us. His last starring role was Dr. Morrison. Carl Harport, take a bow. The Hardys admire your talents."

"Why don't you let me at Joe a while?" Slicer asked. "I have some debts to pay."

"You know my rules," said Bantler sharply. "No violence unless absolutely necessary."

Slicer took a step back and said in a softer voice,

"Whatever you say, Burl." He seemed afraid of the leader.

Bantler turned to the three youths. "Of course, I didn't expect this hurricane," he continued smoothly. "If it hadn't come up, we would have been on our way to Alaska an hour ago. I fear your father's perfect record of solving crimes is coming to an end, Hardys. You did get too close for comfort at times, but there is no way we can now be stopped from destroying the pipeline."

"Burl, this is all very interesting, but I think we ought to be looking for the others," said Harport nervously.

Bantler's eyes flashed with momentary anger at being contradicted, but he calmed himself quickly. "He is right," he told his prisoners. "Alessandro Krazak somehow got the clock working and it tolled several times, as you are no doubt aware. The fool probably thought that someone would notice and send for the police, but who could hear it in such weather? He is still somewhere at large in this house, as are Tonio and Dubek. I would enjoy chatting with you further, but I'm afraid catching them is a more pressing matter. Slicer, show our guests to the dungeon."

Slicer prodded the boys with his gun. "Get going!" They were pushed through a kitchen and down a long corridor, which ended at a door.

"Open it!" the man commanded. Joe obeyed and the three descended a steep staircase into a tunnel.

As they marched along, they could see by Slicer's flashlight that the walls were solid, thick rock. It was damp and moisture covered the stone.

"Here we are. You three stand with your backs to me and your hands high. No funny tricks!"

Slicer unlocked a huge door. "Hey, Radley," he yelled inside, "got some company for you. Three of your friends have come calling."

For some reason, the thug thought that was very amusing and went into peals of laughter as he roughly shoved the young men into the dark. The door slammed, was locked, and they heard him walk away, still laughing.

"Who's that?" came Sam's voice from a corner.

"Sam!" cried Joe. "It's me, Joe! Frank and Chet Morton are here, too!"

"Wait till I light a candle. That Slicer only gave us one and it's pretty small so we don't keep it lit all the time." There was a spark and then a flame flickered. Sam, holding the candle, slowly rose from a pile of hay. He stretched his aching muscles. "Reminds me of when I was in the army and we went out on maneuvers." He grinned at them. "Am I glad to see you!"

"And we're glad we found you!" said Joe. "Are you all right?"

"I guess so. I woke up in an ambulance and I thought I was on my way to the hospital. Instead, I was pushed into a car and brought here. I'm fuzzy about what happened since I saw that machine in the woods. But I feel okay. By the way, we've got a cellmate. Curt, wake up. We've got visitors."

A second person arose from another corner and came forward. "Is that Joe Hardy I hear?"

"Curt Gutman!" exclaimed Frank as the man shuffled into the light.

"Frank! Chet Morton! I hope you've come to take us out of here. I'm sorry that I didn't show up to lay the new carpeting, but as you can see, these guys kidnapped me when I was on my way to work and—"

"Don't worry," Frank said dryly. "You had a real expert as a replacement."

"Boys, bring me up to date, will you?" Sam requested. "What's been going on?"

"We'd better sit down," Frank advised. "This will take a while."

The five of them sat around the candle and Frank narrated the events of the past few days. "So you see, Sam, how it's all beginning to hang together now. But just how Bantler is going to destroy the pipeline is beyond us."

"I can fill you in on that," Sam said. "I saw it in

action." He shuddered. "The fact is that I was its first victim!"

"What!" Frank exclaimed.

"It all began by accident. A few days ago, I was driving through Bayport when I spotted Burl Bantler. He passed me in a pickup truck, going in the opposite direction. I managed to turn and follow him to the Sayer estate.

"He went in, but of course I didn't dare pursue him beyond the gate. I hid my car in the woods and set up a stakeout from behind bushes opposite the entrance."

"I wish we'd known!" Joe said.

"So do I. But I wasn't able to phone you or notify the police. After a few hours, I saw Bantler, Slicer, and a third man I later learned was Carl Harport. There were also two others, a man in a wheelchair and a younger guy."

Joe broke in. "The man in the wheelchair is Dubek Krazak, a scientist from Eastern Europe. The younger man is Tonio Mossesky, also a foreigner."

Sam nodded and continued. "They went into the woods on the mansion side of the road. I followed them. Tonio was carrying some kind of machine, similar in appearance to a hand-held TV camera. They walked about a mile or so when they came to an old shack in a clearing by a stream. They stopped on the south side of the clearing and I hid behind a tree on the north side.

"The scientist—what is his name?"

"Dubek Krazak," Joe said.

"Right. He held the machine, pointed it toward the shack, and then I heard this whirring sound. I tell you, I've never seen anything like it. That building just melted away. It crumbled to a pile of sawdust before my eyes!"

"We saw the residue!" Chet cried out. "My father noticed it and couldn't figure out what happened."

"I tried to get away to call the police," Sam went on. "I would have made it, too, but I hadn't gone more than a few steps when a pack of wild dogs came out of nowhere and charged at me!"

"We ran into them, too," Frank pointed out. "They almost got Joe."

Sam shook his head. "Anyway, I was forced to retreat into the clearing and was spotted immediately. I heard Bantler yell, 'Give me the Annihilator,' and I saw him grab it from Krazak. Then he pointed it right at me and turned it on!"

The boys gasped.

"I have never felt such pain before," Sam went on, "and I've been through some very torturous experiences, believe me. It was as if I had been shot by a million sharp pins. My whole body was in agony. Maybe I would have dissolved like the shack if this Krazak hadn't run his wheelchair right into Bantler and knocked him over. He was yelling, 'No, no, it's not for killing!'

"The pain stopped, but I was dazed. Everything around me was in a kind of haze. I started to run . . . and that's all I remember until I woke up in that ambulance with Harcourt leaning over me. As you said, I must have wandered onto the Morton farm."

Everyone was silent for a few moments as they thought over the strange events of the past few days and their perilous predicament.

At last Frank sighed. "Somehow, we've got to find a way out of here and stop Bantler. He's going to take off for Alaska as soon as the hurricane is over."

Joe looked out of the window. "It looks like the storm is losing its force," he said gloomily. "I never thought that I would hate to see a hurricane end."

"I tried to think of how to escape," Sam said, "but I wasn't able to come up with a practical plan. Curt and I couldn't rush Slicer when he came in with food, for he always held his gun on us."

"With more of us here now, though," Joe said, "we might be able to jump him."

"From what you tell me, I doubt whether he'll return," Sam said. "Why should he? They'll leave and throw away the key!"

"Maybe the police will get here soon," said Chet brightly. "Also, it looks like the Krazaks are on our side now. Maybe they'll set us free."

That hope was immediately dashed. The door was suddenly opened and the two Krazak brothers and Tonio and Maquala were thrust in. The door slammed shut and the newcomers stared around them with helpless expressions.

17 An Evil Plan

"There goes that hope," Chet said gloomily.

"Oh, cheer up," Joe advised. "We've been in worse spots before." But he didn't sound convincing, even to himself.

After a quick evaluation of their predicament, Alessandro sighed. "I'm afraid I must agree with your friend, Joe. Apparently no one heard my feeble attempt for rescue by ringing the clock. In a short while, Bantler and his men will be off to Alaska while we languish here. It may be many days before we are discovered."

"By that time, we'll have starved to death," Maquala cried.

"I am deeply sorry that my invention has brought

all of us such peril," Dubek said in a heavy tone.

"Tell us about the four-headed dragon," Frank suggested.

Alessandro looked startled. "You know about that?"

"We don't really know what it is," Joe said.

"It's better that you don't know," Tonio declared.

Dubek waved a hand at the young man. "What difference does it make now? Anyway, they are entitled to learn what has put them in such great danger. The Four-Headed Dragon is the name of a secret organization behind the Iron Curtain. It is dedicated to overthrowing all forms of tyranny and freeing the enslaved people of Eastern Europe. Once the enemy was the Nazis. Today it is other oppressive governments."

"But what has that to do with Bantler and his gang?" Joe asked, puzzled.

"It will be simpler if we start at the beginning," said Maquala. "My father is the head of the Four-Headed Dragon. When we were forced to leave our homeland, he came to the United States to raise money for our cause. He believed that Americans, who love freedom more than any other people in the world, would be willing to donate funds."

"But he didn't want charity," said Alessandro, "so he decided to give something in return—a machine we called the Annihilator."

Now it was Frank's turn to be puzzled. "And you sold it to Burl Bantler to destroy the Alaskan pipeline?"

Dubek Krazak sighed. "Unfortunately, that has been the result, but we never intended it that way. It was not to be used as a weapon, but as a tool for industrial demolition or in place of dynamite in road construction."

He turned to Sam. "You must believe me," he said urgently. "We never meant to hurt you."

Sam grinned. "Don't apologize. You saved my life."

"You see," the scientist went on, "Burl Bantler is of Hucul parentage. He's a distant cousin of my father. For that reason, I looked him up when we came to this country. He told me he would be glad to help our cause and I trusted him. I did not know about his criminal background, so I told him of my plans to build the Annihilator. He offered to aid me with my experiments and I must admit he was a brilliant assistant."

"That figures," Frank said grimly. "He's known to the police as an electronics genius."

"We found out from bitter experience," Joe added, telling of how well the electronic bug had been placed and how the master criminal had broken through the installed burglar-proof system at the Hardy house.

"We took the Annihilator out into the woods for our first real test," Dubek went on. "It was then that I discovered how vicious Burl was when he tried to kill Sam Radley. After you had escaped, Mr. Radley, Burl revealed his true intention of using my invention, namely, to smash the Alaskan pipeline."

"Could he really do that?" asked Joe.

"Oh, yes, quite easily. You see, the Annihilator is based on high-frequency sound. You have probably heard that an opera singer can break a thin glass with her voice and that a group of marchers stepping in unison can bring a bridge down. That is roughly the principle behind the Annihilator. It emits a sound so high that not even a dog can hear it."

"And there was no way you could stop him?" Joe inquired.

"He threatened us," Tonio explained. "He said he would harm Maquala if we attempted to alert the police." It was quite evident from the young man's expression that the thought of Maquala being hurt was unbearable. "I apologize for the unfriendly way I've been acting, but I thought I could drive you away."

"You never told me," Maquala cried resentfully. "I was not even allowed to learn about the experiments."

"Don't blame Tonio, my dear," said Dubek. "I

made the decision to keep you out of this. Perhaps that was wrong, but I did not want to frighten you." He turned back to the Hardys and Sam Radley. "Bantler went crazy with rage when Mr. Radley escaped. He does not like to fail and has a fierce and almost uncontrollable temper. He was afraid that Fenton Hardy was on his trail. Why else, he reasoned, was Hardy's assistant following him?"

"That's why he broke into our house and Sam's apartment, and later took Curt's place as carpet layer," Frank said. "And that's why he tried to sabotage my father's plane and steal the tape."

Dubek nodded. "It is also why he had Sam Radley kidnapped. Even though he found nothing that showed you were on to him, he felt insecure. He was desperately afraid Mr. Radley would regain his memory and identify him."

"If only I could have remembered while I was still in the hospital!" Sam said wistfully.

"You may have noticed that I was quite cold and a bit impolite when I met you," Dubek went on. "That was done deliberately. I had hoped my inhospitable attitude would drive you away, for I feared for your lives. At that time, Burl was unaware of your presence here since he was in another wing of the mansion. When your friend, Mr. Morton, appeared and informed us that the bridge had collapsed, though, it was evident that you had to remain here. I had hoped to keep Burl oblivious of the fact that you were on the premises. However, when you and Tonio returned to the house after your phone call, Slicer saw you coming through the foyer. Later I had Tonio lock you in when you prowled around the house. I wanted to prevent you from meeting my dear cousin," he said bitterly. "But it was useless. He knew where you were all the time."

"Maybe the police will manage to get here soon," said Joe hopefully. He told the new prisoners about how Frank had transmitted a message to Aunt Gertrude.

Chet shrugged his shoulders. "They won't make it soon, I guarantee you. There's no chance of them crossing over the stream, now that the bridge is gone. That water's going a mile a minute."

"But Bantler is planning to take off as soon as the hurricane dies down," Joe cried. "If he can get out, why can't the police get in?"

"Yes, just how does he figure on leaving?" Curt asked. "He can't go toward Bayport, and the other roads will be in terrible condition. I don't see him going by boat, since the ocean will be rough long after the storm is over."

"He never misses a trick," said Alessandro. "He has a helicopter hidden under canvas on the western side of the house. I even doubt if Emile Grabb knows it's there. I overheard Slicer say that they plan to fly to a small airport in New Hampshire. There they will switch to a larger plane that will take them to Alaska."

"And we're the only people near enough to stop them!" Sam said. He struck his palm with a fist in frustration. "If only we could escape!"

For the past few minutes, Frank had been walking around the room. He turned to the others suddenly. "I think we can," he said.

18 Daring Tonio

Frank opened the one window in the room and banged against the bars on the outside. "Just as I thought. These are loose."

Sam shook his head. "Forget it, Frank. Curt and I already tried to pull them out."

"But there are more people now," the young detective declared. "More arms to pull with."

"Then what? We're on the ocean side of the house," Chet said. "Even if we manage to get those bars out, it's a sheer drop into the water."

"But I see a ledge out there," Frank said. "That may lead to another room. If someone could move along the ledge, get through the window, and slip into the hall, he could let us out!"

"Sounds crazy to me," Chet grumbled, "but I guess it's worth a try."

Joe, Frank, Sam, Tonio, and Chet gathered around the open window and seized the bars. For three minutes, they strained all their muscles. Their faces turned red, but the bars only gave an inch or two.

Then Alessandro strode up and pushed his way through to the window. "Once during World War Two, I traveled with a circus from enemy camp to enemy camp as a spy. I learned a great deal, most particularly how to be a strong man. It was, as the U.S. Intelligence services would say, a 'good cover.' "

He seized the bars, took a very deep breath and held it, then pulled. Slowly, the bars came away from the window!

The others looked at him with admiration. "That is really something!" Chet breathed.

"Yes, there is a ledge here," said Alessandro, sticking his head out into the storm. "But it is narrow and does not look strong. Whoever is going to walk on it must be light and sure-footed." He looked regretful that he could not fill this description.

"It's up to me," said Joe. "I'm the lightest."

He started toward the window, but Tonio held out a restraining arm. "No, my friend, I must be the one," he said in a far more genial tone than he had ever used before when talking to the Hardys. "You are lighter than I am, but I am more used to narrow places."

"He's right, Joe," Dubek said. "I love Tonio like a son and hate to see him taking chances, but he is probably the best qualified."

Joe nodded and stepped aside. Tonio nimbly jumped to the sill, holding both sides of the window. He stuck his head out, then turned back to the others. "I see a window forty feet or so to my left," he reported. "I'll try for that."

Cautiously, he went out on the ledge, his face to the wall of the building. He had only gone a few feet when Joe, who was looking out after him, yelled, "The ledge is crumbling!"

The wood had rotted after years of storms and winds. It cracked apart and Tonio began to fall toward the angry ocean. Joe lunged and grabbed the boy's wrist, but was yanked ahead himself. Just when it seemed that both young men would plunge to their deaths, Alessandro seized Joe's waist and pulled them back.

In a moment, Joe and Tonio were in the room again. Alessandro wiped his brow. "I'm not as strong as I used to be. That was tiring."

"Strong enough for me," Joe cried.

"Thank you," Tonio said, pumping the Hardy boy's hand.

"And now we're right back where we started," said Chet.

"Not quite," Frank said. "There's another alternative." He held up an old, rusty can he had discovered in a corner. "Kerosene!"

"What could we possibly do with that?" Maquala asked.

"Burn down the wooden door, of course," Dubek cried out. "That's what you have in mind, am I right?"

"Yes," Frank answered. "The door is fairly solid, but it is old and dry. It's worth a try. Please listen carefully, everyone. When the fire starts, lie down with your noses to the floor. If the room fills with smoke, you will find that there will be about an inch of fresh air on the floor."

Frank and Sam poured the kerosene until there was a pool by the door while Tonio helped Dubek out of his wheelchair. Sam touched the fluid with the candle. There was a *shoosh* and flames shot up. Smoke swirled above the prone bodies of the prisoners. The door caught fire and the old wood crackled.

It did not last long, though. The fire died, leaving the door charred, but still solid.

"Now what?" Chet groaned.

Just then, they heard a key in the lock. The door opened and Emile Grabb stood in the entrance, shining a flashlight and peering down through the smoke at the prisoners.

"What's going on here?" he shouted. "What are you doing?"

As the smoke poured out of the window, Frank jumped up. "Are we glad to see you!"

The startled caretaker drew back, holding his club high in a defensive gesture. "What are you doing to Miss Sayer's house? All these strange goings-on! First, the clock goes off. I came over and saw three men packing and making a mess of everything. They tried to capture me, but I ran away. Then I smelled smoke and found out you're trying to burn down the place!" As he spoke, his anger grew and his voice became louder. "I won't allow it! Miss Sayer was very kind to me when I was an orphan and she left the house in my care. I won't let anyone harm it!"

"We agree with you," said Frank quickly, "and we'll make it up to you. But there is no time to explain now. Those men you saw are criminals. They locked us up here and are going to escape with a weapon that will harm our country. They must be stopped and there's no time to lose!"

The smoke was slowly clearing and Emile Grabb squinted at the young detective. "You're one of the

Hardy sons, the family Miss Sayer admired. All right. I'll just have to trust you. Come along and we'll try to stop those men."

He turned and ran down the hall toward the stairs leading up to the main floor. The Hardys, Chet, Tonio, and Sam followed him to the door of the wing where the experiments had been conducted.

"Locked!" exclaimed Grabb, trying the knob. "And I left most of my keys back in the cottage." He pounded on the door. "Open up in there!"

"They won't pay any attention," Frank said.

The elderly man snapped his fingers. "I almost forgot. This isn't the only way to get into that wing."

He led the way back to the basement and past the room that had served as their prison. Alessandro was just coming out, pushing Dubek in the wheelchair. "Where are you going?" he shouted.

"Mr. Grabb is showing us another way to the eastern wing," Tonio replied.

"Alessandro, Maquala, and I will go up to the foyer and wait for the police," Dubek said.

At the end of the corridor was a ladder nailed to the wall. Grabb flashed his light upward to a trapdoor. "Come on," he snapped, starting to climb.

They emerged into a "ghost" bedroom, from where they heard the sounds of hurried footsteps in the hall. Frank dashed out just in time to see the crooks run by. Slicer pushed the boy back as he rushed past. Frank fell against Joe and Tonio, who were right behind him. All three lost their balance and tumbled to the floor. By the time they regained their feet and ran into the hallway again, they heard a door being slammed and a lock being turned.

Emile pointed his flashlight in the direction of the sounds. It shone upon another closed door.

Tonio felt defeated. "They'll reach their helicopter in a few moments," he said. "Looks like we've lost them for good!"

19 Helicopter Chase

"You give up mighty fast," Emile Grabb growled. "If we're quick, we can still catch them."

Once again, he led the small troop up the stairs to the huge attic. They peered through a window at the western end of the room. The rain had stopped, although the wind was still high. A pale full moon whisked in and out of the fleeing clouds.

A moment later, Bantler and his men emerged from the house carrying a large bag. They hurried toward a covered object at the edge of a grove of trees.

"It's too far from the ground to jump," Tonio said. "We're no better off than before."

Emile Grabb glanced at him as he reached

underneath the window frame and picked up a rope ladder. "This is for fires," he explained. "We can go down it and surprise them." He fell silent for a moment before adding regretfully, "Only it's going to have to be you to catch 'em. I've got a bum leg." He glanced at Chet. "You'll never get through that window, either. Too fat!" Then he looked at Sam. "Nor you, fellow. You don't look too strong at the moment."

Frank and Joe tossed the rope ladder outside and saw the end hit the ground. Joe slipped out the window first, followed by Frank, with Tonio bringing up the rear. The younger Hardy noted that Bantler and his henchmen were too engrossed in pulling the canvas off the helicopter to see the descent of the three youths. We've got you now! he thought to himself.

He hit the ground softly and waited for Frank, who arrived a moment later. The rope was old, however, and its worn strands broke as Tonio was halfway down.

The young man landed catlike and unhurt, but the sound of his fall diverted the crooks' attention. Carl Harport shouted, "It's the Hardys!"

The three crooks' surprise immobilized them for a few seconds. Then they sprang into action, charging their pursuers.

Slicer was the first to reach the youths, but Joe

was ready for him. Timing his blow perfectly, he buried his fist into the gangster's solar plexus, doubling his attacker up. As Slicer bent, hands clutching his stomach, Joe seized an arm and sent the man flying through the air. Slicer landed heavily several feet away and, Joe noted with satisfaction, remained motionless.

But as Joe turned away from his opponent, Bantler's blackjack crashed down upon his head.

The boy fell, half dazed. Bantler and Harport ran at the two remaining boys, swinging their weapons. Tonio and Frank fought bravely, but soon suffered Joe's fate.

Harport was prepared to hit Frank again as the hapless youth lay on the ground, but was stopped by Bantler's words. "Leave him alone. We've got no time."

"Let me clip him a little," the ex-actor begged. "He and his brother have been such pests to us."

Bantler struck down his crony's blackjack arm. "Revenge is for fools," he snarled. "We have more important things to take care of. Help me lift Slicer and carry him to the chopper. Come on, move!"

They dragged their unconscious companion to the helicopter and unceremoniously threw him inside. Then they picked up the bag containing the Annihilator and placed it next to Slicer.

Bantler turned as he was about to enter the craft

and waved at the dazed youths still lying on the ground. "So long, Hardys. It's been a pleasure to meet you. Best regards to your father." He shut the door and the helicopter's engine began to roar. A few moments later, the craft lifted into the air. Tonio and the Hardys watched it disappear to the north.

Slowly they rose, their heads still spinning from the blows they had received. "You all right?" Sam called from the attic window.

"Yes, but they got away," Joe replied.

"I saw that," Sam shouted, "but maybe they can be cut off between here and Alaska."

The youths looked at one another. They had little hope that the police would be able to catch the elusive and clever Bantler before he destroyed the oil pipeline.

"Poor Dubek," said Tonio. "All he wanted to do was to make a peaceful and valuable invention for your country so he could help the Four-Headed Dragon organization. Now all he has accomplished has been to hurt the free world. He'll be crushed by this." He shook his head.

The Hardys could think of nothing to say to relieve Tonio's gloomy feelings. Silently, the trio started around the house toward the front door.

Suddenly, there was a roar from above. High-beam spotlights floated over the grounds of the

Sayer estate. For a moment, Frank thought that Bantler had returned. Then he caught sight of three hovering helicopters bearing the red and blue stripes identifying them as police craft.

"What do you know!" Joe shouted. "Maybe we still have a chance!"

They waved frantically, chasing the spots of lights on the ground until they were caught in one. A pilot noticed them and the choppers descended.

Emile Grabb and the others had reached the west lawn by the time Bayport and state police poured out of the helicopters, led by Chief Collig. They were followed by two familiar men.

"Dad and Jack Wayne!" Joe shouted.

Fenton Hardy jumped from the craft. "Frank! Joe! Are you all right?"

"A little dizzy from being knocked on the head," Frank admitted ruefully, "but we'll get over that."

"Aunt Gertrude said you told her something strange was taking place here. Why, there's Sam!" The detective strode ahead and grasped his assistant's shoulders. "How are you? I heard you were kidnapped. What's going on, anyhow?"

"Plenty, but there's little time to tell you the whole story now," Sam said grimly.

"He's right, Dad," said Joe. "Bantler and his gang are getting away and—"

"Bantler?" Mr. Hardy repeated, amazed.

"They have the weapon that can destroy the Alaskan pipeline," Frank broke in. "They took off in a helicopter not more than five minutes ago."

"That's quite a lead, but maybe we can catch up!" Jack Wayne exclaimed.

"Right!" Fenton Hardy agreed. "Frank and Joe, you can tell me the story on the way. Come on!"

Chief Collig, who was questioning Emile Grabb, turned around as the Hardys, Sam, and Jack started back toward one of the helicopters. "Where are you going?" he asked.

"To catch one of the cleverest crooks in the world!" Mr. Hardy shouted.

"Okay. You have my permission to fly one of our choppers!" Collig yelled back.

When they were high in the air, Mr. Hardy relaxed a little. "Now tell me exactly what has been happening," he said to his sons.

First, Sam related how he had been injured by the Annihilator, and subsequently kidnapped and brought to the Sayer mansion. Then Frank and Joe told what had happened since the last time they had spoken to their father.

When they were finished, Fenton Hardy whistled. "To think that I have been looking for a man who was working almost in my own backyard and who actually broke into my house!"

"Helicopter ahead about a mile," Jack Wayne

suddenly announced, "at ten o'clock." He pointed slightly to his left.

The moonlight etched the other craft against the night sky as clearly as though it was the middle of the day. Jack's passengers leaned forward anxiously.

"That's Bantler and his gang!" Joe cried.

20 Easy Target

The police craft steadily gained on the other helicopter. Bantler, apparently unaware that he was being chased, was not flying at top speed.

"He's smart," Jack Wayne said. "He doesn't want to catch up to the hurricane . . . and that's to our advantage."

It was not until the Hardys were flying beside the gangsters that the master crook noticed them. He then urged his pilot, Carl Harport, to greater speed by pounding his henchman on the back roughly and pointing ahead.

However, the police craft was a far more powerful machine and the thugs could not escape. Bantler was infuriated and shook his fist in frustration.

Harport tried several maneuvers to get away—sliding off toward the east, flying higher, flying so low as to almost touch treetops—but Jack Wayne kept up with him.

"He hasn't a chance," said Fenton Hardy's pilot triumphantly. "I think we ought to call in at this point."

He radioed Bayport's police headquarters and gave his position and the direction in which they were flying. "Please contact police units and military installations ahead," he asked. "Request them to send up interceptor craft. If we get enough in the air, we can force Bantler down."

"Never!" Bantler broke in. He had monitored the transmission and his voice crackled with anger and hatred. "I'm not going to let you guys stop me when I'm so near. Get away! Get away, I tell you, or you'll regret it!"

"Be realistic," Fenton Hardy replied coldly. "Don't do something you'll regret."

Bantler's answer was a curse, then he turned off his radio. They saw him shake Slicer, who had been holding his face in his hands, still recovering from his fight with Joe, into full consciousness. The two then struggled to open the large bag between them and took out a heavy machine.

"They're going to use the Annihilator on us!" Sam breathed, shuddering as he recalled his encounter with Dubek Krazak's invention. "If it hits us, this copter will crumble into dust!"

In horror, the Hardys, Jack, and Sam watched Slicer balance the Annihilator on Bantler's shoulder. Once again the gang leader's voice sounded over the radio.

"We'll blast you out of the sky as we will do to anyone who is in our way!" With that, Bantler aimed the machine at them.

Jack Wayne swooped downward out of the way. He straightened out about a hundred feet below. Bantler's desperate voice screamed at them over the radio once more. "That won't do you any good! We'll hit you sooner or later!"

Harport brought his craft down to the same level as the Hardy helicopter. Once more the Annihilator was aimed. Once more Jack Wayne skillfully escaped, this time climbing above the attacker.

Harport jerked his controls and the Bantler copter listed to a forty-five degree slant. Then . . .

"Something's wrong!" yelled Joe. "They're going down!"

Harport frantically tried to straighten out, but it was too late. Down, down, down spun the criminals' machine. The Hardys, Jack Wayne, and Sam gazed at the plummeting craft in horrified fascination.

The helicopter smashed into a lake, but the

criminals managed to jump out just before it struck the water. Fenton tapped Jack on the shoulder. "Down," he ordered.

The pilot descended and a moment later they landed gently some distance from the lake's shore. In the moonlight, they saw Harport and Slicer swimming toward the beach.

Then the criminals changed direction. But they obviously did not have the strength to strike out for the opposite side, so they started for a spot about a hundred yards from the Hardy party.

Fenton Hardy pulled two pairs of handcuffs from his pocket and handed one to Sam. "Let's go!" The detective and his assistant hurried toward the gangsters' destination, followed by Jack and the boys.

"Where's Burl Bantler?" Joe cried suddenly.

"Guess he went down with the craft," Jack replied.

"No, there he is," said Frank, pointing toward a struggling figure in the middle of the lake. "Either he doesn't know how to swim or he's got a cramp."

The youths sprang into action. Peeling off their jackets and shoes, they dove into the water. They swam as fast as they could, keeping their eyes on the desperate Bantler. They reached him just as he was sinking, grabbed him, and began the torturous return trip.

When they arrived, Sam and Fenton were waiting with their captives. Fenton slipped handcuffs on the man who had eluded him so long and then put a coat over his shivering body.

Before they got into the helicopter, Bantler looked at Frank and Joe curiously. "Here I tried to kill you and yet you risked your lives to save me. Why?"

Joe grinned. "Well, Mom and Aunt Gertrude said you did a fine job on the new carpets and we thought you deserved something for that."

The three criminals were taken to the Bayport jail, then Mr. Hardy and his companions returned to the Sayer mansion.

"That is the end of the Annihilator," Dubek Krazak said when he heard his invention was at the bottom of the lake.

"Why?" Fenton Hardy asked. "You can build another one, or we might recover this one by dragging the lake."

The scientist smiled wanly. "Why do that? It has only brought evil. It has proved to be an instrument of death and destruction!"

"But it can be an instrument for good," Fenton replied. "Look at dynamite. It can kill people, but it is also essential in so many worthwhile activities."

"You argue well," said Alessandro, "but we

couldn't rebuild it, anyhow. We have very little money left."

"Don't worry about that," said the detective. "I have plenty of friends who would be eager to invest money to help you."

Tonio and Maquala had been standing together silently, holding hands. Now they came forward to Joe and Frank.

"Tonio has something to say," said Maquala.

The young man looked embarrassed as he struggled to get the words out. "I—we have a lot to thank you for. If it hadn't been for you—" he waved a hand helplessly, "well, I just want to thank you for all you have done and I deeply apologize for the way I have treated you."

Now it was the Hardy youths' turn to be embarrassed. Fortunately, they were saved by Emile Grabb who was looking with dismay at the huge house. "I will never rent the mansion again."

Fenton knitted his brow. "You talk as if it is your decision. I don't understand—"

"I own it!" exclaimed the caretaker irritably. "Abby Sayer left it to me, but only her lawyers know that. I've tried to keep the building in good condition because I promised her on her deathbed I would do so. But the cost of maintenance has been too much for me in the last few years. That's why I told the lawyers to rent it. But no more, never again! Better it should become a ruin!"

"I can see your point, but I have an idea," said Fenton Hardy. "Why not turn the mansion into a museum? People have always been curious about the house. I think they would come from near and far to take a tour of it. You could be their guide and the admission prices would be more than enough to maintain the building."

Grabb snapped his fingers. "That's great! Now I can see why Miss Sayer had such respect for your brains. I'll do it."

The gray streaks of morning began to stretch across the sky. Frank stared thoughtfully into the distance. What would the next day bring? Would there be another challenge for the Hardy boys? He had no idea that soon they would be called upon to solve a strange case called *The Infinity Clue*.

The Hardy Boys® in

The Infinity Clue

The Infinity Clue was
first published in the U.K. in a single volume
in hardback in 1982 by Angus & Robertson (U.K.) Ltd,
and in Armada in 1983

Contents

1 The Trembling Ground

Frank and Joe Hardy scanned the wide valley that appeared before them, as their yellow sports sedan rounded the crest of a hill. In the distance, a huge cylindrical tower rose from the valley floor.

"Looks like a giant barnacle," Joe remarked to his older, dark-haired brother, Frank.

Biff Hooper, a tall, muscular high school friend of the two amateur detectives, leaned forward from the backseat. "You're looking at the cooling tower. The reactor itself is in the building next to it."

Biff's uncle, Jerry Hooper, was a nuclear engineer at the Bayridge Nuclear Power Plant, located outside Bayport. He had invited the three boys on a private afternoon tour of the facility. The summer had just begun and the Hardy brothers were eager for new adventures.

A few minutes later, the yellow car arrived at the power plant's front gate, where a uniformed guard checked identifications before letting the boys pass through.

"There's Uncle Jerry," Biff said, indicating a man dressed in a white smock who stood at the entrance.

"I'm not sure you'll find this very exciting," Mr. Hooper warned as he shook Frank's and Joe's hands and led them inside. "Nuclear power is produced by a fairly simple process. No wild flashing lights or bizarre sounds like in science fiction movies."

The group followed him along an elevated steel walkway through several levels of the immense structure.

"Is that the reactor?" Joe asked, having traced a huge pipe to its source.

"It's the tip of the iceberg, so to speak," the engineer replied. "Most of the reactor is hidden."

Frank gazed at the strange device. "Isn't a nuclear reactor like a contained nuclear bomb explosion?"

Mr. Hooper smiled. "Yes, it's similar. But it's in no danger of blowing up." He explained that water traveled through the pipes at temperatures of six hundred degrees, nearly three times the boiling temperature for water.

"Is that what's making that low rumbling noise?" Biff inquired.

"Low rumble?" his uncle asked as a look of concern crossed his face.

The group stopped and listened. A dull sound seemed to come out of the earth itself, growing by the second in intensity.

"I hear it too!" Joe cried, breaking their tense silence. "It's getting louder!"

By the time the blond youth had finished his sentence, they not only heard the rumble, but also felt the steel walkway vibrate.

Suddenly, a chorus of alarms blared warnings throughout the power plant. Fear that the whole building was about to explode gripped the young visitors, and all eyes turned to Biff's uncle for direction.

"Follow me!" Mr. Hooper frantically ordered as he went back down the steel walkway. By the time they had descended to the next level, the plant was shaking violently. Pipes began to crack, gushing huge clouds of steam. The boys stumbled and groped their way along, trying not to lose their footing.

"Watch out!" the engineer called back as a pipe broke near him.

The scalding hot steam that shot from it made the visitors' journey along the shaking steel walkway all

the more dangerous. Finally, they arrived at the control room, where men were already at work on the problem.

"Where's Joe?" Frank asked suddenly.

"He was behind me!" Biff exclaimed, as he, too, realized Joe wasn't with them.

Without hesitation, both boys ran from the control room. Although the rumbling was beginning to die down, the alarms were still blaring and the hot steam cloud cut visibility almost to zero. They called Joe's name, but the noise made by the hissing steam, the alarms, and the rumble all but drowned out their voices. To be caught by a direct spray of steam, they knew, could cook them like lobsters in a matter of seconds.

Just then, Frank stumbled over something. "Joe!" he gasped, finding his brother's body face down on the concrete floor.

Cradling the boy's limp form between them, Frank and Biff carried him through the plant toward safety. By the time they reached the control room, the rumbling had stopped. Mr. Hooper and the other engineers threw switches on the control panel, activating cut-off valves to the damaged pipes.

Frank and Biff laid Joe on a couch in the adjoining lobby. Frank could see that his brother wasn't burned, but had received a nasty lump on the head.

"Wha-what happened?" Joe asked as he slowly opened his eyes.

"You must have slipped," Frank replied, relieved that Joe was apparently all right. "Lucky for you to have landed on your thick head or you might have been hurt!"

Joe smiled thinly at Frank's kidding, but his expression became serious as Mr. Hooper approached to take a look at him. "I meant, what happened to the plant?"

All eyes turned to the nuclear engineer. His face was pale. "I'm afraid we had a minor earthquake. It seems to be over now, however, and the situation is well under control."

Frank, noticing the ashen look on Mr. Hooper's face, asked, "What might have happened if the quake had been worse?"

Mr. Hooper frowned. "The effect could have been disastrous. Had the reactor core cracked or the cooling system broken down, it could have contaminated the area for miles with radiation. Fortunately, nothing like this appears to have happened. But for safety's sake, you boys had better leave the plant immediately."

He gave them special suits to guard them against possible exposure to radiation in the plant. Now able to stand, Joe put on the suit with the help of his brother, and the three left the building. Their yellow sports sedan was still in the parking lot, unharmed by the quake. Leaving the protective suits with the guard at the front gate, the trio headed back to Bayport.

"This isn't an earthquake-prone area," observed Frank. "In fact, I've never even heard of a tremor around Bayport."

"Neither have I," Joe agreed, and switched on the radio for a broadcast on the strange event.

The earthquake, a local station reported, had affected an area about twenty miles wide, including Bayport. It registered between two and three on the Richter scale, making it a fairly small quake. Experts were, however, perplexed. No tremors had ever been recorded in the area.

"It may have been a minor quake," Joe said, feeling the lump forming above his forehead, "but this bump is anything but small!"

A worried expression came over Biff's face. "I hope everyone's okay back home!"

Frank and Joe shared Biff's concern, and they rode back to town anxious and quiet. On the way, they passed fallen telephone poles and fences. Cattle, dazed by the event, had just begun to settle down to grazing again.

By the time they reached Bayport, it was clear that the city had received much less of a jolt than the power plant. A few windows were shattered and electricity was out. A report came over the radio that the nuclear plant had been badly shaken, but the current would be restored as soon as the engineers had cleared up minor difficulties.

After dropping Biff off, Frank and Joe headed homeward.

"It could have been a lot worse," Joe remarked.

"Don't count your blessings yet," the older Hardy warned. "Earthquakes have aftershocks, sometimes as strong as the quakes themselves." He paused, then pointed to the side of the road. "Hey!" he exclaimed. "Isn't that the Mortons' car?"

A blue Ford had run off the road into a ditch. Nobody seemed to be inside.

"Looks like it," Joe answered. "Better pull over."

Chet Morton, a chunky, longtime pal of the Hardys, had often joined them in solving mysteries. He lived on a farm just outside of town.

"Do you think Chet was on his way to our place?" Joe asked, finding the vehicle unoccupied.

"He must have known we weren't home," Frank mused.

The brothers hopped back in their car. After driving a few blocks, they turned on Elm Street and parked outside their house. Night had fallen, and with the power off, homes and street lights were dark.

"Has Chet been here?" Joe asked Mrs. Hardy

when she greeted her sons at the door, holding a candle.

Instead of answering, she smiled. "I have a surprise for you. It's in the dining room."

Frank opened the dining room door. Seated at the table were Chet, Aunt Gertrude, Iola Morton, and Callie Shaw.

"We've been waiting hours for you two," Aunt Gertrude scolded. "Dinner is long cold!"

"Sorry," Frank apologized. "We got caught in the earthquake." He knew his aunt had a soft spot in her heart for her nephews, and that she tried to hide it behind her stern and authoritative manner.

Joe looked questioningly at Chet. "We found your parents' car."

"Don't look at me!" Chet defended himself. "She was driving." He pointed at his sister.

Pretty, pixie-faced Iola, who often dated Joe, blushed. "I guess when I felt the rumbling, I panicked."

"That clears up one mystery," Frank said with a chuckle. "But it's still a mystery to me what everyone's doing here for dinner."

"We thought we would all like to have one last meal together before we possibly never see you again," Chet said offhandedly.

"Oh, stop being so melodramatic," Mrs. Hardy said with a chuckle. Then she turned to the boys. "I invited your friends to dinner when I learned about your trip to Washington, D.C."

"What trip?" Frank was dumbfounded.

His mother handed him a slip of paper. "The German ambassador called this morning with a message from your father!"

2 Unwelcome Visitors

Frank held the message up to the candlelight, read it, then passed it to his younger brother. It said:

SMITHSONIAN MUSEUM OF NATURAL HISTORY.
TUESDAY ELEVEN-THIRTY. CONTACT H. W.—
BEWARE INFINITY

The Smithsonian Museum of Natural History, the boys knew, was a small part of the Smithsonian Institution, a vast enterprise of scientific research and learning located in Washington, D.C.

"I wonder how this fits in with Dad's case," Joe mused.

Fenton Hardy, the boys' famous detective father, was presently in Germany investigating a ring of

terrorists believed to be involved in the production
of sophisticated weaponry. Sponsored by the German government, Mr. Hardy's work was top secret.
He couldn't even contact his own family but had to
communicate through the German ambassador in
Washington, Gerd Kriegler.

"The ambassador said his son, Fritz, would meet
you at Washington National Airport at eleven in the
morning," Mrs. Hardy told her sons as they began
their candlelight dinner of roast beef and mashed
potatoes.

Frank stared at his plate. "Beware infinity." He
mused on his father's curious warning over the word
that meant never-ending, or forever.

Joe shared his brother's concern over the cryptic
note. "I wonder why Dad didn't send us more
information on the case," he whispered to Frank.
"He must know more about the dangers behind
'infinity' than he let on in the note. The message
sounds like it was communicated to Kriegler hastily,
as if Dad was in a tight spot at the time."

"I don't know," Frank answered, still appearing
to be lost in thought. "Maybe Ambassador Kriegler
will fill us in on the details when we get to
Washington."

"I sure hope he does."

"There will be no whispering at the table," Aunt

Gertrude spoke up sternly. "If you two have something to talk about, you can either share it with all of us or save it until we've finished eating."

"We were just discussing our upcoming trip to Washington, Aunty," Frank said, not wanting to spoil the party by expressing their concern over their father.

"Actually, it's too bad you have to go," Iola spoke up. "There's a dance at the high school this weekend, and we were hoping you'd come with us."

Joe made a face. "I hate to miss it," he admitted.

Everyone talked about the dance, and the infinity clue was momentarily forgotten.

After dinner, Iola and Callie, a vivacious blonde who was Frank's girlfriend, offered to wash the dishes if the boys would do the drying and stacking. They all set to work.

"Why don't you come with us?" Joe asked Chet.

"No way," answered the chunky boy as he cleaned the dessert plate by consuming the uneaten portions. "This time you're talking about foreign terrorists, the worst kind of bad. Anyway, I want to spend a few days studying up on earthquakes."

"Too bad," Joe said as he winked at his brother, "because we'll be staying at the German Embassy, where I hear there's a European chef preparing gourmet meals every day."

"Also," Frank put in, "the Smithsonian Institution probably has an authority on seismology who would love to discuss earthquakes with you."

Chet weakened at the thought, but stood his ground. "I still say no thanks. No terrorists for me."

Frank decided not to press the point any longer, thinking it better to let Chet sleep on it and dream about great cooks serving him fantastic culinary delights. "Well, if you change your mind, we'll be flying down early in the morning."

After finishing with the dishes, Joe got some heavy rope from the garage and they all went to tow the Mortons' blue Ford from the ditch. In a few minutes, it was on the road again, and the visitors were on their way. The two sleuths returned for a good night's sleep.

"I'm still curious about that quake," Joe commented.

"I am, too," Frank agreed. "I plan to ask some questions myself when we get to Washington."

The next morning, Frank and Joe woke early and had just eaten breakfast when Chet appeared at the front door with a suitcase.

"I smell bacon," he announced, sniffing the air.

"You just missed it," Frank teased, "but we're glad you made up your mind to come along."

The phone rang and Joe picked up the receiver.

"Is this the son of Fenton Hardy?" came a male voice with a thick German accent.

"Yes," Joe answered hesitantly. "Who's this?"

"Never mind," the man went on. "I am calling to say that they have found out about your father. For your own good and for his, too, do not become involved in this matter."

There was a click, and the anonymous caller hung up.

"Who was that?" Frank asked.

"He didn't say," Joe replied, and related the message to his brother.

Frank shook his head. "If Dad's in trouble, it's important we get to the bottom of this as quickly as possible. We'd better not tell Mom, though. It may have been just a crank call and there's no point in worrying her."

The sun was well up in the sky by the time the Hardys' plane reached Washington. There the aircraft was put in a holding pattern over Washington National Airport. The pilot circled the runway for close to a quarter of an hour before getting permission to land.

Frank looked at his watch as the plane's wheels finally touched the runway with a dull thud. "We don't have too much time," he announced to his companions. "The ambassador's son was supposed to meet us here fifteen minutes ago."

"I'm sure he's waiting," Joe said. "I just hope it won't take too long to get our bags."

Soon, the boys were inside the terminal building, which was crowded with rushing air travelers.

"All these people!" Chet sighed. "Do you think Fritz'll find us here?"

Just then came an announcement over the airport loudspeaker: "Frank and Joe Hardy, please come to the information desk."

"Must be Fritz," Joe remarked.

The announcement was repeated, and the boys hurried through the crowded waiting room toward the information counter. When they arrived, however, Fritz was not there, nor was anyone else except a man behind the desk.

"I'm Frank Hardy," Frank told him. "My brother and I were paged."

"Yes," the clerk nodded. "Someone left a message for you." He handed the sleuths a folded piece of paper.

FRANK AND JOE— AM BEING FOLLOWED. WAIT OUT FRONT WHILE I SHAKE HIM—FRITZ

The brothers exchanged glances. Chet was already beginning to wish that he hadn't come. They picked up their baggage and hurried toward the front entrance of the terminal building.

"He'd better shake him fast," Frank said, anxiously looking at his watch. But ten minutes passed before a small, red sports car swung up to the curb where the trio was waiting.

"Frank and Joe Hardy?" the young driver called out. He had broad shoulders, straight, blond hair, and a wide grin that never seemed to leave his face. "I'm Fritz."

Frank introduced his group to their host, who spoke English as well as the Hardys spoke German, which they had perfected on a recent case in the Rhineland.

"I'm sorry I didn't know there were three of you," Fritz apologized. "My car is not made to hold that many people."

His red sports coupe was, in fact, very small. Frank and Joe had to curl up with their chins on their knees to fit in back. Chet, for once advantaged by his large frame, got to sit up front.

"Who was following you?" Frank asked the German youth.

"I don't know." Fritz shrugged. "But he was in a dark gray Peugeot, and had been on my tail since I left the embassy. I called the airport from a pay phone to leave that message for you at the information desk. I sure didn't want to pick you up with that guy on my back. Who knows what he wanted. I finally lost him, I think." Fritz checked the rearview mirror to make sure the gray sedan wasn't behind them.

"Did you get the license number?" Frank inquired.

"I tried, but the plate was covered with mud."

"Probably on purpose," Joe put in.

"Since our government began cracking down on terrorist activities, my father has received several threats from unknown sources," Fritz told them. "We have had to be very careful."

"Especially since kidnapping has become so popular among terrorists," Joe added.

"Correct," Fritz said. "We try to vary our daily routines to make it difficult for them to attempt something like that. But let's forget about that right now. I don't even like to think about it."

Returning to his cheerful self, Fritz was anxious to talk about Frank and Joe's adventures as amateur detectives. Chet, proud to have helped solve a number of cases, related *Mystery of the Samurai Sword* to Fritz. Joe couldn't keep a grin off his face while Chet dramatically told how a reclusive Japanese business tycoon had vanished, and how the sleuths had traced his disappearance to the secret behind an ancient Japanese samurai sword. Chet's role in unraveling the mystery was greatly exaggerated, but Joe restrained himself from correcting his friend's account.

Frank, however, wasn't listening. "I hope it's not too much farther," he said, interrupting Chet's story. "We have five minutes left."

"We're almost there," Fritz replied as they passed the Lincoln Memorial and turned up Constitution Avenue.

Being early summer in the nation's capital, the grounds along Constitution Avenue were filled with tourists. Several blocks farther up, the Washington Monument jutted from a hill, and beyond that were the buildings of the Smithsonian Institution.

"We'll be passing the White House on the—" Fritz stopped short. "Oh, no!"

Traffic was slowing down in front of them, blocked by a large group of young people, many of whom were carrying protest signs. The crowd had spilled out onto the avenue in front of the White House, reducing traffic to a single line of cars.

"Looks like a demonstration of some sort," Joe said.

Motorists made their way slowly and carefully through the mob of protesters, who were shouting in chorus and waving signs. The White House, home of the President, could be seen through a high iron fence.

"What's their gripe?" Chet asked.

"Nuclear power," Frank told his friend. "An article in the news this morning said there would be a demonstration here today. That earthquake near the power plant scared a lot of people."

"I agree it wasn't any laughing matter," Joe put in as he felt the bruise he had received the day before.

He then rummaged through his bag and pulled out his camera to get a picture of the demonstration. But as he aimed the camera, one of the protesters turned toward them. With uncommon quickness, the man charged the red sports car, swinging a sign over his head.

"Watch out!" Frank cried.

Too late! The demonstrator wielded the sign like a club and jumped on the car's hood.

Smash!

3 Museum Closed

The front windshield shattered, spraying glass all over the car's occupants. Fortunately, they had had time to shield their eyes from the flying fragments. When they looked up again, the protester was already disappearing into the crowd.

"Let's get him!" yelled Joe, jumping from the car with Frank, Chet, and Fritz.

Suddenly, a large group of people rushed the car. The four boys prepared to defend themselves, even though they were hopelessly outnumbered.

"Are you guys all right?" called one youth as he ran toward them. "Is anyone hurt?"

Frank and Joe relaxed, realizing that the protesters were coming to their aid.

"We're okay," Joe said sharply, addressing the boy, who was about his age, with long, sandy hair and freckles. "But our windshield is smashed to pieces thanks to one of you. Is this supposed to be a demonstration or a riot?"

The youth's feelings were clearly hurt. "I'm sorry about what happened," he apologized. "This is a peaceful demonstration, and whoever did that wasn't one of us. What did he look like?"

Having shielded their eyes from the glass, none of the foursome had gotten a good look at the attacker.

"He must have been an old man," Chet said. "He had white hair."

Frank nodded. "I saw the white hair, but there was something else about him, something strange."

Joe held up his camera. "I tried to get a shot of him when he attacked us. I hope I caught him."

"We're late!" Frank nearly jumped when he saw the time. "It's a quarter to twelve!"

Leaving the protesters scratching their heads, the foursome climbed quickly back into Fritz's sports car and headed down Constitution Avenue toward the Smithsonian.

"It looks like someone is out to get me," Fritz said, "and whoever it is, he means business."

He stopped in front of a large stone building capped by a massive dome. "Here we are," he announced. "The Smithsonian Museum of Natural History." He deposited his passengers, and, after promising to meet them at six o'clock, drove off to shop for a new windshield.

A sign was attached to the museum's glass door. It read:

CLOSED FOR EXHIBIT CHANGES

Joe tried the door. "It's closed all right," he said in frustration.

Frank cupped his hands against the glass and peered into the dark museum. "There's a guard inside," he said.

The young detectives banged on the door and waved wildly to get the guard's attention. Finally, he got up reluctantly.

"What's the matter with you kids?" the stout little man asked, opening the door only a crack. "Can't you read? The museum's closed."

Literally sticking his foot in the door, Frank said, "We have an appointment to meet someone here at eleven-thirty."

The man looked at his watch. "Well, you're late for your date and the museum is closed all week. So I'd say you blew it." With that, he shut the door and returned to his post.

"Boy, he sure thinks he's running the show," Chet grumbled.

"And he's enjoying it," Frank added, when a pickup truck swung around the corner from behind the museum. A canvas tarp covered a load of cargo in back. Two cars full of men followed the truck, and all three vehicles turned up the avenue.

"I bet those are the guys we're supposed to see!" Joe said, angry that they had nothing to pursue the group in.

The three youths watched helplessly as the caravan of vehicles mingled with the traffic on Constitution Avenue and disappeared from sight.

"Let's check in back," Frank suggested. "There might be more where they came from."

The sleuths raced around the huge museum building where they found a small parking lot that was reserved for museum employees. To their dismay, no one else was on the way out.

Frank and Joe felt the hoods of the few cars that were left in the lot, checking to see whether the engines were still warm from recent use. None were.

"What are you doing that for?" Chet protested. "We're looking for people on their way out, not on their way in."

"That's why we're the detectives and you're not," Frank kidded his buddy. "Always look for clues, even if you're not sure what they're good for at the time. Later on, they might turn out to be valuable."

"Hey, Frank, Chet!" Joe called from the far corner of the building. "There's a basement entrance here, and it's unlocked!"

Frank and Chet hurried toward Joe. Steps led down to a door that the blond sleuth held open, and the three boys entered a dimly lit corridor.

Old museum exhibits that had been dismantled over the years were jammed into storage rooms on either side. One was filled with stuffed mammals, another with jars of pickled sea animals. "This place gives me the shivers," Chet whispered.

Near the end of the corridor, beyond an open door, was what looked like a classroom. A group of chairs were set up facing a desk and blackboard. The odor of pipe tobacco pervaded the air.

"Do you think the men were in here?" Chet asked.

"I don't know," Frank replied, "but the tobacco suggests *someone* was here recently. There are nine chairs. The same number of men were in those vehicles. I counted."

The boys started to look for clues in the makeshift classroom, hoping to get some idea who the men were and what they were up to.

"Hold it right there!" a voice suddenly shouted from behind them. Standing in the door frame, a white-haired old man held a shovel threateningly in his hands.

"It's him again!" Chet cried.

Still wary from the assault on Fritz's car less than a half hour earlier, the boys made ready to defend themselves against the white-haired man. But he didn't advance on the sleuths, he just stood guard at the door, holding the shovel like a baseball bat.

"What are you kids snoopin' around here for?" he demanded sternly.

"What are you trying to prove by threatening us with that shovel?" Joe responded with a question of his own.

"I'm planning to bring you three thieving little hoodlums to justice!" the man growled. "Now, you can either give yourselves up or we can wait like this until help comes."

"Thieving little hoodlums?" Chet cried indignantly.

"Wait a minute," Frank said, then addressed the old man. "You think we're here to burglarize the museum?"

"Of course. What else would you be doing down here?" the man sneered.

"Why did you smash our car windshield at the demonstration?" Joe took over the questioning.

"Smashed windshield? Demonstration? What in the world are you talking about? I've been here in the museum, doing my job."

"This isn't the same guy," Frank told his brother.

"There was something strange about that other one."

"You work here?" Joe asked the white-haired man.

"That's right. I'm the custodial engineer," he replied proudly. Then his expression changed. "Wait a minute, I'm the one who's asking the questions. If you kids ain't thieves, then you won't mind going to Mr. Boswell's office and explaining your business to him."

"Who's Mr. Boswell?" asked Frank.

"Museum curator," the old man replied as he stepped back into the hallway, inviting the boys out of the room.

With the custodial engineer behind them, the trio marched to the curator's office.

David Boswell was a serious but kindly looking man about their father's age. His face broke into a grin when he realized he was speaking to the sons of Fenton Hardy. "Your dad worked on a case for the Smithsonian years ago when you were toddlers. Fine man, he is."

Frank told Mr. Boswell that in fact they were following up a lead for their father.

"Well, to be honest, I'm tickled to have Fenton's sons here on a case. You'll have to forgive Jason," Boswell added, referring to the janitor. "I've given everyone working in the museum special instructions to be on guard against intruders. You see, we've been rearranging some things, including our mineral exhibit. That's why the museum is closed for the week. There are some very valuable stones in that display, and we don't want to take any risks, especially since the security alarm system has been temporarily disconnected. So I hope you'll understand why we're a little touchy about strangers prowling around."

Frank and Joe apologized for entering the museum without permission, but explained that under the circumstances they had no choice.

"I'll try to help you any way I can," Boswell replied, easing back into his cushioned desk chair.

Frank informed the curator of their father's cryptic message to be at the Smithsonian that day at eleven-thirty and to find someone with the initials "H. W." He also asked about the men the young detectives had seen driving from the museum.

"I can't help you on your father's note," Boswell said, knitting his brow. "There was nothing scheduled for eleven-thirty as far as I know, and the initials H. W. don't ring any bells. But I can tell you that those men were a team of geologists who use that meeting room from time to time. Their activities are supported by the museum, and it's all on the level. But if you want to know more, I can refer you to the head of the geology department."

Boswell jotted a name and office number on a slip of paper and handed it to Joe. "Ask for Professor Simmons."

The three boys found Professor Simmons's office in a far wing of the museum, but the geologist was out for a late lunch. He would be back about three.

"Now that's a good idea," Chet said. "Let's find ourselves a good place to eat."

On the way out, the boys left Joe's film at the museum's photo lab to be developed, then they strolled into the Washington Mall grounds. At one end stood the United States Capitol, and far down at the opposite end was the Lincoln Memorial, which they had passed earlier. The Washington Monument rose in the center, and large government and Smithsonian Institution buildings lined the Mall on either side. Thousands of tourists filled the area with activity.

After wandering for a while, the boys bought hot dogs and sodas from a sidewalk vendor, then sat outside the Lincoln Memorial and dangled their feet in the Reflecting Pool, a shallow, man-made lake.

"I hope the ambassador hears from Dad soon," Joe said, swishing his feet in the cool water. "I'd like to know he's okay."

"It would also give us a chance to warn him about the phone call we received," Frank added. He finished his hot dog and washed it down with one last gulp of soda. "Right now I want to hear what Professor Simmons has to say about those geologists."

A blue Frisbee sailed through the air in the direction of the sleuths. Chet, seeing that it would land in the water if he didn't catch it, got quickly to his feet.

"Watch this!" he shouted.

Just as the blue Frisbee passed over their heads, Chet leaped into the air as high as he could, which was only a few inches. He snatched at the floating disc but it sailed past them, landing out in the lake.

Kaboom! A tunnel of water shot up as the Frisbee exploded, drenching not only the three youths but several startled tourists who were walking by.

Frank and Joe looked in the direction from where the Frisbee had come. They saw a figure dart from behind some bushes and run across the Mall toward the Washington Monument.

"That's him!" Joe exclaimed, seeing the bomb thrower's white hair in the sunlight as he sped into the crowd.

4 Rent-A-Terrorist

Frank and Joe, both stars in track and field at Bayport High, took up the pursuit. Dodging tourists as if they were part of an obstacle course, the two Hardys kept the culprit in sight. But he was too fast and the boys knew he would soon be able to elude them in the crowd.

"Keep after him," Frank panted, running next to his brother. "I'll see if I can cut him off on the far side of the Monument. It's our only chance."

Joe quickened his pace, bearing off to the left in the hope it would force the assailant to veer to the right, around the Monument. Frank also stepped up his pursuit. He had learned in track to conserve energy for a final burst of speed at the end of a race.

Now he sprinted up the hill, thinking of the Washington Monument as the finish line.

At first, the plan seemed to work. The bomb thrower had arched up the hill toward the Monument where the two sleuths planned to converge. But when Frank and Joe reached the spot, the man was gone!

Exhausted, the brothers returned to the Reflecting Pool, where they found Chet wading knee-deep in the water. He had collected several pieces of blue plastic, all that remained of the Frisbee.

"You guys couldn't catch that old man?" Chet kidded as he handed over the fragments to Frank and Joe for inspection.

"We lost him in the crowd," Joe admitted.

"Hey," Frank said, examining one of the pieces, "did you notice this?"

Chet nodded. "Sure, someone drew a number eight on it, whatever that means."

"Look again." Frank turned the bomb fragment on its side.

Joe snapped his fingers. "It's the sign for infinity! This must have been what Dad was trying to warn us about!"

The symbol for infinity, ∞, looked exactly like the number eight lying on its side. The boys remembered the sign from physics class.

"Boy, I wish we had nabbed that guy," Joe said in

frustration. "That was no firecracker he heaved at us."

"And we thought it was Fritz he was after." Chet groaned.

The threesome returned to the museum and found Professor Simmons back from lunch. He was a cordial man with thick glasses, a bow tie, and buck teeth, which he showed the trio in a broad grin.

Joe went right to the point, questioning him about the team of geologists they had seen leaving the museum.

"They're doing research on the earth's crust. Why do you want to know?"

"It may be relevant to a case we're working on," Frank explained. "At this point we just want to find out something about them—who they are, what they're up to."

"Let's see," the professor said, as he folded his hands on the desk in front of him. "They came from Europe not long ago to undertake various expeditions along the Eastern Seaboard. From what I understand, they plan to research configurations in the earth's mantle, which requires that they drill a series of core samples, as well as take soundings. The team uses the museum as a kind of home base for their research. They were here this morning to pick up some equipment. You must have seen Dr. Werner on his way out."

"Dr. Werner?" Joe inquired.

"Dr. Werner heads the team. He's a well-known and respected man in his field."

"Do you know Dr. Werner's first name?" Frank asked.

"My, my, these questions are getting stranger by the minute. His first name is Hasso, Dr. Hasso Werner. Why? Have you heard of him?"

Frank and Joe exchanged quick glances. Hasso Werner could well be the "H. W." they were looking for!

"It's possible we have heard of him," Frank told the museum geologist. "How can we get in touch with Dr. Werner?"

Simmons threw up his hands. "I don't have any idea. Although we try to support his research as much as we can, we don't keep tabs on his whereabouts. I expect they were on their way to a new expedition site, although I couldn't tell you where it is. I'll be happy to call you when Dr. Werner returns, but that probably won't be for at least another week."

"I'm not sure we have that much time," Frank said in a low tone. "But I'd appreciate it if you'd let us know as soon as you hear from him."

Frank gave Simmons the German ambassador's phone number and told him they would be there for several days.

Chet had been waiting anxiously for the meeting to be over, and when it was, he took the opportunity to ask a few questions of his own.

"Do you know anything about that earthquake near Bayport?"

Simmons shrugged. "That was certainly unexpected. My only guess so far is that there may have been a weakness in the mantle that had gone undetected. Although there hasn't been any seismic activity in that area, it is possible for geological forces within the earth to build up to a sudden and unexpected rupture of the crust."

"I thought earthquakes were caused by known faults in the land," said Chet, having heard about the San Andreas fault in California.

"Most of them are," said the professor. "That's why I'm so puzzled by this one. In fact, I'm eager to get Dr. Werner's report. He's an expert on such things, and his research may give us some insight into this matter." He smiled and extended his hand to the boys. "I guess we each have our own mysteries to solve. Good luck on yours."

The three visitors thanked the professor, then headed for the photo lab, where they had left Joe's film.

"You're just in time," the operator announced as he emerged from the darkroom with wet sheets of photographic paper. He laid the prints on a table and the young sleuths gathered around.

"I got him!" Joe said, pointing to a figure caught in the act of charging. "But the color looks bad. His face is all washed out, and his eyes are . . . pinkish."

"Did you use a flash on the camera?" the darkroom operator asked Joe. "That often causes a reddish reflection off the eyes."

"No, I didn't," Joe replied, knitting his brow. Suddenly, he realized why the man's appearance seemed so strange. "There's nothing wrong with this picture," he said. "This is an albino."

Frank snapped his fingers. "That's right. It explains why he was able to run so fast. He's not an old man at all."

"You mean he really looks like that?" Chet challenged the two sleuths.

"An albino," Frank explained, "has no natural pigmentation, so his hair is white as snow. The blood vessels under his skin and in his eyes give him his only color—pink."

Chet studied the photograph for a few seconds. "Boy, he sure is a mean-looking guy."

Frank grinned. "I don't think being an albino makes you mean. But at least he'll be easy to identify if we see him again." He then checked his watch. "Fritz ought to be out front to pick us up."

"Great, I'm about ready for some of that gourmet cuisine you guys promised me," Chet said, patting his oversized tummy.

Frank and Joe looked at each other, neither one wanting to tell Chet what they had in mind for him.

"Actually, we were hoping you could do us a favor," Frank finally said. He watched his friend's expression drop to one of gloomy expectation.

"What kind of favor?" Chet asked.

"We need you for a stakeout here in the museum tonight," Joe said.

"You expect me to sit all by myself in this dark place while you two go off to the ambassador's for a big gourmet feast? Do you take me for a fool? This is your case, not mine."

Chet folded his arms and acted like the subject was closed. But secretly he was eager to help. This could be his big chance to show off his sleuthing talents.

"Look, Chet," Frank began, "Dad's message told us to be at the Smithsonian, but it didn't say whether it meant eleven-thirty in the morning or at night. We just assumed it was during the day. But now I suspect the action may be tonight, and we'd like you to keep a lookout."

"Why choose me?" Chet asked.

"Joe and I have a lot to discuss with the ambassador. If we didn't think you could handle this as well as one of us, we wouldn't ask you to do it."

"That's all I wanted to hear." Chet beamed, and agreed to keep watch in the building.

The three boys returned to Boswell's office. The curator gladly granted Chet permission to stay that evening. He gave them a key to the basement door, which would be locked for the night.

Frank and Joe then left Chet in the museum and met Fritz, who was waiting in his car out front. A short while later, they arrived at the gates of the German Embassy, which Fritz opened with a remote control switch on his dashboard.

"One of our new security gimmicks since the threats began coming in," he explained.

Inside the elegant embassy, Ambassador Kriegler greeted Frank and Joe wearing nothing but a towel around his waist. An energetic man, he gripped their hands and shook vigorously.

"Excuse me for the way I am dressed," the ambassador apologized. "I have been in the sauna. Be with you in a few minutes."

Fritz, proud of his Washington home, showed the two visitors around the building. They met Herman, the chef, who was already at work preparing dinner in the kitchen. Simmering pots and saucepans filled the room with delicious smells. Then

Fritz took the brothers up a winding staircase to show them his room. But before they got there, an electronic beeping signal came from a panel in the wall.

"Someone's climbed the fence," Fritz said in an anxiously hushed tone.

"Let's go," Joe commanded, pounding back down the staircase to the front door.

In a few seconds, all three boys were outside scanning the embassy yard, which was surrounded by a high fence. Upon a quick inspection of the grounds, it was clear that they were free of any intruders.

"Must have been a false alarm," Fritz deduced. "Sometimes a bird or squirrel will trigger the system. It's happened several times already and is becoming a nuisance."

Frank stood in the driveway and took one more look around. He wasn't sure at all that it had been a false alarm. Yet, the intruder clearly wasn't there now. The three youths returned inside.

The first course for dinner was a gourmet fish stew, which the ambassador ladled out into bowls for his guests. Both Frank and Joe hesitated before trying the dish, but once they had tested it, they dug in hungrily.

Frank told Ambassador Kriegler about the day's

414

events, and asked whether he knew anything that might aid in their investigation.

Kriegler frowned thoughtfully. "I'm expecting to hear from your father again soon. When I spoke with him yesterday, he gave me the message for you and promised to call again this evening."

"And he didn't tell you anything more than was in the message?" Frank asked.

"No." Kriegler shook his head. "I know he was on the trail of something. When he called me, he seemed anxious to relay his information and get off the line as quickly as possible. He may have been making the call at some risk of being caught. I guess he thought it was important that you boys get to the museum in time to follow up on his lead."

Kriegler paused and ladled more stew into the sleuth's bowls. A fish head ended up in Joe's, pointing straight up at him. To be polite, Joe pretended not to notice, but he suddenly lost his appetite for the delicious dish.

"As for the albino who seems to be on your trail," the ambassador continued, "he sounds to me like a man known in terrorist circles as the White Rabbit, or Rabbit for short."

Joe snapped his fingers. "Because white rabbits are albino, pink eyes and all."

Kriegler nodded. "Not only that. He is also

415

famous for his agility and quickness. I'm sure you learned that when you tried chasing him."

"What's his business?" Frank inquired.

"He's a bomb expert," the ambassador replied. "He once worked as a mercenary soldier in Europe. Since then, he's gone underground and hires out as a free-lance saboteur for terrorist organizations." Kriegler's expression turned grave and he spoke slowly for emphasis. "He's a very dangerous man who takes a fiendish pleasure in inventing different types of bombs, and who has little respect for human life."

Frank and Joe shuddered. "I hope Dad calls tonight," Frank said. "This Rabbit may be part of the gang he's investigating."

Kriegler frowned. "You're right. And the infinity sign may be a trademark of sorts for the Rabbit."

"An emblem suggesting that there's no end to his destruction?" Joe wondered.

"I don't know," the ambassador replied. "I'll check with my government for any further information on him."

Suddenly the same thought crossed Frank's and Joe's minds. Chet was alone in the museum right at this moment, and the Rabbit might be taking the opportunity to try a new bomb out on their best friend!

5 A Lively Dummy

The museum storage room was nearly dark. Only a light at the end of an adjoining corridor enabled Chet to see whether anyone entered through the basement door.

Chet had borrowed an American Indian costume and sat cross-legged in a museum exhibit, pretending to be one of the dummies who were grouped around a fake camp fire in front of a tepee. Earlier, this had seemed like a great idea to Chet, a perfect disguise with a good view of the hallway. But after several hours, the costume was growing uncomfortable and his legs were getting cramped.

"Maybe I'll be a lying-down Indian for a while,"

he muttered under his breath, and stretched out, putting his head on the lap of one of the dummies.

On the far side of the storage room was an Eskimo, just visible in the dim light coming from the hallway. Chet suddenly noticed that he seemed to be staring at him!

The young sleuth froze, locking his eyes on the dim figure dressed in sealskins. It moved! Chet screamed silently to himself. But when he strained to see the figure better, he could tell it remained rigid.

This is ridiculous, Chet thought; I'm playing with dummies, and I'm beginning to feel like one myself.

Next to Chet was a fake piece of meat roasting on a spit. It reminded him of how long it had been since they'd had lunch. He wasn't used to missing a meal.

Suddenly, Chet stopped breathing. The basement door at the far end of the hallway opened, then closed gently. He remained motionless as a man approached, wearing a ski mask pulled over his face. The man passed the doorway to the storage room and continued down the hall. Then his footsteps could be heard climbing a stairway to the main floor.

Chet breathed a sigh of relief. Whoever that man was, he didn't look friendly enough to tangle with.

Chet decided to wait a few minutes, then he would sneak out to call Frank and Joe. But just as he was about to leave the room, the man began to descend the stairs.

Chet quickly resumed his cross-legged position in the Indian exhibit and waited for the night visitor to pass.

Then an idea sprang into the boy's head. This might be his big chance to capture the intruder! But the thought was quickly smothered when he saw the masked figure approach in the dim light. Why should I risk my neck? he argued silently with himself. It isn't even my case.

Just then the man apparently heard a noise. He ducked into the storage room and crouched behind the door, only a few feet from the Indian display! Chet's mind went into a panic. Should he jump the man and be a hero, or should he play it safe and just watch as Frank had instructed him to do? He tried to screw up his courage to attack the masked intruder. But before he could, he heard more footsteps coming from the end of the hall. They grew louder, then stopped.

All was quiet for what seemed to Chet like an eternity. The masked figure pressed himself against the wall, waiting without a sound. Chet's body ached from the rigid position he had assumed. He scarcely dared to breathe. Then the footsteps started up again, growing softer as they went back down the hallway.

Now's my chance, Chet thought as the sounds disappeared. But before he could jump up, his stomach let out a low grumble! Startled, the masked figure swung around toward the Indian display.

Grruuup! The boy's tummy betrayed him again.

The man took a step toward him to inspect the dummies. Chet knew he had to do something, or he would be caught! He watched as the masked intruder began to look closely at the figures, touching one after the other. He seemed to be almost as scared as Chet of what would happen.

"Wawawawawawa!" Chet let out a piercing war whoop and sprang to his feet. Then he began dancing like an Indian warrior around the fake fire.

At this, the strange man nearly jumped out of his skin. He shrieked, turned on his heels, and fled from the room. Chet stopped his rantings as the intruder ran down the hall and out the basement door.

A second later, however, another figure appeared at the door to the room. It was a museum guard! "All right, what's going on in here?" he demanded, flipping on the light switch to reveal the young warrior standing amongst the dummies.

"I—I was just—" Chet began, but couldn't find the right words.

"You're coming with me," the guard announced and grabbed Chet by the arm.

An hour later, Frank and Joe arrived at the police station. Still in his Indian costume, Chet sat glumly on a bench in the waiting room.

"I'm glad to see you two guys!" Chet sighed. "I've never felt so stupid in my life!"

"How, Chief Sitting Fool," Joe quipped.

"Ah, cut out the jokes," Chet grumbled, "and let's get out of here."

"You're free to go?" Frank asked.

"Sure. They called Boswell's house and got the whole story. I tried explaining everything to that museum guard before he dragged me here, but he was so gung ho about his job, I couldn't get through to him."

"What about that guy you saw in the museum?" Joe questioned. "Can you describe him at all?"

"Just that he was medium height, medium build. He wasn't the man who attacked us."

"We know who that albino is," Frank explained. He related the ambassador's story as they returned to the red sports car, which Fritz had let them borrow.

"Wow, he sounds too dangerous for me!" Chet remarked with a shiver as he sank into the front seat.

"We also called Sam," Joe spoke up, referring to Sam Radley, a detective who often assisted Mr.

Hardy on cases. "He's going to dig up what he can about Dr. Werner."

"What about your dad? Has he been in touch with the ambassador today?" Chet asked.

"He was supposed to call, but never did," Frank replied, his tone hiding his worry. "Must have been too busy to make it to a phone."

For a while, the three boys rode through the streets of the nation's capital in silence.

"Hey!" Chet blurted as his foot hit something crinkly. He bent down to pull a brown paper bag from beneath the seat. He opened it and his eyes lit up. "It's a can of food, and am I ever hungry!" Then he realized there was no can opener, so he sat back in his seat with a groan.

"Let me see that," Frank said anxiously. He reached over and grabbed the can from Chet. Examining it closely, he found a small figure etched in the bottom of the can. "It's the infinity sign!" he shouted, and instantly hurled the object out the window.

The can rolled into a sewer. A moment later, they heard a muffled explosion and saw a flash of flames shoot from the sewer drain.

"That was too close for comfort!" Chet breathed, wild-eyed.

"I bet the Rabbit planted that thing at the embassy," Joe growled. "He must've got in and out of the premises so fast that we thought the alarm had gone off by accident."

"That man's becoming a real menace," Chet put in, now more angered than stunned. "I wonder how he knew we'd all be in here when the bomb was set to go off."

"He didn't," Frank spoke up. "There must have been a radio controlled detonator that the Rabbit could set off when just the right people were in the car."

When the trio returned to the embassy, they told their story to Fritz and the ambassador. As a result, Kriegler had several security guards placed around the embassy.

In the morning, the boys sat down to a continental breakfast, which was no more than a cup of coffee and pastry.

"This isn't much to go on," Chet whispered to Frank and Joe.

"Come with me," Fritz said, noticing the chubby boy's dismay over the light meal. "We'll go out to the kitchen and rustle up some real grub, as you Americans say."

Chet followed Fritz in search of ham and eggs, while the Hardys discussed their plans.

"I'd like to go back to that meeting room the geologists were using," Joe said. "We didn't really have a chance to search it thoroughly yesterday."

"Good idea," Frank agreed. "I also wonder what that masked guy was doing in the museum last night. It certainly wasn't any ordinary business!"

After breakfast, Frank, Joe, and Chet returned to the Smithsonian in Fritz's car, having searched it for bombs before leaving. They unlocked the basement door with the key the curator had given Chet, and returned to tbe geologists' meeting room. No papers were left lying around, and the wastebasket was clean.

Frank went to the blackboard. It had been erased, but a few faint lines were still visible. He studied the chalk markings, which seemed to be part of a map.

"Look over here," he said, stooping down.

In the lower corner of the blackboard, they could make out the words, "low clay."

"What do you imagine that means?" Joe asked.

"Your guess is as good as mine. Maybe if we ask Simmons, he'll have an idea."

The boys left the meeting room and climbed the stairs to the museum's main floor. Rounding a corner into the front hall, they spotted a cluster of policemen.

"I wonder what's up," Frank murmured.

Seeing the young detectives approaching, the police turned to face them.

"That's them!" Boswell shouted, stepping out from amongst the cluster of officers and leveling his finger at the trio.

In an instant, the policemen surrounded the boys. "You're under arrest!" one of the officers thundered.

6 A Fortune in Bad Luck

Frank, Joe, and Chet were stunned by the words of
the policeman, who stood before them. He flipped
his badge at the trio, identifying himself as Detective Barnes from the local precinct.

"Under arrest for what?" Joe blurted.

"We have reason to believe you stole a valuable
gem from the museum last night," the detective
told Chet, then turned his piercing hazel eyes
toward the Hardys. "And we have reason to believe
you two conspired in the theft!"

"Why would we want to steal any—" Frank
began, but was cut off by the angry curator.

"I don't know who you kids are, but you sure

tried to pull a fast one on me with that phony story," Boswell said acidly.

"We don't have any idea what you're talking about!" Joe cried in defense. "I'm Joe Hardy. He's my brother Frank, and this is Chet Morton, just as we told you yesterday! And we didn't steal any gem!"

"Hold on, Joe," Frank said calmly. He then addressed Detective Barnes in an even tone. "Please explain what this is all about."

"The Faith diamond, which is worth a small fortune, was stolen from its display case sometime during the night," Barnes began. "Curator Boswell tells me you three were caught breaking into the museum yesterday morning. After convincing him that you were involved in an investigation of some kind, you were given a key to the basement entrance and permission to spend the night here."

"I was on a stakeout," Chet agreed.

The police detective continued. "Late in the evening, Chet Morton was caught acting suspiciously in the museum. He was taken to the police station and subsequently released. This morning, the diamond was missing."

"And to think I was fool enough to tell them the security system had been disconnected," Boswell growled. "As far as I know, you three faked the whole thing, names and all. Now let's see some identifications."

The boys pulled out their driver's licenses and handed them to Barnes.

"So that's what that guy was up to last night," Joe whispered to his brother.

"Sure seems like it," Frank agreed.

While the police looked at their licenses, Frank told Detective Barnes about Chet's encounter with the mysterious night visitor.

"I still have to take you to the station," Barnes informed them. "Those licenses could be stolen, and you're the only suspects we have at this point. Also, I'd like you to fill me in on this investigation you claim to be on, as well as on the man you say broke in here last night."

Before leaving the museum, the boys were searched by one of the uniformed policemen, then were led to a waiting squad car. Several reporters tried to question them as they climbed in, but they made no comment.

At the precinct station, Detective Barnes questioned Frank, Joe, and Chet at length about the reasons for their visit to Washington. He then called the Hardy home in Bayport to confirm the story.

Aunt Gertrude answered the phone, and not only corroborated the boys' testimony, but indignantly accused the detective of slandering her nephews.

She had Barnes on the line for five minutes, letting him know Frank and Joe were fine boys, good students, upstanding citizens, and had probably solved more cases than he had in his whole career. The boys could hear the excited voice of their aunt and had difficulty suppressing grins.

Finally, with a groan of relief, the police detective handed the receiver to Frank. "Your aunt wants to talk to you."

"Thanks for the character reference, Aunty," Frank said as he took the phone.

"Don't 'Aunty' me!" came Gertrude Hardy's no-nonsense voice. "What do you mean by smearing our good name up and down the East Coast?"

"What did you say?" Frank raised his voice in alarm.

"I just heard it on the news!" Aunt Gertrude went on. "Sons of well-known detective, Fenton Hardy, suspected of stealing Faith diamond from Smithsonian. I nearly fell off my chair!"

Frank assured his aunt that the matter was being cleared up and that they should be free from all suspicion soon.

"I suggest you see that you are," Aunt Gertrude said abruptly. "And please try to be more careful from now on."

Once Aunt Gertrude was off the line, Detective Barnes offered to reiease the boys, provided they would not leave the city without notifying him. "You understand you are still under suspicion," he added.

The Hardys promised to keep in touch, and the detective took them back to the museum, where they had left Fritz's car.

"I've always been a big fan of your father's," said Barnes as they drove through the city. "And I hear that you two do quite a job following in his footsteps."

Frank and Joe thanked the detective and waited for him to get to the point he seemed to be making.

Barnes continued. "As long as you are still under suspicion, I thought you might be interested in helping me with this case. I could use you, and the sooner we get to the bottom of this, the sooner your names will be cleared."

"We were thinking the same thing," said Joe. "Are there any clues at this point as to who might have done it?"

"Nothing. Chet's description of a man of medium height and build who wore a ski mask is of little help. But there is an interesting story behind the gem that would be worth looking into."

The detective glanced at Frank and Joe to make sure he had aroused their curiosity, then continued. "The Faith diamond is reputed to bring bad luck to its owners. It was recently acquired by the museum through the will of a man named Arthur Rutlidge. He was a wealthy horse breeder who had been having a devastating run of bad luck with his racehorses. He disappeared in a storm while boating, and presumably drowned."

"Do you think the diamond brought him all that bad luck?" Chet asked.

The detective grinned. "I doubt it. But he willed the stone to the Smithsonian just prior to his disappearance. That's the part I find curious."

"Did Rutlidge know Curator Boswell?" Frank queried.

"I believe they knew each other well," the policeman answered. "Why do you ask?"

"I'm not sure," Frank said thoughtfully. "It's odd Rutlidge would leave the gem to the Smithsonian so shortly before his death, as you said."

Detective Barnes dropped the young sleuths off at the museum, where Fritz's car was still parked.

"Hey, we never had a chance to ask Simmons what those words 'low clay' meant!" Joe said, snapping his fingers.

"We'd better leave that one alone for now," Frank answered. "I doubt either Boswell or Simmons will be very cooperative with us until we clear up the question of the stolen diamond."

The boys were quiet for a moment, then Frank said, "I wonder if Mr. Boswell knows more about this than he lets on. He seemed particularly anxious about the theft, and he was a good friend of Arthur Rutlidge's. Something might add up."

Chet raised his eyebrows at Frank's suggestion. "Are you thinking that Boswell might have taken the stone himself?"

"I know the idea is farfetched," the dark-haired sleuth admitted. "But whoever entered the museum had to have a key to the back door. And it seems odd that the man had a ski mask on, as if he was worried that someone might recognize him."

"I see your point," Joe said. "But the idea is so far out I can't believe it. Anyway, what do we do now?"

"I'll think about it," Frank answered as he squeezed into the driver's seat of Fritz Kriegler's tiny car.

Upon returning to the German Embassy, the three sleuths were met by another gathering.

A group of radio and newspaper reporters waited outside the gate and crowded around them as soon as they arrived. Frank made a short statement for the journalists, saying that the Hardys were in no way connected with the diamond theft, and had been released by the police.

Just then, one of the reporters reached through the open car window and shoved a note into Joe's shirt pocket. Without saying a word, he turned and crossed the street.

Once the newspapermen had left, Joe pulled the note from his pocket and read it aloud: "'PIER SIX AFTER DARK BE THERE WITH DIAMOND. WILL PAY $.'"

"Someone must think we really took that stone," Chet observed.

Frank looked back across the street for the man who had delivered the message, but he was gone. "That's right," he said. "Someone who wants it badly enough to pay for stolen goods."

"Pier six must refer to the city dock," Joe remarked.

"Who cares where it is," Chet spoke up. "We don't have the diamond anyway."

Frank operated the switch on the dashboard to open the embassy gates. "Diamond or not," he said, "this is our chance to find out who wants it and why."

Joe frowned. "I think perhaps we're being set up."

"So do I," Frank concurred. "I'd want Chet and Fritz to be there for cover."

"You plan to walk right into this trap, and I'm supposed to rescue you, is that it?" Chet asked with a tone of disbelief.

"Think of us as live bait," Joe answered. "We'll attract the fish and you can reel him in."

"At least you can help turn the odds in our favor if we do meet with trouble," Frank added.

Once inside the embassy, Frank and Joe described their plan to Fritz. He and Chet were to dress in disguises and be at pier six of the city dock by nightfall. The German youth eagerly agreed to participate in the plan, and he went upstairs to look for material for a disguise.

Frank looked at his watch. "We have a few hours left before dark. Ought to be plenty of time for a little ghost hunting."

7 Unwilling Jockeys

Joe looked at his brother questioningly. "Ghost hunting?"

Frank smiled. "Not real ghosts, but the questions people leave behind about themselves after they're dead. Arthur Rutlidge willed that diamond to the museum very shortly before his boating accident. It's possible that someone associated with him knew he would have that accident."

"You're saying that the drowning may have been on purpose," Joe stated, picking up his brother's thought.

"It's possible. Anyway, Detective Barnes told me that Rutlidge had a horse-breeding farm outside of town. It might be a good idea to check the place out. I'll call the police and tell them we're going. They'll tell whoever is at the manor to let us talk to them."

Less than an hour later, Frank and Joe were driving through thoroughbred racehorse country. Rolling hills covered with dark green grass provided plenty of room for the fast animals to run.

"That must be it," Joe said, indicating an old manor house and several stables set off the road on top of a hill.

Frank turned the red sports car up the long drive. Arriving at the manor house, the boys were met by an old butler who escorted them inside.

The butler introduced himself as Wilkinson as they sat in the living room. "May I bring you some tea?"

The Hardys declined the offer and explained that they were interested in the events surrounding Rutlidge's boating accident.

Wilkinson shook his head. "I was employed by Mr. Rutlidge for close to forty years. He was a grand man, a gentleman and one of the finest breeders in the country. Then a few months ago, everything began to fall to pieces for him."

"How do you mean?" Joe asked.

The butler made a sweeping gesture with his arms. "I mean everything. His best horses could no longer run. Nobody would buy the horses because it was believed the animals were hexed. And then one day, he went sailing on the bay and never came back."

"Why were his horses supposed to be hexed?" Joe questioned the old butler.

"It was that cursed diamond of his. I knew it would get him some day, but he wouldn't let go of it, even when it started to ruin him."

Wilkinson pulled a silk handkerchief from his jacket pocket and gently dabbed his forehead. "I tried persuading him to sell it. I believe several offers were made, although I'm not sure what the conditions were. Anyway, Mr. Rutledge refused them. He just laughed at the idea that the diamond had any special powers, and seemed almost determined to disprove the superstition. You can see where that got him."

"Who offered to buy the Faith diamond from Rutledge?" Frank queried.

Wilkinson shrugged. "I don't know. Whoever it was never came here in person." The butler looked quizzically at the boys. "Why are you asking these questions?"

Joe explained that the valuable gem had been stolen from the museum the night before, and that they suspected the theft might be connected with Rutledge's accident.

"Are you suggesting that this is all part of a plot?" the butler said, raising one eyebrow.

"Could be," Frank answered tersely.

"Is that Mr. Rutlidge?" Joe asked, pointing through the open door to a photograph hanging in the hallway of the old manor house.

A number of pictures covered the walls, mostly of winning thoroughbreds the former horse breeder had raised and owned. In the photograph Joe indicated, a middle-aged man with graying temples stood proudly beside a black filly.

"It was the last picture taken of him," Wilkinson told them. "As a matter of fact, that filly he's with is called Faith. Mr. Rutlidge named her after the diamond. She's a very fast horse now, and she'll be entering her first major race this week."

"This was Rutlidge's way of proving that the Faith diamond didn't have supernatural powers?" Frank asked.

"Exactly." The old butler nodded. "He hoped to clear away the superstition once and for all by actually naming a winning horse after the diamond. Unfortunately, the gem got him first."

"Do you really believe that the diamond has the power to bring bad luck to its owners?" asked Joe, not yet sure whether Wilkinson wasn't exaggerating the story for their benefit.

"All I know," Wilkinson said, as he leaned forward and folded his hands, "is that Mr. Rutlidge isn't the first owner to have met with an untimely end. The last proprietor was lost in an avalanche while skiing in Chile, and the one before him was the victim of a rare tropical disease. Then Mr. Rutlidge, rest his soul, took his sunfish sailboat out for the afternoon and never came back. The next day, the Coast Guard found it washed up on shore all broken up. They concluded that he was caught in a thunderstorm, was thrown off the boat, and drowned. I say he was just another victim of that gem. I hate to admit it, but there's just too much evidence pointing to that stone for me not to believe it has evil powers."

"What about his will?" Frank asked. "He left the diamond to the Smithsonian shortly before his accident. Do you know why?"

"No, I don't. But I do know that his sister, Meg, was quite upset when he made the alteration in the will. They were very close, so when Mr. Rutlidge did this without so much as an explanation, she was surprised and disturbed."

"Does the name Boswell mean anything to you?" Frank asked, changing his line of questioning. "He's the curator of the Smithsonian Museum of Natural History."

Wilkinson brightened. "Oh my, yes! Mr. Rutlidge and Mr. Boswell were childhood friends, and the two saw each other quite often." The butler's smile dropped from his face. "In fact, Mr. Boswell was here for a visit just a couple of days before the terrible accident. Why do you ask?"

"No particular reason," Frank said offhandedly. "Just trying to be thorough. By the way, did Boswell know Meg Rutlidge well, too?"

"Of course," Wilkinson replied. "She's known him all her life."

"How can we get in touch with her?" Frank asked.

"She lives in Baltimore. But you should ask the head trainer, Max, for her exact address. Right now they're trying to settle the estate. Both Meg and Max are supposed to get part, and they're negotiating for it at present."

Frank and Joe thanked Wilkinson for his help. Then they left the old manor house, walking down the hill behind the building to the stables where they found Max. He was shorter than both brothers, and had coarse black hair that seemed to be uncontrollable. His hands were too big for his body.

"Yes, I know the diamond was stolen," Max said after he heard their story. "It was on the radio this morning. Say, aren't you the guys who are supposed to have taken it?"

Frank explained that they hadn't stolen the gem,

and were presently trying to track down the thief who had.

"Well, what brings you out here?" Max asked as he led a horse from its stall and saddled it up. "Mr. Rutlidge gave the diamond to the Smithsonian, and everyone around here is happy to be rid of it. Nothing but bad luck, that stone."

"We find the circumstances of Mr. Rutlidge's streak of bad luck somewhat curious," Frank said. "Especially since he willed the gem just prior to his accident. It was almost as if he knew what might happen, and was trying to prevent someone from getting his hands on it."

Max shot a sharp glance at the young detectives, then grinned. "Why don't we get you a couple of horses and talk about it while we take a ride?"

"Sure, why not?" the boy replied.

The trainer saddled two mares for Frank and Joe. They started out in a trot over the rolling hillside, then slowed to a walk.

"These used to be fine racehorses," Max said as he pulled alongside Frank and Joe. "Trained them myself. Too old to race anymore, though. We just use them for breeding."

Upon further questioning, the boys learned that Rutlidge's sister had wanted the Faith diamond very much, and had prepared a case to get it back legally from the Smithsonian. Max gave them her address in Baltimore.

Suddenly the sleuths' horses took off as if out of the starting gate of a racetrack. The jolt nearly knocked the boys out of their saddles. Frank managed to grab his reins when his thoroughbred spooked, but Joe had dropped his, and now he hugged the animal's neck as it sped at a full gallop across the field.

However, he gradually began to lose his grip. He tried in vain to slow the animal, which seemed to be driven by some invisible force. Finally, Joe's arm slid from the horse's neck. He grabbed a piece of the saddle, but his balance was going.

"Hold on, Joe!" Frank yelled. He had gained some control over his horse and was pulling alongside his brother. "Jump!" he shouted, urging Joe to leap from one speeding animal to the other.

"I can't!" the younger Hardy yelled back. His foot had become twisted in his stirrup. If he fell now, he would be dragged along under the frenzied racehorse! Yet he knew he wouldn't be able to hold the saddle much longer.

Then, just as suddenly, both horses slowed down and came to a stop. The wild impulse that had possessed them left them the same instant.

"These old beauties still have plenty of steam left in them," Joe groaned as he disentangled himself

from the stirrup and climbed down. "I wonder what caused them to spook like that."

Max rode up to the Hardys. "Are you okay?" he asked worriedly.

"We're alive," Frank answered with a frown.

"I'm sorry," Max went on. "Sometimes these thoroughbreds get the idea they're back at the racetrack, and they just take off, each trying to outrun the other."

"You could've warned us," Joe grumbled.

Max shrugged and turned back toward the stables.

"Do you think he knew these horses would spook?" Joe murmured to his brother.

"It might have been a good way to put an end to our questions," Frank replied, watching Max disappear up the hill.

"Let's ask *him* a few questions, like where he was last night when the diamond was stolen," Joe said hotly.

Frank shrugged. "I don't think he'd cooperate. Meg Rutlidge might be a better bet at this point. Boswell didn't tell Detective Barnes that she had been trying to reclaim the stone. If he was trying to cover for someone by accusing Chet of the theft, it may have been Meg!"

"But Chet saw a man enter the museum," Joe argued.

"That doesn't mean she didn't have something to do with it."

The two sleuths took their horses back to the estate. Max had gone, and one of the stable hands led the animals to their stalls.

"We'd better return to town," Joe said as they walked to the car. "We have an appointment at the city dock."

It was dark by the time the two arrived in Washington. The dock was located along the Potomac River in the heart of the city. When he found the pier marked number six, Frank pulled the red sports car over to the curb and stopped.

"Well, here we are," he murmured. "I just hope Chet and Fritz are around. This could be trouble."

8 A Clever Deal

Pier six was empty except for two people fishing from the end of the dock. They wore wide-brimmed hats and brightly colored shirts. Figuring them to be Fritz and Chet, the Hardys chuckled at the corny disguise and strolled out on the pier to let them know they had arrived.

"Pssst," Frank whispered loudly as they drew near, "seen anyone around?"

"Nobody but you guys!" a rough voice answered as the two fishermen jumped to their feet and lunged at Frank and Joe!

Caught off guard, the boys found themselves in the clutches of two strange thugs before they could react.

"We'll take that stone now," Frank's captor demanded. He was a big man with a low, gravelly voice.

"What about the money?" Frank challenged, playing along.

"We'll let you have the money when we see the stone," the man replied, tightening his wrestling hold on Frank.

"That sounds fair." The older Hardy pretended to give in. "But I left it in the car. I'll go and get it for you."

"Go ahead. But if you try anything stupid, remember your brother is with us," the hefty man snarled.

He released Frank, who took one step down the pier, then whirled around and caught him with his fist just above the jaw. In the same instant, Joe hooked his foot around his captor's leg and brought him to the ground.

Fists flew for a few rounds between the battling pairs at the end of the pier, but Frank and Joe were in better physical shape and soon gained the upper hand over their tiring assailants.

Just then, one of the men hesitated for a second and gestured to his companion to retreat. Both took off down the pier with Joe in pursuit. Frank, however, stood still and stared out across the dark water. He had seen one of the men glance beyond him just before they broke off the fight, as if looking for a signal from somewhere out in the anchorage that lay beyond the docks.

"What happened to you?" Joe said accusingly to his dark-haired brother as he returned from his chase. "I couldn't handle both of those guys all by myself."

"I think I know who arranged this little surprise party," Frank answered. "See that ship anchored over there?"

Joe peered out on the water. A sixty-foot motor yacht lay in the bay, gleaming in the moonlight.

"Someone was on deck watching the whole show through binoculars," Frank went on. "When I spotted him, he put down the glasses and ducked beneath the railing."

The Hardys hurried to a small marina nearby, where the lights were on. They knocked on the door, and a portly, red-faced dock master greeted them.

"Did you see a couple of guys on the pier with fishing poles and wide hats?" Joe queried.

The dock master let out a big belly laugh. "You'd be lucky to catch a boot in these waters. Nobody with any sense would go fishing around here. Now if you're looking for crabs, that's a different story."

"So you haven't seen two men with fishing poles," Frank interrupted.

The portly dock master shook his head.

"What about the yacht anchored out in the basin?" Joe asked. "Do you know anything about it?"

"Sure do. A fellow named Jensen owns that beauty. Wayne Jensen is his name. He's been moored out there for a couple of months." The dock master paused. "Say, you youngsters look like you've been in a fight or something."

"We were mugged," Frank said tersely, "And we think Mr. Jensen could have had a hand in it."

"I hardly think Mr. Jensen has to mug people to make money," the portly man told them, his deep laugh bubbling up again. "But if you'd like to discuss it with him, I'll let you use a dinghy to row out there."

The brothers thanked the dock master, who led them to one of several dinghies he had tied at the dock. Just as Frank and Joe were getting in, though, two figures appeared in the darkness equipped with fishing poles and wide hats.

"Are those the fellows you were talking about?" the dock master asked.

Without answering, Frank and Joe ran to intercept the muggers. The two tried to avoid them but Frank and Joe stopped them in their tracks with flying tackles. The four landed together in a heap on the ground.

"Hey, what are you guys trying to prove?" a youthful voice cried out.

The Hardys immediately realized that they had just tackled Chet and Fritz! The four got to their feet and dusted themselves off as Frank and Joe apologized and explained their mistake.

"What took you so long to get here, anyway?" Frank questioned his friends. "We could've used your help a few minutes ago."

Fritz explained that he and Chet had come on a couple of motorcycles he kept in his garage. When they left the embassy, the same gray Peugeot that had followed him to the airport had pulled out behind them. He and Chet then took different routes, finally shaking the sedan.

Chet drew a rolled up newspaper from his back pocket. "The evening paper just came out. It mentions our names in connection with the diamond theft."

Joe opened up the paper to a small article on the theft. It said that the trio had been released, but were still under suspicion.

"Come on," Frank told his blond brother, "with a little luck, we might be able to clear this thing up tonight."

Leaving Chet and Fritz at the dock to stand guard, Frank and Joe climbed into the dinghy and rowed out to Wayne Jensen's boat.

The night was clear, and the light from a full moon glittered off the surface of the calm Potomac River. As the sleuths drew near the large motor yacht, they could see a man on the aft deck watching their approach. The boat was even more luxurious than they had guessed from a distance. It looked to be capable of long ocean voyages.

The man aboard the yacht stood up and dropped a ladder over its side.

"Howdy, boys. What can I do for you? I'm Wayne Jensen," he said with a Texas accent as they pulled the dinghy alongside the sixty-foot vessel.

"He's not the phony reporter who put the note in my pocket," Joe said. "But no doubt he's the one who hired that guy."

After obtaining permission to climb aboard, Frank explained that he had some merchandise the man might be interested in.

Jensen eyed the two youths suspiciously. "What are you talking about?"

"Look," said Frank, "we saw you with your binoculars, watching us as we were jumped on the pier. So don't play innocent."

"Yes, I saw the fight," Jensen admitted, "and I got my binoculars to see what was going on. I would have called the police, but you seemed to be handling the situation very well by yourselves. Probably a couple of muggers, right?"

"No. We had a date with those guys. They were going to buy something from us," Frank said slowly.

"Oh?"

"And we're ready to sell it to you if you have the money!"

Jensen's smile left his face. "I still have no idea what you are driving at, but whatever it is you're involved in, you're barking up the wrong tree."

Frank put his hand in his pocket. He was clearly carrying a small, round object, which he played with in his pocket. Jensen stared at it for a second and a look of anxiety crossed his face.

"What are you boys trying to peddle on me, anyway?" he asked.

"Just a stone," Frank answered.

"What kind of stone?"

Joe handed the Texan the newspaper and pointed out the article on the stolen diamond. The man quickly read it.

"Are you telling me you have this gem with you?" Jensen said coldly. "I could see to it that you're arrested."

"We're not saying anything," Frank answered. "But if you want to buy what I have, this is your last chance to make an offer."

Wayne Jensen sat still, glaring at his visitors.

"Okay," he said at last, "I'll give you fifty thousand for it."

"The stone's all yours," Frank said evenly as he pulled a large pebble from his pocket and flipped it at the wealthy yachtsman.

9 *The Racer's Edge*

Anger flashed across the Texan's face. "Just what are you trying to prove with this stupid charade?" he snapped, hurling the worthless pebble overboard.

"We want to know why a man like you is so anxious to get hold of the Faith diamond, even as stolen property," Joe told him. "If you don't mind answering a few questions, we won't tell the police that you had us attacked and offered to buy the gem."

"You can't prove anything," Jensen replied hotly. "Now get off of this boat before I have to throw you off!"

"Certainly," Frank said. "It was a pleasure meeting you."

The boys climbed down the ladder into their dinghy, feeling like sitting ducks. They did not breathe easy until they had reached the pier and joined their friends.

"What happened out there?" Chet asked as he grabbed the painter from Joe and fastened it to a piling.

"Frank's quite a salesman," Joe said proudly. "He almost sold a piece of gravel for fifty thousand bucks."

"I just wanted Jensen to admit he was after the gem," the older Hardy said. "Now we have to figure out why."

Fritz gazed at the motor yacht gleaming in the pale moonlight. "It looks like your friend is making his getaway!"

They could hear the sound of the yacht's engines starting up, and two men were on the bow pulling up the anchor. In less than a minute, the sixty-foot cruiser was on its way out of the basin and into the Potomac River.

Upon returning to the dock house, Frank and Joe questioned the dock master as to where Jensen might be headed. The jolly man could tell them only that the yacht sometimes left for one or two days. He wasn't sure where it went, but it couldn't go far in that time.

"Has Jensen bought any charts lately?" Frank asked.

"I seem to recall that he has," the dock master answered, scratching his head. "I believe he bought several of the Potomac River and Chesapeake Bay area. He also got one of Baltimore Harbor."

Thanking the dock master for his help, the four youths returned to the embassy. They kept an eye out for the gray sedan that had followed Chet and Fritz earlier, but it was not in sight.

"Do you think the Rabbit was driving that Peugeot?" Chet asked once they were in the German Embassy.

"Either he was or someone else who's very interested in us," Frank replied. "I hope the ambassador heard from Dad today. I'm getting edgy about this whole business."

But Ambassador Kriegler still had not received any word from Fenton Hardy. Frank and Joe had a fitful night's sleep.

In the morning, Frank called Detective Barnes for further information on the diamond theft. The police detective told them that he would run a check on Wayne Jensen, and that as yet he had no substantial leads on the missing gem.

Then Frank contacted Sam Radley in Bayport,

who reported that Dr. Hasso Werner was a very well-known geologist who taught at a German university. He was a good family man, and his record was clean.

"Maybe Dr. Werner's team is on the level after all," Joe commented. "It could have been just plain coincidence that they were meeting in the museum on Tuesday."

Frank shook his head. "Too many coincidences are adding up. Werner has the initials H. W., he's German, and he was there that morning. On top of that, there's something too secretive about him and his party."

"And we still don't know where he is." Joe shrugged, seeing his brother's point. "We ought to pursue that clue we found on their blackboard. 'Low clay' just might lead us to the geologist. If Dad is in trouble, we shouldn't be wasting our time chasing the diamond."

"Unless the theft ties in with Dad's case," Frank pointed out. "It's also quite a coincidence the Faith diamond was stolen the same day we got here."

The blond sleuth nodded. "I just wish Dad would call to fill us in on some of this stuff and tell us he's okay. I'm also shaky about the Rabbit. We haven't had a bomb thrown at us for two days, and it makes me wonder whether he isn't cooking up something really nasty."

"It's possible," Frank said, trying to play down the thought. "But I have a feeling that the Rabbit's job is over. Even if he didn't blow us to bits, he diverted us from the case long enough for us to lose the scent."

"Let's sure hope so!" Chet piped in. "One more sign of that guy and I'm back in Bayport!"

Over breakfast, the amateur detectives decided to pay a visit to Meg Rutlidge in Baltimore. They borrowed Fritz's two motorcycles since he was using the car. The bikes were German-made, light and swift. In less than an hour the boys were in Baltimore, a major port for commerce on the Eastern Seaboard.

Meg Rutlidge lived in a townhouse in the center of the city. She was hesitant to talk to Frank and Joe, but at last convinced of their sincerity, she opened up.

"Yes, I've been trying to reclaim Arthur's diamond from the Smithsonian," the kindly, refined woman said. "My brother had always promised me I would have it someday. Then his racehorses began performing poorly and that old superstition about the stone's power to bring bad luck came up."

"So Mr. Rutlidge changed his will, giving the diamond to the museum and protecting you from its so-called curse?" Frank guessed.

Meg nodded. "He told me when he changed the

will that he was doing it for my own good. He said he was convinced the gem had some kind of evil power. The funny thing is, until that day he had always laughed at the superstition. He even had a young racehorse named after the diamond, just so he could dispel the myth."

"Your brother's butler told us about the horse," Joe said. "She's supposed to run her first major race in a couple of days."

"Yes, but Arthur won't be there," Meg said sadly. She sat silently in thought for a moment, then went on. "In any case, I thought it was very strange that he had that change of heart over the diamond. He knew the gem had about as much supernatural powers as the kitchen sink. He couldn't have been in his right mind when he made out that new will."

"And that's why you made your case to reclaim the Faith diamond from the museum," Frank deduced.

"Yes," the woman answered softly. "Only now there's no diamond to reclaim. I hope you boys find the thief who took it."

"Did a man named Jensen ever offer to buy it?" Frank queried.

"Not that I know of," Meg Rutlidge said. "If an offer was made, Arthur didn't mention it to me."

"What about the museum curator, Mr. Boswell?" the older Hardy asked casually, but watched for her response to the name. "I hear that you and Arthur were both good friends of his."

"Arthur was and I still am," Meg replied, giving no sign of being jarred by the question. "Why do you want to know?"

The sleuths explained that they had a hunch the curator might know more about the diamond's theft than he let on. The fact that Arthur Rutlidge's accident left some peculiar questions of its own, and that he was a friend of Boswell's, might tie in with the case.

Meg stared out the window, distracted by a thought. "David Boswell phoned me this morning," she said at last. "It was just a social call. He apologized for the loss of the diamond, knowing how much I had wanted it back. We talked about it for a while. But I couldn't help thinking that there was something else he meant to tell me and didn't."

"Does he believe in the stone's curse?" Joe asked.

"No. He's even helped me in my case to reclaim the diamond," Meg said, leaning back in her chair with a sigh. "He was planning to testify on my behalf that Arthur must have been out of his mind when he changed the will."

Convinced that Rutlidge's sister knew nothing about the gem's disappearance, Frank and Joe thanked her and left. They mounted their motorcycles and drove down to the harbor to see if Jensen's ship was there. The harbor was busy with traffic, but the large yacht wasn't among it.

The sleuths then made a stop at a special museum of horse racing, a small brick building near the harbor. A collection of films was available to the public for viewing, and the brothers picked out one in which Rutlidge's entry had lost unexpectedly. In a small viewing room, they threaded the spool into a projector and turned out the lights.

By stopping the film, running it in reverse, and then forward again in slow motion, Frank and Joe could see that Rutlidge's horse seemed to break stride during the race just as it rounded the far turn.

"Look at the way its ears perk up just before it loses its pace," Joe said. He stopped the projector, freezing the animal's motion as it rounded the turn.

"It sure appears as if the horse sensed something that made it falter," Frank agreed. "Almost as if it was trained to react to a signal."

"You think someone conditioned it to lose?" Joe asked, finding his brother's idea hard to swallow.

"Let's just say it might be time to ask Rutlidge's trainer, Max, a few questions."

The boys returned the film, left the museum, and rode over the hilly country roads that led to the Rutlidge estate.

They were not far from the city, however, when Joe's bike developed engine trouble. He had to coast down a hill and pull into a service station.

"I'm a biker myself," the attendant told the Hardys as he stepped away from the gas pumps to inspect Joe's motorcycle. "Haven't seen any like these around here, though. I bet I can fix 'em anyway."

The lanky young man wheeled Joe's bike into the garage and brought out a set of tools he used on his own machine. "Are you guys on the way to the cliffs?" he asked.

"What cliffs?" Frank inquired.

"I take my bike there all the time," the young man said as he pointed with a wrench to a motorcycle in the corner of the garage. "Best biking in the area.

Frank glanced at the bike. It was covered with yellowish mud. "Looks like you drive it hard," he observed. "That mud's pretty thick."

"It's not mud," the youth answered. "It's clay, yellow clay. You get that down at the cliffs."

Frank and Joe instantly had the same thought. Could the words "low clay" they had found on the geologist's blackboard have been what was left of "yellow clay?"

"These cliffs are made of yellow clay?" Frank asked to get the story straight.

The lanky gas station attendant looked up from his work. "They're called the Yellow Clay Cliffs."

"You didn't see a group of scientists down there recently, did you?" Joe asked. "They would be drilling the ground?"

"So that's what those guys were up to," the youth said, his interest showing. "Geologists, huh? I saw them working at the base of the cliffs just this morning!"

10 Follow the Yellow Clay Road

Frank and Joe decided to put off returning to the Rutlidge estate. While Joe helped to fix his motorcycle, the older Hardy made a phone call to Washington. Since the boys were still officially suspects in the diamond burglary, they had to make regular contact with the police to inform them of their whereabouts.

Barnes had dug up some material on Wayne Jensen and related his findings over the phone. Jensen had indeed made a fortune. But a great part of his earnings were either undocumented or suspect, and were centered around dealings with foreign concerns.

"Let's go," Joe called out as his brother returned from making the call. "My bike's humming like new."

He took a few laps around the pumps to make sure the engine was working properly, then waved to the station attendant and wheeled back on the road. Frank took off after him.

In time, the steep hills gave way to much lower and flatter terrain covered with thick underbrush. Following the gas station attendant's directions, the two sleuths took a road that led down to the shores of the lower Potomac, where the river emptied into the wide Chesapeake Bay.

The road followed the river for a short while before the terrain began rising again. In moments, the boys found themselves on a narrow lane, cut high into the wall of the bluffs that towered above the water. The bluffs were jagged from erosion, and the road wound around them in sharp curves.

It continued rising until it reached the top of the bluffs, more than a hundred feet over the river and bay. There, dense pine forest covered the land. Except for a few dirt lanes running into the woods, there were no signs of civilization in the area.

Taking it slowly along the dangerous terrain, the Hardys kept an eye out for the geologists. At one spot, the cliffs suddenly became a deep yellow hue.

Now the brothers traveled over a hard clay surface, making traction considerably worse for the motorcycle tires.

"That guy at the gas station has got to be some kind of daredevil to take his bike out here for kicks," Joe shouted above the noise of the engines.

"When this stuff gets wet, it must be especially treacherous," Frank called back.

Following the dangerous road for another mile, the sleuths came to a point where the yellow clay ended. Beyond it, the ground once again became dirt brown.

"We must have missed them," Joe said, swinging his motorcycle around. "Let's take it slower this time."

The boys drove back and forth over the area of the bluffs marked by the yellowish clay, but they saw no sign of the geologists whom the gas station attendant had told them about.

Joe braked his bike and waited for his brother to catch up. The day was growing hot, and he used a rag from his back pocket to wipe his neck and forehead, grimy with a combination of dirt and sweat.

"Do you think they've already packed up and left?" Frank asked as he pulled alongside Joe's motorcycle.

"I don't know," Joe responded. "Maybe we

466

should try exploring some of those dirt paths leading back in the woods."

They started their bikes up again, heading toward the top of the bluffs.

Just then, a pickup truck came from around a corner in the road. Both boys swerved hard to avoid the oncoming vehicle.

"That's the geologists' truck," Joe yelled. The Hardys spun their bikes in a one-hundred-and-eighty-degree turn and started down the road after it.

Following at a distance, they trailed the pickup back to an area where the road widened. The truck parked on the shoulder. A man got out and climbed down a small trench cut diagonally in the steep bluff.

Waiting until he was out of sight, the brothers drove up to the truck and peered toward the water. On the beach at the foot of the bluff were the geologists! The equipment they used for boring core samples was in operation. It was an elaborate rig and most of the men were working on it. A makeshift dock had been built nearby.

"Werner must be among them," Joe said excitedly as he started down the crude path.

"Wait a minute," said Frank, grabbing his brother's arm. "If we barge in like that, we might blow our chances of finding out what they're up to."

"You're right," Joe agreed, and climbed back to

the road. "Those men may not be as harmless as they seem."

Staying out of sight, the young detectives mounted their motorcycles and headed down the yellow clay road. They found a small fishing village further along the shoreline, a couple of miles from where the cliffs began.

"Can we rent a skiff with an outboard somewhere in town?" Frank asked a group of men who sat in rocking chairs on the front porch of the village's general store.

"You boys want to go fishing?" one of the men asked, bringing his rocker to a stop.

"In a way, we do," Frank responded.

The man stood up from his rocker. "Come on along then. I've got something you can use. It's ten dollars a day, not including the cost of gas."

The brothers agreed to the fisherman's terms.

Joe went to inspect the skiff to be sure the engine worked, and to check for leaks. Frank, meanwhile, called Chet and Fritz from the general store and asked them to meet the Hardys in the village as soon as possible. He also suggested that they bring along the disguises they had used the previous evening, and get two more for Frank and Joe. They would also need a tent, sleeping bags, and camping supplies.

An hour later, Fritz's sports car pulled up in front of the general store.

"We have everything you guys asked for," Chet announced. "What's the plan?"

Frank told him that, disguised as a group of boys out on a fishing trip, they would "accidentally stumble" on Werner's team. They could set up camp on the beach near the geologists, pretending to be just a bunch of curious youngsters.

"So the idea is to play dumb," Joe put in. "That should be easy for some of us."

Still embarrassed over the episode in the dark museum, Chet ignored Joe's kidding. "Just wait. You'll be glad I came along."

Donning sunglasses, hats, and fishing poles, the foursome manned the skiff and headed down the shoreline. As they rounded a turn under the bluffs, Joe slowed the boat. The others threw out lines, as if trolling for fish. The geologists looked up from their work when they saw the young people approach, and Joe turned their boat toward the beach.

"Howdy!" Frank called out with a big smile. "What's going on?"

The men returned the greeting with rude stares, then resumed their work. Frank, Joe, and Chet got out of the skiff and walked up the beach, joining the workers around the equipment.

"Are you drilling for oil or something?" Joe asked with a hokey accent. "Gee whiz, that sure is a weird contraption you've got there."

A slightly balding man of medium build stepped from the machinery. He had dark eyes and a neatly cropped beard. "What do you want?" he asked with a thick German accent.

"Oh, we're just fishing," Frank answered. "Weren't getting any bites, though, so we thought we'd say hi and find out what's going on."

"We're taking core samples," the bearded man replied tersely.

"Then you're scientists?" Frank asked.

"Yes, and we're very busy. So if you will excuse us."

"Hey, this stuff is neat," Chet said as he wandered around the drilling equipment. "What are these things for?" He pointed to a couple of long cylinders lying on the beach.

"Boring rods," the scientist answered. "Don't touch anything."

"Why are you taking core samples around here?" Frank pursued the questioning.

A large, burly man came over to him. "Get out of here. You are bothering us," he ordered.

"Sorry," Frank said, backing off. "We were just curious. We'd be happy to help with the drilling if you are behind schedule or something."

"We don't want your help," the burly man replied gruffly. "We want you to get out of here."

The four boys, seeing that they would be physically evicted from the site unless they left on their own, prepared to go back to the skiff.

"Nice to meet you," Frank said with a smile and extended his hand to the bearded scientist. "By the way, I'm John Sterret. I didn't catch your name."

The man, happy to be rid of the nosy boys, quickly shook hands. "I'm Dr. Werner. Sorry we're too busy to chat."

The sleuths returned to their boat, where Fritz had already started up the motor in case trouble erupted.

"We should've let him know who we were and why we're here," Joe said to his brother.

"Maybe later," Frank decided. "Right now we're not sure if he's friend or foe. The odds would be against us if Frank and Joe Hardy were names that spelled 'enemy' for Werner."

"If you saw what I saw, you'd be glad you gave him that phony name," Chet spoke up. "That man is no friend. One of those cylinders had the infinity sign drawn on it!"

11 Sunset Oystermen

Joe shot an astonished look at his friends, then at the team of geologists on the beach. "You mean, Werner's in cahoots with the Rabbit?"

"Cool it," Frank urged his brother. "Don't pay any more attention to them. Just head this thing down the shore."

The boys threw out fishing lines as Joe motored the skiff around a bend in the high bluffs. Once they were out of sight, they drew in the lines and took off their disguises.

"This seems like a good spot to set up camp," Frank said, indicating an area where the bluffs had eroded enough to provide a naturally protected section of the beach.

The foursome pitched Fritz's tent at the foot of the yellow clay cliff. Frank and Joe collected driftwood, as Chet and Fritz prepared to make supper. By the time the sun began to set over the wide, still waters of the lower Potomac, the boys had a pot of beef stew bubbling over a crackling fire.

"I feel like a gypsy camping on the Rhine River," Fritz remarked wistfully, remembering the natural beauty of his own part of the world. "Now all we need is a violin and a tambourine."

"I feel like an early American explorer," Chet said, and gazed over the water. The far shore was lined with a dense forest that broke off at the point where the Potomac fed into the bay. "Only now we don't have to worry about hostile Indians or wild animals. We can just enjoy the sunset over the river."

Joe, relaxing against a log, chuckled at his chunky friend's observation. "No, we don't have to worry about wild animals, just bomb-throwing terrorists. If given a choice, I'd go for the animals."

The four youths sat in quiet thought as the sun turned a deep red hue and sank into the horizon. A boat loaded with oysters came into sight. Moving slowly with its heavy cargo piled high in the middle, it made an odd silhouette against the sunset. Two men were aboard and, noticing the camp fire on the beach, watched the four boys as they went by.

"They must be from the fishing village," Joe said. "Looks like they made a good harvest today." He stood up and waved at the oystermen, who returned the wave before disappearing around the bend.

"I wish we had some of those fresh oysters to make a stew," Chet put in.

Joe let out a groan. "How can you think about food right now? I'm stuffed."

"Wait a minute," Frank said. "This isn't oyster season. Those couldn't have been fresh oysters."

"Are you suggesting that the boat was full of rotten oysters?" Chet said.

"Look," Frank told him. "Oysters are not in season during the summer. They're only harvested in the months that have an 'r' in their spelling—September through April. I don't know what those guys are up to, but they're sure not oystermen!"

Suddenly, Frank and Joe had the same thought. The boat might not have been on its way to the fishing village at all!

"Let's check on the geologists," Frank said to his younger brother.

Both boys got to their feet and jogged down the beach in the direction of the drilling site. It was dark by the time they arrived. The oyster boat was nosed up on the beach and several men were in the process of unloading something.

Hoping the men were too busy to notice them, the two sleuths crept closer to the drilling site to get a better look. Concealed under the mound of oysters were several core cylinders, which the men unloaded and carefully carried up on the beach.

Frank nudged his brother's arm and pointed to the pickup truck parked on the bluff road. As the geologists finished their business, the boys scaled the steep path up the bluff. They climbed in the back of the truck, covered themselves with the canvas tarp, and waited.

In a few minutes, they could hear two men approaching. One of them was clearly Dr. Werner. The other sounded like the one who had threatened the boys earlier. In listening to the two talk, Frank and Joe learned that his name was Roget. Although he spoke German, he clearly had a French accent.

The two men climbed into the cab of the pickup. A second later, the engine started up and they were on their way down the bluff road.

"This guy drives like a maniac!" Joe exclaimed in a whisper as the truck sped around the sharp bends in the road, tossing its hidden occupants back and forth under the canvas tarp. "Next time I hitch a ride, it'll be with someone who I know can drive."

After some adjustment of their bodies, they found that they could brace themselves between the sides of the truck without getting thrown around too much. Once settled, they discussed their next move.

"The geologists, or whatever they are, were using those oyster shells to cover their cargo of core cylinders," Frank observed. "They wanted it to appear as though they were going out empty in the morning, then returning in the evening laden with a harvest of oysters."

"But they were really going out full at night and coming back empty in the morning," Joe finished Frank's deduction.

"Exactly. Also, there were nine geologists at the Smithsonian for Werner's meeting. Only five were at the drilling site. If the two men in the oyster boat were part of the team, that leaves two remaining men unaccounted for. They might be where the cylinders were coming from."

"Do you think the Rabbit is one of the two missing guys?" Joe asked nervously.

"No. He was busy hassling us while the meeting was being held. But Chet saw the cylinder with the infinity sign on it, so that proves he's associated with this outfit. In any case, I have the impression that Dr. Werner isn't the head honcho in this operation. We ought to stay under cover for the time being until we can determine a little more clearly just what's going on."

The young detectives felt the pickup truck turn off the road and go up a gravel drive. Soon it came to a stop. They waited for the men to leave, then peeked out from under the tarp. They found themselves outside a small bungalow set back in the woods at the top of the yellow clay cliffs. The two cars that they had seen leaving the Smithsonian were also parked in front of the house.

"This must be where the gang's staying," Joe said excitedly.

Frank was puzzled. "If those are the cars that carried the geologists, why aren't they down at the drilling site? It doesn't make sense. How do the men get back here to sleep without their cars?"

"Perhaps they camp at the drilling site," Joe said.

The older boy shook his head. "I didn't see any tents or camping gear there."

"Well, maybe they travel on the oyster boat," Joe suggested. "It seems to me we should follow that boat and see where it comes from."

Frank nodded. "That might be the answer. But let's try a little old-fashioned eavesdropping first."

The sleuths threw off the tarp and hopped from the pickup truck. The sky was overcast, making it darker than it had been on the previous evening. This provided good cover for the boys to sneak up on the house without being noticed.

Lights were on in the bungalow. Dr. Werner and

Roget could be seen through the window engaged in conversation. The Hardys stationed themselves outside and listened. The muffled voices were barely audible. Roget did most of the talking, appearing loud and argumentative.

Frank and Joe crept around the bungalow, hoping to find an open window. But as they did, Werner stood up and went to the door. A ferocious-looking dog jumped to its feet. It was a Doberman pinscher that had been lying in a corner. Werner opened the door, letting the animal out.

The Doberman sensed Frank and Joe almost immediately and emitted a low growl.

"Let's get out of here," Joe cried under his breath.

As soon as the boys dashed away from the house, the vicious dog began barking. It lurched forward in pursuit, and before they knew it, the amateur detectives found themselves cornered at the top of the cliff. The Doberman's bark turned into a bare-teethed snarl when it found its prey trapped. The dog approached slowly and deliberately. Neither boy dared move.

"When I say jump, jump," Frank said, just barely moving his lips. The beach lay far below, but the incline of the bluff face would help break their fall. If they were lucky, they would get away with only minor injuries!

12 A Mysterious Signal

The beast drew closer, exposing canine fangs, until it was no more than a few feet from the frightened youths.

Suddenly, the Doberman's ears perked up. It seemed to linger in a moment of indecision, first looking back at the bungalow, then turning toward Frank and Joe with a snarl. Finally, the animal reluctantly retreated from the cliff and returned to the bungalow.

"What happened?" Joe gasped, amazed by the abrupt shift in their fortune.

"Werner probably called the dog back inside," Frank answered. "And not a second too soon."

"I didn't hear anything," Joe said.

"Remember the werewolf case?" the older Hardy asked, referring to *Night of the Werewolf*, a recent mystery the brothers had solved by tracking down the secret behind a killer beast that glowed in the dark.

"Yes, the crook in that case was using a dog whistle," Joe said, slapping his forehead for not having thought of it himself. "Werner must have used one of those things too!"

"Right," Frank went on. "The pitch of the whistle was too high for us to hear. Only dogs can . . . Wait a second!" Frank's voice rose in excitement. "Max, the horse trainer, had something hanging around his neck that looked like one of those whistles. I hadn't thought of it before, but there's no reason why an ordinary dog whistle couldn't be used on a horse!"

"It might account for the strange way those two horses spooked on us," Joe said, snapping his fingers.

"Not only that," Frank put in. "It might also account for the way Rutlidge's horses lost those races. They may have been trained to respond to a whistle!"

Vowing to return to the Rutlidge estate as soon as possible, the amateur detectives walked back down the bluff road.

But before they had gone more than a few

hundred feet, the geologists' pickup truck swung out of the driveway. Its headlight beams nearly caught Frank and Joe in the road, but the boys dove out of the way and threw themselves face down in a ditch as the truck sped past.

"I wonder if they're going back to the drilling site," said Joe as he stood up and tried to wipe off the sticky yellow clay smeared on his knees and elbows. "Maybe another shipment is coming in."

The two sleuths watched the truck disappear around a curve. A minute later it appeared again in the distance, rounding the next bend in the cliffs. It came to a stop on a promontory, pointing out over the dark expanse of the bay. Then its headlights flashed on and off three times.

"They're signaling," Joe said, as he watched the truck's lights flash again.

For a moment nothing happened. Then from far out on the bay came three answering flashes.

Immediately, Frank drew an arrow in the clay with his finger. It pointed in the exact direction of the answering signal. By reading the stars, he soon determined that the flashes had come from east by northeast.

"I'll bet that's where the oyster boat started out," Joe deduced.

"And possibly where our two missing geologists, if not the Rabbit himself, are located," Frank added.

The brothers continued, hoping to find a route down the bluff without having to go all the way back to the drilling site. Luckily, they discovered a shallow groove cut diagonally in the clay all the way to the beach. Taking it slowly, the boys descended along the groove, ending up a short distance from camp.

"Hey, what happened to you guys?" a worried Chet asked, as his bedraggled friends stumbled into camp.

Frank and Joe told their story to Chet and Fritz, then curled up in sleeping bags and fell fast asleep. They didn't wake until the smell of sizzling bacon wafted into their tent in the morning. Putting on a clean set of clothes, the brothers stepped out into the sun.

Chet sat in the sand with an open book in his lap. "I've been reading up on earthquakes," he said, flipping the page. "Did you know that tidal waves are caused by earthquakes in the ocean floor?"

"Yes, Chet," Frank replied. "Did you know that your bacon is burnt to a crisp?"

Chet dropped his book and forked what was left of his breakfast from the pan. With a shrug, he discarded the charred bacon, then put a few fresh strips in. "As I was saying," he went on, as he sat down with his book again, "tidal waves can travel hundreds of miles in a few minutes, and rise as high as a hundred feet or more by the time they hit shore. Can you imagine sitting at the beach when a hundred-foot wave suddenly comes out of nowhere? That's as big as a building!"

"Have you read about any quakes like the one we had in Bayport?" Joe asked.

Chet sniffed. "That one was too small to even count. There are around fifty thousand earthquakes every year."

"If it had damaged that nuclear power plant much more, it would've counted for plenty," said Frank, remembering how frightened Biff's uncle had been that the reactor core might have become cracked.

Conversation among the boys stopped when the oyster boat came into sight around the bluff. It was empty of its phony cargo.

"If we could do it without being spotted, this would be the perfect time to follow those guys," Joe remarked as he pulled his hat brim over his eyes to avoid the possibility of being recognized.

"Except we *would* be spotted," Frank said. "Also, we should pick up an extra can of fuel before we go on any long trips in the bay."

After breakfast, Frank and Joe took the skiff back to the fishing village. Fritz and Chet stayed to mind the camp and keep a lookout for any new developments.

At the village, the brothers found the man who

had rented them the skiff. He supplied them with an extra fuel can, and asked, "Did you catch anything yesterday?"

Frank shook his head. "No. We were thinking about heading farther into the bay, east by northeast. Any good spots out that way?"

"East by northeast? That ought to take you around Chapel Island. Not sure you'll find much fish there, except you might hook a bass if you're lucky."

"What's Chapel Island like?" Frank asked as he filled the fuel tank from a gas pump outside the general store.

The fisherman's face screwed up in a curious expression. "It's a strange island. Some folks moved there close to two hundred years ago, and to this day the same families live there, descendants of the original settlers. They don't mix with mainlanders. Stranger than that, for all appearances they still are living in the eighteenth century. Still speak the Queen's English."

Frank and Joe exchanged glances. Had the signals the night before come from Chapel Island?

Before heading for the small island, the two youths called Ambassador Kriegler from the general store.

The German ambassador sounded worried. He still had not heard from the boys' father, and was sure Mr. Hardy was in trouble. Frank told him they had found the infinity sign on one of the geologists' boring cylinders, then asked just how powerful a bomb the Rabbit might be able to build.

"We've had reports that the terrorists he's working for have been making some very sophisticated arms," the ambassador replied. "In fact, we believe they're capable of turning out small nuclear bombs of tremendous power."

"Nuclear bombs?" Frank cried into the receiver loud enough to attract the attention of several people in the store. He hushed his voice. "You mean those cylinders could be . . . ?"

The ambassador's tone was serious. "As I said, I wouldn't put anything past him. I also think it's time to get federal agents on this case. You boys have been running a terrible risk."

The older Hardy pleaded with Kriegler to give them a couple more days, explaining that they had already established a cover and were on the way to solving the mystery.

"One day is all I'll give you," the ambassador replied. "Then I'll have to turn this case over to the United States government."

Frank hung up the phone. Then, remembering something, he picked it up again and began to dial. "I forgot to call Detective Barnes," he told Joe while cupping his hand over the receiver. "He must be wondering what happened to us."

"Where in the world are you boys?" came the police detective's irritated voice over the receiver. "I let you go with the understanding you would help me with the diamond theft. The next thing I know, you're off chasing geologists, and you don't even bother to call with your whereabouts. I don't want to remind you again that all three of you are still under suspicion."

"I'm sorry," Frank said soothingly, "but this is the first chance we've had to call since yesterday afternoon. We're hot on the trail of our other case and we don't have much time left on it."

"Look," Barnes told the sleuth, his voice becoming weary. "This whole department is on my back for letting you leave the city. I promised the captain that you were working on the diamond theft. When he asks what you've uncovered so far, what am I supposed to say to him?"

Frank told the detective about their visit with Meg Rutlidge, their feelings about Boswell, and their suspicion that Max used a dog whistle to throw races.

"Okay, okay," Barnes said finally. "I'll look into Boswell, although it sounds crazy to me. But you two had better go back to the Rutlidge place and check up on this dog whistle theory of yours. And I mean now, or I'll have to ask you to come back to town."

Hanging up, Frank looked at his brother. "This leaves us between a rock and a hard place." He shrugged. "The ambassador is only giving us one more day before he sends in federal agents, and Barnes tells me if we don't work on the diamond case, we'll have to return to Washington."

"So we'll have to act fast," Joe concluded. "The Rutlidge place isn't far from here. If we leave now, we could be back before noon."

The sleuths put off their trip to Chapel Island and borrowed Fritz's sports car, which had been left at the village when they rented the boat the day before. Soon they were on the road toward Baltimore, figuring out ways they might be able to prove their theory about the dog whistle.

"Here we are," Joe announced, spotting the Rutlidge estate from the roadway and turning up the long drive toward the manor house.

The old butler, Wilkinson, greeted them at the door. "Max isn't here right now," he informed the sleuths in response to their questions. "If you would like to come in and wait for him, though, you are welcome to. I'll make some tea."

"Hold on," Frank urged Wilkinson as the butler

started toward the pantry. "We don't have that much time. Do you mind if we go to the stables and take a look around?"

"Go ahead," Wilkinson replied, showing them to the door.

At the stables, Frank and Joe found a dozen or more racehorses in their stalls.

"Look at this!" Joe said excitedly as he pulled a small, silver object from a peg on the wall.

Frank studied it for a second. "It's a dog whistle all right. Let's try it out."

"Hey, who are you?" a voice suddenly boomed from the other end of the stables.

Joe quickly stuffed the dog whistle in his pants pocket and turned to find a boy about his age running toward them. He was short, with straight brown hair and a thin face. In a moment, he stopped in front of Frank and Joe, told them he was the stable boy, and demanded to know what they wanted. His manner toward the visitors was haughty and condescending.

"The butler said we could come down here," Frank said coolly. "We're looking for Max."

"What for?" the stable boy asked, folding his arms and eyeing the two sleuths with an air of superiority.

Joe nudged his brother and took over. "We were

thinking of doing some riding," he told the boy. "In fact, this looks like a good horse right here." Joe motioned with his head toward a black colt.

"Max wouldn't let you ride Blue Lightning. Anyway," the boy continued with a smirk, "you guys wouldn't be able to handle him. That's a fast horse. He'd throw you in a second."

"But you're so great you could ride him with no sweat," Frank challenged the cocky youth.

"That's right!" the boy shot back, grabbing a saddle from a rack on the wall.

Frank and Joe exchanged winks as they watched the stable hand saddle up the young racehorse. Then he led Blue Lightning outside and mounted him.

"Watch this!" the stable boy shouted and gave the thoroughbred a kick.

Blue Lightning took off, galloping at full speed over the breeding farm's rolling fields. Frank and Joe watched as horse and rider rounded the far end of the pasture and started back. The stable boy was, in fact, a very good jockey, maneuvering the high-strung animal expertly across the field.

"Okay, do it now," Frank told his brother when the horse was about halfway back.

Joe lifted the dog whistle to his lips and blew. Suddenly Blue Lightning lost his stride, faltering noticeably and slowing down.

"Let's go," Frank said, looking at his watch.

They hurried from the stables, leaving the cocky jockey out in the field to wonder what had gone wrong.

"So our theory was right," Joe said, driving the red sports car back toward the yellow bluffs. "But it still beats me what it has to do with the stolen diamond."

"I don't know," Frank commented. "Let's give Barnes a call when we get back to the fishing village, though. Then we'll go to Chapel Island. The day's awasting."

A short time after the sleuths arrived at the village, they were out on the bay in the rented skiff, heading east by northeast. A light breeze made a slight ripple in the surface of the otherwise calm waters, and visibility was good but for a thin haze on the horizon.

"I think I see the island," Joe said after a while. He shaded his eyes from the sun and peered ahead.

A church steeple could be seen in the distance, as if rising out of the bay. A few minutes later the outline of the shore appeared beneath the steeple!

13 Island Hideout

The day had grown hot and humid by the time the sleuths' skiff reached the banks of Chapel Island. Joe attached the painter to a bush limb that hung over the water, and the two boys hacked their way inland through dense foliage.

"There's a road over here," Frank said after he had gone about thirty feet into the thick bushes.

A narrow dirt lane wound its way toward either end of Chapel Island. Using his penknife, Joe notched a groove in the bark of a tree, marking the spot where the skiff was tied.

"Which way do you think we should go?" the blond youth puzzled aloud, looking first in one direction, then the other.

Unable to determine which was the better way, Frank made a guess. "We can't get too lost in a place this size. Let's try this way." He then started down the road to the left, which seemed to head more toward the main body of the island.

The narrow lane followed the edge of Chapel Island, looping around the far end and continuing to the back side. Tracks in the dirt indicated that the road was used by horse and buggy, but these were the only signs of habitation the brothers could find as they walked through a forest of bushes and tall trees. The mosquitoes, which thrived in this kind of weather, were bothering them now and then, but it was bearable.

On the far side of the island, Frank and Joe came across a cemetery. In it were several dozen gravestones dating back to the 1700s. Curiously, many of the names on the markers were either Stone or Levenston, with few exceptions.

Joe stooped to inspect a monument dated 1706. "This looks like the oldest one here," he said. "Samuel B. Levenston. Could have been the first settler."

"Thou art wrong!" hailed a voice from the roadway.

The sleuths, who had been too busy looking over the graves to notice a horse and buggy coming down the road, now stood up as a man in simple black clothes and hat addressed them. He had dark, bushy eyebrows and a sharply chiseled nose.

"Jacob F. Stone was the first man to settle here," the stranger continued, pointing to another grave which was dated 1712. "Samuel Levenston was but the first to pass away upon this isle."

With that, the man's bushy eyebrows furrowed and he regarded the visitors with interest. "Now tell me," he said. "Why doest thou come here? And where art thou going?"

Taken aback by the buggy rider's odd blend of early English and modern dialect, Frank and Joe stood mute for a few seconds before answering. Finally, Frank spoke. "We would like to visit the island church. Are you going that way?"

"Verily, there is but one road. And to the church it leads," answered the man. "Come, I will carry thee hence." He made room for the two boys on the buggy seat.

Once aboard, Frank and Joe introduced themselves.

"And I am Jeremiah Stone," the driver answered. He chucked the reins and his horse started slowly down the road. "We have few strangers come to our island. May I ask what brings thee here?"

"We're looking for some men who might be here," said Joe. "They would also be strangers, possibly posing as oystermen."

Jeremiah Stone looked questioningly at his passengers. "Would these men be friends of thine?"

"Not at all," Frank said quickly. "We have reason to believe they're part of a dangerous gang of terrorists."

The driver frowned. "Mainlanders always bring trouble with them. Yes, I have read about terrorists in the newspapers. Methinks the world is now a very sinful place indeed."

"Is that why you speak early English and drive a horse and buggy instead of a car, to escape the modern world?" Frank queried with a hint of challenge in his voice.

Jeremiah Stone's voice rose in reply. "Ye think our community backward and stupid? We want no part of thine evil world. We choose to live here in peace as did our forefathers. But still trouble comes. Terrorists! I hope thee finds thy terrorists and begone."

"If you help us, we will be gone soon," Frank said calmly. "Have any other strangers been here recently that you know of?"

The man's disposition softened. "It is true there is a newcomer. He too, like all mainlanders, is unfriendly and Godless. He hides in his cottage, does not attend church, not even on the Sabbath. Some of us have tried to befriend him, but he will not be swayed."

"Can you take us to him?" Joe asked.

"If thou wisheth," Jeremiah responded.

Turning a corner in the dirt road, the boys found themselves entering a small community. Old Victorian houses, decorated with gingerbread latticework, clustered about a wooden church. White picket fences lined the unpaved street. Women wearing calico dresses and carrying parasols strolled by. Men wore clothing similar to Jeremiah's. They watched the young visitors with curiosity, tipping their hats at the buggy.

"Most of the tombstones in the graveyard have the names Stone or Levenston on them," Frank remarked. "Are the people living here direct descendants of those original settlers?"

"Many are indeed," Jeremiah answered. "Jacob F. Stone is my great-great-great-grandfather's grandfather, and most of those thou seest are related to either him or Samuel Levenston."

"Isn't there danger of too much inbreeding?" Joe asked.

"The church sees to it that we are in no such danger," Jeremiah answered defensively. "We have been careful to bring new blood to our community by marrying outsiders. But the newcomers must choose to live according to our heritage."

As the man spoke, he used less and less of the old English. It became clear that the church played a very strong role in the survival of the island community, and that the English they spoke was more the result of following the language in the Bible than it was of carrying it on from previous generations. This made the sleuths wonder all the more about the meaning of the signals that might well have come from the church steeple.

Jeremiah stopped in front of a cottage at the edge of town. The lawn was overgrown with weeds, and a television antenna stood on the roof.

"The newcomer lives here," Jeremiah announced. "He hides away and watches television, an evil machine which we who live here shun. His name is Jonathan Welsh."

Frank and Joe noted that none of the other houses had antennas.

"Why did he come here if not to share your way of life?" Frank wondered aloud.

"I do not know his reasons. He just arrived one day with his pockets overflowing with money and bought the house. Many of us did not want him here, but we needed money for supplies from the mainland. Now methinks it was a grave mistake."

The two sleuths went to the front door of the cottage and knocked, but no one answered. The sound of a radio or television was faintly audible. They knocked again without success, then Frank yelled Mr. Welsh's name through the closed door.

"Let's get out of here," Joe urged, afraid that the man in the cottage might be concocting an unpleasant surprise for the young detectives. "That might be the Rabbit in there, or worse."

"I thought of that," Frank said. "But I doubt he would want to blow a cover he went to such lengths to make just to get rid of us. I suggest we ask Jeremiah to see if he can lure him out. He may have more luck."

Jeremiah agreed to try convincing the cottage's occupant to open up. Frank and Joe hid in some nearby bushes where they could see the front door clearly. In a couple of minutes, Jeremiah had talked the new island resident into opening the door just wide enough to stick his head out.

"Well, he's not the Rabbit," Frank whispered. "But he still could be part of the gang."

Joe stared intently at the face in the door. Then he snapped his fingers. "That man is Arthur Rutlidge! Remember that picture of him hanging on the wall of his estate?"

"Yes!" Frank exclaimed under his breath. "So he's not dead at all. That whole boating accident was a fake!"

Both boys sprang from the bushes and ran toward the cottage. Seeing them coming, Rutlidge slammed the door.

"Mr. Rutlidge!" Joe yelled through the door. "We

know it's you in there. Whatever you're afraid of, we have nothing to do with it."

After a short pause, the wealthy horse breeder spoke from behind the door. "Who sent you here?"

"We weren't sent by anyone," Frank answered.

"Then how do you know who I am?"

Frank explained that the diamond Rutlidge had willed to the museum had been stolen, and that they had come across Rutlidge's photo during their investigation of the theft. "We also believe your trainer, Max, was involved in throwing those races," Frank added, hoping the information would inspire Rutlidge to let them in.

The horse breeder opened the door. "Come in," he said anxiously, motioning to Jeremiah and the Hardys.

Once they were inside, Arthur Rutlidge quickly shut the door. He took Jeremiah aside and spoke in a threatening whisper, making him promise not to mention what he had overheard to anyone. The island resident nodded and departed.

Arthur Rutlidge turned toward Frank and Joe. "What's this about my diamond being stolen? And how did you find me here? What do you want?"

"First tell us why you faked that boating accident and went into hiding," Frank replied directly. "Did it have something to do with the Faith diamond?"

Rutlidge looked nervous. He had lost weight

since his picture with the horse had been taken. He also appeared tired and worn, like a hunted man who couldn't sleep at night. "I had to do it," he said slowly. "My life was threatened because of the diamond."

"So you changed your will and pretended to have the boating accident," Frank put in.

"That's correct. My sister, Meg, was to have the gem. But to protect her and the diamond, I willed it to the Smithsonian, where I thought it would be safe until I came from hiding and could reclaim it. I had suspected that the races were purposely thrown. Once people thought I was dead, I hoped the culprit would expose himself by being careless."

"We think he did," Frank said, and explained how Max had probably used the dog whistle when he had taken the boys riding. "As soon as we realized your trainer blew the whistle to throw our horses, the rest fell into place."

Rutlidge nodded. "So that's how it was done." Then his expression changed and he looked keenly at his guests. "Still, I would like to know how you tracked me here."

"There was a team of geologists in the museum the day the diamond was stolen," Joe said, watching the horse breeder for his reaction. "In following them for other reasons, we stumbled on you. Quite a coincidence, don't you agree?"

Frank took up the questioning. "Maybe you aren't telling us all you know."

Rutlidge flinched, then regained his composure. "I can't tell you any more than I already have." He sat up, having heard something on the television in the next room. "Come with me."

The brothers followed Rutlidge to the den. A horserace was being broadcast over the set.

"One of my horses is in this race. Number seven, Faith," he said as they sat down.

"The one you named after the diamond to disprove the curse," Joe observed.

"Yes. Since I am not dead, the gem actually still belongs to me and not the Smithsonian. When I come out from hiding, it will be clear that the stone's powers are a hoax, that it belonged to me all along, and that my horse ran well in spite of it."

"Providing Faith does run well," Frank cautioned. "And providing the diamond is recovered."

The race began. Faith had a slow start and was several lengths behind the leaders as they came into the initial turn. By the time the horses were halfway down the first stretch, however, Faith had moved up into the pack and was gaining slowly. Rutlidge clenched his fist, urging his horse on as she rounded the far turn and broke outside to challenge the leader. The finish was neck to neck, with Faith taking it by a nose!

Rutlidge shot out of his seat and clapped his hands. "Just wait till they find out I'm still alive! They'll eat their words about that diamond causing my horses to lose. I'll get Max and Jensen behind bars before they know what hit them!"

Frank jumped up from his chair. "Did you say Jensen?" he exclaimed in surprise.

14 The Swarm

Rutlidge blinked, opened his mouth to say something, then stopped. "I . . . I've told you enough already," he murmured at last. "For your own good, drop this investigation right now. It isn't safe here!"

"Is Wayne Jensen behind all this?" the older Hardy brother persisted. "Did he try to force you into selling the stone by purposely bringing on your misfortune?"

"I think you boys ought to leave," the horse breeder said sharply. Then he sank wearily back in his chair. "Go back home."

Seeing they would get no further with the frightened man, Frank and Joe left.

"He sure is worried about something," Joe said as

they walked down the dirt road toward the church.

"Being cooped up like that can drive a guy nuts after a while," Frank said. "But it makes me wonder whether the Rabbit has more targets than just us."

Arriving at the Chapel Island church, the brothers found the minister and questioned him about recent visits from strangers. If the flashing signals had come from the steeple belfry, he might have seen something.

The aging cleric's mouth bent down at the corners. " 'Tis an interesting thing thou asks, for a man who is a stranger to mine eyes has of late joined our evening services. A crude man he is, but I be pleased that he came amongst us to find peace with God. I only hope it is not too late," the minister added, shaking his head. "Doest thou know this man?"

"His name wouldn't be Jonathan Welsh, would it?" Frank asked, referring to the name Rutlidge had used to conceal his identity.

The minister shook his head. "No. I have visited Mr. Welsh. He is a good man. I can see that quite easily. But he is deathly afraid of something he will not speak of."

"Too afraid even to go to church?" Joe questioned.

"Afraid even to leave his cottage," the minister

answered. "Do you boys know something of his troubles?"

"Yes," Frank told him. "And whoever the stranger is who attends your evening services may be part of the problem. Do you have any idea where he lives?"

The minister told them the man had come from Mosquito Island, a low and marshy place that was inhabited only by oystermen during the cooler months of the year, when oysters were in season.

"I was surprised anyone would be there in the summer months," the cleric continued. "The little island swarms with mosquitoes. A soul could be gobbled up by the devilish creatures. One hardly can believe they are God's creation."

Thanking the minister for his help, the brothers left the old church. They followed the dirt road to their skiff, which was still tied to the branch where they had left it.

"I envy those people in a way," Joe commented as he got the outboard motor running and propelled the boat away from the island. "No worries about the modern world with all its problems."

"Don't kid yourself." Frank chuckled. "There were plenty of troubles a hundred years ago, too. Now we just have different kinds."

Following the shore, the boys rounded Chapel

Island. On the far side, another island appeared, lower and smaller than the one they had just visited.

"That must be Mosquito Island," said Joe, angling the craft away from shore.

"And there's the oyster boat!" Frank cried.

The same boat that had delivered the cylinders to the geologists emerged from a winding channel leading into the island. Joe throttled the outboard and sped off in the direction of the boat. The men aboard were looking out into the bay, away from the skiff, and the boys approached the oyster boat from the rear. Once the skiff was within fifty feet of the slow-moving craft, Joe gave it full throttle.

"Let's see their reaction when we pass them," he said. "Maybe it'll give us some clue as to what they're up to now."

When they heard the outboard, the phony oystermen looked back. Suddenly, they swung their boat hard to the left.

"Hold on!" Joe shouted to his brother as he turned the skiff abruptly to avoid hitting the boat broadside.

SMACK!!

The skiff swiped the side of the larger vessel. Both boys were thrown overboard as it flipped from the impact. By the time they had gathered their senses, they were in the water and the oyster boat was on its way across the bay.

Both Hardys were excellent swimmers. They made it back to the overturned skiff, then maneuvered it toward the nearby island by paddling and kicking.

"That wasn't the best idea we've had all day," Frank said wryly as they pushed the skiff up on a sandy beach.

"There wasn't much time to think of a better plan," his brother answered. "I just hope I can get this motor to work. It took in a lot of water."

Frank gazed beyond the beach. Mosquito Island seemed nothing more than scrubby bushes and marsh. Yet, the oyster boat had come from a marked channel. Somewhere up that channel had to be a landing. "I'm going to do some exploring," the dark-haired boy announced.

While Joe tried to clear the bay water from the outboard's fuel line, Frank worked his way inland, hoping to find the oystermen's base of operation. Within a few minutes, however, he came bounding back through the marsh at a full clip, waving wildly at the air around him.

"What happened?" Joe cried in alarm.

Without answering, Frank hurtled past his brother and dove headlong into the water. A moment passed before his head popped up again. "Mosquitoes," he sputtered. "I thought they'd eat me alive!"

Joe couldn't hold down his laughter. "I thought you had seen a ghost!" he bellowed, then doubled up in laughter again at the thought of his usually composed brother running like a madman from an army of mosquitoes.

Frank, although covered with bites, had to smile himself. "Okay, okay," he said at last. "That's enough. What about the motor?"

Joe's grin left his face. "I'll need tools to get it working, and they're back at the camp. Luckily, though, I found oars wedged under the seat. At least we can row back."

Taking turns at the oars, the sleuths made their way toward camp.

As the bluffs drew closer, Frank pointed ahead. "Doesn't that look like a 'V' to you?"

Joe stopped rowing and gazed at the face of the bluff. A huge letter "V" was cut in the yellow clay, extending from the top of the cliff almost to the water. "One of those grooves must have been what we used to climb down to the beach last night," he deduced. "What do you think it means?"

"Maybe it's the Roman numeral for five, or 'V' for victory," Frank guessed.

Stumped by the purpose of the huge letter, the boys continued rowing. By the time they arrived at camp, the sun had set. They were both sunburned and exhausted, and hoped Chet had a meal waiting for them. Neither Chet nor Fritz, however, was there.

"They were supposed to wait for us," Joe said anxiously.

Frank went to the tent and got a flashlight. He scanned the beach until the flashlight's beam landed on two sets of tracks leading away from camp. No unfamiliar footprints or signs of a scuffle were visible. "At least they left camp at their own will," he declared. "We'd better follow their tracks in any case."

Summoning their last reserves of energy, the tired sleuths jogged down the beach in search of their companions.

Suddenly, Frank turned off his flashlight and motioned for his brother to stop. In the darkness, someone was running toward them!

15 Kidnapped!

"Frank! Joe!" the figure hollered in a German accent.

"It's Fritz!" Joe shouted, running to meet him.

"Are you all right?" Frank asked the ambassador's son when the three of them were together.

"I think they got Chet!" Fritz gasped.

"Who got him?" Joe cried.

Fritz took a few seconds to catch his breath. "We . . . we were watching the geologists. The oyster boat came again, so we tried to get a closer look. They spotted us. I got away, but they must have captured Chet."

"Let's go!" Frank commanded his brother.

Leaving Fritz, who was too exhausted to run any

farther, Frank and Joe took off down the beach. They reached the geologists' drilling site to find the oyster boat gone and no one around. Without stopping, they scaled the bluff and ran along the road until they arrived at Dr. Werner's bungalow.

The pickup truck was parked outside. Inside, two men were roughly interrogating the geologist. Frank and Joe moved closer to the window. The Doberman was tied to a couch. The dog snarled and barked as one of the men, Roget, slapped Werner across the face. He was demanding something of the German, and threatening that he would put an end to him. The second man busily ransacked the house, pulling out drawers and ripping through furniture.

"The Rabbit," Frank murmured, identifying the man as the albino terrorist.

"Now's our chance," Joe said eagerly.

The brothers burst through the front door. Caught off guard, Roget and the Rabbit were struck by Frank and Joe's fists before they were able to react. But they recovered in an instant to return the punches.

"You two will pay for this!" the terrorist spat as he prepared to strike Frank again.

Frank ducked the Rabbit's fist and landed a stiff upper cut squarely on the man's jaw. The terrorist flew back against a chair, dizzied by the blow. Frank got ready to pounce, but the Rabbit quickly jumped up and hoisted the chair above his head.

Meanwhile, Joe was still exchanging blows with Roget, but was beginning to lose the upper hand in the fight.

Just then, the Doberman broke from its leash and lunged at the Rabbit. The terrorist brought the chair down heavily on the ferocious dog. It yelped with pain as the wood splintered against its back, but it only became more vicious as a result and lunged again. The Rabbit dodged the beast and ran for the door. Roget followed. In a few seconds, the two men were tearing out of the driveway in the pickup truck.

Werner, who had left the room during the fight, returned and calmed the excited animal.

"Where were you?" Frank said angrily to the geologist. "We could have used your help."

"You made a mistake in coming here," the bearded man spoke evenly. "I was in no danger."

"No danger?" Joe cried in disbelief. "Those two guys had it in for you! Do you know who that albino man is?"

"Yes. And I also know who you are. You are Joe Hardy and that is your brother Frank."

The brothers were stunned by the geologist's words. Finally, Frank spoke. "If you know who we are, maybe you can tell us what happened to our friend Chet."

"Or what happened to our father," Joe put in sharply.

The scientist's eyes narrowed. "I warned you to stay out of this and you did not listen."

"*You* warned us?" cried Joe. "When did . . . ?" Suddenly, he remembered the mysterious phone call they had received in Bayport. The man had spoken with a thick German accent. "You called us," he said, snapping his fingers.

Werner nodded. "If you had taken my advice, your friend would not be in trouble."

Joe made a move to grab the geologist, but stopped as the Doberman bared its teeth in warning.

"The Rabbit will be back," Werner went on. "Now I hope you are impressed that you should not be meddling. You know too much as it is. Your father and your friend will not be safe if you insist on pursuing this further."

"Look," Frank said, taking a step toward the geologist. "The federal government will be sending men down here tomorrow unless we give them a reason not to. So you had better cooperate with us. We saw the infinity sign on those boring cylinders and we know what they are."

Werner stared at Frank, not sure whether to believe his story. "I will tell you where your friend is," he said at last. "But I cannot tell you any more. You may call these government men if you wish, but remember, your father's safety is at stake. If you value his life, you will ask the government to stay away."

"Where's Chet?" Joe demanded.

"He is being held captive on Mosquito Island, several miles—"

"We know where it is," Joe said.

While Joe stayed with the geologist, trying to pry more information from him, Frank went into a back room of the bungalow and called the ambassador. Kriegler agreed to hold off sending in federal agents unless he did not hear from the boys by the following afternoon.

He was shocked to learn that Dr. Werner was involved with the terrorists. "The man has an excellent reputation," he said. "I can't believe he would do anything wrong."

"He might have been forced into cooperating with the gang," Frank said. "There's something very strange about this whole thing."

"I know," Kriegler said. "And it worries me that you have no help down there. Be extra careful, will you?"

Frank promised, then hung up and went back

into the living room. Joe had not had any success in shedding more light on the mystery. Werner's dog stood guard in the corner, ready to spring if the boys made a move toward his master.

"Come on," Frank said to his brother. "Let's find Chet."

The two sleuths left the bungalow and walked toward camp. On the way, Frank related his conversation with Kriegler.

"I'm glad he's holding off for another day," Joe said. "I just hope we can crack this case in the next twenty-four hours!"

"First thing we have to do is to find Chet," Frank decided, "and before we do, we have to fix the outboard and get a few hours' rest."

Back in their tent, the two exhausted youths fell asleep instantly. But by the first light of dawn, Frank and Joe were up and working on the skiff's motor. Fritz made a quick breakfast for them, and soon they were on their way in the gray morning light, heading east by northeast, while the ambassador's son remained to spy on the geologists.

The water wasn't as calm as it had been the day before. The wind had picked up and the small skiff bounced over choppy seas.

"If this gets any rougher," Frank called from the bow, "our boat won't be able to handle it. She's getting shaky as it is."

515

The wind increased and a line of dark clouds appeared on the horizon, moving rapidly down the bay in the direction of the boys.

"I'm going back to shore," Joe said, uneasy over the approaching storm. He swung the boat around. "We'd better wait this thing out."

As the skiff headed toward the bluffs, the wind and waves grew in force. Soon the storm was almost overhead. As the cliffs drew near, the brothers could make out someone scraping letters in the yellow clay with a shovel.

"That's Fritz!" Joe yelled. "He's writing something!"

The boys watched intently as Fritz's message became clear. BOMB it said in bold letters.

"Bomb?" Frank exclaimed. "He must be trying to warn us!"

Frank and Joe looked up and down the beach for any sign of the Rabbit. When they brought the skiff closer, Fritz waved his arms, frantically motioning for them to get away. But the storm was almost upon them!

Suddenly, something landed in the water near the skiff and exploded.

Kaboom!

16 Stormy Crossing

A column of water shot in the air, nearly swamping the small boat.

"Up there!" Joe hollered, as he pointed toward the top of the looming yellow bluffs.

Standing on the cliff's edge, silhouetted against the stormy sky, was the Rabbit. He hurled one small bomb after the next from his perch high above the two youths, who bobbed like sitting ducks in the rough waters.

"Let's get out of here!" Frank urged as another bomb barely missed their bow.

Giving it full throttle, Joe swung the skiff around. The bombs hit the water like a barrage of mortar shells, and he had to zigzag away from the shore to make a difficult target for the Rabbit.

By the time the sleuths were out of range of the terrorist's assault, dense, black clouds had rolled in overhead, bringing strong winds and a heavy rain with them.

"Hold her into the wind!" Frank shouted.

"I'm trying!" Joe answered, knowing he must direct the small craft into the oncoming waves to prevent it from being capsized.

But the waves, driven by the whistling gale, had grown too short and too steep to keep the skiff's nose angled at them. Frank searched the compartments under the seats for life jackets, but either the boat wasn't supplied with them or they had been lost in the encounter with the oystermen.

"Take her back in," Frank ordered.

"What about the Rabbit?" Joe cried, his clothes soaked with rain. "He'll be waiting for us."

Frank hesitated, unsure of his decision. The waves and wind grew with each second. "Take her ashore," he repeated at last.

A bolt of lightning shot from the dark sky, for a fraction of a second illuminating the wet, frightened faces of the two youths. Joe turned the skiff back toward the bluffs, now barely visible through the driving rain.

"I'll head her downwind," he said, hoping they could lose the Rabbit by landing farther along the shore under cover of the storm.

Again lightning lit up the sky. For an instant, the

sleuths could make out the figure at the top of the bluffs. The terrorist walked along the cliff's edge, steadily following the skiff as it moved down the coast. Joe imagined he saw the Rabbit grin, as if pleased by this game of cat and mouse.

"Watch out!" Frank screamed, warning his brother of an oncoming wave that threatened to swamp the tiny boat.

Joe's attention left the bluffs as he made a desperate effort to avoid the wave. But it was too late. The skiff was caught by its stern and turned on its end with an abrupt twist. A second later, both boys found themselves in the water. Their boat was quickly swallowed up by the churning seas.

Desperately, the young sleuths tried to swim toward shore. But the driving waves and wind were against them, and washed them even further into the stormy bay.

Just then, seemingly out of nowhere, a boat appeared, crashing through the waves in the direction of the helpless youths. It was an old, wooden sloop with a single raked mast. Frank and Joe yelled and waved at the approaching vessel. When it was close enough, the skipper threw a line with a life ring attached to the end. "Hold tight!" he yelled from aboard the sloop as the brothers grabbed the life ring.

Wet and shivering, they were soon pulled onto the boat's deck by a sturdy old man in a yellow rain slicker. "Go below and dry yourselves," he ordered.

Joe started to thank him for saving them, but the sailor interrupted by repeating his command. Then he returned to the sloop's tiller without another word.

In the boat's cabin, the boys found towels and blankets. Removing their wet clothes, they wrapped themselves in the blankets and huddled below deck until the storm was over. The dark clouds rolled away as quickly as they had come, and warm sunlight greeted the youths as they emerged from the cabin.

The sloop was manned solely by the old sailor, who had removed his rain slicker. Long, white whiskers flowed from his leathery skin. "You kids were stupid to be out here in this kind of weather," he scolded. "You're very lucky I spotted you. That skiff didn't have a chance in this storm."

Frank thanked the skipper for rescuing them, and explained that they had not expected the storm would be so severe.

The man's steel gray eyes softened. "Most of the time the bay is as gentle as a pond," he said, gazing across the expanse of water. "You could sail a dinghy from one end to the other. Then, just when you think she's a piece of cake, one of these thunder-bumpers will blow down out of the north. Can hit you like a brick before you have a chance to trim your sails, and all at once it's like being caught in a big washing machine. Many a skipper has learned the hard way to have respect for these waters."

The old salt paused for a moment to let his words sink in, then continued in a lighter tone. "I've seen it raining frogs from the skies during these storms."

"Raining frogs?" Joe asked, not sure if he had heard correctly.

The sailor chuckled. "Sometimes the wind comes up so hard and fast, it picks up little frogs from the shore and blows them out in the bay. Had a few land on my deck."

Finding the story hard to swallow, Frank just nodded politely and changed the subject. "You're a crabber?" he asked, having noticed some crab pots piled in the sloop's stern.

"In the summer I am," the old man replied. "The rest of the year, I'm an oysterer. Been at it my whole life."

"Do you know Mosquito Island?" Joe queried.

The white-whiskered skipper looked curiously at his two passengers. "Spent many a year working out that way. What makes you ask?"

"We have a friend who's being held captive there," Frank said directly.

The old salt's curiosity turned to surprise as the boys explained that the island might be the head-quarters for a gang of terrorists, who presently held Chet at their mercy. Without hesitation, he volunteered to take them there.

"This could well be dangerous," Frank warned. "Those men would as soon get rid of us as swat a fly."

"When you're my age, you haven't time to be scared of anyone," the skipper said with a glimmer in his eyes. "By the way, my name is Jake, and the boat's called *Marybelle*."

"Frank and Joe Hardy," Frank introduced himself and his brother.

Jake acknowledged it with a grin, then let out the sloop's sail and set course for Mosquito Island. The boys changed back to their clothes, which they had hung out on deck to dry. The wind was still fresh from the north, and the old sailing vessel made good time as it cut its way through the choppy bay waters.

"Mosquito Island is next to the island I came from," Jake told the sleuths.

"You lived on Chapel Island?" Joe asked.

"That's right. I'm descended from the original settlers."

"Are you a Stone?"

The old skipper nodded. "Jacob Stone the Sixth. How do you know about the Stones?"

Frank explained how they had visited Chapel Island the day before and met Jeremiah Stone. Then he asked why Jake had left the island.

"Wanted to get out and see the world," was the old man's reply. "I got itchy with all their talk about how evil it was. Made me go and take a look for myself. I've been around the world several times on boats, and believe me, I've seen more than my share of it. Now I'm thinking of going back to the island and retiring there in peace. Only from what you boys tell me, even Chapel Island has trouble brewing on its back porch. It's a shame."

"Well, with your help," Frank said, "we might be able to put an end to it right now."

Jake sailed the sloop around Chapel Island, and the smaller, mosquito-infested island came into view.

"Take the tiller," the skipper told Frank as they approached.

Frank took control of the sloop's steering while Jake stepped down into the cabin. The old man reappeared a moment later with a bottle of greenish liquid, which he applied to his face and arms. He then handed it to his passengers. "Here, put this on. It'll keep those mosquitos from eating you alive."

The boys doused themselves liberally with the homemade insect repellent. It smelled like rotting fish.

"Phew!" Joe exclaimed at the odor. "I sure hope it works."

Rounding Mosquito Island, Jake sailed into the channel, which was lined with thick underbrush, and negotiated his way expertly along its winding course.

"There's the landing," Joe said in a hushed tone as they rounded a corner.

A run-down wooden shack and a dock were the only constructions at the landing site. The oyster boat wasn't there, and there was no sign of anyone. Noiselessly, Jake pulled up to the dock and the two sleuths hopped from the boat.

In crouched positions, Frank and Joe crept toward the wooden shack. If someone was inside, they wanted to catch him by surprise. Frank motioned for Joe to sneak behind the shack while he tried the front entrance.

After listening intently for a few minutes, Frank opened the door with a swift kick. It flew back without resistance, and he prepared to defend himself.

At first, the shack did seem to be empty. But as the young detective's eyes adjusted to the dim light, he saw three figures lying on the floor, bound and gagged. Just then Joe came back, and both boys rushed inside.

"Dad!" Joe cried out.

17 The Chase Quickens

Fenton Hardy and Chet, both bound by their wrists and ankles with heavy rope, made anxious noises through their gags. The third captive was a girl with long, chestnut brown hair. She stared at Frank and Joe with fear, not knowing whether they meant her harm or not.

"See if Jake has a knife," Frank said to his brother.

Joe ran back to the sloop while Frank quickly untied the captives' gags. Mosquito bites covered their exposed faces and arms.

"What happened? What are you doing here?" Frank asked his father, who was supposed to be in Germany.

"I'd like to know the same thing from you," the famous detective replied with a smile. "But I'm certainly glad you came. We haven't much time left. I'll tell you all about it later. Right now let's get these ropes off."

Using the sharp edge of an oyster shell he found on the floor, Frank started cutting his father's ropes. Joe returned with Jake's rigging knife, which he used to free Chet and the girl.

"Boy, I'm sure happy you guys showed up." Chet groaned as he rose to his feet. "I must have been lunch for five hundred mosquitoes!"

"Well, now you know what it's like to be the eat*ee* instead of the eater," Joe kidded his pal.

"All I know," Chet replied, swatting his arm as another mosquito prepared to dine, "is that I want to get off this island, and pronto!"

The chestnut-haired girl, realizing that the boys were there to help them escape, let out a flood of words in German. Teary-eyed, she thanked her rescuers. She seemed to be about sixteen. Joe began to question her, wondering how she became mixed up in this affair. But Mr. Hardy insisted that they make their escape without hesitation.

Hurrying from the shack, the group boarded the old sloop. Jake hoisted his sail. In a few minutes, they were back on the bay.

Mr. Hardy listened eagerly to his sons' story. "It

all seems to fit," he said, once the boys had finished recounting their adventures. "The Rabbit was hired by a terrorist organization called Vici, which means 'I conquered,' in Latin. Vici, in turn, is under contract by a Middle Eastern group involved in the illegal export of oil. The man who tried to buy the stolen diamond from you, Wayne Jensen, is the American connection for the Middle Eastern organization."

The young detectives seemed puzzled. "But why does Jensen want the diamond?" Frank asked.

"And what is the gang doing here?" Joe added. "And why are the geologists involved?"

Frank frowned. "Wait a minute. You say Jensen is involved in oil dealings, Dad?"

Mr. Hardy nodded.

"I wonder if there's a nuclear power plant near Yellow Clay Cliffs," Frank went on.

"As a matter of fact, there is," Mr. Hardy replied. "It's a couple of miles west of the cliffs."

"That's it!" Frank cried out. "I think I know what that gang is up to!"

Joe and Mr. Hardy caught on the same instant.

"You mean they're fabricating earthquakes to sabotage nuclear power plants in order to further their oil interests?" Joe asked his brother.

"It's possible," Mr. Hardy said. "I learned that the terrorists were actively producing small and powerful nuclear bombs, but I didn't know for what purpose. I was on the gang's trail when they transported the bombs to a waiting freighter on the coast of Spain. Unfortunately, I was captured while attempting to save this young lady from being kidnapped aboard the ship. I was then taken on the same freighter myself, where I was kept prisoner until we arrived here a little over a week ago."

"Do you know who the girl is?" Frank asked.

"No. But I overheard the men saying that the last piece of the bomb was being taken to Yellow Clay Cliffs today, and that the whole thing would be over by this evening."

"But if the gang is causing the earthquakes with the bombs, what is Dr. Werner's part in this?" Joe spoke up.

Just then the German girl, who had been trying to understand what she could of the conversation, became excited. "Werner!" She exclaimed. Speaking in her native tongue, she told them that she was Katerina Werner, Dr. Hasso Werner's daughter. She had been kidnapped from her home in Germany while her father was working on a geology project in the United States.

Joe snapped his fingers. "That explains why Dr. Werner got mixed up with the terrorists! They forced him into serving them by kidnapping his daughter!"

"It also explains why Werner wanted us to stay out of his way," Frank put in. "He was trying to protect Katerina, and he didn't want us to become victims of the Rabbit and his gang. That's why he tried warning us off the case!"

The sun began to sink below the horizon as the sloop neared the mainland shore. Jake, now almost as anxious as his passengers to apprehend the gang, steered a steady course toward the geologists' drilling site. Mr. Hardy continued to discuss the mysterious case with his sons. Katerina gazed ahead. Her thoughts were filled with worry about her father being in the clutches of the terrorists, who might try to dispose of him once their mission was completed.

"We'll be getting there before long if this wind keeps up," the old sailor said, judging their distance from the yellow cliffs.

Frank stood up and surveyed the approaching shore. But they were still too far out in the bay for him to see any signs of activity on the beach.

"How did you come upon the information about the meeting at the Smithsonian?" he asked his father as he sat down again.

Mr. Hardy grinned. "I discovered some communication between two members of the terrorist ring," he replied. "At the time, I didn't know what it meant, or else I would have given you more specific instructions. Shortly afterward, I was captured. I'm glad the message got to you through Ambassador Kriegler, even though it was a dangerous mission."

"We've had some close calls," Frank admitted. "And it looks as if we still have a rough time ahead of us. If the Rabbit means to use his bomb tonight, none of us are safe by a long shot."

"We also left the ambassador's son, Fritz, in a bad spot," Joe put in.

The detective appeared thoughtful. "Our only hope is to catch the men before they have a chance to carry out their plan," he declared. "We should also contact Kriegler as soon as possible. We're outnumbered by those in the gang, and Kriegler might be able to get his men down here in time to pitch in. Werner may also be of great help to us once he finds out his daughter is safe."

When their father had finished speaking, Frank and Joe stationed themselves at the sloop's bow. Night had fallen as they drew near the beach. The oyster boat was not there, and the site was abandoned. The drilling equipment had been removed! Jake ran his boat up on the sand, and his passengers climbed out.

"We're too late!" Chet moaned, seeing that the cylinders were gone as well.

"We'll have to warn the power plant," Mr. Hardy

declared. "And we'll have to catch those crooks. If the Rabbit can set this bomb, he may also be able to deactivate it. We'll have to act fast!"

"I can get you to the power plant," Jake volunteered. "My place is just a short trip up the coast and I have my car there."

All except Frank and Joe returned to the sloop.

"I'll contact Kriegler from the power plant," Mr. Hardy called to his sons as he boarded the boat. "Do what you can to find those men. But be careful!"

The brothers turned and began to scale the steep path up the bluff face. Once up to the clay cliff road, they ran in the direction of Werner's bungalow.

18 Night Rendezvous

The lights were out in the geologist's house. But the pickup truck was in the driveway, and another car was parked next to it.

"A gray Peugeot," Frank muttered. "I bet that's the car that trailed Fritz and Chet to the dock!"

"But where are the men?" Joe asked, puzzled. "They didn't leave their truck so they could hike their way out of this wilderness!"

"No," his brother agreed. "They must be around somewhere."

The two stopped in their tracks, not knowing in which direction to go. The night was calm, the only sound the constant chirp of crickets and the washing of waves on the beach far below.

"The oyster boat," said Frank in a hushed tone. "It wasn't at the island or the drilling site. Maybe that's how they're making their getaway!"

The boys hurried to the edge of the bluff and looked out over the dark water.

"We lost them," Joe cried in frustration. "They probably went back to the island to pick up their hostages. I bet we went right by those creeps on our way here."

"Ships passing in the night," Frank reflected, searching the water below them with his eyes.

"Hey, look!" Joe said suddenly. He pointed at the horizon, where a light flashed dimly in the distance. "Signals from Chapel Island again. Maybe that's where they are!"

"You could be right," Frank said, growing excited. "Arthur Rutlidge might be part of this thing after all. Also, those signals mean at least someone is still over here to communicate with."

The brothers all at once sensed that they might not be alone on the bluff. They drew away from the cliff's edge to some bushes on the other side of the road, listening intently.

The light repeated its signal at short intervals, as if expecting responding flashes. The boys kept their eyes open for an answer from their side of the bay. But the signal continued with no response.

Frank nudged his younger brother. "Doesn't it

look like Morse code, three short flashes and one long one?"

Familiar with the old method used to send messages by telegraph, Joe watched as the signal repeated itself. "Yes," he said at last with a nod. "In Morse code it would stand for the letter 'V.' Do you think that could have something to do with the 'V' we saw on the face of the bluff?"

"Not just that," the older boy answered. "Remember what Dad said? The terrorists' organization is called Vici. That could be their pickup signal, and the 'V' on the bluff could be the pickup point."

"I've got an idea," Joe said after a short pause. "Come on, hurry!"

The two sleuths returned to Werner's bungalow. In less than a minute, Joe had the geologists' truck hot-wired, and they drove it out of the driveway onto the bluff road. Stopping on the promontory where Roget had signaled with his headlights, Joe flashed out the letter "V" in Morse code. They could see an answer in the distance and noticed that the signal became increasingly brighter and clearer, as if the source was getting closer.

"Wait a second," breathed Joe. "Those flashes are coming from a boat, not Chapel Island. Someone out there thinks we're the gang, and is about to pick us up!"

Frank looked at his brother. "That's great, but

what do you plan to do when they get here?"

"I don't know," Joe answered. "I just hope Dad brings help soon."

The sleuths watched as the boat drew closer. Their father and the federal agents would not arrive for a while, so they climbed down the cliff to the beach, hoping the darkness would somehow make it possible for them to take advantage of the situation. But they were still without a plan.

Suddenly, a voice spoke up behind them. "What are you doing here?"

The boys wheeled around. Dr. Werner stepped out of the shadows, glaring at them. "How many times do I have to tell you to stay out of this?" he cried out. "You have no idea what danger you are causing for yourselves and others."

"Your daughter Katerina is safe, sir," Frank told him quickly.

The geologist's jaw dropped and his eyes grew wide. "My—my daughter? What are you talking about?"

"Your daughter was being held captive on Mosquito Island with our father and our friend," Frank continued. "We rescued her and she's now with our dad at the power plant to warn them of the upcoming nuclear explosion. Do you still want us to stay out of this?"

Overcome with relief, Werner nearly fainted. In a moment, however, he composed himself and thanked the boys. "What can I do to show you my gratitude?" he asked.

"You can help us capture the men who put you up to this," Joe told him. "A boat should be arriving here soon and we'll need your help to get aboard."

"Yes, I know. I will gladly help," the German geologist replied.

Just then the boat, which had been giving the "V" signal, appeared out of the night, coming toward the beach at a rapid pace.

"It's Jensen's yacht!" Joe cried, recognizing the sixty-foot cabin cruiser.

Werner waved as the large boat's spotlight scanned the beach. Frank and Joe ducked behind a log lying in the sand. The spotlight beam rested on the geologist, and the yacht slowed as it eased its way into the landing spot at the beach. A boarding ladder was thrown from the bow by a deckhand. Werner started up the ladder and reached out for the sailor to pull him aboard.

Then, with a quick yank, he grabbed the man's hand and pulled him over the side. At the same moment, the two young sleuths jumped from behind the log. Before the deckhand could yell for help, they knocked him out. Then Frank and Joe boarded the yacht behind Werner. They quickly overcame a second man on their way to the cabin. When they threw open the door, they found a startled Wayne Jensen at the yacht's controls.

Jensen shot an acid glance at Frank and Joe, then stared at the geologist. "So you decided to double-cross us, eh, Werner?" he said maliciously. "You know what will happen to your daughter if you don't cooperate."

Werner's eyes became slits. "Tie him up," he said to the Hardys, then pushed Jensen aside and took control of the yacht himself.

Finding spare rope in a storage compartment, the sleuths bound the struggling oilman's hands and feet. Werner backed the sixty-foot yacht away from the beach and turned it around.

"Where are the others?" Frank asked the geologist.

"Probably on Mosquito Island," Werner replied. "Jensen was going to pick them up first, then come by and get me. I don't know why they changed their plan."

Joe explained that they had signaled Jensen from the bluff.

"Very clever," Jensen sneered, struggling with his ropes. "But I'm afraid you're a little late for the big coup."

Frank looked anxiously from Jensen to Werner,

remembering that the bomb was probably soon to go off. "Are we too late?" he asked.

The geologist sighed. "I hope not. I will explain everything, but right now there's a signal being given to us ahead."

Werner steered the yacht toward a light that flashed the "V" code. It came from the direction of Mosquito Island.

"We're expecting help at the drilling site soon," Frank said. "If we can get the gang on board and take them there, we'll be all right."

Werner glanced at the sleuths. "That may not be such an easy trick. When those men find their hostages missing, they will be very angry, and very suspicious, especially the Rabbit." The geologist switched on the yacht's searchlight. "There they are now, on the oyster boat."

The craft was just off the small island. It carried not only the albino terrorist, but Werner's entire team.

"Those men aren't really geologists, are they?" Joe said to Werner.

"No. They're members of the Vici terrorist gang," Dr. Werner answered bitterly. "I'm the only real geologist among them. The big one, Roget, is their leader."

As the yacht made ready to intercept the oyster boat, the sleuths gagged Jensen. Frank put on the oilman's captain's hat and jacket, then took the controls while Werner went forward to assist the men aboard. Joe crouched in the corner of the cabin, ready to spring if anyone tried to enter.

Soon the two boats met.

"Where's my Katerina?" Werner said angrily to Roget, pretending to be upset that his daughter was not on the boat. "It is over now and you must return her to me."

Roget stepped up on the yacht's deck. "We will give her back only after the Rabbit has received his payment," he lied, as if the girl were still in their clutches. "We have hidden her."

Following Roget came the Rabbit. His white hair and pinkish skin appeared ghostlike in the moonlight. "I will receive my payment tonight," he hissed threateningly to Werner. His pink eyes shifted about, focusing only for an instant on the geologist. "If I am not satisfied, your precious daughter will die!"

19 Delicate Cargo

"You've said enough," Werner interrupted the terrorist. "I will see to it that you are given what you deserve."

The Rabbit mumbled something under his breath as he turned from the geologist, watching the rest of the men climb on deck and file into the yacht's stateroom. Only a short hallway and a door separated the terrorists from the sleuths in the control cabin.

All was quiet while Frank put the cruiser in gear and headed toward the bluffs, where he hoped Mr. Hardy would be waiting with the federal agents. The oyster boat was left drifting in the bay.

Suddenly, the door leading from the stateroom to

the control cabin opened part way. Dr. Werner's voice could be heard from the other side.

"He will discuss it with you later," the geologist argued. "Mr. Jensen told me he doesn't want to be bothered with the subject right now."

"I have no more time to waste with either you or Jensen," the Rabbit grumbled, and the cabin door opened further.

Frank pulled his cap down, hiding his face. Joe pressed himself against the wall to one side of the door. If they could take the Rabbit quickly enough, he wouldn't have time to cry out an alarm to the others.

"Do you hear me, Mr. Jensen?" the Rabbit challenged. "I must be paid tonight, or nobody will go anywhere."

In a frantic gesture, Werner grabbed the terrorist's arm, pulling him back into the hall before he had a chance to recognize Frank. "You will get nothing until my daughter is given back to me!" the geologist shouted in a display of wild desperation. "You lying cheat! You told me Katerina would be on the oyster boat with you!"

Werner kept yelling as he wrestled the Rabbit down the hall away from the yacht's control cabin. Several minutes later, he reappeared, his jacket torn and his jaw bruised. "Well, it worked," he told the two sleuths with a grin. "Are we almost there? I don't know how much longer I can hold these people off."

"We should be arriving soon," Frank replied.

"Dad better be there with help," Joe put in anxiously.

As the huge motor yacht moved through the water, Dr. Werner and the young sleuths watched intently for the bluffs to appear out of the darkness.

"I will now explain to you what happened," the geologist told the boys in a hushed tone. "I did not know at first what the Vici gang was up to, only that they had Katerina and I was to cooperate with them. All they told me was that they were testing something underground, and that I was to be in charge of boring holes for the tests. It was not until the first earthquake that I began to understand their intentions."

"The earthquake at Bayridge?" Frank asked.

Werner nodded. "Yes. The gang had developed a small nuclear bomb in the shape of core cylinders. Its explosion caused a minor earthquake." He paused for a moment, then went on. "At that point, I became very suspicious of their plan, so I tried to listen to what was being said behind my back. It turned out they had been hired by someone to sabotage nuclear power plants and make it appear as

543

if natural earthquakes caused the damage."

"We figured that," Frank said. "The Bayridge plant almost had a serious problem."

"We were at the facility when the quake hit," Joe added.

"Then you know what I am talking about," Werner whispered. "But that was only a test for the real show down here. The bomb that the Rabbit planted at the foot of the bluffs is three times more powerful than the one in Bayridge!"

Frank shot an accusing glance at the geologist. "And you were willing to go along with risking the lives of perhaps thousands of people to save your daughter?"

"I wanted to thwart their scheme," Werner replied solemnly. "I thought up a plan of my own. That's why I tried to prevent you boys from interfering."

Seeing the embarrassment on the youths' faces, Werner quickly added that if it had not been for them, the plan to save his daughter would not have worked.

"But the bomb has already been set," Joe said in alarm.

"It will go off," Werner told them. "But I studied the geological formation of the earth very carefully before we chose a drilling site. I misled the terrorists into believing the spot I picked would cause a severe quake. In fact, however, I selected a particularly poor place to set the bomb. The earth should absorb nearly all of the explosive's power without affecting the surface to any great extent."

"Are you sure of your calculations?" Frank asked.

"Yes and no," the geologist replied tensely. "The bomb will definitely not be as strong as Vici had planned. But exactly what its effect will be is impossible to know. It is set to go off at midnight, so we'll find out shortly."

Frank glanced at his watch. It was just past eleven o'clock. The bomb would explode in less than an hour. "How did Vici expect to fool everyone with the earthquakes?" the dark-haired sleuth queried. "Geologists would soon learn that they were caused by the bombs, wouldn't they?"

"I expect they would," Werner shrugged. "But the terrorists were hoping that the mysterious quakes would take a while to investigate, giving them time to cause a number of such incidents before being found out."

"There are the bluffs!" Joe said suddenly, turning their attention. Out of the night, the yellow cliffs rose up rapidly in front of them. A cluster of figures were visible on the beach. "It must be Dad and the federal agents!" The blond-haired youth's voice cracked with excitement.

Frank headed the craft toward shore. "We'll have

to act fast," he said, taking command. "I'm going to ram her up against the beach."

The yacht slackened speed only a little as it neared the dock. Frank wanted to hit the beach with enough impact to temporarily panic the gang members. Werner went to the bow, where he would be able to shout a warning to those waiting below the cliffs.

With a crunch, the yacht smacked the piling. The terrorists, unprepared for the sudden stop, flew against the walls of the stateroom. By the time they recovered, Dr. Werner had already hopped off the boat to alert the federal agents to take cover.

"Let's get them!" Frank exclaimed, abandoning the yacht's controls. The boys ran onto the deck and, with swift blows, greeted the dazed terrorists as they filed out of the stateroom. Soon, the brothers were joined by several federal agents. The fighting on deck became heavy. Both sides were evenly matched at first, but as more agents climbed aboard, they managed to subdue the gang members.

From the corner of his eye, Frank saw one of the men creep noiselessly over the side. Almost invisible, he moved quickly across the beach and began to scale the bluff. "The Rabbit's getting away!" the older Hardy called to his brother, who was helping to handcuff one of the oyster boat operators.

Both boys took off after the albino terrorist. By the time they reached the bottom of the bluff, however, the Rabbit had already made it to the top.

"We can't lose him," Joe cried, scrambling upward as fast as he could.

Once on the yellow clay road, the sleuths raced in the direction of Werner's bungalow. They feared the Rabbit would make his escape in the gray sedan, and expected that at any second the vehicle would come speeding toward them from around a bend. But when they arrived at the house, they found themselves witness to a peculiar scene.

Fritz and Werner's Doberman had the terrorist cornered in the driveway. The boy held the dog by its leash, preventing the angry beast from pouncing upon the Rabbit.

"Makes a good rabbit dog, don't you think?" the ambassador's son told Frank and Joe with a restrained chuckle.

The Rabbit's eyes, in fact, had the wild look of a cornered animal. He glanced from Fritz to the Hardy brothers, and a fiendish grin spread over his face. "I've been waiting for you punks to show up," he sneered, then drew an object from his jacket pocket. "Now that I have all of you together, I have a little present for you."

"It's a bomb!" Joe cried.

20 Eruption

The terrorist cocked his arm to heave the bomb.
Fritz let go of the ferocious dog, and before the
Rabbit had time to deliver his goods, he was on the
ground. Frank grabbed the bomb from the man's
hand and carefully placed it some distance away. It
would go off only on impact.

Pulling the Doberman off the Rabbit, the boys
quickly used Joe's belt to bind the albino's hands
behind his back. The cornered terrorist struggled
violently, but finally realized that he was helpless
against the young detectives.

"That's what's known as a quarterback sack,"
Frank quipped, referring to a football play in which

the quarterback is tackled before he has time to throw the ball.

"Right," Joe said, speaking to the now calmed dog. "You made a pretty good play."

"The game is not over yet," the Rabbit spat out.

"It's over for you," Frank replied sternly.

The three boys hoisted the man to his feet and led him down to the beach, where Mr. Hardy and the team of federal agents had the other terrorists tied together in the sand. The dog followed.

Seeing Dr. Werner and Katerina, the Doberman bounded toward them with glee. It jumped on its hind legs, and, putting its front paws on the girl's shoulders, wagged its tail and licked her in greeting.

"Stop it, Alex!" The girl giggled as she tried to avoid the animal's tongue.

Dr. Werner began to laugh too, in good spirits for the first time since Frank and Joe had met him.

Just then, Detective Barnes stepped out of the shadows. "Hi, boys. Just thought I'd come down to see what you were up to." The hazel-eyed police detective smiled.

"How did you get here?" Frank said with a puzzled expression as he shook Barnes's hand.

"Oh, I had been in touch with the ambassador,

and when he told me a little about what was going on, I decided to tag along."

The two sleuths took the detective aside to discuss the diamond theft. Barnes told them that he had followed up on the hunch they had about the curator.

"Boswell had some crazy notion that Arthur Rutlidge was still alive, and that, after giving his diamond to the museum, he then proceeded to steal it."

"I don't think he stole it," Frank said. "At least, he said he didn't."

"What do you mean he said he didn't? The man's dead."

"No, he isn't," Frank replied, and explained that they had found Rutlidge hiding out on Chapel Island under an assumed name.

Barnes's eyes widened as he listened to the story. "But why would he do that? It doesn't make sense."

Frank told Barnes about Rutlidge's plan to disprove the diamond's curse. "He felt that if he was still alive, he was legally the owner of the diamond. If his horse, Faith, won the race, obviously the curse did not work."

The detective shook his head. "Well, I sure would like to ask him some questions."

Dr. Werner interrupted the discussion. "I want to thank you again for all you've done," he said to the two boys who had saved his daughter. "Please let us repay you by inviting you to visit with us in our country soon."

The brothers thanked the geologist and told him they had been to Germany once before, but would love to go again.

The Rabbit, who had been listening to their words, let out a wild laugh. "In a few more minutes we will all be blown to bits," he spat. "When my bomb explodes, everything will come tumbling down."

The good humor disappeared from the faces in the group. Hearing the Rabbit's threat, Chet stood up from where he had been sitting on the beach. He looked at the high bluff wall that loomed overhead.

"Let's get out of here." He gulped, fearing that when the quake hit they would all be smothered by the cliffs tumbling down on top of them.

Jake had worries of his own. The quake could possibly cause a tidal wave of enough size in the bay to wipe out his birthplace, Chapel Island.

"Is it true what he's telling us?" Mr. Hardy asked the geologist.

"The bomb ought to have little or no effect," Dr. Werner replied, fixing his eyes on the terrorist.

The Rabbit's face went blank for a second before a sneer again formed his expression. "You have no idea how powerful it is," he said in a biting tone. "The one we set off in Bayport is nothing compared to this one."

"I took that into consideration," Werner answered evenly. "But the configuration of the earth below us ought to absorb nearly all of its impact."

The Rabbit struggled to kick the geologist, but Frank and Joe held him in place. "Believe what you will, Werner!" the Rabbit responded, his voice breaking into an eerie, high-pitched squeal. "But you will learn better very soon."

Although everyone thought the terrorist's threat was nothing more than a scare tactic, the mood of the success was broken. Katerina leaned silently against her father's shoulder. Sensing the change of spirit, the Doberman lay down with its head between its paws.

The somber mood lasted only a moment, however, before a thought occurred to Werner. He smiled. "I have something that you boys might be interested in." He proceeded to pace off steps on the ground, beginning with the spot where the hole had been bored. Counting twenty-five paces, he bent down and dug at the sand with his hands. In a moment he stood back up again, holding a jar. "Here," he said, unscrewing the lid and presenting the jar to Frank and Joe. Inside was a large gem, which twinkled as it caught the moonlight!

Joe's eyes lit up. "It's the Faith diamond!" he exclaimed. He poured the priceless gem into the palm of his hand and stared at it in wonder. "How did you get it?"

"I stole it from the Smithsonian," the geologist answered with a grin.

"So it wasn't Rutlidge after all!" Barnes exclaimed. "Boswell just thought it was."

Frank turned to Werner. "So you're the one who broke into the museum that night. Tell us about it."

The geologist chuckled. "Yes, I did. It was part of the plan I mentioned to you earlier."

"But why?" the older Hardy brother queried.

Werner cleared his throat and began to explain. "The diamond was to be the Rabbit's payment for his services. It was Jensen's job to get it for him. When I learned of this, I was determined to procure the gem myself and hold it until my daughter was released to me. That was the only way I could be sure of getting her back."

"So the Faith diamond was what the Rabbit and Roget were demanding from you the night we showed up at your bungalow." Joe put in.

"Yes," Werner said. "And it's a good thing you came. These men were much harder to deal with than I expected. They were prepared to beat it out of me."

The albino terrorist, now handcuffed and bound

by his feet, thrashed in the sand. "That's mine!" he shouted in anger, staring greedily at the gem.

Paying no attention to his rantings, Werner continued. "What I discovered was that Jensen had been trying to buy the stone from a man named Arthur Rutlidge."

Frank and Joe both wanted to interrupt at this point, but they restrained themselves.

"However, Rutlidge was not interested in the deal," Werner went on, "so Jensen tried less honest ways to make him sell. I believe the gem is reputed to bring misfortune to its owners, and Jensen contrived somehow to make it appear that the stone was affecting Rutlidge's horses."

Unable to contain themselves, the two sleuths told the story of how Max had used a dog whistle to cause the diamond owner's horses to lose races.

"We found Rutlidge hiding away on Chapel Island," Joe added. "He was supposed to have been drowned in a boating accident."

Werner raised his eyebrows in surprise at the youths' story. "You boys have certainly been doing a good job." He grinned. "That boating accident was my idea. But now I am getting ahead of myself. When Jensen's plan to make Rutlidge sell the diamond did not work, he began to threaten his life. That is when I made my move. I contacted Rutlidge. After convincing him that I was on his side, I told him to will his diamond to the museum, then to fake the boating accident. I arranged for him to take refuge on Chapel Island."

"And when the diamond ended up at the Smithsonian, you would steal it and hold it as collateral for your daughter," Frank added.

"It would also mean the stone still belonged to Rutlidge, but at the same time it would get Jensen off his back," Joe put in.

"Right." The geologist beamed. "It was a good deal all around."

"But if you were planning to trade the stone for Katerina," the dark-haired Hardy puzzled, "how was Rutlidge supposed to get his diamond back?"

Werner shrugged. "I hoped I would be able to get my daughter before I paid the Rabbit. But I would have gladly given him the gem if that had been necessary to insure Katerina's safety. Rutlidge agreed, by the way." The geologist then hugged his daughter gently and was silent.

Frank let a moment pass before speaking again. "I have only one more question, if you don't mind." He waited for Werner to nod before going on. "What was the purpose behind sabotaging the power plants?"

"Jensen represents some very shady oil merchants in the Mideast," Werner replied. "I suppose they wanted to discredit nuclear power by causing the quakes. Public opinion would then turn against nuclear energy and the price of oil would increase. But that's only a guess."

When the questioning was over, Katerina rewarded each of the boys with a kiss on the cheek. Chet blushed, having become attracted to the chestnut-haired girl. "Hey, let me take a look at that diamond," he said, trying to hide his embarrassment. He took the stone from Joe and held it up in the moonlight. "I bet this thing would pay for a lot of chocolate sundaes. I wonder how people ever got the idea it would bring bad luck. You'd have to be pretty superstitious to believe something like that."

Just then, a low rumble came from the earth. The ground began to tremble as the sound grew louder. Everyone froze for a moment.

"Here, take this thing back!" Chet cried, shoving the diamond into the geologist's hands.

"Quick, get on the yacht," Mr. Hardy ordered, worried the yellow clay would break off the bluff wall and bury the beach.

The group hastened to Jensen's cruiser, but by the time they were aboard, the trembling had stopped.

"Well, that was your earthquake," Werner told the Rabbit with a laugh. "Not much of a show for all the trouble you went to."

The terrorist growled, but did not reply.

Joe gave Chet a friendly slap on the back. "Now what were you saying about how stupid people were to believe in that diamond's powers?" he chided. "You sure were in a big hurry to get rid of it when the rumbling started."

"I was afraid I might drop it in the sand and it would get lost," Chet defended himself. "Of course I don't believe in that silly superstition."

No one knew at this point that Chet would soon have to worry about another superstition in *Track of the Zombie*.

Frank chuckled at his friend's excuse. "Okay, let's pack up our camping gear and head for Washington," he announced. "If we leave now, we'll make it back to Bayport in time for breakfast."

"Not so fast," the boys' father told them. "That skiff you sank is worth quite a bit of money. I'm afraid it will have to be paid for." Mr. Hardy watched his sons' faces pale as they realized their entire summer savings would be used up in paying for the skiff. "But since it was for a good cause," he added with a twinkle in his eye, "I'll cover it."

The Hardy Boys Mystery Stories

by Franklin W. Dixon

Have you read all the titles in this exciting mystery series? Look out for these new titles coming in 1988:

Armada

The Three Investigators

Brilliant Jupiter Jones, athletic Pete Crenshaw and studious Bob Andrews make up the Three Investigators. Read more about their baffling mysteries in these new titles, available from Armada in 1988:

No. 41 The Mystery of the Creep-Show Crooks
No. 42 The Mystery of the Cranky Collector
No. 43 The Mystery of Wreckers' Rock

Armada